BRITANNIA:
THE WALL

BRITANNIA: THE WALL

RICHARD DENHAM

&

M J TROW

ISBN 978-1-913762-50-6

First published in 2014.

This edition published in 2020 by BLKDOG Publishing.

A catalogue record for this book is available from the British Library.

Cover art by Andy Johnson.

www.blkdogpublishing.com

THIS SERIES IS DEDICATED TO TRISTAN

CURA DAT VICTORIAM

'He carried the sword and the buckler,
He mounted his guard on the Wall,
Till the Legions elected him Caesar,
And he rose to be master of all.'

Rimini: Marching Song of a Roman Legion of the Later Empire
From *Puck of Pook's Hill*
Rudyard Kipling.

LIBER I
CHAPTER I

Valentia, Autumnus, in the year of the Christ 367

It was cold on the heather ridges and the distant mountains stood like grey ghosts in the early morning. The only sound was the guttural scream of the rooks wheeling on the air currents. Their bright eyes saw everything; the hares darting in the tangled purple, the water, bright and babbling over the stones. And they saw four men trudging with their heavy loads, their studded boots smashing through the bracken at the stream's bank.

Leocadius had lost track of how far the four of them had marched since dawn. All he knew was that the pole had worn a groove in his shoulder and he was glad to let it drop, along with the corpse of the deer they had killed. He unhooked the shield slung over his back and threw it and his leather cap onto the grass. Leocadius was nineteen and already he was having his doubts about a soldier's life. His boots were heavy. His mail was heavy. And he didn't want to think about the weight of the shield. He looked across, beyond the still face and glassy eyes of the kill and watched Justinus.

The old man was a born soldier, three decades old if he was a day. He was a circitor, two ranks up from the bottom where Leocadius was. How had he stood it this long – the monotony of the Wall? Justinus had laid down the trussed deer too, but he was not resting. He was standing with his shield still strapped to his back, watching the skyline. Did the man never give up?

Vitalis nudged Leocadius and passed him the leather canteen he had just filled from the brook. The water was icy already, for all the summer had just gone and there was an early winter in the wind. Leocadius looked at the lad, just a year his junior. He was trying to grow a beard to make him look like a legionary, but he was still a boy underneath it. You could see it – a softness that did not suit a life on the frontier at the edge of the world, guarding a bloody wall.

'What are they?' Justinus asked the others.

'Rooks,' Leocadius took a long swig, without really looking.

'Rooks be buggered,' Paternus was climbing to his feet. He was actually older than Justinus but his face was softer, his eyes twinkled more kindly and he had less of the Roman about him. 'They're ravens.'

Vitalis stood up too, watching the great black birds wheeling and diving in the steel of the sky. The wind had got up and it stung his eyes now so that focus was difficult.

'So?' Leocadius was still sitting, rubbing his calves and trying to get some feeling into them.

Justinus looked at the boy with ill-disguised contempt. 'So the raven is a sign of battle,' he said flatly. 'They are bringers of death.' All four men were on their feet now, staring at the circling birds. Paternus squinted into the clouds, looking for the sun but there would be no sign of that today. Justinus had read his mind. 'Banna,' he said. 'They're over Banna.'

Vitalis crouched to grab his end of the pole ready to lift the hunting trophies. 'No,' Justinus said. 'Leave that. If all's well, we'll come back for them.' Leocadius snatched up his weapons and splashed through the stream with the others. Now, he had something else to complain about – his boots were soaking. But complaints were the last thing on Leocadius' mind as they made their way to high ground.

The going was heavy, their shields bouncing on their backs and their swords hitting their legs at every stride. It was nothing for these men to march twenty miles a day, but that was on good roads and a stone surface. There were more sudden ravines and pot holes in Valentia than in the whole of Britannia Secunda and all four hunters found most of them that day.

It was Paternus who stopped first, pointing ahead to where the fort of Banna stood in the grey stillness of the moors. Justinus dropped to one knee and the others did too, looking in all directions. There was nothing.

'What'll we do?' Vitalis asked. He was scared. And he looked younger than ever.

'What we've been trained to do,' Justinus told him. 'We keep together. Now!'

All four were on their feet, jogging forward with their lead-weighted darts in their hands. Each of them had three left, tucked into the hollow of their shields, ready for any eventuality. These little weapons could bring down deer, whispering through the air to reach their mark; they could bring down men too.

'Shields!' Justinus barked and each man swung the oval wood and leather in front of him. Banna was a solitary tower, bobbing on the horizon in their vision and something was sticking up above the crenellated parapet. Vitalis could not make it out. None of them could, at first. Then Justinus stopped in his tracks and the others heard him mutter, 'Jupiter highest and best!'

Each man stood with his mouth open, staring at the tower. A body had been fixed to the tower's top with spears. It had the discs of a centurion dangling from its lorica-clad chest and the four could hear these rattling in the wind. The arms hung forward while the legs were pinioned by the spear shafts. There was no head, just a mass of dry, dark blood around the neck and across the shoulders, crusting the mail.

'That's Piso,' Paternus whispered. 'I spoke to him only yesterday.'

'The day before,' Justinus reminded him. 'We've been gone for two days.'

They had. No one moved. It was Vitalis who spoke first, who said what each of them had been thinking, the reason that no one could look another in the face. 'We should have been back yesterday,' he blurted out. 'We shouldn't have dawdled. One deer was enough; why did we need two?'

'If we'd got back yesterday,' Leocadius hissed, 'We'd have been up there with Piso.'

'Shut up, both of you!' Justinus growled. 'Paternus, to the right. Vitalis, go with him. Leo – you come with me.' In pairs now, the four began to circle the tower. Two days ago this fortlet had housed four contubernia – thirty two men. Now it housed nobody but ghosts. Paternus was first into the cramped compound, springing over the low stone wall and crouching there. He was listening for sounds. Whoever had done this had destroyed a vexillation of the VI Victrix and they had done it with speed and skill. Drusus would have been on guard duty, relived by Cimber, then Lucullus. All of them had eyes like eagles. How could they possibly have been surprised?

Slowly, as his eyes got used to the darkness inside the fort, he made out the bodies lying there. There was Cimber, his naked body riddled with arrows, the eyes gouged out of his head. Who was that lying across his body? Clitus, who still owed Leocadius six denarii for the last game of Hand. Well, he wouldn't be repaying that any time soon. Vitalis took one look at the pale corpses, their eyes rolled to the sky and vomited all over his boots. He felt Paternus' hand on his shoulder, steadying him. 'All right, lad,' the older man said. 'Go outside. Get some fresh air.'

A noise above made both men look up. Justinus had reached the ramparts from the steps on the far side and was staring at what was left of Piso. The man had been primus pilus, the senior centurion of the VI and every other month, he had solemnly made his way from Eboracum in the south to review the troops on the Wall and make sure that all was well. They had all been surprised when he had turned up unannounced a couple of days ago; that was not exactly routine but Wall soldiers did not ask questions of senior centurions and they had just gone about their business with more spit and polish than usual.

Justinus slid the dart back into the hollow of his shield and slung the thing behind him. Then he hauled off his cap and began to lift Piso's body down from its perch. Behind him, Leocadius watched in horror. He had never seen a decapitated man before and he felt sick. Somehow he managed to fight it down and took some of the weight off Justinus. Together, they laid the corpse down on the ramparts. Justinus took one of the dead man's discs in his hand and ripped it away from its leather housings. He kissed the silver medusa's head carved there and muttered under his breath, 'Mithras, also a soldier, teach me to die aright.'

'Out here!' Paternus was calling from the ground to the west. The pair on the ramparts hurried down the steps to join the others. They were standing by the site of a fire, its smoke a memory, its ashes cold. There were bones strewn everywhere, with grey, cold meat still hanging from them. Overhead, the ravens still wheeled, calling to each other in their fury that their meal had been interrupted.

Justinus looked as grey as the ashes he was looking at. 'They go for the eyes first,' he said, 'then the liver and the heart. This ...' he kicked a long bone sticking out from the heart of the fire, 'this is to make a point.'

Leocadius and Vitalis looked at each other. 'What go for the eyes?' Leocadius found his voice first. 'Ravens?'

'Attacotti, boy,' Justinus murmured. 'Wild bastards from across the Hibernian Sea. They eat people and they always start with the eyes.'

'Jupiter highest and best,' Leocadius mouthed.

'What are they doing here?' Paternus asked. 'I've heard of them on Monapia before now . . .'

'And raids up the Itunae Estuary,' Justinus nodded. 'I've never known them come this far east.'

Paternus had already strapped his shield more securely on his back and started jogging away, falling easily into the marching pace.

'Wait!' Leocadius called after him. 'Where are you going?'

Paternus did not look back. 'My family are at the Crooked Bend. *That's* where I'm going.'

'That's where we're all going,' Justinus said, 'But we're going together.'

Paternus ran on for a few more paces, then stopped. He turned to look at the three of them, standing alongside the butchers' shambles that was all that was left of a vexillation. And he knew Justinus was right.

'What about the deer?' Leocadius asked.

'They'll only slow us up,' Justinus said. 'And the bastards who did this haven't vanished into thin air. Jupiter knows which way they went, but if it's south, we're going to run right into them.'

'South?' Leocadius frowned. 'They'd never dare attack the Wall.'

'No.' Something approaching a grin crossed Justinus' dark features, to disappear again like a lightning flash through a lowering cloud. 'Any more than they would have attacked Banna and taken the head of Ulpius Piso.'

'What about these men?' Vitalis asked, gesturing to the desolate little tower. 'They were our contubernia, our friends. We must give them decent burials.'

Justinus looked hard at the boy. 'Lad, if we meet up with the Attacotti, none of us is going to get a burial at all. We'll end up like the deer we caught yesterday. Paternus, take the lead. Leo, Vit, you're next. What is it, Pat? Two hours to the Crooked Bend?'

Paternus nodded.

'Let's do it in one.'

There would be no sun that day. Autumn came early in Valentia, the high country beyond the Wall, the long days of summer shortening quickly to give chill dawns and dusk. The wind lifted as the four crossed the heather. They kept away from the old track that linked Banna to their destination; a Roman road made too clear a target. Whoever had destroyed the little fort might still be in the area. The fire had been cold but that told the Wall soldiers nothing.

Vitalis and Leocadius had never seen action before and bliss may have lain in their ignorance. Leocadius had joined the army out of a sense of adventure. There was little chance of seeing the world when you were a limitaneus, a frontier guard, but the legionary base was Eboracum, with girls. And taverns. And dice. And more girls. Vitalis had no idea what he wanted to do with his life, but he wanted to know what was out there, beyond the Wall. Did the world end there, as some men said, in ice and fire?

Justinus knew it did not. He had been north of the Wall, across Valentia with its wild deer, its grouse, its wolves and its eagles. He had been as far north as that other wall, the Antonine and knew it was no more than a ruin of earth mounds and ditches where the hares ran on a summer's evening and where deer barked in the morning. And beyond *that* wall? Ah, well, that was a question. Men called it Caledonia, but it might as well have been the far side of the moon.

There was only one question on Paternus' mind – where was his family? His wife and baby son? He could hear them as he tramped the heather, the little one gurgling as his mother tickled him. And his mother crying when the boy was sick. They did not allow families to follow their menfolk to the Wall's outposts. Valentia was a frontier, a no-man's land where everybody watched and waited; as if the very air held its breath. No, Flavia would be safe in the cluster of huts south of Camboglanna, high on the bluff of the Crooked Bend, overlooking the river. No Attacotti war band could take a fort like that. The Wall was designed that way. It was fifteen feet high with a parapet above that the height of a man. There were sixteen forts on the Wall, with eighty milecastles and two towers between each. If one section was attacked, the garrisons on either side could come to its aid.

'There!' Justinus had eyes like a hawk and he sprinted past the others to point to the road. 'Arcani.'

They all stopped and crouched in the heather, the spears they had collected from Banna flat to the ground. The circitor was right; Paternus knew that, even if the others were unsure. It was one of the secret ones, men whose people had ruled Valentia long before the Romans came; men who knew a superior race when they met them; men who had long ago sold their souls to the Eagles. This one was riding a shaggy little pony and he was not much of a horseman. He was bouncing on the animal's back like a sack of grain and he had a brace of hares dangling from his saddlebow.

Justinus took a chance. He could see no one else but the lone horseman and he needed answers. He stood up in the heather and cupped his mouth to make his voice carry over the wind. 'Io, Arcanus,' he called in Latin.

The four of them saw the horseman stop. For a moment he looked as if he would ride away to the west, but then he hauled on the animal's rein and trotted over to the Wall men.

'Io, Justinus!' the man called. The younger men had never seen him before, but the others knew him. He was called Dumno, a little, round man, hunched in his Roman horned saddle and he stared at the four, screwing up his forehead with the effort. He reined in alongside the circitor and grinned. 'You lads hunting?' he asked in the peculiar dialect of Valentia.

'You might say that,' Justinus lapsed into his language, leaving the younger men in the dark. 'We've just come from Banna.'

'Oh, yes?'

Justinus tried to read the man's face. He and Dumno went back a year or two. The man, like all his people, acted as an unofficial scout for the Roman army – and a spy, too, from time to time. Many was the time Dumno had slipped a useful piece of information to the garrison of the Crooked Bend; and many were the pieces of silver he had received for it. Justinus stepped closer so that his head was level with the Arcanus's shoulder. 'They're all dead,' he murmured.

'What?' Dumno's eyebrows reached his hairline. 'The entire command?'

'And Ulpius Piso, the senior centurion.'

'Jupiter highest and best!' Dumno had long ago learned to pretend he loved the Roman gods. His own were of no consequence here. 'What happened?'

'That's what I was going to ask you,' the circitor said, 'because that's what we pay you for.'

'I have no idea,' the Arcanus gabbled. 'As Jupiter is my witness ...'

Justinus launched himself with both hands and hauled the man out of his saddle. Alarmed at the sudden movement and loss of weight on his back, the little animal snorted and trotted away.

'My hares!' Dumno turned to run after them, but Justinus held him fast.

'The command was butchered,' he growled low in his throat, holding the man's face close to him. 'Not just killed, as in a fair fight. They were eaten. There was a fire. Charred bones. Meat.' He shook the little hunter. 'Am I speaking a foreign language?' the circitor shouted.

'Sounds ... sounds like Attacotti,' was the best Dumno could do, with Justinus' iron grip on his wolf-skin collar tightening around his throat.

'Doesn't it, though?' the circitor said. And he let the man go. 'So what can you tell me?'

Little Dumno looked at the four of them as he cricked his neck back into place, lifting each shoulder carefully. Limitanei. Wall soldiers. None of them had ever been to Rome in his life; nor would he. What was it about these idiots that made them take on the world? Didn't they know it always ended in death in the heather?

'Nothing,' the little man shook his head. 'As Jupiter is my witness ...'

'Let's not pretend you and the Gods have anything in common, Arcanus. You'd swear you slept with Ceres if your life depended on it. And as of now, believe me, your life depends on it.'

Justinus nodded to Paternus who drew his sword. The long-bladed spatha hissed clear of the scabbard and glinted at Dumno's throat. 'My man Paternus has a family hereabouts,' Justinus said. 'He's worried about them. So worried, I'm worried he might overreact with that blade.'

Dumno gurgled a little with his chin in the air and his eyes rolling. 'Well, I did hear a rumour ...' he managed to choke out.

Paternus lowered the sword point slightly.

'What rumour?' he asked. His dialect was not as good as Justinus', but Dumno followed his drift.

'The Attacotti have come east,' the Arcanus said, 'crossed the Hibernian Sea. There's no rhyme or reason to it.'

'Out of season?' Justinus frowned. 'The summer's gone.'

'Like I said . . .' Dumno smirked. Out of the corner of his eye he could see his pony – and his hares – wandering ever further away. '. . . no rhyme nor reason to it.'

'How do the Selgovae feel about cannibals on their ground?' Justinus asked. He was talking about Dumno's own tribe – he would get the truth or he wouldn't; he would have to watch the Arcanus' face carefully to be sure.

'Oh, circitor,' Dumno put on his humblest expression, 'the Selgovae know that their lands belong to Rome. If the Attacotti have trespassed, it is up to Rome to punish them.'

'Oh, we'll do that all right,' Justinus promised him.

'We're wasting time.' Paternus was already marching south.

Leocadius and Vitalis looked at their circitor. Could this strange little man of the foreign tongue and shaggy pony help them? Had Justinus found anything out that the four did not know already?

'Get yourself west,' the circitor said to Dumno. 'Find out what's going on. When I come back – and I will come back – it will be with a legion at my heels.'

'Vale, Justinus,' Dumno smiled, hurrying to catch his pony. He half turned to the others. 'Valete!' he called to them. Only Vitalis grunted something in return.

The fort at the Crooked Bend was called Camboglanna. The VI Victrix had built it two hundred years ago under orders from the deified Adrianus whom men called Hadrian. It was part of that frontier that separated the civilized from the barbarian, men from animals. Its earth ramparts and white-painted stone towers said 'Here is Rome. Defy us if you will. But you will break on our stones. And you will die on our swords.'

For the last two years, Vitalis and Leocadius had called this place home. Usually it hummed with life: the thud of the VI going about their training, marching and wheeling into line, closing their shield wall and hurling their javelins; the rattle of carts as they rolled north and south through the gates; the clash and hurry of the smiths and the carpenters and the masons. Paternus had lived here longer than that, ever since he had married his Flavia and before the gods had blessed them with a son.

But there was no sound today. Not even the wind had risen over the bluff and there were no guards on the ramparts. No birds, either. No rooks. No ravens. Just a stillness that was alien. The four crouched in the heather. In front of them the flat ground of the vallum would give no cover at all and if there were archers or spearmen behind that crenellated skyline, they would be sitting ducks for their weapons.

Leocadius saw it first. He nudged Justinus and pointed to the stone-lined ditch that stretched away to the east. Half-hidden in the bracken, a warrior lay face down, his legs sprawled, his head a mass of blood. Justinus motioned the others to stay where they were and he scrabbled down the steep ramp of the ditch. In the shadows, the bracken, the soil and the body were wet, for all it was mid-morning by now. Justinus hauled the dead man over. A crossbow bolt was imbedded in his throat, the dark dry blood running in a straight line over his bare chest. And a slingshot had smashed his skull. The garrison at Banna, with the exception of Piso, had been stripped; a legionary's armour and weapons fetched serious money and they could be re-used by any barbarian short of equipment. This man still retained his plaid trousers and a broad leather belt that covered most of his rib cage. His auburn hair was plaited in braids but the most telling thing about him was his face and body. It was covered in blue swirls and circles, old tattoos that marked the brooding darkness of this man's race.

'Picti,' Justinus called to the others. 'The painted ones.' He and Paternus had faced these men before. They were almost certainly from the tribe called the Vectriones who lived on the northern fringes of Valentia in their strange, stone circular houses. They never washed and women ruled them.

The others waited until Justinus had climbed out of the ditch. There were no more bodies lying on the vallum or at the foot of the tower, so the man in the ditch had probably been overlooked when they dragged their dead away for burial. The four edged forward slowly. There were not enough of them to form the tortoise defence, a moving maul of shields and all they could do if they were attacked now was to run or stand and fight. Ahead of them the gate had been smashed off its huge hinges and lay flat on the bloodied ground. The guards of Camboglanna lay beyond that, ripped and stripped as they had been at Banna, their armour gone, their wounds many. On the steps that led to the ramparts arrow-riddled corpses were sprawled in the bizarre attitudes of death.

Justinus looked at their faces particularly, turning a corpse over if it lay on its side or front. They all still had their eyes, some closed, some wide open, staring in silent accusation at the stranger who was violating them again. But Justinus was not a stranger. He was a circitor for this vexillation and if the corpses did not know him any more, he still knew them. Here was Claudio, the demon Hand player. There lay Sixtus, with the fine beard of which he was so proud. The semisallis Atticus had died in front of the granary, now empty of grain. Justinus only knew Flavius Tarquinius by the tattooed name on his arm – Lucia; his head was battered to a pulp.

Leocadius and Vitalis wandered the fort as if in a daze. This was a nightmare, surely, and any minute they would wake up. Banna was one thing. But there had only been thirty men there, give or take. And it was a single tower. Here, in this complex defence system, with ditches and ramparts and walls, there had been well over a hundred men. And that did not count the civilians who lived as camp followers behind the lines.

Paternus had gone and Justinus knew where. While the others turned over corpses, looking for old friends and comrades, the semisallis had dashed through the courtyard, beyond the stone of the fortifications to the wooden huts and lean-tos. There were dead soldiers here too, as if the lines had been driven back from the Wall, desperately fighting all the way. But it was not the soldiers Paternus was interested in. It was the women. It was the children. His hands were shaking as he rolled over one corpse after another. There had been no armour to steal from these people, but several of the women had their dresses ripped or roughly pushed up around their hips. The painted ones had had a field day here. Having slaughtered the men at the Crooked Bend, they had then raped their way through their women. Paternus could hear it all rushing through his blood-filled ears – the taunting jeers of the Picts, the terrified screams of their victims.

He knew his Flavia would not have gone quietly. If she had had any chance at all, she would have taken one of the bastards with her; more if she could. But Flavia was not among the dead. The last scattering of corpses lay along the river bank, one or two face-down in the bloody water. As he stared into each still face, Paternus offered his silent thanks to Sol Invictus, the unconquered sun. This was *somebody's* Flavia, *somebody's* Herminia, but not his. He found three dead babies that were the right age for his, little ones too little to toddle away from the hissing arrows, the slicing iron;

children who could do no more than cry as the painted monsters of their nightmares snuffed out their lives. But none of them was his. Paternus sank to his knees in the mud of the river, rank-smelling with the blood of Camboglanna. Violent sobs shook his body. Unless the Picts had taken his family as hostages, they had got away. They were alive. He felt his chest heave with the tension of it all and he threw up in the mud.

'What do you see?' Justinus called up to Vitalis on the ramparts.

The boy took a while before he answered. To the north, the way the attack had come, Valentia lay silent and vast. Only the ravens circled like tiny insects, high in the grey of the sky, skimming the belly of the clouds to watch for more feasting. To the west, the next milecastle stood forlorn, with as little sign of life as here at Camboglanna. Beyond that, invisible because of the roll of the land, the Wall fell away to Uxellodunum, the next fort. To the east, where the brightest sky hurt the lad's eyes with a sudden break in the clouds, another forlorn milecastle, abandoned and dead. Further east still, Aesica. Was that, too, a graveyard?

'Nothing,' Vitalis said.

He was halfway down the steps again, stepping over bodies, when Justinus shouted, 'The vexillum!' and he was leaping over corpses, running into the eastern tower of the main gate. The other two were with him as he crashed into the chapel. A single shaft of light slashed diagonally onto the altar. There was a stone trough, the housings of the standard of the VI, but the standard itself had gone; the scarlet cloth edged with gold and glittering with the letters 'Victrix'. This was the heart of the legion, the ancient reminder of the men who had marched from the Tiber to the far reaches of the world, under the deified Julius, Adrianus and Marcus Aurelius. These days, each cohort of the VI carried the streaming Draco standard with its snarling mouth and leather wings, but the vexillum carried the battle honours of the centuries.

In the half light in that violated chamber lay the signifer, the standard bearer. He had been wearing his bearskin headdress and part of that was stuffed into his mouth. And his right hand had gone, taken as a trophy no doubt by the bastard who had hacked the vexillum from him.

Justinus led the others out into the daylight. Vitalis felt as sick as he had at Banna but managed to check himself. Leocadius was still looking around in disbelief.

'Where are the others?' he asked. 'The garrisons from Aesica and Uxellodunum? Why didn't they get here?'

'They didn't get here because they couldn't,' Justinus told him. 'Because if we travel the length of the Wall, we'll find the same.'

'That's not possible,' Vitalis said. 'The entire Wall? It's not possible.'

'It might not be the entire Wall,' Justinus was trying to make sense of it too, 'but we're not staying to find out.'

Paternus came padding back up the corpse-strewn slope from the river. He shook his head in answer to Justinus' enquiring look. 'No,' he said. 'They're not here.'

Justinus slapped his shoulder, encouraging them all to hope for the best. 'Eboracum,' he said. 'They'd have got away to the south.'

'Is that where we're going?' Vitalis asked.

'The Hell we are!' Leocadius shouted. 'Nobody tells a Roman army to run.'

'Since when were you such a Roman?' Justinus asked him. 'I thought you'd had enough of soldiering.'

'I thought I had, too,' the younger man said. 'But this . . . there's a score to settle.'

'Yes,' Justinus agreed. 'And the four of us aren't going to settle it here. Pat, see if those murdering bastards have left us any food we can take with us. And fill your canteens, everybody. It's five days march to Eboracum; assuming we don't meet any painted people on the road.' He looked at the three men with him: Paternus, who couldn't find his loved ones; Leocadius, the arrogant, slovenly soldier who suddenly wanted revenge; Vitalis, the man who was a child again in the midst of all this slaughter. Would any of them survive, if they met the painted people on the road?

CHAPTER II

They spent the first night huddled in a copse above a stream, far enough away from the babbling, rushing water to be able to pick up other noises. They took turns to keep watch, straining their eyes through the gloom of the early autumn night and watching always to the north. The mountains loomed dark and mysterious on their horizon and the owls hunted in the black tangle of the trees, startling the watcher with a sudden call as they swept by on soft wings.

No one really slept and as dawn broke, grey and chilly on the crags, they filled their canteens and moved on again. Once more they kept away from the army road that ran south like an arrow, breaking here and there where it crossed a brook or vanished into the thickness of a forest. Men on the run, as the Wall soldiers were, had a straight choice; take the open country where they could be seen a Roman mile away; or trail the woods where every tree might hide the enemy.

Justinus chose the high land. If an enemy could see them, they could see the enemy. And if that happened, then it would be a straight race for survival. The only sure way to keep on the move before hunger and exhaustion overtook them was to find horses. And horses meant Vinovia.

The cavalry fort stood on a low escarpment with woods behind. The Wall men splashed and swam their way across a dozen becks before they found it, and darkness was already on them by the time they crouched in the tall grass and looked across the vallum to the stockade. Vitalis felt his heart sink. It was Banna and Camboglanna all over again. No sound. No movement. By now they were close enough to have heard the thud of the guards' boots on the wooden walkway; to hear the whinnying of the cavalry horses in the paddock beyond. There were no lights, no torches flaring at the north gate; nor any gate. Just the wind of evening moaning across the heather and the beat of the blood in each man's throat.

The general Agricola had built this place when the legions first came this far north, and the XX Valeria Victrix had sawn down every tree and lashed together every fence post. The tribes here were the Brigantes, whose chieftains since Cartimandua of the wild hair had learned to live with the Romans. There had been peace in this land south of the Wall for generations. Until now.

'Nothing,' Leocadius called through the night as the last of the day died behind purple clouds. 'Not so much as a pile of horse shit.' He was right. All four of them had scoured the place from gate to gate. The horses had gone. The stables were empty. Iron mangers stood stripped of hay and the straw in the stalls was cold. Stone troughs still held water but the water was dark under the rising moon and Justinus dabbled his fingers in it, bringing them out bloody.

The Ala whose post this was had not given up easily. Some of them, at least, had gone down fighting. But where were their bodies? A raiding party would have stolen the horses, helped themselves to harness and hay but would they have risked taking the cavalrymen as prisoners? Prisoners slowed men down. They had to be fed and watered. Might as well kill them where they stood. But if that happened, where were their bodies? The question echoed and re-echoed in Justinus' head and whatever other thoughts flashed through his mind that night, it kept coming back to that one.

They talked in the shadow of the overhang of the stables and decided to stay put. Here at least was warm shelter and water from the brook nearby. There was little chance that the raiding party would come back. Other than to burn the timbers down, there was no point. And three of them settled down to their second night without food. Paternus took the first watch. Paternus, whose family were not at Vinovia either.

Dawn the next day was bright and warm, the sun already waking the camp with its gentle rays. There was no horn, no drums, no prayers to Mithras, just three tired soldiers rolling out of the sharp straw and pulling on their coats of mail. They would have to hunt today. Blackberries on the moorland were fat and sweet at this time of year, not yet blemished by a frost but after the initial pleasure of the honeyed juice going down the throat there was no substance to them, nothing to keep a man's body going and they could not warm his soul.

Civilization lay over a long day's march away, at Isurium Brigantium. Justinus had been there once and knew its walls and the bright, mosaic pavements where Romulus and Remus suckled forever from their she-wolf mother and lions sat in the perpetual shade of trees. The four halted just before midday by a milestone of Trajan Decius. Isurium, to a man like Leocadius whose feet throbbed, might just as well have been the far side of the Styx. While Vitalis stood thigh-deep in a wide river, the sun dancing on the ripples, Leocadius sprawled on the long, warm grass. Overhead the sky was cloudless and the only sound he could hear was the rushing of the river and the murmur of the last bees of summer, mumbling over the heather hunting nectar against the winter which soon would come to the land once and for all. He could hear Justinus droning on, now and then, to Paternus, sitting together some yards away and he glanced down to see how Vitalis was doing tickling the fish. The peace of the moment was shattered by the rumbling of his own stomach. Leocadius had come to terms with what had happened. Last night, with Vinovia the cavalry school of ghosts and the awful silence of the stables, it seemed as if the world – at least, the world of Rome – had come to an end. But today was different. Today there was sun and softly waving grass and a babbling river and bees ... all would yet be well.

'Jupiter highest and best!' That was Vitalis' voice. Leocadius sat bolt upright to see his friend thrashing about in the water, making for the bank towards him, stumbling on the rolling slippery stones of the riverbed.

'No! Other way!' he heard Justinus hiss and he and Paternus were sliding down the bank into the water.

'Leo!' Vitalis was waving frantically at him and the fourth Wall soldier plunged into the river. It hit him like a wall of ice after his warm dozing on the hillside and all four of them were crouching up to their necks in water, hiding under the overhang of the branches that formed a canopy on the north bank.

'What ...' Leocadius began but Justinus clapped a hand over the boy's mouth and pointed upwards with his other hand. Leocadius could not see anything above him but the underbrush of leaves and roots, but he could hear well enough. It was the thud of horses' hooves and shouts and whoops from riders racing each other to the riverbank. Vitalis had seen them briefly seconds before and hoped to Jupiter they had not seen him as well. From the angle he had, Vitalis could make out tall men with blond hair and heavy moustaches. They wore loose tunics of dark blue and at the waists of many of them hung heavy, vicious swords with a single edge. Their spears pierced the sky for a while until they reined up and dismounted, letting their horses drink before they did.

Paternus did not recognize their language, but he knew the horses well enough. They were Roman cavalry horses, their withers branded with the mark of the Ala Invicti Britanniciaci. And they came from Vinovia. The Wall men waited in the shallow water, hardly daring to breathe. All of them had their spears in their hands, their shields trailing in the eddying water. Then Leocadius' heart thumped even louder. He had left his cap on the far bank and there it was, in full view of the horsemen who were only feet away. Were they blind that they did not see it?

Justinus had counted twenty horsemen, but that was before he ducked for cover and more may have cantered over the yellow hill in search of water. As the horses drank their fill, the riders pushed past them, laughing and joking, dipping their heads in the river and drinking deep, splashing and pushing each other.

Please, Vitalis prayed to every god he could name, please don't let them go swimming. Any horseman wallowing in the shallows would be bound to spot the Wall soldiers. And then the stream would run red.

Vitalis did not know how long he crouched there. He had been nearly up to his waist in the cold water for longer than the others, trying to catch a fish and he had lost all feeling in his legs. Then, at last, the horsemen had mounted, wheeled their horses away and ridden to the west, not fording the river but following its meanderings for a while before disappearing over the yellow horizon.

The four straightened in the water and grabbed trailing branches and tree-roots to pull themselves out. Leocadius sat on the still-warm grass and wrung out his saturated boots. Vitalis tried to pump some blood into his legs by rubbing his calves and flexing his knees.

'What were they' Leocadius asked his elders and betters. 'More Picts?'

'None like any I've seen,' Paternus said. 'Justinus?'

The circitor was drying his sword blade on the grass. 'I'd like a closer look at one of their weapons,' he said.

'I wouldn't,' Leocadius grunted.

'Those swords,' Justinus said. 'They're heavier than ours and with a longer reach. More like an axe. Unless I miss my guess, they're Saxons, from Germania.'

Vitalis whistled through his teeth. 'They're a long way west,' he said. Justinus and Paternus looked at each other. The boy was right and it made the hair stand up on the back of the circitor's neck.

'Never mind the fish,' he said. 'We'll find a village before nightfall. And we'll help ourselves if we have to.' And he waded back across the river, marching south.

As the sun was setting, the far civilization Isurium was still four hour's march away but hunger was burning in their bellies now and cramps were forcing Vitalis to slow down. Leocadius' already painful feet had not been improved by the wet leather of his boots rubbing on his heels and he slowed down too, hoping he just looked like a good friend keeping another company. In a gentle valley, a cluster of huts stood on the edge of a stream, smoke drifting lazily up from a handful of fires. Scrawny dogs yawned and scratched themselves in the half light and a little girl was shepherding a gaggle of geese into a pen. It was her scream that brought the little village to life, and a dozen armed men tumbled out of their circular hovels, brandishing cudgels, pots and pans, *anything* to see off the marauders.

Justinus held up his hand. 'It's all right,' he said, instinctively falling into Latin. There was only a grumbled response and a ring of surly faces glowered at him in the twilight. He switched to Brigantian and spoke slowly because he was not sure of his words. 'We're from the Wall,' he said, flinging his arm behind him to make sure they understood. 'We've been attacked there. We bring you word. You're in danger.'

A large man with a thatch of dark hair and a heavy beard stepped forward, cradling a heavy club in his arms. 'In danger of what?' he asked.

'Picts,' Justinus said. 'Attacotti. Saxons. You name it; they're everywhere.'

The headman half turned to the others and by now a crowd

19

of women and children had gathered too. There was a silence. Then everybody except the Wall soldiers burst out laughing. 'You're mad,' the headman said. 'The Picts have never come this far south. And as for the others ... who did you say?' He was still chuckling, looking round at his people to share his fun.

Justinus stepped towards him, his spear in his hand. 'Attacotti,' he said softly. 'They eat people.'

Another silence. More laughter, this time louder and more hysterical than before. 'They give you blokes too much wine,' the headman said. 'Or maybe it was the sun today. It's turned your head.'

'Look, you ...' Leocadius had had enough. He was exhausted; his feet hurt; he was hungry and he did not appreciate being the butt of somebody else's joke. Weapons came up to the level, but Justinus raised his empty hand and let his spear fall. He unbuckled his helmet strap and dropped that too. And he looked into the headman's eyes. 'You've got women and children here,' he said, 'and no defences.' He looked around at the huts, twinkling with fires and heavy with the scent of woodsmoke. 'We've come from the Wall, where there are ramparts and ditches and stone towers. Safety, you'd think. But you'd be wrong.' He looked into the eyes of the little goose girl. A mother standing by her, with one hand protectively on her shoulder, hitched her baby closer so that it could latch on to her naked breast. Her eyes were wide with maternal worries and he concentrated on speaking to her, to the heart and hearth of the village, not its head. 'You would be wrong,' he repeated, softly, making the people lean in to hear his news. 'Because behind those ramparts, those ditches, those towers, we've left behind butchered babies and girls raped for sport.'

There were murmurs now as the menfolk jostled nearer their families.

'What would you have us do?' the headman asked. 'Build a Roman fort?'

'I don't know what you can do,' Justinus said, 'And we can't give you protection. We're going south – to Isurium. You're welcome to come with us.'

The villagers muttered together for a while, then the headman spoke again. 'I've lived here all my life,' he said, 'As did my father and his father before him. I'm not running away from any barbarians.' He paused, 'And anyway ... who are the barbarians here?'

Leocadius' hand went to his sword hilt, but Justinus checked him.

'You're not being sensible ...' Vitalis tried to reason with the man; but Justinus knew it was a waste of time.

'At least,' he said, 'Give us some food. We've been on the road now for two days. Berries give you the shits.'

'Tough,' the headman shrugged.

'We'll pay,' Justinus said, dipping into his purse. 'We have coin.'

The headman took a single denarius and squinted at it in the dying light. He saw the jumble of a language he could not read and the laurel-wreathed head of a man he did not know. He bit it to make sure it was metal. Then he threw it to the ground and spat on it. Again, Leocadius jerked forward. This time with his sword half-drawn. Justinus spun round and slapped him hard across the face. Vitalis flinched. He could see the fire reflected in both men's eyes and the muscle jumping with fury in Leocardius' jaw. Then the younger man relaxed and he moved back, letting the sword slide back into the scabbard.

'You'll get no food here,' the headman scowled at Justinus. 'Now, get out of my village.'

For what seemed an eternity, the Wall men stood and looked at the villagers, then Justinus picked up his helmet and strapped it on his head. Then he picked up his spear and the four of them marched into the night.

The villagers watched them until they were a single black speck against the purple of the sky. 'Follow them,' the headman said to the two men at his elbow. 'Make sure they don't double back. Haxo ...' another villager stepped forward, 'Saddle that horse of yours. Get a message to Valentinus. He will need to know about these four.'

They stayed away from the river that night, men too exhausted to march on, and bivouacked in a stand of elms with only the noisy rooks for company. While one kept watch, the others slept with their swords drawn beside them on the ground and their shields for pillows. Nobody was taking off his mail, just in case.

The next day was like the last, with the sun climbing and slanting its rays on the light mist that crawled the ground. Justinus knew they were about three hours march from Isurium where, at last, they would find the world they knew and friendly faces and some explanation of what was happening. Once more, they skirted the road rather than followed it, filling their canteens and eating berries on the way. If Leocadius never saw another blackberry in his life, it would be too soon.

They had been slogging along for nearly an hour and nobody was making small talk anymore. They had exhausted the possibilities – that the Wall had been destroyed, that the world had gone mad, that this was all some hallucination, some dream. Paternus had talked of his wife and son, of happy summer days at Camboglanna, until the tears had filled his eyes and he had had to stop. Leocadius was babbling about his plans once they reached Eboracum. There was a girl he knew there – Paulina of the lovely eyes. All right, she cost two days' pay, but she was worth it. Vitalis was thinking of a girl too, but he did not share her with the others. She was his sister Conchessa and he had not seen her for years, since they were children. The little girl with the geese had reminded him of her, with her fair hair and her grey-green eyes, shining in the twilight of yesterday. Only Justinus kept his counsel. He said nothing to any of them, because the uneasy feeling of the last days was growing inside him. And because the others, even Paternus, would not understand.

He stopped suddenly, holding his arm out to catch Vitalis' arm. 'Cavalry,' he hissed and the four bolted, dashing to the cover of gorse bushes to their right. The ground ahead sloped downwards to a broad valley and the road shone white and straight across the yellow grass, cropped short by hares. The only shelter here were the bushes they were hiding in, keeping their heads down in the sharp spines that scratched and prickled, finding naked flesh no matter how they lay. Justinus peered up above the spikes and saw a knot of horsemen fanning out from the road. Their hair was long and plaited and heavy moustaches drooped to below their chins. The circitor counted eight. And they were Picts, the painted people.

He waved his hand to the others and they all reached into their shield recesses for their lead-weighted darts. Two to one. Justinus did not like those odds; and the fact that these men were cavalry made it worse. They had the advantage of speed and height, their sturdy little ponies coming on at a walk but able to reach the gallop in seconds. At least these were not stolen Roman Ala horses; they were shorter in the leg, the wild horses of the north.

From where they lay, the Wall men could hear snatches of conversation in an alien, guttural tongue. One of the Picts had a deer slung over his saddle bow, its antlered head hanging down almost to the ground. One by one they dismounted and while one began to hobble the horses, the others squatted on the grass, sitting in a circle and passing round a goatskin sack.

Wine. That was what Leocadius could do with about now and he shook his head in disgust that the stuff was going to such waste. All the others saw was the deer. And they could all smell it, turning nicely over a spit, the fat and blood oozing down to make the best gravy in the world. Justinus assessed the situation. Clearly the Picts had no idea that the Wall men were there, but the country was open. If they broke cover, the soldiers would be exposed from all sides and to stand and fight against cavalry was suicide. They would have to wait.

And they waited all that day, the sun burning on their backs, the gorse sticking into their skin. At least they had water and could survive on that, but Justinus knew that his men could not go on much longer without food. The berries they had eaten churned their stomachs and caused violent cramps. Vitalis was hit worst of all and he writhed in the gorse, pricking his face and gritting his teeth in an attempt to keep quiet. Nobody was going to risk conversation, but Justinus kept a running commentary in his head. He could not understand what the Picts were doing. If this was a hunting party, they had their kill already. There was no attempt to skin the deer and cook it. Instead, they broke the hard, black bread they carried with them and munched on that, along with some pale cheese. The wine flowed faster as more goatskins were hauled off saddles and the conversation became more raucous and more slurred. After a while a couple of Picts began to wrestle each other, rolling over in the dust and slapping each other, to hoots of laughter from the others.

It must have been early evening when they finally left. They had lit no fire and the deer remained uncooked as they unhobbled their horses and trotted away to the south, back the way they had come. Once they had disappeared, the Wall men scrambled up out of their painful hiding place, scratched and hot and stiff and stumbled over to the Pictish camp. Vitalis found half a loaf of bread and no sooner was it in his hand than Leocadius slapped him round the head and snatched it from him.

'That's enough!' Justinus growled. 'Give it to me.'

Leocadius hesitated, then threw the bread to the circitor. This was twice in one day the man had made him feel small. Justinus would have to watch his back in future. The circitor put the bread on the ground and cut it neatly in four with his dagger before passing it round. To all of them, bread had never tasted so good.

'What now?' Paternus asked. 'Isurium?'

Justinus shook his head. 'That's due south,' he said, 'the way the Picts went.'

'What?' Leocadius said. 'You can't think they've taken Isurium?'

Justinus looked at the boy, at all of them. They were looking at him, expecting answers where there were no answers, sanity in a world gone mad.

'I think they were guarding the road,' the circitor said, 'And they're probably guarding both roads in and out of the place. We can't outrun those bastards and in the open we can't outfight them. I hope you enjoyed your bread, boys, because that's probably all you'll get until we reach Eboracum.'

The Picts may have taken Isurium Brigantium but they had not taken Eboracum. In their heart of hearts the Wall men knew that that would be impossible for any barbarian. The great walls of the fortress still stood across the Ussos, its towers huge and imposing, each one with a wall of fourteen faces and the height of seven men, each one a rock in a sea of chaos. The ramparts bustled with armed guards, men with shields and helmets and all the trappings of Rome. Eboracum had been the home of the VI Victrix for two hundred years, long before the men of this legion had elected Constantine emperor. The army camp covered fifty acres, its walls holding a city in all but name. And the Wall men had never seen such a marvellous sight in their lives.

When he had fed and rested, Justinus crossed the river into the colonia, the teeming town that had grown up in the camp's shadow. It was still early morning and the shutters were being rolled up and the stalls set out as the market traders began their day's work. The carpenters were already at their lathes and the potters up to their elbows in the grey clay they would fashion into ewers and amphorae. Geese, sheep, cattle and hens were being driven along the narrow streets and the noise was deafening. No one noticed a circitor of the VI wandering past the temple of Serapis where the priests were unbolting the doors to begin the first service of the day. Soldiers in this town were ten-a-denarius for all it was the capital of Britannia Secunda; seen one soldier, seen them all.

Justinus turned the sharp corner to his left. He waited in the shadows, checking that the way was clear. Rialbus the slave was helping himself to water from the rivulet that ran alongside the street and the circitor held his finger up to his lips. The slave had known the circitor since he was a boy and knew what this was all about. He smiled and carried on drawing his water. Justinus drew his sword, slowly and silently and crept towards the open doorway. He turned back and looked at the sky. What was it? Six o'clock? Seven? Perfect. The man he was looking for, with his naked blade glinting in the half light of the doorway, would still be in bed. This was going to be a picnic.

The circitor reached the stairs that ran to the gallery overhead. He stepped lightly, careful not to make the timbers creak and climbed to the half landing. Ahead of him a chink of light streamed in to show a figure curled up on the bed. Justinus took one pace, two. Then he reached out with terrifying speed, hauled back the covers and held his sword at the throat of the man who lay there. Except that no one lay there. His blade tip was tickling a pile of blankets and another sword tip was pressed into his neck, just below the ear.

'Tsk, tsk,' he heard the familiar voice, 'Will you *never* learn?'

He half turned to see a solid-looking man in an army tunic. He was greyer than he remembered, older; but the eyes still sparkled and he could not fault the old man's faculties.

'Hello, Pa!'

The older man threw his sword on the bed and threw his arms around Justinus. He was Flavius Coelius, the hastilarius, the weapons trainer of VI Victrix, an old warrior who had won his right to the parcel of land that came in lieu of a pension. The men held each other tight, stood back and slapped each other on the back.

'Rialbus, you old shit-fly,' the old man called, 'Get some breakfast for my son. And if you're very good, I'll let you have a few crumbs.'

Justinus laughed. There was no slave in the whole of Britannia better treated than Rialbus. He was family.

'So,' Flavius led the way downstairs, 'What news on the

Wall, boy?'

'I'm not sure you're going to believe it,' Justinus said.

Flavius did not believe it. Not at first. He had guarded the Wall most of his adult life and his father before him. Segovae, in the early days, yes – they were always a nuisance. The Picts, now and again, of course. You'd expect that; the bastards killed people for entertainment. That's why they were called barbarians. But the tribes in Valentia, north of the Wall, the Votadini especially, had co-existed with Rome now for decades. No one had ever conquered them as such, but they knew which side their bread was buttered and service for Rome offered riches beyond their wildest dreams.

'So, let me get this straight.' Flavius poured more wine for them both, sitting at the gnarled oak table as they were, 'You saw Picts, Attacotti *and* Saxons?'

Justinus nodded.

'But not together.'

'No, not as such. But they were all operating as one. If we're being strictly accurate, we didn't actually *see* any Attacotti – just what they did.'

Flavius nodded. He looked grimly at the man in front of him, the man he had once dandled on his knee, whose little neck he used to smell, who learned from him how to walk and then to use a sword. And now the baby he once knew was a survivor of something more terrible than Flavius had ever seen.

'The Praeses will need to know,' the old soldier said. Justinus nodded and stood up suddenly. 'I know,' he said, 'And that's where I'm going now. I just wanted to check with you first. You've served the Wall all your life. I wanted to know if this was possible.'

'It isn't possible,' the Praeses said. Decius Ammianus had been the commanding officer of VI Victrix for five years. He was widely reputed throughout Britannia Secunda as a thoroughgoing soldier, dedicated, meticulous and careful, as befits a man who commands a legion and a province; a politician first, a warrior second.

Ammianus sat on his campaign chair in the Principia as the cohorts went through their motions outside, iron studs smashing the ground, shields clashing and interlocking to the shouts of the centurions. Behind him in the darkened office that was the headquarters of the VI, the massive granite face of the deified

Constantine stood impassive on its plinth. In front of him stood three soldiers of the second conturbernia, third cohort of the legion, a semisallis and two pedes, all of them travel-stained and with several days' growth of beard. And they had just told their commander the most extraordinary story he had ever heard.

'Tell me again,' the second officer in the room spoke for the first time. So far he had just watched the proceedings, listened to the tale of slaughter and butchery. He was Fullofaudes, Dux Britannorum, the man who spoke in these islands for the Emperor.

Paternus cleared his throat. 'The Attacotti had hit Banna, sir,' he said, 'and the Picts Camboglanna. We saw more of these further south ...'

'How far south?' the Duke wanted to know.

'Half a day's march from here, north of Isurium.'

'Show me,' the Duke murmured and Ammianus got up and crossed to the map on the far wall that showed all his bases in Britannia Secunda. He pointed for the Duke's benefit. 'Here's Isurium,' Ammianus said. 'Where did you see these Picts, semisallis?'

Paternus aimed a finger at the approximate position. It looked about right but without Justinus, he felt a little out of his depth. What was keeping the man?

'And then,' Fullofaudes was stroking his chin, 'Saxons, you say. Where did you see them?'

Again, Paternus did his best.

'But you didn't actually *fight* any of these people?' the Duke raised an eyebrow.

'No, we ...' Paternus began, but Leocadius cut him short.

'Of course we did,' he said.

The others looked at him. Vitalis opened his mouth to speak but then shut it again.

'Really?' Fullofaudes was a politician too and nearer to the inner sanctum of the Imperium than a mere commander of a legion and a province.

'We were out hunting when they hit Banna,' Leocadius said, looking the man straight in the eye, 'but at Camboglanna we fought our way out. We were the only ones left.'

'Leo ...' Paternus said softly, but his eyes were wild. What was the matter with the lad?

'We fought the Saxons at the river,' Leocadius was in full flow by now, stepping forward, his eyes alight and his arms sketch-

27

ing the story as it grew and flew from his mouth. 'They carry these big swords, heavy, straight-edged. But they were no match for ours.'

The Duke read the boy's face, noted the responses of the others. 'And the Picts near Isurium?'

'We ...'

'Not you.' The Duke cut Leocadius short, holding up an imperious hand and turning his head very deliberately to look into each man's face. 'You. Semisallis.'

Paternus wanted the ground to swallow him whole or the great stone face of Constantine to roar a reprimand. The silence throbbed. 'There were only eight of them,' he said truthfully.

'And?'

Paternus felt Leocadius' eyes boring into him, felt the tension in the lad's body, strung like a bow next to him. The semisallis faltered, then made his decision. 'We disposed of them,' he said.

Another silence. Another eternity. Then the Duke's arrogant features softened in a grin. 'Good,' he said. 'And that's what I shall do.'

It was nearly an hour later that the circitor Justinus reported at the Principia of the VI. He had shaved, bathed and borrowed a coat of mail for the occasion. He knew by now that the four were the first to bring the news of what was happening in the north; no other survivors had reached Eboracum and that could only be grim news for Paternus; his family were not here either.

Justinus had expected to see his commanding officer but instead, sitting on the Praeses' campaign chair, was Fullofaudes, the Dux Britannorum himself. Justinus had only seen the man once but he remembered the patrician bearing, the aquiline nose between the dark, suspicious eyes.

'I understand that you and your men are heroes, circitor,' Fullofaudes said. He was surrounded by adjutants, both military and civil, clerks in pallia carrying scrolls and shuffling papers. He was reminded of the old joke about how many adjutants it took to light a candle.

'Hardly that, sir,' Justinus said, 'But I thought you ought to know.'

'Know what?' The Duke was being obtuse.

'That there are at least three different tribes on the attack, sir. That's unheard of.'

'Ah, yes,' Fullofaudes held out his goblet to a slave for a refill of wine. 'The Attacotti, the Picti and the Saxones. An unholy trio, to be sure.'

'Sir ...' Justinus began.

'Out with it, man,' the Duke sipped his wine, looking up at the circitor with an expressionless face.

The circitor stepped forward, letting the helmet slip from the crook of his arm. 'Sir, I have served on the Wall for sixteen years, man and boy. And my father before me. And his father before him.'

'Admirable,' beamed Fullofaudes. 'But I don't really have time for a history lesson.'

'It is unprecedented, sir,' Justinus was not going to be put off so easily. 'Three tribes – that we know of – worse: three *peoples*, acting together. That's a conspiracy.'

Fullofaudes burst out laughing. 'Well, well,' he said, 'the conspiracy theory of history. I hadn't expected to hear that again – and certainly not from a circitor.'

Justinus stepped back, head high, face grim. The helmet was back in the crook of his arm again and he was staring into the blank, blind eyes of Constantine the Great.

'Well,' Fullofaudes took another draught of wine. 'Given the circumstances, what would you do?'

Justinus was taken aback. '*Me*, sir? I have no idea.'

'Quite,' Fullofaudes smiled, putting the wine goblet down on the table and leaning back. 'Which is why you are a circitor and I am Dux Britannorum. Let me tell you what *I* intend to do ...'

'What?' Decius Ammianus was putting on his parade armour for the review that afternoon and the Duke had caught him a little off guard. 'You're going to do *what*?'

'Sort this nonsense out,' Fullofaudes said. 'It's as well I was here, really. Oh, no offence to you, Ammianus, you're a thorough-going sort of chap, but this ...' he chose his words with care, 'this situation needs a touch of genius. That's where I come in.'

'But sir, at least take the VI.'

'Praeses,' the Duke chuckled, 'these people north of the Wall are barbarians. They may be able to take a milecastle, perhaps even a fort. But they won't stand against an army in the field. And anyway, it won't come to that. You know these riff-raff as well as I do, Ammianus. Hit-and-run; that's their style. It's all smoke and mirrors. I'll need to move fast, so I'll take an Ala... no, actually, an entire Ala is too much. Four turmae should do it; three at a pinch. I'll find their strongholds and destroy them.'

'But they're working *together*,' Ammianus persisted, sensing that his boss might just have gone mad.

'Rubbish!' Fullofaudes chuckled. 'You've been talking to that circitor ... what's his name ... Justinus?'

'No, I ...'

'Trust me, Ammianus,' the Duke clapped a patronising hand on the man's shoulder. 'No barbarians will stand against me. Now, haven't you got a legion to put through its paces?'

CHAPTER III

The barbarians stood against Fullofaudes as dawn broke over the northern moors. For over a week now the Duke had been chasing shadows and his men had watched their quarry vanishing into the mists like ghosts. The three arcani that Fullofaudes had with him knew both sides of the Wall like the backs of their hands, but north or south, they found the same story and had galloped back to the Duke with an identical message. The raiders had been there but had moved on. Yes, they had taken what they wanted – horses, cattle, grain and wine. Anyone who opposed them was hacked down without ceremony and his body hung from the nearest tree.

And there were thousands of them, the arcani said. Numbers that Rome had not seen since the days of Caratacus and Boudicca, ancient enemies whose names Roman mothers still invoked to quieten their mewling children.

'Thousands of them?' Fullofaudes stretched in the saddle, bracing his legs against the warm flanks of his grey. Ahead, on the black treeless horizon, he counted perhaps forty horsemen, strung out along the ridge, looking at him.

'Io, Arcanus,' he summoned the scout Artabanus to him. 'Where are we? What does the land do here?'

The man looked around him as the Roman cavalry stamped and shifted, awaiting the Duke's command. 'The Wall is twenty miles north, sir,' Artabanus told him. 'The fort of Coriospitum, if it's still standing.'

Fullofaudes frowned and pursed his lips. He was tired of all this negativity. Yes, they had come across the odd village looted and burned; a handful of peasants butchered at the roadside. The rest was hot air, rumours from frightened civilians who jumped at their own shadows.

'Over there?' the Duke pointed to the east.

'The scarps are steep there, sir. Not good for horses.'

'And there?' he pointed west.

'There's a river, tree lined. Not ...'

'... good for cavalry; yes, I get the drift. Decuriones.'

The Duke summoned his turmae commanders and the four of them prodded their horses forward. 'What do you make of that?' he asked. He tossed his head towards the horsemen on the skyline.

Marius was the senior man and he spoke first, unbuckling his helmet from his saddle-bow. 'I can't believe they intend to make a fight of it,' he said. 'They'll run.'

The Duke nodded. 'Gentlemen?' He needed the reassurance of the others.

Gregorius was the youngest of them, the man with least experience. 'They can't stand against half an Ala,' he said. 'Look at them – old men and boys on moorland ponies.'

'How did they take a fort?' Cassius Impius wanted to know. The others looked at him. 'Those four lads who came back; they said those bastards wiped out the commands at Banna and Camboglanna, not to mention the cavalry depot. Are we supposed to believe that old men and boys did that?'

Fullofaudes turned in his saddle to the fourth man, Varus. The Duke was not impressed with the fourth decurion. He expected his officers to know their business, accept orders without question and above all, give him the answers he wanted. For the past week, Varus had signally failed to do this last. 'I'd feel happier,' he said, 'if I knew what was on the other side of that hill.'

All the officers checked the skyline again. Apart from the odd pony shifting position, there was no movement. 'Arcanus?' the Duke turned to his scout again.

'There's a gentle slope, sir, and if I remember it rightly, a ravine.'

'A ravine?' Fullofaudes was suddenly interested. 'Which way does it run?'

'East to west, sir.'

'Steep?'

'Deeper than a man. The locals call it, in your language, the mouth of hell.'

Fullofaudes chuckled. 'The mouth of hell,' he repeated. 'I like the sound of that. Take post, gentlemen; on my command, we'll ride the bastards down. Marius, you'll lead from the right.'

'Very good, sir.'

'Sir,' Artabanus the arcanus was pointing ahead. Breaking out from the raiders' line, reluctantly it seemed, a solitary horseman was trotting down the slope and across the broad valley. He was wearing an old wolfskin cloak, much patched and mended and his pony was stout and short-legged. In his hand he carried a staff and tied to it a white piece of cloth.

'They want to parley,' Fullofaudes said, smiling. 'As soon as they've surrendered, gentlemen,' he said to his decuriones, 'we'll hang one man in five. The others can lead us to their villages. I think the boys will have earned a bit of fun by then.'

There was a ripple of laughter from the horsemen nearest to the Duke. Here was a man all right; one who understood the purpose of a campaign. What was the point of a sore arse and blistered feet if there was no wine, women and song at the end of it?

The little horseman had ridden within range of Fullofaudes' horse archers but the Duke was a patient man; and there were rules of engagement.

'Io, domini,' the rider said in passable Latin.

All the officers except Varus laughed. 'I like a man,' the Duke said, 'who knows his betters.'

'Io, Dumno,' Arbatanus waved to him.

'You know this man?' Fullofaudes asked.

'Yes, sir. His name is Dumno. He's from the north. North of the Wall.'

'What is it you want, Dumno,' the Duke asked, 'from north of the Wall?'

'I have a message, sir,' the squat little man said, 'for the commander of this Ala.'

'That would be me,' Fullofaudes said. 'Get on with it.'

'May I have the honour to know to whom I am speaking?' Dumno said. His Latin was better than passable; it was excellent.

'I am Fullofaudes,' the Duke said, 'Dux Britannorum. Who is your message from?'

Dumno half turned in his saddle, leaning heavily on one arm as he twisted his squat body. He pointed a trembling finger. 'Him,' he said, softly. All eyes followed the finger to the horizon. A knot of horsemen had arrived in the centre of the line, including one on a huge black stallion that snorted and pawed the ground. He was a big man, in Roman mail armour but the oddest thing about him was his helmet. It was a cavalry parade model, fitting closely over the head and surmounted by a laurel wreath. It had a plain silver face that flashed blank and expressionless in the brightness of the morning. Fullofaudes had not seen one of these in years. As a boy in Rome he remembered them from the cavalry games when crowds of thousands sat in the Colisseum to watch mock battles, roaring to the wheeling and clash of the squadrons. To see one here, on a bleak hillside at the arse-end of the universe, came as something of a surprise.

And there was another surprise too. Beyond the thin line of horsemen a standard-bearer rode into view. He was carrying a scarlet flag edged with gold – the vexillum from Camboglanna.

Varus felt the hairs on the back of his neck crawling. The rider on the black horse was not moving. He sat perfectly upright, as if he were dead, staring blindly at them all. Varus looked closer. On second thoughts, he was staring at *him*, with a cold, unblinking stare which seemed to peel back the layers of his skin to the bone beneath.

'And who is he?' Fullofaudes refused to be fazed by theatricals. The man might fart thunderbolts and piss ambrosia but when all was said and done, he was a barbarian wearing a stolen helmet.

'Valentinus,' Dumno almost whispered.

'Man of Valentia?' Fullofaudes said. 'I am none the wiser. What is his message?'

Dumno wanted the ground to swallow him up. He wriggled and squirmed in his saddle.

'Out with it, man!' the Duke bellowed.

'He says ...' Dumno took a run at the words. 'He says if you lay down your weapons now and leave your horses, he will spare your lives. He also says ...'

'There's more?' Fullofaudes thundered.

'He also says that you now have no northern frontier worthy of the name. You will abandon Eboracum. And because he realizes that will take some time, he gives you until Saturmalia to do it.'

Only the wind made an answer, sighing through the flying tail of the dragon banner streaming over the heads of the Duke's front line of horsemen.

'Seven weeks,' murmured Fullofaudes. 'He *is* generous. Take my answer back, Arcanus – and be thankful I'm leaving you alive to deliver it.'

'He's got my family, sir,' Dumno blurted out. 'He'll kill them if I don't go back.'

'Calm yourself, Dumno,' Artabanus reached out to pat the man's shoulder. 'The Duke won't let that happen.'

Fullofaudes was less than pleased that this renegade thought he could speak for the Dux Britannorum but he let it go. 'Tell this ... Valentinus ... that in ...' he looked at the one hundred and twenty riders at his back, 'in approximately ten minutes I shall have ridden over his dead body. I think, after that, all negotiations will be a little superfluous, don't you?'

Dumno hauled his rein and with a last despairing look at the Duke, trotted back up the slope. The Roman cavalry watched as the little man spoke briefly to Valentinus on his black horse, gesturing wildly in their direction. Then he kicked his pony through their lines and was gone. A battlefield was no place for Dumno.

'Where were we?' Fullofaudes clicked his fingers and a trooper hurried to his side, carrying the man's helmet with its gilded crest and eyebrow ridge. 'Marius, lead on the right. Cassius, you'll follow on the left.' The Duke scanned the faces of his two remaining commanders as the first two saluted and rode away. This would be a tough call, but he was Dux Britannorum and he made it anyway. 'Gregorius; is this your first action?'

The younger man swallowed hard. 'Yes, sir,' he said.

'Support Marius. I want you on his heels. If you can't smell his horse's farts, you're too far behind and must close up. Understood?'

'Perfectly, sir,' the young man saluted and turned his horse.

'Varus, you have the reserve. If anything goes wrong – which it won't – I expect you to pull us out of it. Do I make myself clear'

'Very, sir,' the Decurion said and swung hard on his rein. Fullofaudes took the helmet from the trooper and buckled it under his chin. Now his face looked nearly as blank as that bastard on the hill. The Duke looked at him again, the dull silver face, the empty eye sockets. He had not drawn his sword and there was no battle-standard at his shoulder. Whatever cold shiver ran briefly down the spine of the Dux Britannorum, he shook himself free of it. This was not going to be a battle. There sat a mob of ill-armed, badly-led cattle thieves and sheep-shaggers. Most of them would run at the sound of advance. Creeping up at dead of night was one thing;

standing against Rome in full fighting trim would be something else.

'Cornicen!' the Duke unsheathed his sword with a rush of iron.

The horn blower trotted forward to take his place behind his commander and to his right.

'The Ala,' Fullofaudes began, 'will ...' He waited until every man behind him was ready, 'draw swords.'

Every man in the second rank of each turma had released his weapon, the long blade of the cavalry that could split a man from knave to chops. Those in the front rank tightened their grip on their spears. They would use them like lances, to jab the enemy out of their saddles while the second rank would ride over them. 'The Invicti Britanniciani will advance, Cornicen. Walk. March.'

The horn blasted out in the morning and the whole line, except Fullofaudes and his trumpeter, moved forward. Horses snorted and tossed their heads, their bits jingling under the dragon standard that whined as the wind blew through it. Hooves cut up the grass, sending clods of earth into the air and the ground, even this early in the morning, was dry enough to send up dust. The Decurion Marius let his horse caracole to the left, assuming the position of the Duke and his own trumpeter blasted his horn, quickening the pace as his first turma rose to marching speed.

Fullofaudes watched the other turma spring forward over the short turf, their helmet plumes swaying as their speed picked up. The lances were still upright, probing the sky and beyond them, the Duke could see the enemy on the hillside, jostling and skittering as the Romans advanced. He could hear their unearthly yells as his own men rode on in silence. Varus' turma was beginning to move, the reserve in support of the others and Fullofaudes, with his trumpeter, took his place in line alongside the decurion he trusted least. Perhaps he should have given this job to Cassius, but it was too late for all that now.

The barbarians were moving at last. Marius squinted under the rim of his helmet. The silver-faced giant was waving his sword, galloping forward with his riders in no cohesion at all. For centuries it had been like this. A disorganized rabble, screaming like the Furies, would hurl itself at the Roman lines, battering against shield walls and going down before the legions. It was the same against cavalry. Sword to sword. Lance to lance. The steady attack of the Roman Ala could smash its way through any barbarian defence ever built. In the open, it would be slaughter.

They were halfway up the slope when the barbarian horse broke. The man called Valentinus was yelling commands to the others and they fell back. Marius' front rank had reached a canter now, the horn braying out its metallic orders. Battle-mad, the lancers on the wings were riding ahead of their commander even though he was bawling at them to keep their line. Two of the spears thudded home, the iron tips skewering two barbarians who were catapulted out of their saddles and lay writhing on the ground, bloody and dying. The hooves of the second rank trampled them, kicking their heads to a crimson pulp and the centre was forcing Marius on to the full gallop.

The timing was so predictable. Still at the trot a hundred paces back, Fullofaudes could have taken bets on how long the barbarians would stand. They had cracked exactly as he thought they would and they were streaming back towards their hilltop, nobody galloping faster than the silver-faced man on the black horse.

The men on Marius' right flank who had drawn first blood were also first over the rise. Whatever concerns they had had about hidden traps on the reverse slope vanished because there weren't any; only the men who had lined the ridge, running hell for leather in the opposite direction. The ground was softer here, Marius noticed, churned by horses. He frowned, confused. The ground had not got like this from the few horses he had seen. His trumpeter sounded the charge and every man in his turma and Cassius' broke into the gallop. There was no stopping them now. This was a field day. True the field itself was narrowing, with steep slopes to the right and stands of elms to the left, but the field itself was empty.

'Turma, left wheel!' Marius ordered and his trumpeter blew the command. The scattered barbarians were galloping like men possessed for the safety of the elms to the Roman left and the half Ala crashed forward across open ground. Fullofaudes laughed. His men had not even bothered to roar their barritus, the battle cry that spread terror on any battlefield where the Romans stood.

Marius saw them first. As his front rank of horsemen thudded towards the line of trees, archers peered out from trunks and roots and a hiss of goose-feather shafts filled the air. Marius went down, his throat torn by an arrowhead. His first line of lancers hauled on their reins, but it was too late to avoid the hail of missiles and within minutes Marius' turma had disintegrated. Gregorius had no idea what was happening. He shouted at his trumpeter to sound the halt but the man was already dead, his horse cantering away with the man sprawled over his neck. Cassius yelled at his men to wheel away from the line of the trees and the whole front rank was now in disorder, cavalrymen jostling each other and their horses rearing and shying as a second hail of arrows hit them. The decurion led his turma horizontally towards the steep scarp slopes which had been to his right. The arcanus had been right about this ground; it was too steep for horses. And Cassius' jaw dropped as he rode towards them. Fanning out across the scarp ridges were more archers. They were roaring defiance and sending volley after volley down into the dip of the land, turning the grass slick and bloody as their shafts struck home.

'Sound the recall!' Fullofaudes shouted to Varus who had halted his line out of bowshot of either body of archers. He swung his horse round to ride back over the ridge as the cornicen's notes blasted in his ear. His eyes widened as he looked up. Along the sky-line over which his half Ala had just ridden, a line of barbarian horsemen were forming up. And what began as a line became a crowd, a mob; more horses than Fullofaudes could match. And on the back of every one was a wild-looking madman with blue swirls across his face who could smell Roman blood ...

It was two days later and a little after dawn that Antonius Bulo was guarding the north-east corner of the VI Victrix camp at Eboracum. There was no doubting it now; winter was on its way and the man was shivering as he stamped his way along the ramparts, worn smooth by two centuries of marching feet. His shield was slung over his back and he carried his spear at the slope. In an hour, Petrucius would relieve him and he could get some breakfast.

It was the call he heard first. A cry; something like a strangled shout to the north. He squinted into the early light. If this was some drunken trader trying to offload trinkets or cheap wine, he'd tell him his fortune. But it wasn't a trader. It was a signifer of cavalry, still wearing the wolfskin over his helmet. He was calling out incoherently, invoking Jupiter and Mercury and any other god he knew, stumbling on bare, bleeding feet as he crossed the vallum, trying to run now that he saw the great fortress wall. Where was his standard, Bulo wondered, the dragon he was supposed to give his life to protect? Where was his sword? His horse? More importantly, where were the other one hundred and twenty men of the Invicti

Britanniciani who had ridden out with Fullofaudes over a week ago?

'Io,' Bulo shouted down to the gate. 'Soldier coming,' and he hurried from the ramparts as the bolts were hauled open and the timbers groaned and the gate guard caught the signifer in their arms.

Claudius Metellus had been signifer of the Invicti Britanniciani for four years. But today, as he stood before his praeses in the candlelit principia, he never wanted to see a cavalry unit again and the praeses wondered whether 'invicti', unbeaten, should be struck from the Ala's name for ever.

Justinus was circitor of the watch that morning, attending the praeses personally, so he stood at the man's elbow as the signifer told his story. Decius Ammianus was not known for his courtesy but the signifer had been through hell in the last few days and the praeses let the man sit. Justinus could see that his feet were cut to ribbons and his left arm was stiff with caked blood.

'The entire command?' Ammianus could not believe it. He sat, even greyer than usual, shaking his head.

'All of them, sir,' the signifer said, 'save me.'

The praeses looked at the man, wondering how it was that one man among so many had been spared. 'And why were you saved?' he asked. The Ala Invicta Britannici were part of the auxiliaries of the VI Victrix; Ammianus expected such men's shields to be picked up in the heather, not to have them come back to tell the sorry tale of a defeat.

'To bring you a message, sir,' Metellus said, 'From Valentinus.'

'Who?'

'The leader of the barbarians, sir.'

Ammianus looked at Justinus. 'Circitor, you know these people, on the Wall. Have you heard that name before?'

'No, praeses,' Justinus said. 'Metellus, did you see this man, in the flesh?'

The signifer nodded. 'As big as a house,' he said, eyes wide in memory of him, 'rides a black horse.'

'What does he look like?' Justinus was racking his brains to think of anyone north of the Wall who fitted that picture.

'I don't know, circitor; he covered his face with a helmet.'

'What sort of helmet?' Ammianus asked.

'I've never seen one like it,' Metellus said. 'It was solid silver and had a face mask.'

Ammianus frowned. Like most of the men stationed at Eboracum, the signifer had been born in Britannia; Justinus had been too. It needed the wide experience of a true Roman to grasp the significance of it. 'It's a cavalry parade helmet,' he murmured, 'And I've never seen one like it west of Gaul either. Tell me, Metellus; the man in the helmet, what was his message?'

The signifer swallowed hard. 'That you ... we ... are to evacuate Eboracum, sir. We are to leave our weapons and horses here. The Picti will escort us to Verterae, at the mouth of the river. Then we are to go home.'

'Home?' the praeses chuckled. 'Where's home for you, signifer?'

'Far to the south, sir,' Metellus told him. 'Ratae Coritanorum.'

'Circitor, you?'

'Further south still, sir,' Justinus said. 'Verulamium.'

The praeses nodded. 'The chances are,' he said, 'that if we left these shores I would be the only one going home.' He looked at both men's faces. 'Brindisium, before you ask. Quite a pleasant little resort, really. I miss it.' But the praeses did not reminisce for long. 'What happened to the Duke?' he asked.

For a long time, Metellus searched for the right words; indeed, any words at all. 'After we were surrounded, Valentinus drove us back to the ravine.' He was almost whispering. In his mind, the man was no longer safe in the principia of the largest army camp in Britannia; he was out again on the windswept moors with dead men and horses all around him and savages in skins and blue paint chanting and whooping as they rode their horses round. Every now and then a barbarian archer would send an arrow singing into the clustered ranks of the half Ala and no amount of parrying with swords or defending with shields could prevent it.

'Then he called out, behind that damned mask of his that we had a choice. We either did what was fine, what was Roman and threw ourselves over the ravine's edge. Or we could surrender and become his slaves.'

'What was Fullofaudes' answer?' Ammianus wanted to know.

'He said he was Dux Britannorum,' the signifer told him, 'and would wipe the arse of no man. He ... he turned to us, those who were left and said it was our choice. He, for one, intended to die with a sword in his hand. He did.' Metellus hung his head and his body shook. Justinus knew the man was crying, broken, perhaps beyond recall.

'What happened to his body?' the praeses asked softly, as if he would rather not know his answer.

'The Attacotti were there, sir ...'

Justinus stiffened. He knew what was coming.

'When ... when the battle was over, they stripped the Duke naked and slung him over a horse. I was tied behind it so all I saw for half a day was the Duke's face.' Metellus' voice had been rising, the words coming faster, louder and shriller, as though forced through his tightening throat under pressure. 'It ...' His voice broke and he coughed, controlling himself with superhuman effort. He took a shuddering breath and began again. 'It had no eyes, sir. Two of the Attacotti had taken them. They ...' he gagged slightly, 'they swallowed them in front of me.'

The signifer sagged visibly in his chair. For him there would be no more war. Decius Ammianus, never the tenderest of men, lifted up the man's chin. His cheeks trickled with tears. 'All right, boy,' he said. 'Get yourself to the surgeon. The medicus can fix your feet and that arm needs attention too. As for your soul, well, Mithras is also a soldier. Pray to him. He'll understand.'

Once the signifer had done his best to salute, he dragged himself away helped by a couple of principia guards. Ammianus turned to see Justinus looking at him.

'Well, sir?' the circitor asked.

'Well, what, sir?' the praeses snapped. It was not every day that the eyes of the Dux Britannorum, right hand of the Emperor, were ripped from their sockets and eaten.

'What will we do?'

The praeses sighed and crossed the room to the map on his wall. 'Fullofaudes must have been surprised about ... here ...' his finger found it, 'if what the signifer has told us is correct. What's that ... three, four days' march?'

Justinus nodded. 'Are we going after them, sir?' he asked. They all had even more of a score to settle now.

The praeses looked at him. 'Are you a superstitious man ... Justinus, isn't it?'

'I worship Mithras, sir,' the circitor said, 'and Jupiter highest and best, of course.'

'I'm talking about omens,' the praeses said. 'When the Duke decided to go off on that mad hunt of his, I offered him a vexillation of the VI. Four cohorts, to be exact. Know what he said?'

'No, sir.'

'He said – and it's rather ironic now, in the light of what's happened – he said, "If I can't wipe out this little difficulty with four cavalry turmae, I don't deserve the Emperor's respect." But he must have seen the look on my face, because he said he would take an eagle, so that the genius of the legion would fly with him.'

'And?'

'It wouldn't budge. I was there, in the chapel, when Metellus tried to lift it. It wouldn't move. *I* tried. The Duke tried. Nothing. It's there still, as though ...'

'... As though the gods knew,' Justinus finished the sentence for him. He felt the skin crawl on his neck.

For a moment the two men looked at each other in silence, then the praeses broke the spell. 'No, circitor,' he said, 'we're not going after them. I am sending a message to the Emperor. With something as serious as the death of his Duke, I can't do less. Then, we are going to double the guard and lock this place down. I want it sealed so that a mouse can't get in. It's going to be a long winter.'

CHAPTER IV

Eboracum

Three days later, the first refugees reached the Ussos, bedraggled lines of peasants in the driving rain. They came to the great north gate of the camp of the VI Victrix and were met with the clash of spears crossed to bar their way.

'We've no room for you here,' the circitor had told them, ignoring the pleading eyes and outstretched arms. He was a family man himself, with children no taller than his boot, but he was a man who had his orders, direct from the praeses himself. No one was to be allowed in unless they carried the necessary papers. And even then, they must be searched. And a second search must be carried out before they were admitted to the Principia.

Over the next week, hundreds of people trickled towards Eboracum, all with their tales of blood and fire. The Picti had struck here, the Attacotti there. Were there Saxones with them, the guards were told to ask. Who knew? One look at the thundering horses, the flaming brands and the villagers had snatched up their little ones and run. Men who stood and fought were hacked down, their heads sliced off and hung from saddle bows already dark brown with blood.

And what were the VI doing about it, the refugees wanted to know. The VI were limitanei, for Jupiter's sake, guards of the frontier. More, they were the largest fighting force in the whole of Britannia Secunda. Were they going to hide behind their impregnable walls for ever?

'It's a fair question,' Leocadius sat with his fist around a goblet of Spanish wine in the tavern along the Via Caesi. The place was out of bounds for soldiers of the VI which was precisely why he was there. Vitalis looked at him and the girl on his lap. What was her name – Lucia? Lucilla? He couldn't remember. After his umpteenth goblet he was having difficulty remembering his own name.

'How do you mean?' he managed, his tongue thick with drink.

Leocadius frowned at his friend, then burst out laughing. 'You are *such* a lightweight,' he said and clinked his goblet with Vitalis'. He leaned as close to the table as he could, allowing for the girl hanging around his neck, breathing hot breath and suggestions in equal measure into his ear. 'What I am saying is, why aren't we out there collecting a few heads of our own?'

Lucia stopped being subtle and ran her tongue over his ear, whispering something that Vitalis couldn't hear and was glad not to. Leocadius laughed again and nodded to the girl. 'On the other hand,' he said, adjusting the arm around her so that his hand was somewhere a little more intimate, 'There's no hurry, is there?' She giggled and squirmed suggestively in his lap.

Vitalis, through the blur of the oil lamps and the raucous laughter at the tables, suddenly felt rather in the way. He downed the last of his wine, shook his head and stood up, after a fashion. 'I'll be saying "Goodnight" then,' he slurred.

'Indeed you will,' a stern voice barked in his ear. He half turned to see Flaminius, primus pilus now that Piso was dead. Vitalis remembered the man from his training days. His bark, men said, was worse than his bite but Vitalis knew different and had the scars to prove it. Even now, in cold weather, the skin on his back crawled and twitched to Flaminius' cane. The thing was gnarled, carved to inflict maximum pain. 'The praeses wants you,' the centurion said. Then he looked at Leocadius. 'And you.'

Leocadius' smile had frozen on his lips. 'If it's just a matter of us being slightly out of bounds, primus pilus ...'

'Nothing to do with that – this time,' the centurion told him.

Leocadius' mind was racing. He had never felt the whip before and had no intention of starting now. 'The girl, then ...' his face lit up. 'I don't even know her name.' He slapped her rump. 'Look,' he held her out to the man by the wrist. 'You can have her if you like.'

'Leo!' Lucia shrilled, frowning, sitting back down on his lap with a bump. She had been passed around various cohorts of the VI before, but she liked it to be at least partially of her own free will.

'Get up,' Flaminius ordered and Leocadius obeyed, letting Lucia slide unceremoniously to the floor. The centurion was a big man and he had four pedes with him, men who were not from Leocadius' cohort. He could make a run for it, but how far would he get? Flaminius was already talking to Vitalis. 'How many have you had?' he pointed to the empty goblet.

'Some,' was all the lad could manage.

The centurion clicked his fingers. 'Ussos. Now,' he said and both lads were hauled away, their arms pinioned by a guard on each side of them, Vitalis trying to force his legs to walk vaguely in the same direction.

'You arsehole!' the luscious Lucia bellowed at Leocadius' back. 'Don't you think you can come sniffing around me again in a hurry.' Her snarl died as her eyes lighted on a handsome young man sitting with his friends at a nearby table. 'Ave,' she said in her best Latin, smiling. She ran her fingers through his curls. 'It's Marcus, isn't it? Ave. Ave.'

The cold of Novembris hit Vitalis like a hammer and they dragged him with the constantly complaining Leocadius north to the river. With the plumed helmet of Flaminius ahead like a battle standard, the seven wove their way through the side alleys in the dark of a smoky evening. Dogs barked in the shadows and the smell of the tanneries wafted on the early night air. Vitalis' head hurt and he suddenly could not think of a damned thing to say. Leocadius, on the other hand, born barrack-room lawyer that he was, could not shut up.

Ahead, against the purple of the sky loomed the towers and walls of the camp where torches flickered like fireflies on a summer's evening. But in front of all that the Ussos meandered, dark and mysterious past the wharves and jetties. Fishing boats bobbed at anchor between the trading ships from Nostrum Mare, their holds still full of amphorae of wine from Iberia, earthenware from Gaul.

Leocadius couldn't believe it as his captors clattered with him down steps that led to the lapping water's edge. It was dark down here and rats scuttled along the timbers where, at daybreak, the whole world would bring their goods to market. 'No!' he screamed. 'What are you doing?' He had his legs knocked from under him and he felt his head being forced down towards the swirling water. Primus pilus Flaminius was kneeling alongside him. 'Think of it as Father Tiber,' he grinned. 'You're making an offering to the river. You.' He nodded to the guards and they rammed Leocadius' head under water. He shut his mouth and his eyes and did his best to hold his breath. How long they held him there, as the veins in his neck bulged with the effort and the Ussos roared in his ears, he couldn't tell. When they finally hauled him out, coughing and spluttering, he could barely stand.

'Next,' Flaminius said as if he was supervising pay day. Vitalis' guards threw him forwards on the steps. Then one of them kicked him viciously behind his left knee and he went down, the sudden pain jarring through the blur of his vision. Then he was under water, eyes open, trying to make sense of what was happening. Bubbles were bursting from his mouth and he felt a terrible pain in his lungs. Lights were bursting in all the colours of the rainbow behind his eyes and his nose and throat burned. Then they jerked him backwards and he roared as the air burst down water-filled passageways and let him live again.

Both men now stood dripping wet and shivering in the cold, looking rather shamefaced at the centurion. 'Best way I know of sobering a man up,' Flaminius said. 'The praeses wants to see you.'

They had marched at double-quick time, which was almost a run and now they stood in the flicker of the guttering torches and lamplights of the Principia. Flaminius and his guards had been ordered away. The lads stood to attention in the near silence, listening to the spit and sputter of the torch-flames and the low wind that moaned forever through every building in the camp, winding its cold fingers into the brain below every other sound. They turned at the sound of footsteps to their left and Justinus and Paternus strode in. The circitor was in his tunic of mail, his sword at his side. Did that man *never* relax? Leocadius wondered. Paternus had been in mid-shave, the stubble gone from one side of his chin.

'Justinus, what ...?' Leocadius began, but a door crashed back and the praeses swept in. All four men clicked to attention and stood facing him. Decius Ammianus was wearing a scruffy tunic that had seen better days and he wore civilian sandals rather than his army boots. He unwrapped a scroll lying on a side table and sat down, crossing his legs.

'Gentlemen,' he nodded to them. 'At ease, please.' The four slid their feet apart and locked their arms behind their backs. The praeses looked at each man in turn. Justinus he knew, a circitor with guts and experience. He was a chip off the old block, because men like Flavius Coelius had *made* the legions of Rome. They had carried the eagles to the far corners of the world and their sons would do so again. Paternus was a semisallis and Ammianus had had to ask the relevant tribune about him. The man was good, the tribune had reported, but less so since he had got back from the Wall. His family were missing and he was fretting about them. The others were faces only but those faces were still glistening with water in the torch flames. The praeses was no fool and he knew the ways of his primus pilus. He would have found the lads pissed in some tavern somewhere and this was his way of sobering them up. Well, Ammianus thought to himself, some have greatness thrust upon them.

'We need heroes,' the praeses said.

Nobody moved. Nobody spoke.

'You men are from the Wall,' he went on by way of explanation. 'To date, you are the only survivors of the Wall.'

Justinus wanted to say that that could not be, that somewhere the Wall must have held, whatever kind of attack was launched against it. Segedunum, in the east; Onum with its fancy bath house; Vercovicium high on its crest – surely nobody could take that. Ammianus read the man's mind from his quizzical look. 'I know,' he said softly, 'It's unbelievable, but we have to face it. And I'm not about to send the VI blundering northwards in an attempt to rectify the problem. The Duke tried that and look where it got him. Walled up here, we're safe. Unless those murderous bastards have got siege engines and know how to use them, they won't make so much as a dent in Eboracum.'

Justinus knew that. He also knew that every fort on the Wall had its own onager, the ballista called the wild ass because of its kick. Stones hurled from this could smash palisades to splinters, cave in skulls and tear ribs apart. If all sixteen forts had gone that meant that sixteen wild asses were at the barbarians' disposal. And once they had one, they may be able to make others.

'You men live in the camp,' Ammianus went on. 'What's the mood? What are people saying?'

Again, no one spoke.

'Come on,' said the praeses. 'Out with it.'

'With respect, sir.' It was Leocadius who put his head over the parapet. 'It's all a little ... well ... doom and gloom, I suppose. Men aren't happy. They want to know why we aren't out there, giving something back.'

Ammianus nodded. 'You ... er ... Paternus ... you're a semisallis. Is that how you see it too?'

'People are afraid, sir,' he said. 'The Wall is all we know. It has stood as a bulwark against our enemies for longer than anyone can remember.'

'Exactly,' the praeses nodded. 'So I want you four to do something about it. In two days each of you will be promoted. Circitor, you will be made a tribune.'

Justinus' mouth hung open. He could never have aspired to this exalted rank if he served a thousand years.

'It will have to be supernumerary at first,' Ammianus went on, 'because, as you know, the legion has its full quota at the moment.'

'Sir, I ...' but the praeses was in no mood to listen to Justinus' protestations and held up his hand.

'Semisallis,' Ammianus looked at Paternus, 'You will wear the lorica of primus pilus – again, supernumerary. Don't get under Flaminius' feet; he won't appreciate it and operating as a team is an alien concept for him. You two,' he fixed his gaze on Leocadius and Vitalis, 'are circitors forthwith. There is one vacancy here, he nodded towards Justinus, 'and I understand Decius Salvinus is about ready to hang up his boots.' The praeses stood up and poured himself some wine. Then he filled four more goblets and handed one to each man. 'Congratulations, gentlemen,' he said. 'The VI salute you,' and he raised his cup.

'Praeses, we ...' Justinus was far from happy.

'You are my standard bearers,' Ammianus said, 'my aquilifers. And I'm asking you to lead in a very peculiar battle. On every street corner, along every wharf, in every shop ...' he looked at Leocadius, 'in every tavern, it will be your job to sow harmony, wisdom and strength. If you hear that there have been atrocities, play them down. If you hear we aren't doing enough, tell them we're doing all we can and that the Emperor is on his way.'

'The Emperor?' Justinus was astounded.

Ammianus nodded. 'Or his representative. And I can assure you, gentlemen, he will not come alone. In the meantime, it is our duty – yours and mine – to keep spirits up. And that,' he drained his cup, 'is a two-edged sword. Defeatism is outlawed from Eboracum from today. If a man spits on a denarius, I want him flogged. If he mutters darkly in corners plotting against us, I want his balls nailed to a gatepost. Anyone who deserts will be brought back and hanged, if necessary in front of his wife and children.' He paused for effect and looked at each man in turn. 'Are we clear, gentlemen?' he asked.

There was another pause. Then, 'Yes, sir,' came the answer.

'Good. Well, then, if there's nothing more ...'

'I have a request, sir,' Paternus stepped forward, even more aware now that he had just been promoted that he still had wet stubble on his chin.

'Primus pilus,' Ammianus was listening.

'I understand that you are sending out cavalry patrols from time to time.'

'I am,' the praeses nodded.

'Permission to ride with them, sir,' Paternus said.

'Why?' Ammianus asked.

'My family, sir,' the new primus pilus said. 'My wife and son. They are out there somewhere. I'd like to find them.'

'Very well,' the praeses said. 'But watch yourself, Paternus. I'd hate to lose my extra first centurion so soon.'

Despite himself, Paternus was smiling.

'Goodnight, gentlemen,' Ammianus turned and the four began to file out. 'Oh, Justinus.'

'Sir.' The new tribune stood to attention.

The praeses waited until the others had gone. 'There was something you wanted to say?'

'Perhaps it's not my place, sir,' Justinus said.

'Stop thinking like a circitor!' Ammianus snapped. 'You're a tribune now, my right hand man ... well, one of them, anyway. And I know it's not going to be a bed of roses. My tribunes have their noses so firmly up their own arses I don't know how they can breathe. They won't exactly welcome you with open arms.'

Justinus knew that. Most tribunes were rich young gentlemen whose families had been Somebody in Rome since the time of the deified Augustus. Men like Justinus from the ranks usually got no higher than primus pilus and that was after twenty years carrying a shield and pounding boot leather. He would be the unmistakeable smell of shit in the bed of roses. 'No, sir, it's not that,' he said.

'If it's playing the spy you're worried about, don't be. That's precisely why I've made you a tribune. No one with a lower rank could hope to achieve anything in the camp. The others can wander the canabae to their hearts' content. I don't care what the riff-raff south of the river think – although, Jupiter knows, we don't need a rebellion on our hands. No, it's the legion I worry about, Justinus. You and I both know we aren't equipped for a field army's work. That's what I've asked the Emperor for. And, Jupiter willing, given fair seas and good roads, we'll have his answer back soon.'

Justinus stood there.

'There's something else,' the praeses said.

'We are not heroes, sir,' Justinus said.

The praeses pursed his lips and crossed the room to refill his goblet. He offered the pitcher to the tribune but Justinus shook his head. 'Your man ... circitor Leocadius ... he's been swaggering around Eboracum for weeks with tales of your glory and prowess.' He smiled. 'I've been told the head count of Picts he killed stands at fifteen now.'

Justinus was shaking his head. 'That's exactly it,' he said. 'He killed nobody. None of us did.'

'What did you do?' Ammianus asked.

'We ran, sir,' Justinus felt better now he had said that and stood waiting for his new rank and quite possibly, his old one, to be taken away.

'I prefer to think of it as a tactical withdrawal,' the praeses chose his words carefully.

'Sir ...'

'Damn it, man,' Ammianus snapped. 'This is not about you. If you have a conscience, swallow it; along with your pride. We are not playing games here, sir. I have promoted you and your boys because of your courage in the face of the enemy, because apart from that gibbering idiot who brought us news of Fullofaudes' cock-up, you are the only people who have even seen these bastards – at least, you're the only ones in uniform.'

'But Fullofaudes ...'

'Fullofaudes was full of shit, tribune,' the praeses said, grim-faced. 'And I have a legion on the edge. These endless trickles of the dispossessed from the north don't help. That's why I don't let them in. We don't need their scaremongering or those buggers outside are likely to forget their oath to the Emperor and join the barbarians. It may be half of them already have.' He stood with his nose almost pressed to Justinus' chin. 'Do I have your full support?' he bellowed, laying stress on every word.

'You do, sir,' Justinus told him. It had to be enough.

The legion hardly ever paraded like this but the praeses had his reasons. Every man who could walk was there, links of mail or bronze scales gleaming in the morning sun. It was as if Sol Invictus himself was smiling on the VI as the great silver eagle was paraded through the massed ranks. The townspeople from the canabae and the colonia were let in in sufficient numbers so that they could celebrate the four heroes singled out for praise. Every centurion was there, every cohort. Only the sick of the Ala Invicta Britanniciani who had not ridden out with Fullofaudes were missing. The nine men and their nine horses would not have impressed anybody and as they were the only cavalry Ammianus had, he kept them out of the way. This would be an infantry affair only.

Claudius Metellus watched from his position in the stands. He was sitting with the wives of the legion and honoured guests, members of the ordo of Eboracum, the civilian committee who ran the town. He was not down there on the windswept parade ground with the dragon standard in his grip; that was because he could not hold one any more. Ever since the field of Hell-mouth, he could barely hold a spoon. Even now, as he watched the other signifers going through their paces, he felt his knees trembling and could not control the shake in his right hand. He did not care whether anyone was looking at him or not because he was far, far past all that. His nerve had gone and he would never be the same.

Flavius Coelius, the weapons master of the legion, stood beaming as his boy received the scarf of a tribune. There were tears in his eyes and he wished his Marcia could have been there to see this day. The horns blasted and the drums rattled and the Adjutant read out the four names and their new ranks. The praeses sat on his campaign chair on a raised dais at one end of the parade ground, the cornicines arranged around him and the eagle glittering at his shoulder. He said a few quiet words to each man – Justinus Coelius, the tribune; Paternus Priscus, the first centurion; Leocadius Honorius and Vitalis Celatius the circitors and then, as they took their places in their respective ranks, Ammianus looked at his legion. The tribunate were, as the praeses could have predicted, haughty in the extreme and they shifted imperceptibly as Justinus stood among them. Across the field, Flaminius grunted out of the corner of his mouth to Paternus, 'Don't let this go to your head, son; I'll be watching.' It was just as well that the praeses could not hear the hissed comments from the ranks of the circitors directed at the new boys.

'VI Victrix,' Ammianus shouted so that his voice carried to every corner of the camp and drifted across the Ussos to the smoky streets beyond. 'Today you have new heroes among you; you who are heroes already. Behold, your heroes. Behold your eagle. In the name of the Emperor!' and he raised his hand. The thousand swords hissed clear of their scabbards while the spearmen raised their weapons high. The archers pulled their bowstrings back to their chests, though their arrows stayed in the quiver. When the praeses' hand came down, sword blades clashed on the oval shields in a rhythmic chant that carried to the far mountains and must have reached the Wall itself. Then the other noise started, the cornicines of the legion braying with their terrifying screams and the deep-throated barritus from three thousand voices – 'Victrix! Victrix! Victrix!'

It was a little thing but it was Ammianus' own and he was just letting the world know who ruled it.

The lamps burned low that night. It had been a day of feasting and celebration and even though Ammianus doubled the guard to the north to watch the night roads and the far horizon, the legion relaxed and drank and ate their fill. So it was early morning before Flavius made his way to the new quarters of his son, in the tribunes' block south of the Principia. The guards at the doorway saluted him. He was the hastiliarus, the weapons master and every soldier of the VI knew him by sight.

'Look at this,' Flavius smiled, throwing his arms wide at the sumptuous surroundings. All his working life as a soldier, he had slept in a contubernia, the eight man unit who ate, slept, fought and died together on some far field. Their beds were hard and unyielding, their food equally so. Under stone or under leather, everywhere was cold, grey and grim. It was the way it had always been. But here, things were different. Justinus' bed was wooden, with a soft mattress and pillows. He had a couch to eat on and low tables of marble brought from Italia. The oil lamps had laughing faces carved in Graecia and the metal ewers, glinting in the half light had the bears of some German forest chasing each other through trees of beaten bronze.

'I can't quite get used to it,' Justinus poured a goblet of wine for his father. 'I'm not sure I ever will.'

'How many slaves have you got?' the older man asked, taking the cup.

'One would be too many,' Justinus said.

'Ah, no,' Flavius laughed. 'One is civilized. I don't know what I would do without old Rialbus.' He looked his only son in the face. 'What's this all about?' he asked, 'really, I mean?'

'Haven't you heard?' Justinus said. 'We're heroes of the Wall – Pat, Leo, Vit. We're all that stands between you and certain annihilation.' He gestured with the ewer, sending a trail of golden wine spraying through the lamp light.

'Justinus ...' Flavius was looking for the words. They wouldn't come.

'I know!' the Tribune bellowed, rounding on his father. 'And I don't like it any more than you do. Oh, I've heard it already, the sniggers, the whispers and I've only been in post for a day. Three weeks ago,' he paced the room, the ewer still in his hand, 'I was a circitor in a godless shithole on the edge of nowhere. I had nothing to worry about but reveille, training and seeing that the camp had enough food. Today ... today, I am second-in-command of a legion that holds the north for the Emperor. I have four slaves to answer your earlier question and, on parchment at least, six thousand men under my command.' He looked at his father and knew he had lost the old man already. 'Out there,' he pointed to the north, 'are massing more men than you and I have ever seen together in one place. By spring – or perhaps by tomorrow – I don't know, they will be able to swallow the VI Victrix whole. We haven't faced a threat like this in three hundred years. Look around you, Pa. Do you see *anybody* in this entire bloody city who knows what the hell to do?'

Flavius looked at the man who had once been the boy swinging from his outstretched right arm. He would give that right arm to help him now, because he saw that Justinus was as lost as he was. And he had never seen that look before; never thought he would ever see it. It was etched on his boy's face. It was a look of fear.

The snow set in early that year and as the little cavalry patrol clattered north out of Eboracum, flurries of it were stinging Paternus' face and powdering his hair. It had to be said, a Roman four-pronged saddle was not the primus pilus' natural habitat and he bounced on the back of his chestnut with every roll of the horse's body. Sometimes he could be comfortable for as many as three or four of the animal's strides and then he would lose the rhythm again and would jar against the leather. He tried not to think too much about how many thousand more strides he would have to endure. They had left camp a little before dawn, cloaks over their mail tunics and helmets buckled to their chins. Only Paternus rode bareheaded, because he wanted to see everything clearly, not to have to peer under an iron rim or over cheek plates. It had been nearly four weeks now since he had kissed his wife and son goodbye and gone out with his little hunting party and already, in a curious way, their faces were growing dim in his memory. He knew he would know them, though, just from a turn of a cheek or a curl at the nape of a silken neck; the little things that makes a beloved wife or precious child unique in a husband's and father's eye and he watched carefully every village they rode through, moving north.

He spoke the local dialect well enough to get by. These were the old lands of the Brigantes as far north as the Wall and the patrol's job was to see just how near the Wall they could get before they sighted the war bands that had killed the Dux Britannorum and wiped out his command. Everywhere they went, Paternus asked the same questions. Had anyone seen a woman and her son, from the North? She was dark haired, a beauty with eyes to drown in and a boy with hair of gold. They were not quite the words he used but they were the words burned into his soul as he rode on through the snow.

The patrol had been forbidden to ride more than a day's march away. The nine horses were more precious to Decius Ammianus than the men on their backs and he would not risk them being away overnight. Overnight meant they were dead and the praeses had no more men to send after them. They were at the edge of their limit when they reached Derventio. The fort had been abandoned and the canabae under the shadow of its walls was a shell of ash and blackened timbers under the snow.

'I remember this place,' the Ala semisallis said, hunched in his saddle against the cold. 'Tertillo the jeweller lived here.' He looked up to the snow-filled clouds on the treeless horizon. 'I wonder who's wearing his trinkets now.'

It was the same wherever they rode. The painted ones and

their allies had been and gone. Villages lay burnt and forgotten, temples smashed and levelled to the ground. Jupiter, Mithras, Sol Invictus, their stone and marble likenesses lay in pieces, half-buried in the earth. Villages still standing were full of frightened, surly people. Yes, there had been a woman and a child who had passed by not three weeks ago, but she was flaxen haired and the child was a girl. On the other hand, fleeing refugees with tales of horror from the North had seen many women, many sons. Most of their husbands and fathers were dead; they had no one looking for them. Had the great and virtuous centurion tried Eboracum, some of the villagers asked. He would be bound to find them there.

Paternus was still out with his patrol that Jupiter's day, trailing the Ussos to the east. The wind was bitter, slicing through the men who guarded the main gate of Eboracum as they leaned on their spears and prayed for the arrival of the relief. A single rider was trotting along the road from the north, his wolfskin hood over his head and his hands encased in hare skins. He breathed in the smoke of the cluster of huts on the vallum and urged his battered pony on at the thought of a fire and hot food.

'Io, the gate!' he called, reining in and cupping his hands.

'Get lost, Brigantus,' the sentry shouted down to him. 'We're not open.'

'I am an Arcanus,' the man shouted back in Latin. 'I have an urgent message.'

'Who for?' the guard wanted to know.

'I think his name's Paternus. He's a semisallis. Don't ask me which cohort.'

Leocadius was circitor of the watch that day and the name of his friend brought him out of the guard room even though he was doing particularly well with the dice at the time and men owed him money. He hauled his cloak over his shoulder and stared down at the little man on his shaggy pony. 'I know you, don't I?' he called.

The little man recognized him too. 'You do, sir. My name is Dumno.'

'What is it you want with Paternus?' Leocadius asked.

'For his ears only, sir,' Dumno said. 'It's about his family.'

Richard Denham & M. J. Trow

CHAPTER V

Dumno told his story between gulps of wine and huge mouthfuls of food. The man smelt from his days on the road and he freely confessed he could not remember when he ate last. As for the wine, excellent – Iberian, wasn't it? It certainly made a change from the half-frozen ditchwater he had been living on for the past few days. He was sitting in the circitors' quarters in the south-east corner of the camp, stuffing his face and wiping the grease from his chin. For all he knew, he was eating dog, but he was past caring about that. 'So it's the same all over,' he spoke with a mouthful of food, 'Rape, murder. You name it. I met this bloke from Caractonium way. He says the garrison there mutinied – killed their officers and went over to the barbarians.'

'No!' Leocadius leaned back and put his goblet down. 'That's not possible.'

'I heard it with my own ears,' Dumno assured him. 'How many men have you got here, masters? Four thousand? Five?'

'On parchment, six,' Leocadius told him. 'In reality, less than three.'

'What? Actually here in Eboracum, or including the lads on the frontier?'

Leocadius did not know.

'Not that there is a frontier now, of course. You're it.'

'No Wall?' Vitalis frowned, staring the arcanus in the face.

Dumno shrugged. 'Oh, the Wall's there all right. You know, stones, mortar. All you haven't got is men to hold it. That was then.'

'Tribune!' somebody barked from the corner and the handful of circitors lounging around the room stood to attention, Leocadius and Vitalis among them. Justinus strode into the building, his sagum wrapped around him against the cold. Dumno struggled to his feet and only then realised just how much he had eaten and drunk. He bowed his head to Justinus and stifled a belch.

'Why wasn't I told this man was here?' the tribune asked, raking the men around him with his eyes.

'It's my fault, master,' Dumno said. 'I hadn't eaten. These gentlemen have been kindness itself.'

Justinus ignored the others. 'The officer at the gate tells me you have a message for Paternus,' he said.

'That's right, sir, I have,' the arcanus said.

'Well?'

'Er ... for his ears only, sir,' Dumno mumbled.

Justinus looked at the man's bowl, wiped so clean with his bread it might have been brand new. 'Well, now you've enjoyed our hospitality,' he said, 'You can give me your news. Come with me.' He looked at Leocadius and Vitalis. 'To your duties, gentlemen,' he said.

Even sounds like a bloody officer, Leocadius thought to himself. 'We'd like to hear this, sir,' Vitalis said. 'Paternus is one of us.'

One of us. The events of the last few weeks had driven a wedge through that. The four men who had run from the Wall were separated now by rank and fortune. But were they? Would they not forever be bound by that one chance factor – that they had been out hunting when the world turned upside down? Could a bond like that ever be truly broken?

'As you please,' Justinus said and he led the way to his quarters.

The green swirling mist that cloaks the northern moors in winter was thicker than Paternus could remember. Once more he was on the road with the cavalry patrol, looking for his loved ones. The droplets of water that had condensed on his helmet rim had turned to ice and he could barely feel his hands around the reins. Staring into the fog was becoming troublesome; in its green depths he started to see shapes that could not be there – pray Sol Invictus they were not there, because the monsters that peopled the murk were not for human eyes to see. He blinked and shook his head. His patient horse plodded on, slipping a little here and there as its hooves clashed on the ice under the snow.

The semisallis who was the real leader of the patrol suddenly reined in and raised his hand. 'There,' he said, in a voice dropped to a whisper. The others followed his pointing finger to a hollow in the ground ahead. Smoke was drifting upward, mixing with the fog to give it a smell of burning wood with an acrid overlay of seared fat. They could all hear now the hum of conversation.

'It's a village,' the semisallis murmured.

Paternus shook his head. 'A bivouac,' he said. 'I see tents.'

He was right. They were low to the ground, sheets of leather fastened together and lashed to the hard earth with ropes. Outside the largest of them, a single wood fire struggled to stay alight in the deep gloom. Paternus felt his heart thump. He blinked, then rubbed his eyes. It couldn't be, could it? A beautiful, dark-haired woman was stirring something in a pot over the fire and the smell of stewing hare was suddenly overwhelmingly on the light breeze that fanned across to the cold, hungry soldiers.

'Flavia!' he blurted out and rammed his heels into his horse's flanks.

'No!' the semisallis yelled. 'Jupiter highest and best! Patrol, swords!' Nine spathas shot clear in the morning and the cavalry broke into a canter, four to the left and five to the right, to encircle the little camp in the hollow. The semisallis did not have a single horse archer with him and if this was going to be a fight it was going to be bloody.

'Flavia!' Paternus had bounced down from the saddle and was running across the open ground, his boots crunching on the frosty ground. A man stepped into his path with a sickle in his hand, but the centurion barely saw him as he batted him aside and reached the girl. She flung herself backwards, grabbing a little boy as she did so, staring wild-eyed at the mad Roman who was running at her. Paternus stopped, his arms dangling by his side in disappointment and shock. 'I ... I'm sorry,' he muttered. 'I ... thought you were somebody else.' The girl was beautiful under the thatch of dark, curling hair, but she was not his Flavia. Paternus was still looking at the little boy, so like his own, trying to bury his face into his mother's dress and did not hear the man with the sickle running up behind him, the weapon flashing silver in the dim light. The semisallis acted first. A cavalry spatha was not known for its throwing properties, but he hurled his anyway and the heavy blade tumbled through the damp air before thudding, point-first into the scythesman's back. The man grunted, his lung ruptured and blood spurted out from his mouth as he went down. Paternus stepped back as the corpse fell forward and he raised his hand.

'Enough!' he bellowed. 'We're friends.'

'Some friends,' a man grunted, kneeling beside the dead man.

'We are the VI Victrix,' Paternus told them, 'Out from Eboracum. Who are you?'

'It doesn't matter who we are,' the man stood up as the cavalrymen rode in closer, their swords still at the ready. The semisallis dismounted and wrenched the spatha out of the dead man's back. 'What do you care, Roman?'

Paternus looked at the man's face, hatred and fear etched in every line. He wanted to tell him that he was not a Roman. His grandfather had fought with the Alamanii cavalry from the forests of Germany to the far north of the Empire's edge. That his father, Tacitus, had had little love for the Empire either. But life to these runaways was not that complicated. 'They are Roman tents,' the centurion said. 'What are you doing with them?'

'Sheltering,' said the man. 'The men who put them up don't need them now.' He pointed through the fog to a rocky outcrop on which a clump of oaks clung to the ledge. Bodies dangled from ropes along the boughs. Roman bodies, hanging in the fog. Paternus and the semisallis left the smoky hollow and crossed to them. The corpses were stiff and blue, the eyes of most of them bulging from the tight grip of the noose, their tongues protruding black. At least the ravens and the Attacotti had not reached them, if there was any dignity in that thought.

'We didn't do that,' the man shouted. 'It's how we found them. We didn't think they'd mind if we borrowed their tents.'

The bodies were naked, so it was not possible to know where the dead men had come from. Every weapon, every vestige of armour had been taken. Paternus turned back to the woman he had frightened moments ago. 'Where are you from?' he asked.

For the briefest of moments she looked at the man with her. 'We are Votadini,' she said. The man opened his mouth to say something but she stopped him with a glance. There was a power there that Paternus had not seen before in a native woman.

'Votadini?' the semisallis repeated, looking around at the others. 'That's a northern tribe. North of the Wall.'

'You're a long way from home,' Paternus said.

'So are you, Roman,' she answered, holding her head high

and holding the boy tighter to her.

The centurion unbuckled his helmet and took it off. 'We'd take you with us,' he said, 'but they wouldn't let you in at Eboracum. I'm sorry.' He turned to where a cavalryman held his horse and mounted. 'What is your name?' he asked her.

'Brenna,' she said. 'I am called Brenna.'

'What of this Valentinus?' Justinus asked. For nearly two hours now he had been interrogating the little arcanus, asking for names, places, numbers of the enemy and their tribes. For one of the hidden people who was supposed to know everything – who was *paid* to know everything – Dumno seemed to be blind, deaf and dumb.

'Don't get me started!' the little man said. Having eaten the circitors out of house and home in their quarters, he was now pulling apart a chicken, tribunes, for the use of.

'But that's exactly what I want to do,' the tribune said, holding the arcanus' arm before he could load in another mouthful. 'You say this man is leading the rebellion. We've heard the name from others too. Villagers our cavalry patrols have talked to. Man of Valentia ... it could be anyone.'

Dumno put the chicken wing down and wiped his fingers on his sleeves. He looked around, just in case the tribune's quarters had ears. 'He's a bastard. One of the Scotti, they say.'

'You've seen him?'

'Only once,' Dumno nodded. 'And that from a distance. Rides a black horse. Wears a helmet.'

Justinus looked at the others. 'The parade helmet. Yes, we've heard about that too.'

'If he always wears a helmet,' Leocadius said, leaning forward in his chair, 'how do we know what he looks like ... when we hang the bastard, that is.'

'Oh, you'll know him, master,' Dumno said. 'Have no fear of that.'

'Our man who came back from the Duke's command,' Vitalis said, 'the signifer. He said they were beaten at a place called the Mouth of Hell. Do you know where that is?'

Dumno shook his head. 'Never heard of it. You're sure this signifer got it right?'

'No,' Justinus said, remembering the state of the man. 'We're not.'

'Sirs,' Dumno thought it best to leave some of the chicken

carcase for the camp dogs, 'I don't know what more I can tell you. Tribune Justinus,' the little man beamed, 'Well, well ... tribune, eh?' and he clicked his tongue. 'Tribune, I thank you for your kindness and your food. Much appreciated. But could I beg one more favour? As you know I've been through hell for the last few weeks. Would it be possible to stay the night? A safe bed? Perhaps a woman if you've got one.'

Justinus stood up, straight-faced. 'Leocadius can help you there, I'm sure. And not in this camp, arcanus. We'll find you a billet in the colonia. And at dawn tomorrow, I will expect you to be on the road north.'

'North, sir?' Dumno chuckled. 'Oh, no, you won't catch me going north again in a hurry. I've a hankering for the warm south. Oh,' he paused on his way out, Vitalis and Leocadius with him. 'What about Paternus ... and my news?'

'He'll be back by nightfall,' Justinus said. 'Or very soon after. And make sure it's good news, arcanus.'

Vitalis drew the short straw. While Leocadius went about his duties in the camp, Vitalis took the arcanus south of the river, through the twisting alleys of the colonia, well away from the straight thoroughfares that led through the canabae to the camp. It was dark already on that short winter's day by the time Vitalis found Dumno a bed for the night. The wine, the food and the woman were all in the price. He did not know it, but the praeses was paying.

Vitalis was glad to leave him there. If truth be told, the little man irritated him. He was interested in one thing – himself – and all his endless curiosity, about the lads' recent promotions, for example, always ended up with an extended whinge about how unfair life was to him.

But Vitalis had made a promise to the praeses, as they all had. He was to listen at doorways, chat to the carpenters and the gardeners, flatter the tinsmiths and hob-nob with the wharfmen. Leocadius was supposed to be doing the same, to check their mood, test their loyalty, quell dissent and scotch rumours. Vitalis had noticed however than friend Leo spent ever more time in the taverns along the quay and most of the people he talked to, when he wasn't playing Hands, were tall, elegant beauties of the night, who would charge four times to a circitor what a humble pedes would have to pay.

It was not one of these that Vitalis was looking for in the

Red Sparrow that night. He just needed a drink. Ever since his promotion he had needed a drink just a *little* more than before. But he had never been a circitor until now – perhaps it went with the rank.

'Well, well, we *are* honoured, aren't we, boys?' There was a crowd of the Second Cohort at the Sparrow that night, drinking and dicing with the locals. Vitalis looked up to see a dozen men looking straight at him. In accordance with regulations he had left his sword and dagger in the camp and if it came to it, he wasn't sure how far his fists would get him.

'It is circitor Vitalis Celatius, isn't it?' The pedes talking was built like a basilica, just as high and just as square.

'What do you want, soldier?' Vitalis asked him.

'I'd like to buy you a drink, circitor,' the pedes said. 'It's not everyday we get a real live hero of the Wall in here.'

Vitalis looked up at the man looming over him. 'You're drunk,' he said.

The soldier grabbed a cup from his table and threw the contents into Vitalis' face. 'So are you, now,' he laughed and the others laughed with him, banging the table so that the cups bounced. Vitalis stood up slowly. 'I hope you're not going to waste any more good wine like that,' he said, and he turned for the door. Here he came face to face with another of the Second's finest, who folded his arms and looked the circitor squarely in the face.

'Stand aside, soldier,' Vitalis said, his heart pounding and his lips, for all they were dripping with wine, oddly dry, 'and I'll forget about bringing charges.'

'Charges?' the man grunted. 'Now what might they be?' he asked. 'If I'm going to receive punishment, I might as well make it worthwhile.' He swung a lazy right arm but he was too slow for Vitalis who ducked and dodged aside. There were five men on their feet now and Vitalis raised both hands backing away from them. 'Now, think about this,' he said firmly. 'Think very carefully.'

'Is that what you said to the painted people,' somebody asked, 'when they came over the Wall?'

'Yeah,' another grunted. 'I'm surprised they didn't turn and run, there and then. That's what I'd have done, Marcellus, wouldn't you?'

There were guffaws all round.

'Marcellus what?' Vitalis asked. His back was to the wall now and he had nowhere to go. 'Just so I get it right in the cohort punishment book.'

The soldier stood so close their noses almost touched. 'Marcellus I'm going to tear your head off and shove it up your arse, you shit-faced coward.'

'Tut, tut,' a voice in the corner stopped him in his tracks. 'I had no idea the Second were so foul-mouthed, had you, Vit? We wouldn't tolerate that in the Third, I can tell you.' Leocadius emerged from the shadows and Vitalis had never been so glad to see him in his life.

'Well, look at that,' Marcellus beamed. '*Two* heroes for the price of one.'

'We come cheaper by the bunch,' Leocadius said and held up his goblet, raising it higher until his arm was at full stretch. 'Here's to the Second Cohort of the VI Victrix,' he said, 'Cocksuckers all!'

Marcellus was still watching the raised goblet and Leocadius' right hand. He was not expecting the dagger in the left. The broad blade rammed through his tunic and stomach. He jack-knifed, grunting in pain not at all dulled by the wine in him. Leocadius gave the dagger a final twist and wrenched it free, pouring the contents of his goblet over the dying man as he went down. Nobody else was moving. Then a second soldier moved to Marcellus' aid, though he was past all that. Leocadius thrust the dagger blade forward. 'Uh-huh,' he shook his head. 'No more heroics. Vit, that man there, the one who first insulted you. Don't you want to have a word with him?'

Vitalis was still shaking from the murder he had just witnessed, but he was a circitor of the VI. More than that, he was a hero of the Wall. He crossed to the man, 'Name?' he said levelly.

'Paetus,' the man did his best to stand to attention.

'You're on a charge, Paetus,' Vitalis said. 'I shall expect you at the Principia tomorrow morning. Eight sharp.'

Leocadius hauled his friend away. 'For Jupiter's sake, Vit,' he hissed in the man's ear, 'You've a reputation to uphold. Kill the bastard. And I guarantee you'll have no more incidents like this one.'

Vitalis looked at the man. He knew he was right. But he also knew he was no Leocadius. The man lived by different rules from him; the dagger in his hand was proof of that. It was not in Vitalis' nature to take a knife to any man's bowels. And yet, he was a soldier. And yet ... he spun back to Paetus. 'On second thoughts,' he snapped, 'outside. There's no room in here and you can't afford the breakages on your pay; and I'm not picking up the tab for you.'

Vitalis strode for the door, Leocadius close behind him, his dagger still drawn. Paetus followed and there was soon a large crowd in the narrow street, the dead man in the tavern all but forgotten. They faced each other, the circitor and the pedes, arms at their sides, legs apart. Leocadius spun the knife in his hand and handed the hilt to Vitalis. He shook his head. 'It's not worth another death,' he said and put his fists in front of him. Paetus' face broadened to a grin and there was more raucous laughter from the mob at his back. 'Fair fight,' the soldier said. 'tell your friend with the fish-gutter to keep out of it.'

Vitalis flashed Leocadius a look. 'My word,' he nodded.

'Right, then,' Paetus smiled. 'Fair fight it is,' and he swung his left leg so that his boot crunched into Vitalis' ribs and the blow threw him sideways to hit the wall of the bakery to his left. There were cheers and whoops and the crowd made room for the fighters. This time Paetus used his fists, driving his right into Vitalis' temple, then hitting his ribs again with the left. Leocadius winced. The soldier was half a head taller than his friend and twice as mean. Vitalis may have given his word that Leocadius would not intervene, but Leocadius had not. He kept his options open and his dagger in his hand.

Paetus swung forward again, arms flailing, but Vitalis still had his speed and he ducked one fist before catching the other on his forearm. He grabbed Paetus by his tunic and pulled him forwards, rolling in the dirt and throwing him bodily over his head. The soldier landed badly and Vitalis drove his fist into the man's face, feeling bone crunch. His knuckles were bloody and raw and Paetus was on his knees, spitting out teeth. Vitalis scrambled upright and lashed out with his left boot, crunching into the man's cheekbone and he pitched forward, moaning.

Vitalis stood, swaying. His hand was swelling already and blood was dripping off his finger ends. Every breath was torture and he knew that Paetus' first kick had broken a rib. The soldier was finished, however. He lay face down in the Eboracum mud. There were no more jeers from the crowd now, no whistles or whoops, just silent, surly faces who looked at the circitors.

Leocadius led Vitalis away, steadying him as they walked. As they reached the bakery, Leocadius turned back. 'If anyone else wants to buy a hero of the Wall a drink or two,' he grinned, 'We'd be delighted to accept.'

'They're dead, Paternus.'

There was no other way for Dumno to put it. It had been nearly midnight when the cavalry patrol had returned with yet more dismal news for the praeses; and Paternus, numb with cold and exhaustion, had made his way to the bath house to wash away the aches of the day and try to get his body to warm up. He had not expected to see the little arcanus waiting for him by the door of his quarters. At first a guard had been allocated to Dumno but the soldier was needed elsewhere and the arcanus waited alone.

'I'm so sorry,' Dumno said, reading the shock on the centurion's face.

'How do you know?' Paternus asked, afraid to hear his own voice in the darkness of the bath house's atrium.

'I've asked around. There were hostages taken at Camboglanna. Six men, four women and three children, I was told. One of the women tried to escape with her child – a boy, it was; two or three years old, he wasn't sure.'

'Who wasn't sure?'

'One of the men I spoke to, a pedes called Titus. Said he knew you, knew your family.'

Paternus nodded. He knew Titus. The pair of them had been in the same contubernia once, repairing the Wall under the stars of a summer's night. But this was winter. And it would be winter for ever for Paternus.

'It's no consolation, I know,' Dumno said. 'I didn't tell the Tribune, but I've lost my family too. Valentinus killed them.'

Paternus looked at the little man. He was right. It was no consolation.

'I thought you'd want to know,' Dumno said.

'Yes,' Paternus muttered. 'Yes. Thank you.' And he stumbled away.

The almanacs of the farmers of Eboracum had been passed down the centuries. When he was not training in camp with the pedes of the VI, passing with the sword, hurling the darts and the javelin, Flavius Coelius could be found turning the clay with his faithful slave. The month of Decembris had thirty one days and the Nones fell on the fifth day. The sun, when it was rarely glimpsed above the grey, northern clouds, was in the sign of Sagittarius, the archer.

The day had nine hours and the night fifteen. And through every one of those fifteen, Paternus Priscus sat on his bed with his back to the stone wall. He saw them with him through every minute of those hours, the girl he had loved and chosen as his own; the boy who would, when the day came carry his own shield along the Wall. She had been fifteen when Paternus had married her and she had dedicated her childhood toys to the gods of the hearth and the home fire. Paternus could see her hair now on their wedding day, piled on top of her head in the old Roman way, pressed into shape by a hot spear-head and bound with flowers. Her veil was the colour of fire and her belt tied with a special knot that only her new husband could undo.

He heard a noise that he realised came from his own throat. It was sob that tore his heart and shook his body. It was dead of night, the time they buried children. He saw his little Quintilian, as if in a dream, washed and laid out in a cold tomb, the cypress branch across his chest. And he knew, as the tears trickled down his cheeks and his lips trembled, that that was not how it was. There would have been no grave for the boy, no weeping mourners. Just screams and shouts and harsh hands pulling him from his mother, as both of them fought for life, just one more minute of life, to be together. Another sob tore out of his chest, turning to a roar, then a whisper. He let his chin drop onto his chest and he whispered his boy's name in the darkness. 'Quin. Oh, Quin.'

The praeses was sitting in his usual chair in the Principia the next morning, and his tribunes stood before him. Decius Ammianus was ill, the cold of winter gnawing at his bones and about now, a sunny villa on the vine-clad slopes of Vesuvius seemed a paradise to him.

'It's agreed then, gentlemen,' he said, shivering a little in his fever. 'Saturnalia this year will be as low-key as we can make it. We'll sacrifice one ox for the Emperor and another for Mars Ultor, but that's it. There is to be no revelry, no parties. And ... I can't stress this enough ... no release of slaves from their duties. My days of stoking the hypocaust for laughs are well behind me, I assure you. Now, more pressing matters. The deserters.'

'Six of them, sir,' Clodius Narbo spoke first. 'Various cohorts. They were caught together sneaking out of the canabae, running south.'

Six, you say?' Ammianus was thinking. 'Very well, since they came from various cohorts, we'll have the whole legion paraded. No arms. Hollow square. Justinus.'

'Sir?'

'You'll arrange it.'

'Sir.' Justinus stood to attention. As the new boy, he expected the most difficult task to fall to him. Even so, he hated it. He had seen men hanged before and he knew the bitter taste it left in the mouths of men watching. It was supposed to encourage the others, but somehow Justinus doubted that. Even so, he was not about to argue with the praeses or defend the men concerned. He was no lawyer and he knew the way of the legions. It had not been so very long since a legion which had displeased a commander could expect decimation – one man in ten, chosen by lot, was clubbed to death by the other nine. The legions were iron hard. And this winter, of all winters, there was a need to keep this one steady. Justinus saluted and marched off to arrange a killing.

It had stopped snowing by execution day. And the whole legion stood on the parade ground, at attention, their weapons back in their quarters, just in case. As officer of the day, only Justinus carried his sword and dagger, his sagum flapping in the wind behind him, watching the rows of grim faces under the helmet rims. There was no eagle standard today, as though the great, all-conquering bird could not bear to look on the degenerates who had defiled it by deserting.

The six stood bareheaded, their boots unlaced, their belts missing. They shivered in the clawing wind that drew tears from their eyes. One by one, on Justinus' command, they climbed onto the low stools below the makeshift gallows. For half a day, the carpenters of the legion had been sawing and hammering, making the frame that would take the weight of six men. The hangman, his head encased in a hood, pulled the rough hemp around the neck of each man. One of them was crying, his shoulders heaving as he tried to keep his balance on the stool. Two days ago, he was creeping through the canabae in the mists of dawn with two of the others. They had stashed their armour but kept their weapons and they all had such plans. There were fields to the warm south where the vineyards grew and dates from Damascus and pretty girls. And wine. No end of wine. Three men from Eboracum could lose themselves forever in Britannia Secunda. And they would soon forget their life with the eagles.

It was not to be. One by one their names were read out as

Justinus took his position in front of them, at the head of the legion. The praeses and the other tribunes watched from nearby, but there were no locals crowding in this day. This was not a day for celebration; not a day the legion wanted to share.

'You have disgraced your legion,' Justinus told them in a loud, clear voice that every cohort heard. 'You have disgraced your Emperor and yourselves.' He drew his sword and raised it aloft. 'Jupiter, highest and best, have mercy on you,' he said. The sword came down, slicing through air and six hooded men of the legion kicked the stools away. Only four of them rolled clear, the men above them twisting and writhing as the ropes bit into their necks and closed their windpipes.

The man who had been crying died first, his sobbing ending in a spluttering choke as the piss rolled down his legs. The two remaining stools were kicked harder and the last two deserters danced in the wind. Some men looked away, sickened by the sight. Others shut their eyes, but the gnarled sticks of the centurions on their backs made them spring open again. Only Paternus was not patrolling with the others, checking morale, delivering a word here, a quick tap there. He stood like a statue with the Third Cohort, watching the bodies twitch and twitch again before they all hung still.

Justinus sheathed his sword and gave the order for the legion to stand down. He heard them mutter and grumble as they marched away in columns of four. And he looked up at the sky. If the Emperor was coming, he had better make it soon. The VI Victrix were a legion on the edge and everyone knew that today's trickle of deserters would become a torrent tomorrow.

Dumno sat in his saddle on the edge of the canabae. He had not intended to stay this long and the tribune would have been furious had he found out, but the soft beds and the good food had held the arcanus like a comfortable vice. Now, though, it was time to go. There had been a hanging, he had been told, this very morning. Deserters. And there would be more. He trotted out from the little guarded gate to the south, shaking his head at what had become of the once invincible Roman army. Then he hauled on his rein and rode for the north.

CHAPTER VI

Eboracum

In March the night was twelve hours long. So was the day. The goddess Minerva watched over Flavius Coelius and his slave as they propped the vines in their trenches in the fond hope that they might grow this year. They made their sacrifices to Mamurius, the shield-maker and hung the ivy in honour of Liberalis. What more could any farmer do?

It was four days after the feast of Liber Pater that the guard at the south gate of the colonia heard it; the noise of an army. It was not yet noon and the spring dew still clung to the grass of the ramparts. It was too wet at this time of the year for the dust cloud that heralded the coming of troops. Vitalis was circitor of the watch and he tumbled out of the guard tower, buckling on his sword and yelling to his men.

'Take post!' he shouted. 'Arellius, what do you see?'

Arellius had the best eyes in the Third Cohort, some said the whole of the VI Victrix. The sky was bright overhead where a pale spring sun threatened to break through the clouds. 'Archers,' he called down to the circitor from his wooden turret. 'Auxiliaries. Wait a minute. They're ours, by Jupiter!' He was jumping up and down as Vitalis' unit ran along the ramparts, clapping each other on the back and cheering. 'I don't recognize their shields.'

Vitalis and the others strained to make out the cohorts moving towards them. There were indeed archers at the front, four lines of grey-coated men with the recurved bows slung across their backs. On their wings the crossbowmen marched with their deadly weapons at the slope on their shoulders. In the centre, although they appeared unarmed, the slingers kept time, leather pouches and slingshots dangling from their hips. Beyond them, as the distance lessened and the braying of the cornicines drifted over the valley of the Ussos, solid phalanxes of infantry marched, singing the old songs the Roman army had sung for years, songs that spoke of all things soldiers love – victory, slaughter, wine and women. Every man wore a glittering coat of mail and carried a spear. Their helmets flashed in the sun that suddenly broke through.

Vitalis did not recognize their shields either. They were blue with a leaping marten in red. But he recognized the next formation; the engineers and camp builders, sweating and grunting under their heavy equipment, the shovels and picks which made the Romans the master builders of the world. And he recognized too the single scarlet flag floating above and behind them. That was a general's sign, a knot of horsemen with lances piercing the sky.

'General officer!' Vitalis sang out and his guard came to attention.

'Gates!' he roared and his men scurried in all directions, swinging timbers and clearing the way. About a hundred paces from the southern wall the army halted and the horns fell silent. Only a single muffled drum spoiled the stillness. The people of the canabae and the colonia, traders, craftsmen, women and children, had joined Vitalis' guard at the gate, jabbering excitedly about the relief force that, thank Jupiter, had saved their lives. The drum suddenly doubled its speed and the archers and infantry slid to right and left to let the officers through. There were two of them, both bareheaded and wearing the lorica and sagum of a general. The man on the dappled grey reached the gateway first. He was older than the other one, with grey eyes and sandy-coloured hair. A huge brindled dog padded alongside the horse of the younger man.

'I am Flavius Theodosius, circitor,' he said to Vitalis. 'Comes Rei Militaris. Any chance you can put us up for a night or two?'

'Where did you see him last?' Leocadius asked. It was raining that night as he and Vitalis hurried along the Via Flos, moving south.

'In the Baths,' Vitalis told him. 'He looked like shit. I spoke to him and he didn't seem to know me. Stared straight through me, as if I wasn't there.'

'Not like him,' Leocadius muttered, but even as he said it he knew he was talking nonsense. The Paternus the lad once knew had gone into a world where they could not follow. The semisallis they had known, at Banna and Camboglanna, had been a man to be reckoned with. He always had a cheery word, a ready smile and his family were always with him. Vitalis had been a new recruit when little Quintillius was born and as such, he had given the baby a lucky charm on his ninth day, as tradition dictates. It was an eagle, tiny enough for the little one to hold, too big to end up in his mouth and it was carved from the jet the craftsmen of Eboracum made into beautiful shapes. Leocadius had known Paternus' Flavia before that, but he understood, without being told, that this was one woman strictly off limits. Leocadius had no problem with that. There were plenty of other fish in the sea or any other body of water, come to that.

But that was then and as the pair hurried through the Eboracum night, they both thought of the man Paternus had become. He went through the motions of his duties as centurion, but there was no joy in it. Occasionally they would see him striding along the north ramparts of the camp, looking out to the hills where his life had once been so sweet and where the bodies of his loved ones still lay, untended and alone. Increasingly, they had noticed him wandering the colonia, among the graves in the cemetery of the Blossom. That was where they were going now.

The grave markers stood at rakish angles under the black of the night and the heavy raindrops bounced off the memorials to the great and good of Eboracum who mouldered there. It was barely possible to read the inscriptions now on the older tombs. But one man had read them. And that man sat, cross-legged on a plinth now, in full armour, the rain dripping off his helmet-rim and running down the naked blade of the sword in front of him. He rested both hands on the pommel and the tip rested on the cold, wet stone.

Vitalis and Leocadius looked at each other. 'Pat?' the younger lad spoke first. 'What's this all about?'

'Yes, come on, Pat,' Leocadius joined in. 'It's raining cats and dogs, man. You'll catch your death ...' He stopped and wanted the ground to swallow him, even this ground with its thousand silent dead.

'Over there,' Paternus said, nodding his head to the west, 'lies Aurelia. I often wonder who she was. When the rain stops, when day breaks, have a look at it, Vit. It reads "My wife most sweet. I was not, I was, I am not, I have no more desires.'''

There was a silence when even the sky stopped crying.

'And there,' Paternus went on, his voice choking with tears, nodding to the north, 'the tomb of Cerellia Fortunata ... happy Cerellia. I hope she was. Look at that one, Leo,' he breathed in sharply, knowing they could not see, in the dark, his own tears where the rain had run. '"Do not pass by this epitaph, traveller,"' he grunted, '"But stop, listen and learn, then go. There is no boat in Hades, no ferryman Charon, no caretaker Aeacus, no Cerberus dog. All we dead below have become bones and ashes, nothing more."' Is that it, Vit?' the centurion asked him. 'Is that all we have and can hope to be? Bones and ashes?' He looked at them, the two young men in their sodden cloaks, dripping on the sacred ground. 'I want you to do something for me,' he said.

Vitalis cleared his throat, struggling to keep his voice strong and firm, with no tremble or break in it. 'Anything,' he said.

'When I have finished here,' Paternus said calmly, unbuckling his tunic with one hand, 'I want you to take me to the north. Anywhere will do. Somewhere on the moors. Bury me there, will you?'

'Pat ...' Vitalis could not help himself now. He was crying, along with Paternus, along with the night.

'Bury yourself!' a harsh voice boomed from the darkness and a cowled figure sprang out of nowhere to stand on a gravestone. He flicked back the hood. It was a tribune of the VI Victrix, but no one snapped to attention or even moved.

'Justinus ...' Leocadius started to say something but a glance from the man made him shut up.

'Stow it, circitor,' he barked and crossed to Paternus, still sitting cross-legged on the tomb, his chest naked now for the sword blade. Justinus looked down at him. 'Well, go on,' he said. 'Do it.'

Vitalis and Leocadius flinched.

'I said "Do it"!' the tribune repeated.

There was no movement from anyone. Paternus could hear the blood rushing in his ears and the thump of his own heart – the heart he wanted to be still. Justinus hauled the blade away from him and held it with the tip probing the skin, just above the rib and over the flutter of his heart. 'What's fine, what's Roman, remember,' Justinus said. 'It's the way of our ancestors, Pat. It's what we do, we Romans. When we've fouled up, when it's all gone wrong, gone pear-shaped. We don't say "I won't let the bastards grind me down". We say "I can't handle this, can't cope. I'll take the soft option. It'll only hurt for a minute or two and then it'll all be over. No more hurt. No more pain." Well, go on!' Justinus stepped forward, so the blade point drew a fine line of beading blood down Paternus' chest. He gasped and collapsed sobbing on Justinus, who held him and then gently grabbed the nose piece of the helmet and turned his face to the sky. He leaned in to whisper into his friend's ear. 'Your family is dead, Paternus. But do you know how you can make them even more dead?'

Paternus shook his head to release Justinus' grip. 'No,' he said, his words coming thickly through the unshed tears in his throat.

'You can kill yourself. When you are gone, who will talk of Flavia and Quin then? Who will remember the curl of her hair, how your boy was growing big and strong? Their ghosts are out there to the north and getting fainter by the day. But in your heart,' and Justinus grabbed Paternus hand and pressed it to his bloody chest, 'they are growing stronger. But only while it beats, Pat. Remember that. So!' He stepped back from his friend and pulled his tunic together, then wiped a surreptitious hand across his eyes, 'You had better get back to doing what you were trained to do. Fight back. Theodosius came today with a field army. Two legions. It's time to make your dead proud.' Justinus tore a bronze disc from his tunic. 'I took this off the body of Piso at Banna. Oh, I can't say I liked him much. He was a bit of a bastard, actually. But he was *our* bastard. And when I took it, I made a vow to Mithras that I would cut out the entrails of the shit responsible. Well, that shit is Valentinus, Pat, and he's still out there. He has destroyed the Wall and he's killed your wife and child. Now ...' he stuffed the disc away and lifted the centurion's sword out of his hand. 'I want you to get that chest patched up. And I want you to pray to Sol Invictus and every other damned god in the heavens. And tomorrow, we'll start to use that sword on somebody else. Right?'

Paternus blinked through the rain, falling again with a steady persistence. He nodded. Suddenly, he could face the world again. The scar on his chest would be there to remind him for ever, as if he needed reminding.

'Mars Ultor,' he whispered to Justinus.

The tribune nodded and smiled. 'Mars the Avenger,' he said. He turned to the others. 'Lads,' he held out a hand and pulled the centurion up off the gravestone, 'see to it that the primus pilus gets home, will you? He's had a rough night.'

While the new legions bedded down as best they could in the rec-tangle of the camp, the *praeses* Decius Ammianus entertained their commanders in his private quarters. He did not know either of them, but he knew the reputation of them both. Theodosius, the Count, came from the town of Corduba, that part of Iberia known as Baetica where the olive oil was to die for and the sun always shone. The Count was civilization itself, urbane, witty, charming. And the *praeses'* own wife, Augustina, clucked around him over dinner as he admired her Damascus silks, her silver, her Samian ware. She, on her part, lapped it up. It was not often that a famous Iberian general came for supper. As soon as she heard the Count was at the south gate she had galvanized her household. When Decius had arrived for his *prandium* she told him to get out – the place was off-limits until the Count arrived. Her army of slaves had set to work, cooking snails, slicing eggs, roasting the best hare, lamb and kid Eboracum could provide. Then her guests all dented cush-ions and ate and drank and flattered as if there were no tomorrow.

It was the other man that Decius Ammianus did not exactly take to. He too was from Iberia, but the cold, wet mountains of Tarraconensis were his home, near the city of Caesaraugusta. The rumour ran throughout the Empire – that on the first day of the life of Magnus Maximus he had swum the River Iberus and flown to the sun to count its rays at close hand. That seemed even less likely now that Ammianus had met him. The man ate with his fingers like an oaf and seemed to have no table manners at all. Any scraps of food the general did not take a liking to, he threw to the mastiff that lolled in the corner, slobbering on the mosaic. It had not helped that whereas the charming Theodosius was content to purr around his hostess, which was no more than polite society demand-ed, his second-in-command was positively leering at the *praeses'* daughter, not yet seventeen and hardly schooled in the ways of the world. Lavina, of course, saw the legendary general differently. His eyes were a bottomless brown and his jaw was square and Roman. He wore his hair short and combed forward, like a soldier, like an Emperor. The touch of his hand on hers as he took the wine ewer from a slave and refilled her cup for her, sent magic chills along her spine and she did not notice the disapproving looks of her mama and papa. Even the man's dog was delightful.

Decius Ammianus was glad when the ladies retired and the

men could get on to more pressing business than the flirting of goats. The praeses was well aware how vulnerable his command had been all winter and he suspected that little snippets of information had been flying with the snowflakes to the barbarians in the north. Accordingly he dismissed the slaves and leaned back on his couch.

'Actually,' Theodosius said, 'They're to the west of you, too.'

'Who are?' Ammianus asked.

'The barbarians,' the Count said, swilling his greasy fingers in a bowl. 'You were speaking a moment ago of the barbarians to the north. They're also in the west.'

'You've been cooped up here too long, praeses,' Maximus said, demolishing what was left of the dates. 'You've lost touch.'

'My first priority,' Ammianus said, feeling as though he were on the receiving end of a court martial, 'was to hold my command. My second was to get a message to the Emperor.'

'Which he got at Augusta Treverorum,' Theodosius nodded, replenishing his wine. 'Do you know it? Impressive gate, the biggest in Gaul, they say.'

Ammianus had heard that too, but he had never been there.

'Unfortunately, the Emperor has his share of problems in the east at the moment. He hasn't been well and then there's his brother ...'

'Man's a vegetable,' Maximus grunted.

'As you say, Magnus,' Theodosius smiled. 'As you say. The point is we're the best the Emperor could spare at the moment.'

'What's your plan?' the praeses asked.

'To beat the enemy,' Maximus said. 'Grind his face in the mud.' He looked up at the horrified faces of the other two and laughed. 'Well, that's the shortened overview,' he said. 'I'm sure Papa Theo has it rather more structured than that.'

Theodosius laughed too but the praeses did not feel inclined to join in. 'As you know, we have with us eight thousand men – I could have done with a bigger barracks, Ammianus – the Jovii and the Victores. They're mostly Gauls and Alamanni; a few Iberians – and they're all good men, tried and tested. I've got cavalry and siege equipment. In short, a field army, which, I appreciate, you've been without.' Theodosius looked at the praeses. 'You look a little dubious, Ammianus,' he said.

'With respect, sir,' the praeses said, 'I have no idea what we're facing – in terms of numbers, I mean. I doubt whether two legions will be enough.'

'So do I,' nodded Theodosius. 'That's why I have two more waiting at Rutupiae. Our intelligence suggests that most of the trouble is in the north – that's where most of the locals have gone over to the enemy. But in case that's wrong or the bastards move faster than we do ...'

'That'll be the day,' grunted Maximus.

'I've got the Batavi and the Heruli waiting in the wings, as it were. They know the country – they were here seven years ago. As you know, the Batavi are particularly good at river crossings.'

'You're thinking of the Thamesis?' Ammianus asked.

'And others. You know Rutupiae was the place the deified Claudius came ashore?'

'I had heard that,' Ammianus said. 'A little before my time, I'm afraid.'

Theodosius laughed. 'Mine too,' he agreed. 'But the lads like a bit of tradition, don't they? And if it's propitious for the gods and they smile on us ... well ...'

The praeses nodded. Eboracum was full of shrines and waystations dedicated to every god in the panoply. He had invoked them all over the last few months.

'My son, of course,' the Count went on, 'is a devoted Christian. Or at least, he is today.'

'Your son?' Ammianus caught the fleeting, withering look that passed over Maximus' face.

'Didn't I tell you? He's commanding the other two legions,' Theodosius smiled. 'Keep it in the family, eh?'

The talk went on for hours, while Ammianus told the generals all he had learned from his cavalry patrols and the tittle-tattle of camp and canabae. It would be Theodosius' and Maximus' job to winnow out the wheat from the chaff. It was the early hours by the time they called it a night.

'By the way, Ammianus,' Theodosius let a slave help him on with his sagum. 'You knew I was on the way, surely?' The slave stepped quickly away as Maximus' dog growled at him.

'No,' said the praeses. 'Not a word. I hope you know that I would have been more prepared had I known. I merely lived in hope.'

'Hmm,' the Count frowned. 'That's odd. I sent three messages. Still,' he shook the praeses hand, clasping his forearm and holding on a touch longer than Ammianus was comfortable with, 'let's hope my messengers to the Count of the Saxon Shore did better, eh?'

The Count of the Saxon Shore was Nectaridus and that dies solis he was a long way from home. The sky had been a dark grey all day and dusk, when it came, had not come a moment too soon. For nearly four hours the battle had raged, all the more fierce because the II Augusta had not been expecting it. A parley, the note had said. It had been signed in perfect Latin by Valentinus and it spoke of a truce. The Wall had gone, it said, but the barbarians had no intention of marching on Calunium. There could be a compromise. The VI Victrix at Eboracum had fought the barbarians to a stand-still and the tribes needed time to lick their wounds and to heal. They were prepared to surrender, not to the VI, who hated them, but to a fair and famous Legion like the II. Nectaridus, they had heard, was a fair and famous man, too. Like his legion at Calu-nium, they had women and children, wives and mothers who needed help.

So Nectaridus had gone, not like a cuckolded fool with horns on his head or like a lamb to the slaughter. He had gone fully armed, with three cohorts at his back and four turmae of cavalry. Out of the dark woods in the middle of the afternoon came the promised children. And only the children, pale, half-starved wraiths like the demons who haunt the forest. They came on in silence, in their twos and threes, then in their dozens until the whole field was full of them.

Nectaridus and his men stared at them. The dull sky pressed down on the men and the advancing children, dulling all sound so that the jingle of a bit rang as loud as a bell. Then the Count shook himself out of the mood and called over his draconarius, his stand-ard bearer. 'Igennus, you're a family man. See what these kids want. And, more importantly, find out where their fathers are.'

So Igennus had trotted forward, the dragon with its long tail streaming above him. And as Nectaridus watched, one of the chil-dren whipped a knife from nowhere and threw it into the draconarius' back. Another did the same and the man slumped over his horse's neck and the dragon crashed to the ground, a doz-en children were on him, hauling him from the saddle and tearing him limb from limb. Nectaridus had given the order to attack, chil-dren or no children but he was already surrounded by their fathers and for the rest of the day had fought a hopeless rearguard action against hordes of barbarians, wielding clubs and war-hammers, swords and sickles, men with long red hair and dark whorls over their skin.

The noise and the slaughter had stopped at last. The children had vanished into the sheltering trees as their fathers had advanced, but now they were back, mingling with the blood-streaked men who had sired them. Their mothers were there too, with wild hair and terrible eyes. All afternoon, the II had roared the Barritus in defiance, until they were hoarse and could shout no more. The yelling of the barbarians had stopped too and an awful silence descended on the field. There were corpses everywhere, mostly Roman dead and Nectaridus could see the rooks and ravens wheeling in the darkening sky. He could smell the same blood on the wind that they could.

All around him what was left of his command huddled tighter. Wounded men were fighting for breath, leaning on comrades. The living held up the dead. Shields were split and bristled with arrows, sword blades glistened red, darkening with the night and time to a sticky purple and then dry brown. No one had any arrows left – they were all embedded in enemy bodies or lying at crazy angles in the ground ahead. All the spears were gone, hurled into the sea of oncoming warriors who had swept away a third of a legion.

In the centre and in the stillness, a figure on a black horse walked out from the barbarian ranks. He wore a sagum like a Roman general and on his head was a cavalry parade helmet, its face a mask of silver glinting dully in the fading light.

'Lay down your arms, Count of the Saxon Shore. You cannot win today.'

'You know me,' Nectaridus shouted back. 'Be so good as to give me your name.'

'Men call me Valentinus,' the rider yelled back, 'And my children here,' he spread both arms to the multitude that stretched to left and right, 'are all anxious to trample on your corpse.'

'Well, then,' Nectaridus unbuckled his helmet with its gilded fittings and carved eagles. 'Let's not keep them waiting.' He raised his sword, 'The legion will advance, trumpeter. At the double ...' The sword came down and the horn blasted, its notes wailing as the trumpeter broke into a run, trying to keep up with the others.

The dragon standard carried by the second cohort disappeared into the mob of flailing arms and legs as shields crunched against bare flesh and bone collided with bone with sickening cracks. Nectaridus died that day and the man called Valentinus had claimed another titled Roman head.

It was still early next morning and the praeses and Count Theodosius were closeted in the Principia, poring over maps and trying to make sense of intelligence reports. On the camp's parade ground, Flavius Coelius was putting a cohort of the VI through its paces.

The Third were drawn up in parade ground order, facing the weapons master with their shields at the rest and their javelins at the slope.

'Skirmish order!' Flavius thundered and the trumpet blasted across the field. The ranks broke up, scattering in what seemed like chaos, forming tight knots of four, each with an archer.

'Cavalry!' the weapons master roared and the trumpet blared again. Every man dropped to one knee and the javelins pointed upwards, ready to skewer the ghost horses that Flavius had warned against. 'That unit there,' he pointed to one group with his gnarled stick. 'Too slow. Do that in the field and your heads would be dangling from somebody's saddle bow by now. Full pack. Twenty circuits of the field.'

The four men winced. It was not too hot a day but the weight of the pack was considerable and they shambled away to collect their helmets and marching gear. The general stopped them, his dog at his heels.

'Whose contubernia is this?' Maximus shouted, seeing no non-commissioned officer with them.

'Mine, sir,' Vitalis clicked to attention in another unit yards away.

'Circitor,' Maximus beckoned him over with a casual finger. He looked at the young man. What was he? Nineteen summers at most. Young for a circitor but not too young. 'How long have you held the rank?' he asked.

'Six months, sir,' Vitalis told him.

'Semisallis before that?'

'No, sir. Pedes.'

'Really?' Maximus raised an eyebrow. Perhaps they did things differently along the frontier forts. 'Somebody up there must like you.' A half smile flitted across his face. 'You will carry out the circuits with them.'

'General ...' Flavius tried to interrupt, but Maximus had his hand in the air and it stopped him.

'Your contubernia, circitor,' he said so that the whole cohort heard him. 'Your fault.'

'Sir,' Vitalis saluted and ran across the ground with the others in tow.

Maximus turned to the weapons master. 'Ten sesterces says the kid doesn't last fifteen circuits,' he said.

'Sir, I ...'

'Sorry, hastilarium,' Maximus smiled, remembering the man's pay, 'Make that five.'

'Let's make it fifteen,' Flavius said, straight-faced. He had no clue how he was going to afford that if Vitalis stumbled, but he was not going to lose face in front of this man.

'All right,' Maximus chuckled. 'Fifteen it is. Have the rest of them paraded, hollow square. I'd like a word.'

Flavius barked the command, the trumpet answered and the ground shook with the thud of studded boots running to position. In minutes the cohort was assembled and a bearded first centurion stood in front of the general. He saluted, thumping his hand across his chest and holding his arm out straight.

'Who are you?' Maximus wanted to know.

'Paternus Priscus, sir, supernumerary primus pilus, Third Cohort.'

Maximus looked the man in the eye. He saw something there and could not define it. A sorrow? The general prided himself on his instant judgement of men; it was something he had done all his life. 'Supernumerary?' he said. 'Where is the real one?'

'I am the real one,' Paternus stood his ground.

Maximus' eyes flashed fire. 'Don't be flippant with me, sir,' he snapped. 'The regular primus pilus; where is he?'

'Officer of the day, sir,' Paternus told him. 'In the Principia.'

Maximus looked the man up and down. Sloppy young circitors, insubordinate centurions. No wonder Ammianus had hidden his legion away all winter. If half the reports he had heard of the barbarians were true, this lot would not last five minutes.

'Circuit one!' the cohort heard Vitalis shout as the knot of offenders jogged past. Their cooking pots clanked on their mail, dangling from the tent posts they carried.

On the edge of the paraded square, four of the nine cavalrymen of the Ala Invicti Brittaniaci stood to their horses, holding the bridles and waiting for the weapons master's next command. It was not forthcoming because General Maximus was giving the orders now. He pushed his way through the ranks who parted like standing corn before him and reached the nearest horse. He patted the animal's soft muzzle, rubbed its chin. Then he walked around it, checking limbs and flanks and withers. 'Long coat, semisallis,' he said to its owner. 'Winter length?'

'We've had no time to trim them, sir,' the semisallis said. 'we've been out most days since Saturnalia.'

'Hmm,' Maximus nodded. 'There are, I understand, only nine of you?'

'Eight, sir,' the semisallis corrected him. 'Clodius Galvo died of exposure three weeks ago. Froze in the saddle.'

'Bad luck,' Maximus said. 'Did he have a family, this Galvo?'

'Widowed mother, sir,' the semisallis said. 'Here in Eboracum.'

'See my clerk later today,' the general told him. 'See she lacks for nothing.'

'Yes, sir,' the semisallis tried to hide his surprise. 'Thank you, sir.'

Maximus strode back into the hollow square of the cohort. 'Circuit two!' Vitalis called as he and his lads jogged past. They were still in fighting trim, although their shoulders ached with the bouncing of their packs and the air rushing through their lungs was torture, as it burned the throat and the back of the nose.

The general scanned the faces of the men before him. A mixed bunch, to be sure, but there may be hope for some of them. He stopped in front of a circitor, a handsome lad with dark, curly hair and smouldering eyes. 'Name?' the general asked.

'Leocadius Honorius,' the circitor said, standing to attention.

Maximus suddenly grabbed Leocadius' tunic and pulled it down so that threads ripped. The general looked up. 'Dark hair, smooth chest,' he said. 'How long do you spend at the baths, circitor?'

'I ...'

'Too long,' Maximus shouted at him. 'A circitor who is more concerned with his looks than his duties is no use to me.' He grinned at Leocadius. 'Keep yourself smooth for the ladies, do you, lad?'

Leocadius looked suitably confused and hurt, all in one well-practiced expression. Maximus turned away, chuckling. Then he turned back, straight-faced. 'What's that?' he asked, pointing to Leocadius' sword.

'A spatha, sir.'

'Specifically?'

'A double-edged infantry weapon, sir. Iron blade. Wooden hilt. Weight ...'

'Yes, yes,' Maximus cut the man short. 'What's it for?'

'Attack, sir,' Leocadius told him, 'and defence.'

'No, no, boy,' the general said softly. 'It's to kill the enemies of the Emperor. Can you use it?'

'Sir?'

'Hastiliarus,' Maximus called Flavius over and took his sword from his scabbard. He turned to face Leocadius. 'Here I am,' he said, 'Imagine me as you will. I am a Pict – see my painted skin. I am a Scot – how do you like my plaid trousers? I am an Attacotti,' he moved closer to Leocadius and whispered, 'I'm going to eat your bollocks with a little fish sauce and a particularly fine Italian wine I've been saving.'

Leocadius drew his sword in one quick movement and lunged for the general, who half turned, batted the blade aside and threw the circitor to the mud. Instinctively, the Third shuffled backwards to give the men room. Maximus' hound snarled and whiffled, whirling round in circles, defying them all.

'Stand fast!' Maximus bellowed. 'You won't have this much room when the painted ones come for you. It'll be cheek to jowl and arse to arse. Not bad, circitor, but not good either. Give point to an armed enemy with enough space and he'll parry every time.'

Remembering his sword had two sharp edges too, Leocadius scrambled to his feet and slashed down diagonally. Maximus caught the blade on his own. 'Better,' he said. 'What else have you got?'

The dog was barking now, like Cerberus himself, teeth bared and ears flat. Leocadius stood there, listening to Vitalis calling out 'Circuit Three' and he came to his senses. He dropped the attack position and stood upright. 'Sir, I can't kill you,' he said.

'Why not?' Maximus asked.

'Because ... because you're a general.' There were murmurs and chuckles in the ranks.

Maximus roared with laughter. 'Generals are mortal too, boy,' he said. 'No, you can't kill me because you haven't the skill.

Hell. You can't even scratch me.'

Leocadius swung in again. His blade banged on Maximus' weapon and then he changed hands, tossing the spatha to his left hand and slicing upwards. Maximus had not expected this and parried for his life. He was too slow and Leocadius' blade slid over his own and gashed his thigh. The general stumbled backwards, cursing through clenched teeth as the pain hit him. 'Stay, Bruno!' he hissed at the mastiff, knowing that, in that instant, the circitor's throat was at risk. It was all or nothing now and Maximus launched his attack. It was so fast that most of the Third missed it and Leocadius' sword sailed into the air to clatter behind the second rank. He himself was kneeling with the general's blade at his throat. Paternus blinked. He wanted to shut his eyes, to blot out what was to come. Then he saw Maximus straighten and throw his sword back to Flavius. He held out a hand and hauled Leocadius upright. A dark stain was spreading over his tunic folds but he seemed not to notice.

'Good move with the left hand,' he said.

CHAPTER VII

'Heroes of the Wall,' Theodosius' voice carried the length of the parade ground.

The four stepped forward: the tribune Justinus, the centurion Paternus; the circitors Leocadius and Vitalis. The trumpets blasted, cornicines greeting the morning and the legion roared its approval. The VI was drawn up in parade order, the eagle glittering at its head. There were flags and music and cheering because Rome was on the march.

Theodosius stepped down from the dais normally reserved for Decius Ammianus. Today the praeses had vacated his chair for the Count; it was only civil since the man was about to take the field. He looked at the men in front of him. 'What you men have been through. What you have done. You have done already what we are about to do. You have faced the biggest threat to the Empire this island has ever seen. And you have come through. As we will come through.'

Cheers roared from the ranks. The Victores beat their blue shields with their swords, the deafening noise swelling beyond the walls of the camp and echoing and re-echoing through the alleys of the canabae to the colonia beyond. All work had stopped and the boats swung idle at their moorings. Looms were half-strung, chisels and mallets lay among the sawdust, wet clay was hardening in the morning. It would have been a field day for the thieves of Eboracum, had not those thieves been standing with the innocent, the honest people of the city, cheering on the soldiers. *Their* soldiers.

Theodosius held out a hand and a staff officer unwrapped an imperial purple silken cloth in his hand. On it lay five gold rings, each one inlaid with the jet for which Eboracum was famous. And on the face of each, four helmets stood in each of the stone's four corners.

'Four helmets,' Theodosius said quietly, 'For the four men who stood when the Wall fell. Wear them. Wear them with pride.' He waited until each man had slid the gold over the knuckle of his right little finger. Then he did the same with the fifth. His eyes burned into the others as he walked slowly in front of them. 'I vow,' he grunted, 'that I shall not take this ring off until the Wall is restored.' His head came up and he raked them all with that fierce gaze of his.

'We vow it,' they said together, saluted the Count and stood back, taking up their respective positions in the lines. Then the cheering of the legions stopped and the trumpets blasted. Theodosius turned and shook the hand of Decius Ammianus, bowed briskly to Augusta and the ladies of the VI and strode for his horse, held by a groom. The grey lifted its head and snorted, scenting the march and the battle and shifted slightly as it felt the Count's weight. The man was not wearing his gilded parade armour today but a plain mail coat with a shield of the Jovii slung from his horse. Only his helmet marked him out as an officer of rank, its comb and cheekplates heavy with gold dragons locked in deadly combat.

He hauled his rein and faced his legions, packed onto the parade ground as they were. 'Our information tells us,' he shouted, 'that the barbarians are to the west. That is where we'll catch them. We will bring them back in chains, to be sold in the market place. That's after you archers have used them as pin cushions.' Raucous laughter filled the Eboracum air. 'The Jovii will lead out, aquilifer.'

The standard bearer hoisted the eagle high and spun on his heel, marching for the north gate. Behind him the eagle party fell into step, all of them carrying scarlet vexilli and long-tailed dragons. The archers followed, their bows over their shoulders and two cohorts of the Jovii behind them, each unit waiting for the moment before making the ground thunder. Theodosius' standard bearer urged his horse forward and the Count took up his position.

'Heroes of the Wall,' Maximus grunted to himself and spat volubly onto the earth of the parade ground. He sat his chestnut waiting for his place in the line.

A long way along that line, in the Third Cohort of the VI, Leocadius was more than a little confused. 'West?' he said to Vitalis. 'Did he say west? I thought we were going east.'

'Leo! Leo!' There was a babble of female voices from the edge of the field. Half the girls in Eboracum seemed to be there, waving at the circitor. Three of them broke through the cordon of guards to throw amulets at their love, the little knots made from Ussos reeds for him to wear close to his heart. Across the parade ground, Lavinia, the praeses' daughter, saw it and suddenly launched an attack of her own. She leapt up from her honoured place on the steps with the legion's ladies and, hauling up her skirts, ran like a madwoman across to where Maximus sat his horse. The general clicked his fingers and the mastiff beside him dropped to his haunches and did not move. When she got there, panting, she reached up with her love token, her eyes shining and bright. The general looked down at the dark eyes and long, flowing hair. He smiled. He did not have much shame when he was seventeen either, but he still felt awkward that he had bedded his best friend's mother. He took the love-knot and tucked it into his tunic, saluting her as he wheeled his horse away, falling into line at the head of the Victores, the dog ambling alongside.

Near the dais, Decius Ammianus strolled closer to the ladies' steps. 'Remind me to have a word with your daughter, Augusta,' he said quietly out of the corner of his mouth.

For over an hour the legions of Theodosius' field army, along with two cohorts of the VI and a unit of engineers in full pack, streamed through the gate of the camp and out onto the bleak moors to the north.

Clodius Narbo half turned to his commanding officer once the fuss was over and the remaining cohorts of the VI became watchmen again. 'I don't know about you, Praeses,' he said, 'But I feel strangely alone again.'

Ammianus nodded, unbuckling his helmet and running his fingers through what was left of his hair. 'I know what you mean, Clodius,' he said. 'Let's pray to Jupiter they all come back.'

Half a day's march north of Eboracum, the army of Theodosius split up. The tribune Justinus took his engineers and his cohorts of the VI north east, past Derventio which was a camp no more. If there had been bodies here, they had gone now and thistles grew on the camp's ramparts and grass was sprouting from the grey stones. They bivouacked there that night, under the leather tents they dragged on their wagons. Justinus had ordered the wheels be greased so that they made as little noise as possible, trundling north-east. They followed the twists of the river Derventio the next day, the cavalry lent to them by Theodosius riding ahead, on the flanks and at the rear, watching the grey, bare hills.

On the second day the forward scouts rode back to report a settlement ahead, a villa. It was still inhabited with people going about their business and all seemed well. Even so, Justinus was taking no chances. His men were tired of hard tack already and some hot food would not come amiss. But Fullofaudes had ridden into a trap; it was the way of the barbarians.

'Battle order!' he shouted and the column scattered, forming ranks behind their shields with the archers on the wings. The cavalry spread themselves left and right, forming a curve on the sloping ground. Then they advanced, the cohorts kept in check by Paternus marching ahead with his carved stick, keeping time and mending the pace. The only sound was the measured tread of boots on the boggy ground. It had not been long that the snows had melted from these uplands and the grass still lay damp and flat. The Victores horsemen slowed their pace over the rough ground to the south west, where gorse bushes and tangled roots of stunted trees broke the marching line for a moment. To the north east, on the left flank, the going was easier and the horsemen were trotting ahead of the infantry. 'Mind your pace, circitor,' the tribune called out and the cavalry reined in.

'Vexillum!' Justinus ordered and the scarlet flag of the VI was hoisted high behind him. There seemed little point in secrecy now, since five hundred men were on the march, pouring over the little hill and sweeping down into the valley. The villa that lay there, sheltered from the winds, had no defences at all. Its roofs were pale red with imported tiles and smoke drifted up from a furnace behind the barn. Geese hissed and flapped at the arrival of the cohorts and the first lambs of the spring bleated piteously and hid behind their mothers.

The cavalry curved their formation around the outer wall so that the cluster of buildings was surrounded. A squat, balding man came scurrying out of the front door, hauling his sagum onto his shoulder as a slave fussed with the brooch that held it.

'Welcome!' the little man beamed. 'Welcome. I am Virius Cocidius. Welcome to my home.'

'Justinus Coelius,' the tribune said and swung down from his saddle. 'Pat.' The first centurion joined him. 'We're from Eboracum.' Justinus looked around him. The cavalry were right; all seemed well. 'You've had no trouble here?'

'Trouble?' Cocidius was grinning like a gargoyle in the Baths.

'Trouble,' Justinus repeated. 'Pictish trouble, for instance.'

Cocidius' grin faded. 'You'd better come in,' he said. 'I'm afraid I can't offer you much. There ...' he looked at the phalanx outside his kitchen window, '... are rather a lot of you.'

'Centurion,' Justinus barked to the officer commanding the First Cohort. 'Stand the men down. I want the cavalry up on the hills, every direction.'

'Sir!' the man clicked to attention and dashed off, shouting orders as he ran.

The heat from the floor was welcome after hours on the moors but there seemed precious little else in the way of comfort. Cocidius invited Justinus and Paternus to sit on hard, wooden chairs, while the master of the house stood. There were no couches, no tables, no statuary. And only, as it turned out, one slave.

'They've all run away,' Cocidius aid. 'All my people. At the moment I have enough fuel to heat the house, but once that's gone, I have no one to chop the trees. I'd offer you some wine, gentlemen, but ... likewise ...'

'What happened?' Justinus asked.

'Picts,' Cocidius said. 'They came just before Saturnalia. They killed my steward and some of the men.'

'Your family?' Paternus asked, unbuckling his helmet.

'Gone, thank Jupiter. My daughters are married – in Londinium. My wife, Jupiter rest her, went of a chill three years ago. But the bastards took everything else. They offered me a straight choice. Either I handed over everything I had or they'd burn my house down. And the trouble is, they'll be back.'

'How do you know that?' the tribune asked.

'That was the deal,' Cocidius shrugged. 'The reason I'm still talking to you today. It's spring now – I've got new lambs for the taking, goslings. And this,' he tapped the gilded brooch on his shoulder, 'the last piece of jewellery I've got.'

'Did these Picts have a leader?' Justinus asked.

'They did,' Cocidius told him.

'You didn't catch his name, I suppose?' Paternus cut in.

'The others called him Talog or something like that.'

'Not Valentinus?' Justinus checked. 'You didn't hear that name?'

Cocidius shook his head.

'What did he look like?' Paternus asked, 'this Talog?'

'What do any of them look like?' Cocidius shrugged. 'Seen one, seen them all. Wild, red hair, body covered in that bloody blue paint. Barbarian doesn't begin to describe it.'

'No Roman helmet?' Justinius asked. 'With a silver face mask?'

'No,' Cocidius frowned. 'I don't know who you're looking for, Tribune, but I've seen no one like that.'

'Just as well,' Justinus said. He stood up. 'Master Cocidius, we're bound for the coast and I can't spare any men. You and your slave are welcome to come with us ... if you can spare some of your geese and sheep too, that would be an advantage.'

Cocidius stood up too, his nose level with the tribune's chin. 'This is my home,' he said, 'and Picts or no Picts, I will die in it. I've got an old sword somewhere. I'll try to take as many of them with me as I can.'

Justinus nodded. On the way out he touched the little stone statuette of the hearth god, Lares, and walked out into the yard. Paternus walked with him. Outside, the geese were honking madly as soldiers were grabbing for them, slipping ropes around their feet and hoisting them over their shoulders.

'Stop that!' Justinus ordered. 'Put them back. And, soldier ...' The infantryman nearest dropped the flapping bird and stood to attention, 'Ask next time.' And he strode for his horse.

It was two days later that they reached the sea. A spring sunshine warmed the earth now and the clouds, such as they were, threw huge shadows floating over the high moorland. The wind blew horizontal, flattening the grass and bending the trees still further where they had bent to the winds of the German sea for so long.

'There,' Justinus pointed to his machinator. 'That's where the Count would have us build our tower.'

Rutilius had been chief engineer to the VI for years now and he knew his business. 'We'll need to sink deep,' he said. 'These winds will topple any wall over twenty feet unless our foundations are secure.'

'How long will it take?' the tribune asked. The high land was flat up here with a rugged peninsula jutting out into the sea. His men could build a temporary camp in three hours, perhaps less, but a tower would need to be stone-built and the stone would need to be quarried, dragged from the shingle beach itself.

'Give me two months,' Rutilius said.

'I'd want the Forum of Rome up in two months,' Justinus laughed. 'You've got four weeks. After that, I'm taking my boys away and you can build the bloody thing yourself.'

'Fair enough,' Rutilius chuckled. He knew he could do it in three, but it was important not to let senior officers know how easy these things were – they might get ideas above their station.

'Is it me, Vit?' Leocadius downed his shovel that night and sat back on the earth rampart he and his men had just finished, 'or are we balancing on a bloody rock at the arse-end of nowhere, looking out over a sea which is empty?'

'Saxons,' Vitalis wiped the sweat from his forehead and felt his back click as he sat down. 'I overheard Justinus and Pat talking yesterday. There's talk that this barbarian conspiracy, if that's what it is, is bigger than we imagined. There may even be Franks involved.'

'Franks?' Leocadius frowned, taking a hearty swig from his leather canteen. 'Who the hell are they?'

'The world is bigger than we are, Leo,' Vitalis told him with all the experience of his nineteen years. 'North of the Wall is a frightening place. Not just *our* Wall, here in Britannia, but anywhere. Who knows what lies beyond?'

'Hm,' Leocadius was not impressed. 'Men,' he said, yawning. 'Men like us. No more, no less.'

There was a clanging of iron on iron, the call to eat. 'Thank Jupiter,' Leocadius said. 'And to think,' he stood up and spread his arms around him at the half-finished fortifications, 'all this fun and food too. They spoil us, they really do.'

Mario Fabricius had lost all feeling in his fingers. For the last four hours he had strolled the new ramparts of the VIth's makeshift fort on the eastern headland, trying to keep warm. What a god-forsaken place this was, in the middle of nowhere, with winds blowing ice into his face. His nose was dripping and his mouth had stopped working hours ago, which is why it took him a moment to gather his thoughts and force his lips to move.

'Trumpets!' he yelled. 'Picts. North-east.'

They were almost the last words he said because a stone shot bounced off his helmet, knocking him off the earth wall. Leocadius sniggered in spite of the situation. He could not stand Fabricius – the man had been a pain in the circitor's arse ever since he had been promoted. He had the heart to check that he was all right, though, once he had grabbed his sword and shield and climbed out of his tent. The trumpet was waking the morning and all around him was chaos. Men half asleep tugged on mail coats and buckled on helmets. He could see Justinus and the centurions clawing their way up Rutilius' ladders to the top of the ramparts.

'Archers!' Justinus was bellowing and everybody but the cavalry was out of their tents and crowding below the earthworks. The Ala Jovii were saddling their horses, wondering what had happened to the scouts Justinus had thrown out to the north and west. They did not have to wait long to have their question answered. One of them was being dragged along the level ground in front of the earth wall. He was tied by his right ankle to his horse that ambled forwards, pausing every now and then to crop the short grass. The cavalryman's arms hung limp by his side and his mail coat was ripped and dark with his blood. As for his head, that was in the grip of a tall horseman on the low ridge to the west of the half-finished camp. He held it aloft, impaled on a spike and shouted at the Romans.

'He wants to know,' Justinus said, trying to keep his voice level as he caught the snatches of Pictish on the wind, 'whether we want our man's head back.'

'Along with his,' said Paternus, standing up alongside the half-built palisade and preparing to attack.

'Not yet, Pat,' Justinus held him back and looked his friend in the face. 'There'll be a time. Circitor,' he shouted down the slope to where the cavalry were forming up. 'I want five of your fastest horses saddled and ready. When I say you head south I don't want to have to repeat myself. Take a message to Eboracum. To the praeses.' He looked back to the line of Picts who outnumbered his little force two to one. 'Tell him what happened here.' He turned back to the circitor again. 'The rest of you men, dismount. Up on the walls with the rest of us.'

The circitor chose his five men who stayed in their saddles and the others grumbled, tethering their mounts as they did so. What was the point of being a cavalryman without a horse? Those bloody foot-sloggers would never understand.

'What do you make of it, Pat?' Justinus was still bareheaded and he was only now buckling on his sword.

'Ladders,' Paternus frowned. 'They've got bloody ladders.'

Justinus nodded. 'Like tits on a bull,' he said. This was not the Pictish way. The wild northmen roared themselves into a frenzy before a battle, egging each other on, drinking themselves silly and painting their bodies with their devilish designs. Then they ran at everything; earthworks, shield-walls, testudos, cavalry – it did not matter. They were battle-mad and they fought like demons, snarling their outlandish battle cries and dying by the dozen. But no Pictish raiding party that Justinus had heard of came prepared to break a siege. Is that how they had taken Banna? Camboglanna? The tribune squinted to see more clearly in the early light. If the Picts had a wild ass with them, the onager machine that smashed palisades to driftwood, then there was no hope.

'Do you speak our language?' the horseman called.

'We do,' Justinus shouted back, not raising his head higher than he needed above the ramparts. Young Fabricius was still having his head bandaged by the medics.

'Why are you here?' the Pict shouted, 'on our sacred ground?'

'*Your* ground?' Justinus shouted back. 'The last time I looked this was Brigantes country, specifically, I believe, Gabrantovices. But for the last three hundred years, it's been Roman. You're lost, Pict. Get yourselves north of the Wall again and we'll forget all about this unfortunate business.'

There was a pause, then mocking laughter drifted across the open moor. 'What Wall is that, Roman?' the Pict shouted. 'Haven't you heard? A little wind from the north blew it down.'

'We know,' Justinus yelled. 'That's why we're here. To rebuild it.'

More mocking laughter. Suddenly, Paternus had leapt forward, over the low palisade and was rolling down the ramparts. He had left his shield behind and crouched in the ditch before springing out and darting across the open space, making for the meandering horse and its headless rider.

'Arrows!' Justinus screamed and the recurved bows bent back as one, the deadly arrows hissing through the air like rain. A horse went down, its neck skewered by three shafts and half a dozen men pitched forward or fell back. The rest caught the arrows on their limewood shields, the iron tips smashing through the timber to drive splinters into their faces. Paternus had grabbed the horse's bridle and was running to the gate alongside it. He was not horseman enough to leap onto the back of even a trotting animal, so he kept plodding doggedly on as Pictish arrows and slingshots hissed around him. He reached the rampart and half a dozen men manned the make-shift gate to the side to let him in. They carried the dead man to the far ditch and laid him in it with as much ceremony as the moment would allow.

'Centurion Priscus!' Justinus bellowed and Paternus hauled himself up the ladder to the tribune's side. Justinus looked at him. Had he stopped the man from ripping out his own entrails just to see his head sliced off by a Pict? He glowered at his friend. 'No more heroics, Pat,' he said. 'I need you here. I need you alive.'

'They're coming!' someone shouted. He was right. Justinus had not heard the bray of a carynx for a long time. Many of the men on the ramparts had never heard it.

'Mother Minerva,' one of the youngest said, his head below the parapet. 'What's that?'

'It's nothing, lad,' an old circitor told him. 'It's a pipe with a reed up it. A chance for the painted people to blow a lot of hot air, that's all.'

Justinus and Paternus watched them come on, in a silence that they had never seen before. There was no wild rebel yell, no headlong rush. They were actually marching, not as a real legion might, for sure, but in a close approximation of it. There were six ladders, rough hewn from spruce or some other northern tree, but, thank Jupiter, no siege engine. That meant the Picts would have to reach the earth ramparts first, scrabble up them and *then* place their ladders. And all the time, Roman bows and Roman slingshots would be carrying out their deadly work.

Justinus gnawed his lip. He could see their archers were hanging back, along with their leader who still held the head-pole in his hand. And he understood why. They were there to provide cover for the infantry going in now. If they could fire fast enough and accurately enough, they would be able to riddle the defenders on the wall and sweep the ramparts clean. Once up the ladders and over the palisade, it would be every man for himself and, in that confined space, no chance of driving them back.

The tribune turned to the centurions around him. 'On my command,' he hissed. 'I want every archer and slinger we've got to hit those bastards on the hill. Let them take a few steps forward so we're sure they're in range. Everybody else, stand fast.'

The centurions hurried away to do Justinus' bidding. Paternus still stood there. 'Supernumerary, remember,' he smiled. 'I'll just stand here, if that's all right,' Justinus lowered his head so that he could see over the points of the palisade. The new-cut wood smelt sweet and strong in his nostrils. 'Now!' he bellowed and the hiss of arrows punctuated his word. The Picts had not expected this. The dense mass marching forward in an ever more ragged line saw the volley sail harmlessly over their heads, but it wrought havoc among their archers. Not a man had unleashed his bow before the Roman arrows were scything into them, thudding into unarmoured bodies and snaking into bare heads. The few shieldmen they had with them tried to race across and catch the shafts on their timber, but it was a losing battle.

'Archers!' Justinus shouted. 'Below!' Now his bowmen arched over the palisades and sent their arrows smacking into the mass of Celts nearing the ramparts. Dozens went down, blood spurting over mail and blue-painted bodies. The few Pict archers left on the hill were firing back now, their arrows clattering on the camp's timbers and occasionally finding their mark. An archer of the VI toppled over the palisade to be hacked to pieces at the bottom of the slope. Another fell backwards with a shaft through his windpipe, blood bubbling from his lips.

Again and again, Justinus' archers reloaded, sliding their arrows from their quivers and drawing their strings back to their chests. The animal gut pinged on their leather armbraces and they bent their backs again, sending the oak shafts through the morning air. But the ladders came up, first one, then two more. A soldier grabbed the upright ends and pushed it away from the wall but an arrow squelched into his eye under the helmet rim and he died instantly. More and more of the soldiers on the ramparts hauled the ladders aside. Pictish spears were being hurled by now, their blades etched with monsters and gods that no man could understand. A scattering of Romans fell as some of these struck home, the impact of them flinging men off the wall walks.

'Javelins!' Justinus roared as his centurions along the line were yelling the same thing. Roman spears hissed downwards now, gravity adding to their power, slicing through blue-painted shoulders, backs and chests. Now the Picts were roaring. The eerie silence of their advance had given way to the old yells, the curses heaped on Roman heads since the days of Agricola. This was more like it, Justinus thought to himself, in the odd moment he had time to think at all; this was war in the old way. And in the old way, victory always went to the Romans. Then, he had too much time to think and he saw the body of Ulpius Piso at Banna and smelt again the charred remains of his men. Victory always went to the Romans? He was not so sure.

As he looked along the ramparts, he realised that all the ladders now held steady and up them streamed the Picts in great and desperate numbers. Swords and axes were clashing on the legion's blades and bouncing off the legion's shields. One by one the sections of the wall were falling and men were jumping off the ramparts before they were pushed. The archers were useless now; they could not fire for fear of hitting their own men. And in the mêlée, soldiers could not use their darts for the same reason. Now it was sword to sword and the Roman line on the palisades was as broken as the Picts.

Justinus threw himself to the ground, rolling upright and grabbing a shield from a dead man. 'First cohort,' he yelled at the solid ranks facing him. 'Battle order.' Above the screaming of the Picts and the clash of iron on the ramparts, the cornicen shrilled out its notes and the unit slid into position. Shields were locked across the front, their iron rims overlapping for maximum protection and the javelins came down to form a vicious wall of iron spikes. The tribune knew the Picts. They would run onto those spikes all day, dying in their hundreds for whatever mad gods they worshipped.

'Third cohort,' Justinus sword was in his hand. 'Split. Paternus, I want half your men to the right, on the wings of the First. The other half to the left. On my command, you will close in. Understood?'

'Very good, sir.' Paternus dashed across to his circitors to make it happen. Justinus was creating a cul-de-sac of death. There would be Roman spears in front of the Picts and Roman spears to both sides. If a man emerged alive from that, it would be a miracle.

'Parting of the ways, Leo,' Vitalis said as the cohorts separated.

'See you beyond the Styx,' Vit,' and he was gone.

Two heroes of the Wall running to the sound of the cornicen.

'Vexillum!' Justinus roared and the flag of the VI Victrix shot skyward.

A strange stillness fell over the camp. Only the groaning of dying men broke the silence. The Pictish screams had stopped, the roar of their hundreds; and terrible heads came slowly over the parapet, men with long red hair and bodies naked to the waist, circled and snaked with blue. In the centre, a tall man was the first to place his feet on the ramparts the legion had failed to hold. In his hand he was holding the head of a Roman cavalryman by the hair and he threw it over the corpse-strewn parade ground so that it bounced and rolled at the feet of Justinus.

'One of yours, I believe,' the Pict said.

CHAPTER VIII

'Loose!' That was a Roman command and it had not come from Justinus or anyone inside the half-finished camp. The Picts swarming over the palisade were falling forwards, sideways, back. There were arrows in their bodies. Roman arrows. One by one, the ladders fell away from the skyline in the camp. Now was the time. Now, while the Picts were in disarray.

Justinus could not see what was happening beyond the palisade but the bray of the cornicens to the west confirmed what he already hoped. Perhaps only Mithras knew who was out there, attacking the Picts from their rear, but it had to be heaven sent.

'Third cohort,' the tribune yelled, taking his place at the head of the First, 'Battle order.'

Paternus' men broke their formation and dashed into position behind the lines of the First. 'Attack!' Justinus yelled and the whole formation moved forward. If the Picts had not seen a Roman legion, or even a vexillation on the attack before, they saw it now. The tribune stepped over the cavalryman's head but in the mêlée behind him there were no such niceties and it was kicked from foot to foot, rolling in the mud.

'Javelins!' Justinus shouted and the front rank hurled their weapons into the milling Picts. The painted warriors were hopelessly trapped now. Some of them ran forward, yelling their battle cries that froze the blood. Justinus hacked with his sword through a man's ribs and all but caught another on his shield. The warrior lost his balance and fell under the boots of the First cohort that smashed down, cracking his skull and grinding his face into the ground his chieftain had called sacred.

With their backs to the earth bank, the Picts had nowhere to go. Some tried to claw their way back up the ladders, but Justinus' archers had a clear field now and their arrows brought them down, adding to the murderous chaos at the foot of the ramp.

By now the lines of the Third Cohort had closed in, ramming their heavy swords into naked bodies and batting dying men aside with their shields. Paternus dashed like a madman along the line. He had thrown down his shield and swung the spatha with both hands, yelling at each enemy he met, daring him to come on. A Pictish sickle grazed his forearm, darkening the mail with blood and arrows bounced off his helmet. But no one was going to stop Paternus today. 'Quin!' he bellowed as he shattered the red-haired skull of a warrior, shouting out the name of his cold, dead son.

The Picts were backing away, trying to parry the Roman sword thrusts as best they could. But the half naked men, isolated, surrounded, beaten, could not hold for long and one by one they threw down their weapons.

Leocadius and Vitalis had never fought like this before. They had never fought at all. The curly-haired circitor saw his blade slick with another man's blood and laughed. He eased his tunic aside above his belt. The blow he had felt to his chest had left a purpling bruise but that would only impress the ladies of Eboracum even more when he got back. Their amulets were still there, the love knots pressed and tangled in the lining of his tunic. Vitalis' blade was red too, and he felt sick at the cloying smell of blood all around him.

Justinus leaned with both hands on his sword hilt, the point rammed into the earth. He and his men had fought the Picts to a standstill and they faced each other now over a low wall made of the Pictish dead. One by one the warriors threw down their weapons and stood with their arms folded, defiant even in defeat. In their centre, the most defiant of all was the chieftain who had thrown the cavalryman's head, who had challenged Justinus in the first place.

'What is your name?' the tribune asked him, in the flat vowels of Caledonia.

'Talorc,' the Pict grunted. His shoulder had been sliced by a Roman sword and he had difficulty taking each breath.

'Are you called Valentinus?'

The Pict looked at the tribune for a moment, then he laughed; even though it hurt and even though he was bleeding.

'Valentinus is twice as high as me,' he said, 'and twice as wide. When he speaks, thunder shakes the trees and sparks flash from his eyes. You will know him when you see him.'

There was one of those odd stillnesses that fall over a battle-field. The only sounds were the moans of the wounded and of dying men calling for their mothers on the ground they had given their lives for. Beyond the palisade was stillness too and then the clatter of wood on wood. The prongs of a ladder appeared over the parapet and they were followed by a familiar face.

'Salvete,' Magnus Maximus grinned. He was looking at Justinus. 'When are you going to finish this camp, then?'

When they had hauled the dead away and while the prisoners were guarded that night, the medics went about their business. By the light of flickering torches, they cauterized gaping wounds with irons red-hot from the furnace. They wrapped the Pictish sword-slashes in lint soaked in vinegar. They set broken bones with wet leather and splints. Then they prayed to Asclepius, the god who made broken men whole. And they hoped for the best.

The three men who lounged in the Count's tent that night could all have done with a bath and the healing oils and practised rubbing of the masseurs. As it was they had to make do with Theodosius' campaign wine and the roast piglets they had taken on the march. Bruno the mastiff particularly appreciated the bones and the sound of his crunching filled the camp.

'I really am very sorry about this, Justinus,' the Count was saying as his slave refilled everybody's goblet, 'but it was necessary. I had to let everybody think your little command was on its own. Even you. The root of the problem lies back in Eboracum. That's why I made a big thing about marching west. You were attacked because the Picts thought I was miles away, going in the wrong direction. Magnus, has that chieftain cracked yet? What's his name?'

'Talorc,' the general stretched out on his makeshift couch. 'He's the strong, silent type, unfortunately. If we had his woman here, his children ...' he shrugged, 'as it is, I wish we had a few like him in our legions.'

Theodosius nodded. 'We have to accept,' he said, 'that there is a spy at Eboracum. Somebody is feeding these painted people the information. Every time the praeses farts I suspect this Valentinus knows about it. That's a hole we'll have to close.'

'Crucifixions in the morning, Papa?' Maximus yawned. It had been a long day and he had not once drawn his sword during it.

Theodosius chuckled. Whenever Maximus called him that, he wanted something. 'Nice try, Magnus,' he said. 'You know as well as I do the deified Constantine outlawed that as a mark of respect for the Christ.'

'Ah,' nodded Maximus, 'but the more recently deified Julian ...'

Theodosius held up his hand. 'I'm not going to argue the law with you, Magnus,' he smiled, 'and I'm certainly not going to argue religion; we'll be here all night.'

'Hangings, then,' Maximus said. 'I can live with that.'

'Some, yes,' the Count sipped his wine. He had not drawn his sword either, but he was getting too long in the tooth for this sort of campaigning. It was a young man's job. 'We'll hang the leaders. The rest can go home.'

Maximus was not smiling now. 'Go home?' he repeated.

'Certainly,' Theodosius said. 'We still don't know what we're facing here. What have we got here today? A thousand Picts, can't be more. And a lot of those are dead. Tribune, you're the local boy. Are there any other tribes among our prisoners?'

'A handful of Brigantes, sir,' Justinus told him. 'Renegades with the promise of Roman loot shining in their eyes. But this is a Pictish war band. More than that, it's a Pictish army.'

'Are you splitting hairs, tribune?' Maximus asked.

'No, general, I'm not. I've faced Pictish raids before. So have most of us along the Wall. They are like watersilver, striking defenceless villages on their ponies and scattering before we can find them. I've never known them take on a camp before, even an unfinished one. And ladders – they had ladders with them.'

'And what do you make of this?' Theodosius wanted to know.

Justinus looked at both men. 'Valentinus,' he said.

'Go on.' The Count put down his cup.

'The man hits the Wall, first the outlying fortlets, then the Wall itself. He ambushes a Duke, for Jupiter's sake. And today he all but destroyed a marching camp.'

'You think this Valentinus was behind today's little escapade too?'

'I do, sir. The man *thinks* like a Roman, wages war like a

Roman. He's got the measure of us.'

'No, no,' Maximus was on his feet, pouring himself another draught of wine. He looked down at the dog, who looked up at him, licking his lips in anticipation. 'You know you don't like this stuff,' he said to the animal, reaching down as he turned back to the others and scratching the animal's back. He turned to Justinus. 'He's been lucky so far, that's all. And from today his luck ran out.' He turned to Theodosius. 'Why aren't you killing them all?'

'Because we can't kill them all,' the Count told him flatly. 'Behind every Pict under guard tonight there is a father, a brother, a son. Behind them are the womenfolk who will feed them, carry the water, dress their wounds. And the old who will give them shelter. We are two legions, Magnus, three if you count the VI. We can't fight an entire nation.'

'But they're not a nation,' Maximus insisted. 'They're tribes. They can be broken.'

'And they will be,' Theodosius assured him. 'Justinus, that survivor from the mouth of hell, the signifer ...'

'Claudius Metellus,' the tribune said.

'That's the one. Yes. Why did Valentinus let him live?'

Justinus nodded. He understood. 'To bring the rest of us a message,' he said.

'Precisely,' the Count smiled. 'And that's what I intend to do tomorrow.'

They had flayed Talorc with iron-tipped whips, concentrating on the man's torn shoulder. His screams had filled the night, exactly as Maximus had intended they should. And the next morning, two legions and a vexillation stood in all the pride of war, their helmets shining in the sun, their shields bright again after the bloodying of the previous day.

The Picts stood in a circle, roped together by wrist and ankle. Any man who tried to run would drag two others with him and they in turn would drag more. It was tried and it was tested. There would be no escape. The engineers under Rutilius were already at work, repairing breaches, hauling timbers upright, shovelling earth. This time there would be no interruptions and the fresh men of the Victores who had barely broken into a sweat yesterday were toiling in the warm sunshine, stripped to the waist.

Talorc was brought across the vallum, empty now of weapons and bodies. For the last three hours the Picts themselves had been forced to dig a huge pit, three men deep. Five men had collapsed, exhausted, dying of their wounds as dawn broke in the purple sky to the east. They became the first occupants of the pit, but not before the Jovii had lashed some of Rutilius' palisade timbers together and made a grid in the pit's depths. Roman and Pictish bodies, stripped of their armour, were flung in, men from the conturberniae mumbling the old prayers and invoking the gods old and new – 'Mithras, god of the morning, our trumpets waken the Wall. Rome is above all nations, but you are over all.'

'What is that?' the tortured chieftain still had the strength to point to the pit.

Among the officers, only Justinus spoke the man's language, harsh and guttural as it was. 'It's a funeral pyre, Pict,' he said. 'We're going to burn your people along with ours.'

'You can't!' Talorc tried to break free but the ropes and the guards held him fast. 'My men must be buried, their bodies laid in the sacred earth. It is our way.'

Another man who spoke the Pict's language yelled from the Third Cohort of the VI. 'You should have thought of that before you made war on women and children, you bastard.' Justinus looked along the ranks but he had no need to seek out the face. Paternus, the first centurion, stood with his hands gripping each end of his gnarled stick, his face impassive, his eyes dead.

'Point out your leaders,' Justinus said to Talorc. The man was barely standing, his skin ripped to shreds by the work of the farriers' whips, huge weals across his pale blue skin as though the men of the Jovii had tried to carve new designs in his flesh. 'Point out your leaders and you have my word we will not burn them. They will have a proper burial.'

'You can go to hell, Roman!' Talorc spat at him.

The tribune shrugged at Theodosius, waiting on his grey at the head of the Jovii, the scarlet flag and the silver eagle at his shoulder. The Count did not need to understand Pictish to know the chieftain's answer. 'One in twenty,' he shouted to the centurion in charge of the prisoners. 'Take them to the palisades and string them up. That man,' he pointed to Talorc,' will watch them and then he will follow them.' He turned in the saddle to look for Justinus' chief engineer. 'Rutilius?' he shouted.

'Sir?' the man's bare head popped up over the parapet.

'Now we'll see how strong your walls really are.'

The line of roped Picts milled and threshed, trying to make

the selection process as difficult as possible, but relentlessly men of the Victores hauled on the ropes, pulling them along, counting one to twenty and then taking that twentieth man. Finally, struggling and kicking, a total of thirty five were cut free of the others and dragged through the side gate of the camp. They were hauled up the ladders and made to stand on the wall walk at the top. Below them they saw the legions that had defeated then, drawn up as on a parade ground, silent and still. The man who led them, the tall sandy-haired man with the grey eyes who could have passed for a Pict himself turned his horse and walked it along the line of shields on the ground beside each man.

'What you are to witness,' he shouted, 'is an execution. The men who are about to die are warriors. Yesterday they were prepared to die facing you and today they will. I do not have to remind you that men dying for the pleasure of the crowd belongs to our barbaric past. We don't do that now. And we don't find another man's pain amusing. Anybody who I see so much as twitch his lip will join these men. Do I make myself clear?'

The legions grunted their answer in one fierce shout. Then, Theodosius gave the signal and the first man was thrown over the parapet, the noose around his neck jerking tight as his body hit the timbers of the palisade and his feet kicked. For a minute, perhaps two, he writhed in the air, his eyes rolling and his lips frothing with blood. Then he died. But before he did a second man was thrown over and a third. All along the palisade the Picts had failed to hold, bodies twitched and danced, the piss and shit trickling down their legs. Talorc tried to look away, but every time he did, a pedes hauled on his hair and wrenched his head back painfully. If he tried to close his eyes they were slapped open again.

For nearly an hour the hangings went on, then it was the leader's turn. He followed the others, stumbling up the ladder, shivering with shock and the pain in his body. On the parapet, they slid the rough hemp noose around his neck and stood watching for Theodosius' command. The Count sat his horse impassively and dropped his raised hand. Then the twisting figure of Talorc sailed through the air where the others dangled. His heels bounced off Rutilius' uprights up which the Picts had scrambled the day before and the horizon bobbed in his distorted vision. Through bulging eyes, he saw the Romans, grim faces under identical helmets, men with no souls, no hearts. He saw the bastards at their head, the arrogant shits called generals and that bloody dog alongside. And he saw the land, not his land, it was true, but land like it, flatter and warmer than the glens and mountains of Caledonia. The weight on his neck was unbearable. He was choking, his windpipe tightening and his airways closing as he fought. His hands twisted and stretched behind his back but he could not break free. He threw himself forward once and then back. And then he saw the land no more and his body shuddered, his heels kicking a staccato tattoo on the palisade.

Now only the wind moaned. The sun of the early morning had gone and iron-grey clouds were massing in the west. Theodosius nodded at Justinus who walked his horse towards the great mob of prisoners. They stood silent, unwilling witnesses to the deaths of the chosen. And they calmly waited for their turn. There was a thud as Talorc's body, cut from its rope, hit the ground. Followed by another. And another.

Justinus nodded to the guards who drew their daggers and hacked through the ankle ropes of the Picts and then freed their wrists. The warriors from the cold north looked at each other, frowning and rubbing their bleeding limbs. What new treachery was this from the Romans?

'You are free men,' the tribune shouted at them. 'Go home. Home to your loved ones. And there you have a choice. Either you cross the Wall and leave us alone or we will come looking for you. And we will not execute one in twenty. We will execute you all. Every man. Every woman. Every child.'

For a moment, no one moved. Then, a man broke away at the back and started to run. He half expected an arrow or a javelin between his shoulder blades, but there was nothing. Apart from the guards, the Romans still stood stock still, shields at their sides, spears in their hands pointing to the sky. Someone followed him, then another and soon all of them were scurrying away, unarmed and defenceless, the wounded being helped along by those that still had the strength.

Then there were only a handful of prisoners left in the shadow of Rutilius' camp. They were still shackled and they looked at Justinus with fear written all over their faces. There was no wild red hair here, no swirling blue paint. 'You men,' the tribune said, raking them all with a solemn face, 'Are Brigantes and Gabrantovices. At least they,' he jerked his thumb in the direction of the fleeing Picts, 'have some excuse. They're barbarian to the bone from some gods-forsaken hellhole in the north. But you men ... you're from south of the Wall. You've lived alongside us all your lives. So did your fathers and their fathers. Why? Why have you turned against us?'

'Valentinus says ...' a young voice called out and it was immediately silenced.

Justinus singled out the speaker. He was Gabrantovices for sure and he was no more than thirteen. His tunic was ragged and filthy and he wore no boots or sandals. There was an ugly purple bruise across his swollen forehead and his left eye was half closed. But it was the old red line around the boy's neck, shiny and taut with scar tissue that caught the tribune's attention. He held up the lad's chin. 'You're a slave,' he said. 'A runaway.'

The boy blinked, but said nothing. Justinus moved so that he was in his eye line. 'What did Valentinus say?' he asked.

'Shut up, boy,' someone nearby growled and Justinus half turned, slapping the man across the head with the back of his hand.

'Talk to me,' the tribune had not taken his eyes off the boy.

'Valentinus says the day is coming,' he blurted out, tears filling his eyes.

'What day, boy?' Justinus asked.

'The day,' the lad repeated. 'The day when the Romans will sail from these shores. And we will be free.'

'Free?' Justinus chuckled. 'You see this?' He held out his scarf. 'It's the badge of a tribune. And it's just as much a collar as the iron one you used to wear around your neck. Nobody's free. Not now. Not ever.' He turned away. 'And by the way,' he said, 'I'm no more Roman than you are. I am of the same clay as you. The only difference between us is which side of the eagles we stand on.'

The tribune unbuckled his helmet. 'You can believe in Valentinus and his day,' he said to the Brigantes, 'or you can believe me when I tell you that Valentinus will face his own day first. And it will end in his death. I can promise you one thing – I will be there that day. And I will see it with my own eyes.' He slid his dagger from its sheath and looked hard at the man he had just slapped, then he cut his ropes and those of all the others.

Virius Cocidius was reduced to drawing water from his own well. And those days he kept that old sword, the one he knew he had around somewhere, close to hand. That evening, as the sun was setting behind the tall elms, it was slung over his shoulder. His slave, Lupo, was sawing wood, the rhythmic song of the blade drowning out the soft pad of hooves plodding down the hill.

It was a snort from one of those horses that stopped Lupo in mid-cut. Cocidius turned and let the rope go in his surprise, the bucket hurtling down with an echoing rattle followed by an eerie splash. Two riders were coming down the hill, mail shirts gleaming in the dying light and shields strapped to their backs. Cocidius would never see fifty again and his old trouble had been playing him up recently. Even so, he had vowed to every god of his household that he would take no more insults from the Picts. 'Lupo!' he called, 'Save yourself.'

The slave just stood there.

'Damn it, man, you're free,' Cocidius hissed. 'I release you. Go on. Go on.'

'Io, Virius Cocidius!' one of the horsemen hailed him as he reached the flat ground.

Under the helmet, the farmer recognized the face and almost fell over with relief. He felt a little silly with his sword in his hand and sheathed it quickly, having no intention of even trying to skewer the tribune Justinus Coelius or the rather severe young centurion who rode at his elbow. Behind them a running lad had just stopped running and stood looking ahead at Cocidius' villa in awe.

'Gentlemen,' Cocidius crossed to them. 'I can't tell you how good it is to see you. Can I offer you some ... water?'

Even that would take a while as Cocidius remembered where his bucket was, even assuming it was still in one piece.

'No thanks,' Justinus said. 'We're on our way south. But I've something for you.' He twisted in the saddle and motioned the boy forward. 'Master Cocidius,' the tribune smiled, 'I couldn't help noticing when I passed this way before, you are rather short-handed. This is Gracco, or at least, that's his Roman name. He's strong and he's got all his teeth. Can you find a use for him?'

Cocidius took a step forward and looked at the lad. He could smell him already and his face was a mask of mud and bruising. His feet were cut where he had been jogging through the bracken behind the horsemen. The boy bowed his head and held out his hands. He had been bought and sold before. He knew the drill.

'I've something for you, too,' Paternus said. He turned in the saddle and hauled something out of the leather bag tied behind him. It was the head of a Pict and he held it up by the hair so that the dead eyes bulged at Cocidius and the blue tongue stuck out at him, seemingly defiant even in death. 'Is this the man who stole your goods?' Paternus asked. 'The one called Talorc?'

'Er ... I think so,' Cocidius was horrified. 'It's just that, he looks so ... different.'

Paternus stuffed the head back into his saddle bag and took up the reins.

'The gods shine on you, Virius Cocidius,' Justinus said. 'I doubt you'll see any more Picts coming this way.'

'Gods defend you, gentlemen,' the farmer said and watched as they rode away. 'And thank you.' He turned to the boy in front of him. 'Well, lad,' he said. Do you know what a hypocaust is?'

Gracco's Latin was passable and he did his best. 'I think so, sir,' he said. 'It's heating, under the floor.'

'That's right,' Cocidius beamed. 'Do you know how it works?'

'No, sir.'

'Right,' Cocidius sighed. Officers of the VIth Legion had just rid his estate of raiders and brought him a slave, for nothing. It would be churlish to expect everything. 'Well, look, this is Lupo. He'll crank up the hot water for you and you can have a bath. And then, something to eat, I expect, yes?'

No one had moved.

'Lupo?' Cocidius said. 'Are you still here?'

'Er ... there's just one problem, Virius,' he said. 'You set me free a minute ago.'

'The hell I did!' the farmer said. 'You're starting to hear things now. Get on with it, man,' and as his faithful slave shuffled past, he caught him a nasty clip around the ear. 'And that's Master to you, ingrate!'

It was a day later that Justinus and Paternus clattered along the road that led to the Principia of the VI. Theodosius and Maximus were marching back to Eboracum at the head of their legions, having left four turmae of cavalry and two cohorts to protect Rutilius while he finished his watch tower and planned another one, further north.

Decius Ammianus was delighted to see his officers back and even more delighted to hear their news. But he had news of his own and it was grim. He was staring at a map when two of his Wall heroes arrived and he was still staring at it when they left, anxious to

111

get some sleep and take stock of the situation.

'It could have happened here,' the praeses said, tapping the land to the west. 'Cornovii country. Or here.' He pointed to the sweep further south, 'the lands of the Dobuni. If truth be told, we haven't the first clue where it happened. But what happened is without question. A messenger arrived yesterday, wore out four horses getting here. The younger Theodosius got the news at Rutupiae. Nectaridus, the Count of the Saxon Shore is dead. And the messenger said the man who killed him is someone whose name they hadn't heard in the south before – Valentinus.'

'Valentinus,' Magnus Maximus slammed his goblet down on the praeses' desk. He was looking at the same wall map that Ammianus seemed to have been staring at for two days now. 'The man's like a will o' the wisp. Here we are chasing him south of the Wall and all the time he's in the west. How the hell can he be in two places at once?'

'Because he's very good, Magnus,' Theodosius said. 'We've got to face it. I've fought all over the Empire. So have you. I've never come across anyone quite like him. So ...' the Count's face took on a look that Maximus knew well. A plan was forming in his brain. 'If he can be in two places at once, so can we. Ammianus.'

'Count.' The praeses looked up.

'Send for your Wall heroes. I'd like a word.'

'Justinus ...' Leocadius whispered, then caught the look on the man's face. 'Tribune. Can you tell me what the hell is going on?'

Justinus looked at him. 'You were there, man, just as I was,' he said. 'The Count is going south to Rutupiae to join his little boy. General Maximus is staying in the north. Pat and I will rebuild the Wall by all accounts while you and Vit have a high old time in Londinium.'

'Well,' Vitalis said, 'I'm not complaining, but why ...?'

'Londinium is the biggest city in Britannia,' Justinus said. 'Sooner or later Valentinus is likely to try to take it. That little business on the cliffs last week is just a palate tickler. He'll be really pissed off now we've given his Picts a bloody nose. Tell them, Pat.'

The centurion shrugged. 'I'm no master of strategy,' he said, 'but I think the idea is for Magnus Maximus to come from the north; Theodosius from the south and they'll catch Valentinus between them.'

'And what are we going to do?' Vitalis asked. 'We're circitors, for the gods' sake. We aren't going to add a great deal in the scheme of things.'

'No,' Justinus said flatly. 'You are heroes of the Wall.' He looked Leocadius in the eye, into the face of the man who had created that stupid lie in the first place. 'That's your place in the scheme of things. The people of Londinium don't know what it's like up here; they don't have a Wall or anything like it.' He thrust out his right arm, with the ring glowing black and gold in the firelight of the camp. Paternus did the same so that their rings clinked together. Then Vitalis, then Leocadius. The heroes of the Wall, standing together against the world.

Then, they broke up. They were soldiers, with duties to perform. On their way across the parade ground as another velvet night descended on Eboracum, studded with stars, Leocadius put his arm around Vitalis. 'What are we going to do in Londinium, Vit?' he laughed. 'You'll be amazed.'

LIBER II
CHAPTER IX

Rutupiae, Aestivus in the year of the Christ 368

The bireme butted its way south from the mouth of the Abus, dark grey waters flecked with foam. For much of the time the oars were locked horizontally and the wind did the work, roaring through the canvas of the single sail. Theodosius had left his transports in the river shelter, in case things had not gone his way against the barbarians and he needed to get his legions away in a hurry. He left most of his ships there now for the same reason. He and Maximus had defeated one small army or a very large raiding party, depending on one's take on life. That was not the end of it, by anybody's reckoning.

Leocadius thought he had died and was lying in fields of Elysium already. The ship's hold was rank with the smell of slaves condemned to a slow death chained to their oars, but up on deck, the wind whipped the white caps and the flags strained on their ropes. He had never sailed before and he loved it, the roll of the ship and the slap of the sea. He loved it even more when, every night, he sat on the quarter deck at the stern with the Count and his staff, drinking Theodosius' wine and eating his roast mutton that the chef had been preparing all day. He was impressed that, even on a warship moving south through troubled waters, men of Theodosius' rank did things in such style. The talk was of Londinium, of streets paved with gold, of renaming the city Augusta. There were speeches and toasts, to the Emperor, to the Count, to the general Maximus and the total destruction of Rome's enemies.

Vitalis was there too and by the third night, he found himself drawing away from the others, resting his elbows on the rail as the stern torches threw their weird reflections on the waves they slid past. He had never sailed before either, but he could not share Leocadius' obvious thrill. To him the sea was an alien place, forbidding, chilling, always on the move. He could still remember how he had felt back in the colonia at Eboracum when the centurion Flaminius had dunked him in the river. Imagine that a thousand times over, where there is no one to pull you out, no one to rescue you from the dark and the deep.

'Tell me about the Wall,' a voice in the half light made him turn. He had seen the man as soon as he had got on board, but not until now without his elaborate damascened helmet. The hair was flaxen and spread out over his shoulders and the Latin, though good, was clipped and strange.

'What do you want to know?' Vitalis asked.

There was a roar of laughter from Theodosius' table nearby. That sounded like one of Leocadius' filthier jokes.

'Everything,' the flaxen-haired man said. 'I've never seen it. Or these barbarians who swarmed all over it. I'm Stephanus, by the way.'

'You're from Germania?' Vitalis shook the man's hand.

'Vetera on the Rhenus. Ever been?'

'Er ... no. I'm just a circitor.'

Stephanus took the boy's shoulders and stood squarely in front of him. 'No, you're not,' he said. 'You're a hero of the Wall. We've heard all about you boys from the Count. It's an honour to be serving with you.'

Vitalis could not tell from the man's tunic and loose trousers what he did; Stephanus seemed to have read his mind. 'I'm with the Ala Heruli,' he said. 'Under the Count's son.'

Neither man had noticed Theodosius slip away from the increasingly raucous table and join the pair. He clapped a hand on Stephanus' shoulder. 'Don't let this man bore you to death, Vitalis,' he said, sipping his wine. 'That's the trouble with the Alamanni – can't shut up. He hasn't got on to his Pannonia campaigns, has he? No, he can't have. You haven't quite glazed over yet. I have known him leave whole rooms fast asleep and snoring.'

'That's an appalling slur!' Stephanus took an exaggerated

step back.

'Yes,' Theodosius laughed. 'It is. Actually, Vitalis, you'll never find a more professional soldier. If I ever have to face the wrath of the gods with my life on the line, I would want this man at my back.'

Stephanus laughed too. 'Vitalis here was telling me about the Wall, Count,' he said.

'The Wall?' Vitalis looked at the two great men smiling at him. He looked across at Leocadius, thumping the table with hilarity and off his face with drink. And he suddenly felt rather ashamed. 'The Wall was nothing,' he said.

Rutupiae was the largest of the forts of the Saxon Shore, whose Count had been slaughtered somewhere in the west. Theodosius' bireme, oars churning now through the sluggish waters off Tanatus passed under the great stone towers and horns from the walls sang out their welcome. The Count's scarlet flag flew from the masthead and he was wearing his scarlet cloak today. All along the river bank, lines of mailed soldiers stood to attention as his guard of honour; the Batavi with their bright, hoop-painted shields and the Heruli with their red and white circles. 'Io, Stephanus,' Vitalis heard the cavalry roar and the German waved to them from the deck. His face was covered now with a spangenhelm as elaborate as the Count's, except the Count was bareheaded that morning, smiling at the local women who thronged the quay. Leocadius was smiling at them too, but for altogether different reasons.

On the quay itself, under an Eastern awning of purple silk, Theodosius the younger sat like an Emperor on his throne. Vitalis looked at the man, who he guessed was about his age. It was like looking at the Count through a mirror of distorted bronze. His eyes were darker. So was his hair and he had a curious way of holding his head, as though he had a permanent smell under his nose.

The hortator was shouting orders to the oarsmen and the oars came up to the level before sliding inwards into the bireme's hull with a thunder of timber, spraying rainbow drops of river water high into the air. Ropes were thrown and the anchor splashed down, the sailors leaping onto the quayside and hauling on the cables. The half-drooped sail was furled and the ship made secure but the Count was already springing over the side, landing safely on the stone much to the relief of everyone. Stumbling ashore had not been a wise move since the deified Julius had been driven back from these shores centuries before. It had been a sign that the gods did not approve. But today they did and the spring sun shone on Count Theodosius as surely as it shone from his arse.

Father and son hugged each other. 'Salve, Comes,' the boy said in formal greeting, then, as they went off arm in arm, 'Good journey, Pa?'

Leocadius and Vitalis had never known such luxury. The mansio in the camp was huge and the quarters reserved for the heroes of the Wall expensive and well appointed. As they soaked away the stresses of the voyage in the steam of the caldarium, Vitalis gave vent to his thoughts.

'How's Pat going to cope, Leo?' he asked.

Leocadius shrugged. The hairs on his chest were growing again and he would have to have the slave work on those. 'Who knows?' he said. 'Mithras, maybe; Sol Invictus.'

'I can't get it out of my mind,' Vitalis said. 'The last time I saw him at Rutilius' fort. He was like a madman, hacking about him with both hands. No shield. No attempt to defend himself at all. You know he took that Pict's head away with him? That's no way for a Roman to behave.'

Leocadius nodded and closed his eyes, resting his elbows on the warm marble. 'Yes, I did notice that. Better that, though, surely, than threatening to fall on his sword every hour?'

Vitalis looked at his friend through the steam and did not much like what he saw there. The Wall ring glittered on his finger and his wet hair was plastered to his forehead. Later, he would lie patiently while the masseur worked his muscles and scraped the curved strigil over his skin. Then he would grip the bronze bars fixed to the wall and curse every misfortune under the sun as an attendant ripped the hairs from his chest and legs. And, despite himself, Vitalis found himself smiling. For Leocadius, hero of the Wall, nothing was more important than vanity.

The Theodosii, father and son, had finished their dinner that night and, with the family talk over, it was time for a council of war. Both men's staff filed into the room, laden with maps and scrolls of parchment. Clerks scuttled this way and that, sharpening quills and setting up inkwells, ready to record the moment. The German Stephanus was there, as commander of the Heruli cavalry, his opposite number from the Batavi and the tribunes of both legions.

There were also two circitors from the VIth Victrix, a forgotten unit somewhere in the frozen north – Leocadius and Vitalis.

'What more do we know about Nectaridus?' the Count asked once they were all assembled.

'He set off for the west about a week before we arrived,' his son told him. 'God knows why he left the strength of Rutupiae. Apparently – and I'm quoting the few survivors who made it back – he was "responding to rumour".'

'What rumour?' Theodosius the elder wanted to know.

'That this fellow Valentinus had come south, skirting the Cornovii territory, if our reports are accurate. He appeared before Glevum ...'

'Glevum?' Stephanus did not know the country as well as some of the others.

'Old base of the XXth Valeria Victrix,' the younger Theodosius told him. 'He appeared there and went away. The garrison beat him back.'

'This garrison, sir,' Vitalis broke in. 'Do you know its size?'

All eyes turned to him. Introductions had been brief and to the point. This man and the curly-headed one wore the uniforms of circitors, yet here they were, hobnobbing with a Count and his heir.

'Er ... about three hundred, I believe,' the younger Theodosius said, only now taking the opportunity to look Vitalis up and down. 'Glevum is a sizeable colonia; stout walls, I understand.'

There was a silence. 'It's not him,' said Vitalis.

'I beg your pardon?' Theodosius was sitting upright, his face even narrower in the candlelight, a frown furrowing his forehead.

Leocadius agreed. 'It's not Valentinus,' he said. 'If the garrison of Glevum is as small as that, he would have taken it. *Has* he taken it ... sir?'

The younger Theodosius narrowed his eyes. First one, now the other of these upstarts had had the impudence to challenge him and that was unacceptable. The elder Theodosius, however, was still looking on benignly, glancing across to his son for the answer. Everybody else was staring at the floor, except Stephanus, who appeared to have what looked, to Theodosius, like a smirk on his face. 'No,' he said sharply. 'As far as we know, he has not. We have had no reports of that. Anyway, Nectaridus seems to have underestimated him. He took three cohorts west. The survivors say they were ambushed south of there. We think he was on the way to his fortress at what the locals there call Caerdydd. If he could have made it to Isca, he'd have been safe.'

'Isca?' Stephanus had heard the name, but he was unsure where.

'Base of the II Augusta,' the Count told him. 'Just as the VIth have been at Eboracum for ever, so have the II at Isca.' He winked at Leocadius. 'What makes you think it wasn't Valentinus at Glevum?'

Leocadius shrugged. 'From what we know of the man, sir, he doesn't try and fail. If he thought Glevum was too strong, he wouldn't have so much as strung a bow.'

'He's testing us,' the Count said. 'Putting his toe in the water, so to speak. He's probing our weaknesses, noting our strengths. Even so ... Glevum; Caerdydd; Isca; he's a long way from home.'

'Further than you think,' the younger Theodosius said. All eyes turned to him now. 'There are other rumours,' he said.

A silence.

'Well, come on, boy,' his father said. 'Don't leave us dangling. You're among friends.'

Theodosius was not so sure. There was something about these new men he did not like. But he had been well brought up. His father had spoken and that was enough. At least for now. But he was not going to let the old man get off that lightly. 'We understand,' he said, 'from our friends in the north,' he swept his glacial smile in the direction of Leocadius and Vitalis, 'that there is some sort of conspiracy involved; several tribes all working as one.'

'That's right,' the Count nodded.

'And they appear to be fighting in a new way, for barbarians, I mean. A Roman way.'

'Right again,' the elder Theodosius said. 'What of it?'

'What do you know about Aetius Varro, father?'

'Varro ... Varro ...' the Count was thinking. 'Yes, I remember. Didn't he challenge the Emperor over taxation? Saw himself as something of a man of the people, didn't he, for all his aristocratic breeding?'

His son nodded. 'He was charged with treason in Rome four years ago, but because of his previous service – he'd fought in Dacia under the Emperor's brother – he kept his head and was exiled instead ...'

'... to Britannia,' the Count finished the sentence for him. 'Mother of God, you're right.'

'I don't follow,' Vitalis said.

'Oh, it's all quite logical,' the elder Theodosius smiled, 'and it explains a hell of a lot. It's why he fights like a Roman – he *is* one. And all that nonsense with the masked helmet. It's a symbol, to him at least.'

'Do you know him, sir?' Leocadius asked. 'By sight, I mean?'

'No.' The Count shook his head. 'I have not had the privilege.'

'But why would they fight for him?' Vitalis wanted to know. 'The Picts, the Scotti, the Attacotti? Why would they throw in their lot with an enemy?'

'Because he's not an enemy,' the younger Theodosius said. 'My father said it all. He is a man of the people; has an uncanny ability to make the humblest peasant believe he's on his side.'

'Every problem,' the Count said, 'every thorn in the flesh of the people of Britannia, they lay at the door of the Romans. You should talk to a Gaul – they're even worse.'

'But he can't possibly think he can overthrow Rome,' Leocadius threw his arms wide.

'He doesn't need to,' the Count told him. 'He's already destroyed the Wall, God knows how many towns and villages. People have gone over to him in droves and they're probably still doing it. He's wiped out vexillations of two legions and killed the Dux Britannorum and the Count of the Saxon Shore; I wouldn't mind having a war record like that.'

The room fell silent.

'So, what do you propose, father?' Theodosius asked.

The Count blew on his fingers, aware that all eyes were on him, playing for time, measuring his words. 'We don't know what this man looks like, whether he's Aetius Varro or a pig's bladder. And we don't know how far his ears reach, either. I *know* there were people in Eboracum who were feeding him information. Why don't we see what's happening in Londinium?'

'Consul! Consul!' There was a thunder of sandalled feet on the stairs at the back of the basilica and Julius Longinus thrust his head out from under the covers. For a moment he did not know where he was or what time of day. It had to be day because the shafts of sunlight were streaming into the room and falling onto his bed.

'What the hell is it, Albinus? Can't you see I'm busy?'

'A thousand apologies, Consul.' The slave hurtled into the room, stopped short and bowed. 'There's an army at the bridge.'

'Don't talk ... what?' Longinus tried to sit up. 'An army? Are you serious?' He hauled up the covers and shouted at the girl writhing around on top of him, 'Will you stop doing that?' he screamed and then, more gently, 'you'll hurt yourself. Not to mention me.' He dragged the sheets off them both and she screamed, doing her best to cover her nakedness. Normally, Albinus would have appreciated the view, but today his mind was elsewhere and his heart was in his mouth.

The Consul was staring out of the window, trying to crane his neck far enough round to see the bridge.

'It's all right, Consul,' Albinus gabbled, trying to keep them both calm. 'They *are* ours.'

'Ours, you feeble-minded idiot! Of course they're ours. Who's leading them, that's the question.'

'The Comus Rei Militaris, sir,'

Longinus nearly dropped the sheets. 'Theodosius? Here? Why wasn't I told? Get the boys up here. I'll need my robes – all of them. And wine – the good stuff; Theodosius'll know the difference.'

The slave scuttled away in a slap of sandal.

'And get my wife out of bed,' the Consul called after him. 'I want her in the forum with all her ghastly people.' He grimaced ruefully at the girl and was gone.

Leocadius had never seen anything like it. The capital of Maxima Caesariensis was a city three times the size of Eboracum, with merchant ships riding at anchor along wharves bustling with people. To be fair, the bustling had stopped when the dust of Theodosius' army became visible and as the Batavi and the Heruli stared at the dockside, the people of the dockside stared right back.

Trumpets were blasting somewhere in the maze of narrow streets behind the waterfront as the garrison of Londinium tumbled out of their sacking and took post at the bridge head and fanned out along the wharves on either side. Red-tiled roofs, of shops and workshops and houses disappeared into the smoky distance and the stench of the tanneries crossed the river. Somewhere in the centre the basilica stood square and imposing, five times the height of a man and beyond a little stream to the west, the governor's palace was thronged with officials struggling into robes of office.

A heavy man wearing the robes of a consul was being carried in a litter along the waterfront towards the bridge, shouting at his struggling slaves to get a move on.

'Now there's a sight you don't see often,' Leocadius nudged Vitalis. 'Some purple-shirt shitting himself to welcome us. Makes your heart glow, doesn't it?'

At the bridge-head, the man half fell off his litter before his slaves came to a halt and he hurried across the bridge on foot, a small army of hangers-on fluttering with him, all of them panting in their exertions under the noonday sun.

'Salve,' he wheezed, 'Salve, Comes Rei Militaris, great Theodosius. I am Julius Longinus, Consul of Maxima Caesariensis. Welcome to Londinium.'

'You want a what?' Longinus could not help himself. He had not meant to be rude to the Count, but it just slipped out.

'A triumph,' Theodosius said, frowning. 'Surely you've heard the word.'

'I have indeed, sir,' the Consul said, 'but it's been two hundred years since ...'

'Oh, I know it's a little old-fashioned,' the Count apologized, 'but I'm a traditionalist at heart. A bit of old-fashioned ceremony – the crowd love it.'

'I'm sure they do, Count,' Longinus said, clicking his fingers so that a slave poured more wine for his visitors. 'But ... there's no easy way to put this ... didn't they stop triumphs because of the risk? I mean, troops in the city? Armed men with limitless power, for all they were supposed to leave their weapons at the gate. I don't have to paint you a mural, I'm sure.'

'Ah, but that was Rome,' Theodosius reminded the official. 'The eternal city has always had her problems.'

'Yes, well, she's not alone there,' Longinus muttered. 'Look, Count, I have to be honest. It's not a good idea. I've got Christians on the rampage, adherents of Mithras and Sol Invictus wherever you turn. Then there's crime ...'

'Crime?' Theodosius raised an eyebrow.

'Yes.' Longinus gulped from his goblet. 'I've never known it so ... well, organized.'

'Perhaps a few troops on street corners wouldn't come amiss, then. Anyway, I'm more concerned about the military situation. On the way here we fought half a dozen skirmishes – I've got prisoners shackled south of the river.'

'Well, yes,' the consul conceded, 'that *is* a worry. Oh, we've had no trouble here in the city as such. There are stories, of course. A few villas looted, the odd village burned to the ground. But that's beyond my jurisdiction. I have no authority.'

'But I do,' Theodosius said, looking at the man flapping before him. 'The Duke is dead, so is the Count of the Saxon Shore. Whether you are aware of it or not, we are in the middle of a rebellion, Longinus.'

The consul looked at the Count, like a man suddenly facing his own mortality. 'You'd better see this,' he said and crossed the room to a cabinet full of scrolls. He pulled one out and showed it to Theodosius. The Count read it. It was written on vellum, in excellent Latin and it was a death threat.

'I don't know who that lunatic is,' Longinus nodded at the parchment, 'but if he seriously thinks I will surrender my garrison and calmly hand over the biggest city in Britannia ...'

'Oh, he does, Consul,' Theodosius said. 'That lunatic has already wiped out the Wall and we believe he was responsible for the death of Fullofaudes and Nectaridus. When you see that name,' he tapped the written word 'Valentinus', 'you should be very afraid. When did you get this?'

'Last week,' Longinus said. 'Some scruffy little peasant brought it.'

Theodosius strode to the window. From the front of the governor's palace, he could see the sunlight dancing on the river and the white-sailed fishing boats coming in with their catch from downstream, nudging their way in to the crowded quayside. 'We must look to your defences, Consul,' he said. 'You need a wall, here, all the way along the waterfront. Twenty feet high.'

'A wall?' Longinus turned quite pale. 'And who's going to pay for that?'

'You are, Consul,' Theodosius told him. 'You and the good people of Londinium. Now, about my triumph ...'

It had been so since the days of the Republic. A conquering general came back from a campaign, laden with gold, silver and precious stones. He bought captives, defeated warriors in chains for the rapturous crowds to spit at and kick as they shambled past. At the city gates, that general had to ask permission of the Senate to enter; he had to kneel and make obeisance to the genius of the city of Rome.

That day in Londinium, as the June sun scorched helmets and burned grass even in the marshes across the river, the Senate met Julius Longinus, an increasingly worried man. He had hastily convened a meeting of the Ordo, the city council, and, in the spirit of democracy which the Republic had stolen from the Greeks, told them all exactly how it was going to be. The Comes Rei Militaris was going to bring his legions into the city and the entire Ordo would turn out to see it. They would all put on their finest robes and their best grins and they would *love* it. Was that, Julius Longinus wanted to know, understood?

And there they were, under the awnings in the forum, Longinus on his dais being fanned by a slave with the only ostrich-feather fan in the country, waiting to greet the conquering heroes. The roar of the people told them how near the heroes were and minor officials clinging precariously to the roof-tops of the basilica watched them come on.

At the head of the column, Count Theodosius was the *vir triumphalis*, the man of triumph. He rode his grey hung with ribbons in its plaited mane and tail, the count's parade armour shining in its gilt and bronze, the scarlet sagum dangling to his leopard-skin boots. At his elbow rode his son, equally resplendent in his white sagum and plumed helmet. Both men smiled and waved at the crowds who threw petals at them and cheered wildly.

'You know, Pa,' young Theodosius said, 'I could get used to this.'

The Count knew his history. The list of all-conquering generals who had fallen foul of Rome was long indeed. And Emperors today were ten to a denarius. He chuckled and murmured to his boy the old warning. 'Remember you are mortal. Look behind. Look behind.'

Behind came a knot of Theodosian attendants, the fawners and hangers on who went with the territory. And behind them, the prisoners from the Thamesis marshes, chained to yokes that cut grooves into their shoulders. There were no great generals here, no Jugurtha or Zenobia or Vercingetorix, none of the terrible names of the past who had made Rome tremble. These men had no names that either Theodosius could be bothered to find out or to remember. The Count only wanted one man to be there, on his way to a slow strangulation – Valentinus. And his day would come.

The triumphal way was lined with people, laughing, waving, eyeing the marching legions of the Heruli and Batavi with adoration, suspicion, greed or horror, depending on their standing. Paulinus Hupo was delighted. His role today was to blend in, so he had left his flash robes behind and had had his slave shave his head so that he looked just like another dock-worker. In the crowd on both sides of the Via Triumphalis, his people were quietly going about their business, slitting silently with their razor-sharp knives and separating solid citizens from their small change. Paulinus knew only too well that times were hard and every denarius counted.

Behind the Heruli with their painted shields and tall spears, two bulls were being dragged along for the ritual sacrifice. Tradition dictated that they should have been pure white, but the consul had not had long to prepare for this and Theodosius had to settle for a black one and a brown one with white markings. The animals plodded up from the river, garlands on their brows and little boys on their backs. No one could smell the blood yet.

A thunderous applause broke out as the animals thudded past. Decius Critus was the priest of Mithras and normally the man walked in shadows, watching his back. They had burned his temple down years ago in this city of heretics and the cult he spoke for met in secret, deep in the bowels of the city by the stream called the Walbrook. But the bull was *their* bull, its throat slit by the god Mithras himself at the dawn of time and this was a good sign. Mithras was the soldiers' god. And eight thousand soldiers were marching through Londinium.

From his place just outside the forum, Dalmatius the Bishop was furious. They were bringing sacrificial bulls into the heart of his city, the city of Christ. He looked around him, as did his priests in their robes with the Chi-Rho, the shepherd's crook and looped cross of martyrdom on their chests and backs. Everybody was cheering, laughing. This was a holiday when it should have been a holy day. He would stop it. This disgusting pagan spectacle had gone on for long enough. And he tried to push his way through the crowd, but the crowd held him back.

At the gates of the forum, Theodosius dismounted and his son followed suit. Only two men followed them into the open square, both wearing the uniforms and scarves of tribunes, the new rank bestowed on them by the count. Leocadius and Vitalis were walking with kings today, perhaps even walking with the gods.

All four men unbuckled their helmets and knelt before the consul Longinus, the military power subservient to the civil. He made the sign of the cross over them, as befitted an officer who served the Christian emperor of a Christian state and the Theodosii crossed themselves accordingly.

'Salve Flavius Theodosius. You and your men are welcome to our fair city, Count.' Longinus raised his voice so that the watching crowd lining the forum could hear. 'What we have, is yours.'

Behind her father on his dais, Julia Longinus could not take her eyes off the handsome young tribune with the dark curls kneeling in front of her. He had noticed her too and he smiled so that excitement shot through her like a sudden wind blowing away propriety and sense.

'Salve, Julius Longinus,' Theodosius offered the usual response. 'We are your men, pledged to the defence of your fair city. We will obey her laws and respect her people, as God is our witness.'

Standing alone in a corner of the forum, where the morning sun had not yet reached, a young man smiled at the Count's words – '… as God is our witness.' His name was Pelagius. And one day he would change history.

CHAPTER X

Londinium, Ver

For three days and three nights the festivities continued. They put on plays in the amphitheatre south of the fort and Leocadius fell asleep in two of them. Vitalis was taken on a tour of the city's oyster beds and pottery workshops as one of the younger Theodosius' staff. He had never yawned so much in his life. The Count was busy throughout this time marching along the river front, in earnest consultation with his son's engineers, checking the lie of the land and the speed of the river's current. The Thamesis was tidal – any fortifications along its banks would have to take that into account. The ditches of the days of Diocletian would have to go – they served no purpose. And if the walls, of grey ragstone and red tile, were to be the height of three men, there must be flanking towers a man higher, large enough to take the weight of ballistae, the massive catapults that hurled rocks and flaming pitch into enemy formations, spreading fear and hideous death in equal measure. And these towers must be built to the east, too. That was the most likely direction of any attack, if it came by sea. And the talk turned to the bestiality of the Saxons and the Franks.

On the last night of the triumph, Julius Longinus threw a magnificent dinner, for selected guests only, at the governor's palace by the Walbrook. The Theodosii were there, of course, and their respective staffs and the tribunes of the two legions. Vitalis had been backed into a corner by a publisher, who proceeded to explain to him the different qualities of vellum and ink and what a tragedy it was that society was going to the dogs and that nobody read these days.

'I can't begin to tell you,' Longinus was saying, sotto voce, to the Count, reclining on the next couch, 'how many shrines there are in this place. The chap before me had the temple of Isis pulled down – people were throwing stones at it. There are half a dozen to Jupiter Highest and Best, of course; more Mother Goddesses than you've had hot dinners; you can't move for pots with Mercury's name on them; and don't get me started on Sol Invictus.'

'What about Mithras?' Theodosius asked. 'A lot of my lads are adherents, one way or another.'

Longinus eased himself closer to the man because he knew very well, the walls of the governor's palace had ears. 'Bit of a sore point, actually. The temple of Mithras used to be just behind us, a couple of hundred paces up the Walbrook.'

'Used to be?'

'Taken down ... or, to be more precise, desecrated by the Christians. Er ...' the consul checked himself. 'I'm not giving offence, am I?'

The Count chuckled. 'Not to me, no,' he said. Then he too closed to the consul. 'But I wouldn't be so careless in front of my son. He takes this Galilean fellow very seriously.'

'And you don't?'

'God, no,' Theodosius held out his goblet to a passing slave. 'There's plenty of room in our pantheon for one more. It's just that ... well, it's the official religion of the state now, isn't it?'

'God help us, yes,' Longinus said, waiting for the slave to top him up too. 'You've met Bishop Dalmatius, have you? Pompous git, sitting over there, boring everybody to death?'

'Sadly, yes,' Theodosius sighed. 'He bent my ear on the way in about how he disapproved of the bull sacrifices in my triumph.'

'Yes, well, he would,' Longinus grunted. 'I'm sorry about that.'

'Not half as sorry as the bulls, I'll wager,' Theodosius winked.

'What? Er ... no, no indeed. No, it's the man's brass neck I can't stand. Do you know he's started referring to the north-east gate as his? Bishop's gate, he calls it. How ludicrous!' Longinus took a deep draught of his wine, but his small, grey eyes soon found another target for his suspicion. 'Who's that, Count?' he asked. 'The tribune over there who seems to have his eyes glued to my daughter's cleavage?'

Theodosius followed his host's gaze. 'That? That's Leocadius, hero of the Wall.'

'Are you really a hero of the Wall?' Julia asked him, her eyes wide in the candlelight.

'Can you doubt it?' Leocadius asked, smiling. 'You see this?' He showed her his jet ring that glowed in the myriad flames that danced and flickered in the room. 'The Count over there has one just like it. So has my friend, Vit ...' he looked around for him but couldn't find the face. 'He's here somewhere. It's a token of the stand we took against the barbarians.'

'You've fought them?' she asked. Her eyes shone with excitement and her mouth was moist and slightly open, almost as an invitation. If she were a tavern girl, he would be kissing that mouth now, his hand exploring her thigh, but this was not the time.

'Oh yes.' He summoned a slave to add more wine to the girl's goblet. 'Many times.'

She looked at him, the deep, dark eyes and the black hair that fell in ringlets over his tribune's scarf. His teeth were white and even and he smiled a lot. 'Tell me about them,' she said, leaning forward.

Leocadius shook his head. 'Soldiers' tales, lady,' he said. 'They are not for your ears.'

'I *am* the daughter of the consul,' she said, sitting upright. He was staring at her breasts, rising and falling under her pale blue gown and she suddenly felt hot and uncomfortable. No, perhaps uncomfortable was not the right word.

Leocadius shrugged. He was taking a calculated risk, but he knew it would be worth it. 'Very well, consul's daughter,' he said. 'The Picts are the painted people. They're from the far north, Caledonia. Have you heard of it?'

She shook her head.

'Wild, remote place. End of the world. They paint their bodies ...' he reached forward and traced a finger over her cheek and chin. She blinked but did not move. 'They believe it protects them,' he went on, his voice dripping like honey trailing his finger down the contours of her neck and over her right shoulder. 'Keeps them safe from harm.' His fingers crept lower, under the tie of her gown, searching for her breast. 'They paint themselves ...' he paused and dropped his voice to an almost inaudible whisper, ' ...

everywhere.'

'Everywhere?' she gulped. 'The women too?'

'Oh yes,' Leocadius lowered his head towards hers, their lips close in the candlelight, 'the women too. I have seen ...'

The clearing of a throat brought them both upright again, the tribune sipping his wine in all innocence, the consul's daughter adjusting her dress. Julius Longinus loomed over them.

'Julia,' he said sternly, 'You're neglecting our other guests.' And he held out a rigid arm. 'Forgive me, tribune,' he said, without a smile.

Leocadius half rose and half smiled. There would be another time.

The Heruli and the Batavi were two of the legions who rarely fought apart. They had a reputation as hard fighters and hard drinkers and as Vitalis wandered north along the bank of the Walbrook that night, he had proof of both. He had seen them in action already, along other river banks to the east, rounding up rebels, killing some on the orders of the younger Theodosius, letting others go on the orders of his father. It was a topsy-turvy world. Now Vitalis saw the legions at leisure. Three men lay outside a taberna, heads resting on each other's shoulders, fast asleep. Another was crawling along one of the consul's new pavements on all fours, making wild roaring grunts as he wrestled with the demons of drink. Around the corner a semisallis of the Batavi had got lucky with one of the ladies of the town as they jerked backwards and forwards arch-style, which was often the way with ladies of the town.

'What are you looking for, soldier?' a male voice murmured in the shadows. Vitalis whirled round, his dagger blade naked in his hand.

'Not you,' he said.

The voice chuckled. 'No, no,' it said, 'Do you take me for a Greek?' A man walked out into the moonlight. He was tall, with a greying beard and, for all the night was warm, a fur-lined cloak.

'I'm not taking you for anything,' Vitalis assured him. He was still pointing his dagger at the stranger, waiting.

'You're the tribune Vitalis, aren't you?' the cloaked man said. It was not really a question.

'You know me?'

'I know *of* you,' the man told him. 'You're one of the heroes of the Wall.'

Vitalis' heart fell. That label was beginning to be stitched to his shirt. Soon it would be tattooed on his skin, like a Pict. 'Am I?' he said. 'What business is it of yours?'

The cloaked man shrugged. 'Let's just say I have an interest in men like you. Not, of course, that there *are* many men like you.'

'I don't enjoy riddles,' Vitalis snapped. 'Who are you and what do you want?'

'I am Decius Critus,' the man held out his hand.

'That's half my questions answered,' Vitalis did not take the outstretched sign of friendship. The more he learned of Londinium, the less he liked it.

'God of the morning,' Critus said, 'God of the noontide and the sunset ...'

'... God of the midnight ...' Vitalis took up the prayer.

'Look on your children in darkness,' Critus whispered. Then he smiled, 'You even have the look of Cautes about you.'

Vitalis lowered his knife. 'You're a priest of Mithras,' he said.

Critus nodded. 'And are you one of his children?' he asked.

'No,' the tribune told him, sheathing his dagger. 'I know plenty of men who are ... or perhaps I should say were. There were shrines aplenty along the Wall – Brocolitia, Vindolanda ...'

'And they are no more?'

'I don't know,' Vitalis told him. 'I haven't been back. Not for a while. Perhaps one day ...'

Critus looked at the lad's face. 'You're lost, aren't you, boy?'

Vitalis looked at the priest. There was a light in his eyes he could not recognize and had never seen before. 'We've lost our shrines, too,' Critus said. 'But we've rebuilt them. Not far from here. It's a portal to another world. I can take you there. There, where the great bull dies.'

Vitalis shook his head. 'No,' he said. 'Perhaps another time.'

Critus smiled. 'Mithras has all the time in the world,' he said. 'When you're ready.'

'Yes, I ...' but Vitalis was already talking to himself. The priest of Mithras had vanished into the shadows from where he had come.

It was nearly dawn when Leocadius wove his way unsteadily from the governor's palace. He was tempted to run his head under one of the fountains to try to clear it, but he might not survive that and memories of the Ussos still came back to haunt his dreams from time to time. The city that never sleeps was already stirring, bleary eyed men making their way to the river front, women hauling water and children unbolting shutters that had kept out the night and all who flourished in the darkness. Soon the drovers would be on the road again from whatever mansio they had laid their head in, bringing their sheep and their cattle through the Bishop's gate to the north.

It *was* only his fourth day here and Leocadius *had* had a heavy night, so it was not surprising that he had not strayed too far from the governor's palace before he realised he was lost. The buildings here were too tall to make out the walls of the camp and the river mist that wreathed these mean streets did not help. He was also aware, through the blur of his senses, that there was a curious echo to his steps. When he stopped, they stopped. He stamped one foot, then the other, as though he was back on the Wall again in some grim and frosty watch to the north, trying to get some feeling into his feet. There was no echo this time but as soon as he walked on he heard it again.

Leocadius spun round, his head reeling as he did so. There was no one there, just a mangy dog wandering crossways and disappearing up an alley. In fact there were several alleyways off this street, the ground beaten flat and hard by a million sandals over time. Leocadius reached the next one and slipped silently around the corner, dagger in hand, waiting.

Nothing. No shrouded figure hurrying past, no drunken sot weaving his way home. Leocadius took stock. The alleyway he was in smelt like a sewer and was clearly home to an army of black rats that sniffed the air for this newcomer and squeaked their annoyance at his intrusion. They scurried away as he walked on, keeping his dagger in his hand and his hand by his side. The next time he half turned, he saw someone. A large dark figure, just a silhouette that filled the space between the shacks. There was no room for a knife fight here, Leocadius realised and anyway, he had sunk too many at the table of Julius Longinus to be able to do himself justice. So he walked on, quickening his pace and trying to walk straight.

Another figure filled the space ahead, as large and dark as the one behind him and he was forced to stop.

'Well, well,' a voice croaked. 'We've got a lost one here, Antoninus.'

'Looks like we have, Gillo. Shall we offer him directions?'

'Yes, let's,' Gillo said. 'Having got our fee first, of course.'

Both of the men spoke Latin with the peculiar twang of the Thamesis.

'Touch me and you're dead men,' Leocadius said, hoping the tone of his voice would send the necessary message.

'Ooh!' Antoninus wriggled in mock fear. 'I'm quaking in my sandals, Gill, aren't you?'

'Quaking, Ant,' his partner in crime nodded. 'Wait a minute,' he flicked up the fringed tassels on Leocadius' sagum. 'This bloke's army, Ant. A bloody officer, no less.' He peered closer at Leocadius' scarf. 'What's that?' he asked. 'Tribune, isn't it?'

Leocadius' knife came up, but he was far too slow. Gillo winced as the blade nicked his arm but Antoninus swung a lead cosh that thudded against the tribune's temple and he fell heavily, hitting his shoulder on the far wall as he went down.

'The bastard cut me!' Gillo sucked the blood from his arm and drove his foot into the fallen man's ribs. 'The bastard!'

'No, lay off, Gill.' Antoninus stopped him. 'Don't ask me why, but I think Paulinus is going to want to have a word with this one. You do know who he is, don't you?'

'He's a bastard,' Gillo's arm was beginning to stiffen already. 'That much is obvious.'

'Yeah, yeah, of course. But that's not all. He's a hero of the bloody Wall, he is.'

The two horsemen cantered onto the high ground to the south of the river. Below them, Londinium stretched east and west to its century-old walls, the river sparkling in the sun and the maze of streets packed with people.

'Too many forests,' Stephanus said. He was wearing his mail this morning but his shield and helmet he had left in his quarters at the fort.

Count Theodosius was forced to agree. He had gone through three days of feasting and celebration but now it was time to get back to work. To the west, where a sizable tributary emptied into the Thamesis, a narrow wooden bridge led to the gate the people of Londinium had named after their ancient king, Lud. Beyond that, the newest gate of the city formed the north-west corner. That was the way Valentinus would come if he came from the site of his defeat of Nectaridus; and he would come out of the dark forests that Stephanus did not like, the ones that reminded him of his home. It had happened over three hundred years ago, but every Roman soldier had been told the tale of the Teutoberg Forest, when three legions had been hacked to pieces by the Germanii and their corpses nailed to trees. Not a good place to fight; not a good place to die.

To Theodosius' north, beyond the large and expensive villas that lay beyond Dalmatius' church, another gate lay to the west of the camp. That had its own gate, low and turreted and then the wall ran east, unbroken, with the sluggish Walbrook trickling under it, until it reached the gate that Dalmatius was now calling his own. There was a final gate to the east and the gravestones of the cemetery beyond shone like white dots against the green. This was the way the Saxons would come, if they came at all, hitting the coast and sailing up the river, their warships churning the brown water and their swords sharp and ready. And always, Stephanus had said it, forests.

'On a clear day,' Theodosius said, half to himself, 'You can't see for ever.'

One thing was clear to both men. There was little chance of Valentinus attacking from the south. He could pick off the cluster of houses and the little quayside that lay directly below them, but then he would have to cross the Thamesis and there was only one bridge. The Count could hold that all day, like Horatius of old, while his Batavi, like the water-serpents they were, would wreak havoc in the marshes to the south.

'Looks like we've got some building to do,' Stephanus said.

'Yes,' Theodosius nodded. 'Leave that to me. In the next week, I want you and my son to ride west. Take half the Heruli, mostly cavalry. I have no intention of repeating the mistakes of Fullofaudes, but neither can I spare more men from here. Have you had a look at the town's garrison yet?'

'Yes,' Stephanus nodded. 'And I'm not impressed.'

No,' the Count sighed. 'Neither am I. And there aren't enough of them to man the entire wall, should it come to that.'

Stephanus smiled. 'But we've got the heroes of the Wall here, Count,' he winked.

Theodosius gave him an old fashioned look. 'Yes,' he said. 'Haven't we.'

Leocadius could not make the words out very clearly. They were written in a bad hand at a crazy angle halfway up a wall. The Latin was average at best, but he got the gist. 'If you can read this, cock-sucker, it's probably too late.' He tried to move, but his head throbbed and opening his mouth was agony. There was a rattle of links and he realised he was chained to the ground by an iron ring.

'It's not very good, is it?' A shaven headed man was loung-ing on a wide chair ornately gilded and hung with silk, 'The writing, I mean. I was going to have it removed but it has that cer-tain air of menace I rather like.'

'Who the hell are you?' Leocadius asked, although the voice did not sound like his own.

'Well, that's refreshing,' the other man said. 'People usually come out with "where am I?" – such a cliché, don't you think?'

Leocadius pulled at the fetters that held him. He was able to sit up, but the bonds on both wrists prevented any more than that.

'In answer to the question you didn't ask, you are in Via Flumensis. It's a long street and I doubt you'll find the exact ad-dress again. In answer to the question you did ask, my name is Paulinus Hupo, general dealer.'

'General dealer in what?' Leocadius wanted to know. There was dried blood on his face and neck, browning the white of his scarf, but his purse still felt sufficiently heavy on his hip and the Wall ring was still on his finger.

'Oh, the usual,' Hupo shrugged. 'Wine, salt, oysters, gold, silver, opals … people.'

'Slaves, you mean.'

'Not necessarily,' Hupo smiled. 'Take you, for instance. You are Leocadius, the newly appointed tribune of Theodosius' field army; the man who saved the Wall.'

The story was growing with the telling. 'You've heard that?'

'Oh, we've all heard it. Banna, Camboglanna – bloodbaths, they say. And of course the cavalry at Vinovia deserting, saddle, bridle and tethering ropes like that. Shocking.' The bald man shook his head.

'I didn't know about that,' Leocadius said.

'Didn't you?' Hupo beamed. 'It's common knowledge down here. Look, Leo … er … you don't mind if I call you Leo? I could use a man like you.'

'What for?' the tribune asked.

'Oh, this and that. See through there?' Hupo pointed through an archway to a courtyard where a fountain played. It was as big and impressive as Longinus' in the governor's palace. 'That's marble from Anatolia. The figurines are from Gaul. I only drink wine from Germania and my missus is positively dripping with emeralds from Egypt.'

'How nice.' Leocadius' grin was acid.

'Well, yes, it is. To use the language of the street, I've got a nice little number going here.'

'You're an importer?' Leocadius was trying to follow the conversation.

'After a fashion,' Hupo said earnestly, as though discussing some high point of philosophy. 'I believe appropriator of goods *from* importers would be more accurate.'

'Oh, so you're a thief.' The tribune understood it now.

'Tut, tut,' Hupo frowned. 'Such a word. And on the Sabbath, too – that's the holy day of the Christians.'

'Gripping,' Leocadius grunted. 'Are you going to undo these chains?'

'No,' Hupo stood up. 'I have ... people for that. We'll meet again, Leo. Count on it.' And he had gone.

It was nearly noon when Vitalis crossed the square. A single bell was tolling and men, women and children of all classes were solemnly trooping in its direction. A large man riding a donkey rode at their head and at the door of a crumbling temple he eased himself out of the saddle while attendants fussed around him and placed an odd-looking pointed cap on his head. He looked around and saw Vitalis looking at him.

'Are you going to join us, my son?' he called, raising the first two fingers of his right hand over each supplicant who shuffled past him, nodding in his direction. Men tugged off their caps and women bobbed. Children too slow to do either got a clip around the ears from their elders.

'Join you?' Vitalis repeated, 'For what?'

The man left the blessing to an underling in the robes of the Chi-Rho and crossed the square to him. 'For divine service,' he said. 'I am Dalmatius, the Bishop of Londinium.'

Vitalis knew who he was. He had seen him drinking and feasting in the basilica and at the governor's house. He thought it best to introduce himself but the bishop held up his hand. 'No, no, my boy. I know who you are – and may I say what an honour it is to meet a man who has killed so many pagans.'

'I ...'

'No, no,' the bishop was clearly not going to let the man get a word in edgeways. 'I know it is the Lord's tenet that we must turn the other cheek and must not kill, but He cannot have meant us to include the heathen in that. Won't you join us?'

Vitalis looked at the old building into which the people trickled to the tolling of the bell. It was plastered white, with cracks running all over it in the blistering sun of noon and on top of its porticos, headless gods looked down on the square. A huge Chi-Rho had been painted below the gable.

'Yes, I know what you're thinking. It used to be a temple to Jupiter non-believers still call "highest and best". Blasphemy of course. And as soon as I have the funds, I shall tear this abomination down and build a real church, in the shape of the cross on which our Lord suffered, probably somewhere near my gate in the north east.' The bell was tolling faster now as some shaven-headed priests inside swung it frantically to and fro. 'You should hurry, my son,' the bishop said. 'The Count's son will be along presently. Wouldn't do to keep your Lord and master waiting ... either of them.' And he sketched the sign of the cross in the air. 'In nomine patri ...'

'So you're the hero of the Wall?' a soft voice purred in the shadows of the courtyard along the Via Flumensis. Leocadius' head jerked upright. He had been locked into this half-crouched position now for half a day and was grateful that the noonday sun did not penetrate Hupo's gloom this far. From somewhere he heard a bell tolling in the distance but could not tell the direction.

'I'm one of them,' he said.

'Which one are you?' a girl undulated from the archway, her dark blonde hair tumbling over her shoulders and her dark brown eyes burning into his.

'Leocadius,' he said. 'And you?'

'You can call me Honoria,' she said and proceeded to click a small key into a padlock just out of Leocadius' reach. As soon as his wrists were free, he grabbed the girl from behind, twisting one arm up behind her back and holding his dagger at her throat.

'You're hurting me,' she grimaced.

'That's the general idea,' he hissed, prodding her chin higher with the blade tip. 'You work for Hupo?'

'Now and again,' she said, finding talking difficult with her head thrown back to save the dagger point from pricking her neck.

'You're his woman.'

'No,' she shouted angrily and broke free of him. Leocadius was surprised. The girl was strong and had clearly caught him off his guard. He put it down to having been cramped on the floor for so long. 'I am nobody's woman,' she snarled.

Leocadius looked at her. She moved like a cat, slow and graceful, her body swaying in delicious curves under her dress. Expensive jewellery glittered at her wrists and throat, the one that Leocadius had come so close to slitting.

'I'm sorry,' he said. 'I apologize.' He pointed to his swollen head, purple under the hairline. 'The man who did this, where will I find him?'

'You won't,' she said, relaxing. 'And let it stay that way. Londinium is a dangerous place ... unless you know the right people.'

'Are you the right people?' he asked her.

'I might be,' she smiled. 'Come on, let me look at that head. Your wrists need some attention, too,' and she led him through the archway into the marble courtyard where the fountain played. A slave arrived with a tray, wine and goblets and filled them both. Then another turned up, this time carrying pots of unguent and bandages of lint. Honoria sat Leocadius down and passed him a cup. Only now did he sheath the dagger. Only now did he let himself be touched.

She poured a white liquid onto some lint and carefully wiped and patted the gashed temple. Leocadius winced, despite himself. 'And here's me,' she said, 'thinking you were a great hero. And you're just a little boy.'

'Not so little,' he said, running a hand along her hips towards the opening of her robe. 'Honoria; that's funny.'

'What is?' She ignored the wandering fingers and kept stroking his head.

'My name is Honorius. Leocadius Honorius. What would you call that; fate?' His face was close to hers and his lips closed onto her mouth. He could smell the sweet fragrance of her hair, some exotic oil no doubt that Paulinus Hupo had appropriated from somewhere.

She looked up at him, her eyes wide. 'No, she said. 'I would call that one of the feeblest lines I've ever heard.' And she suddenly slapped another piece of lint on Leocadius' forehead.

CHAPTER XI

Brigantia, Autumnus

The fire was burning in the officers' quarters of Arbeia that night, the wood shifting and crackling as the sparks flew upwards. The centurion Paternus was not warming his toes with the others; he was wandering the granaries of the camp, filled again with the fruit of the harvest. A stiff wind was blowing along the Tinea, a river usually lost in the green, swirling fog of the north-east.

Over the last two months, men of the Jovii and the Victores, under the watchful eye of the engineer Rutilius, had built four sea towers and rebuilt Arbeia, the most easterly of the forts of the Wall. While the cavalry threw out screens to the north and west and general Maximus rode with them, the tribune Justinus felt a little like his old man, putting the legions through their paces in the confines of a marching fort. Day after day he watched them jumping in full armour, now landing on two feet, now on one, leaping to the numbered squares the centurions had marked out. It strengthened the leg muscles and gave accuracy and precision to work at close quarters with sword and spear.

Paternus watched the day vanishing into the west and the darkness rolling in over the sea. When they had reached Arbeia, the place was a shambles, rotting corpses strewn by the river bank, clustered deeper by the gates. The wolves of the Wall had loped, grey and silent, over the stones when blood was still warm and had snarled and bickered at each other, fighting over the choicest cuts. Then the foxes had come in the night and the rooks and ravens in the day before they left the real carrion to the rats.

The Romans had dug a huge grave pit to the south of the fort and laid the bones in it; Roman, Scotti, Pict, who could tell. Seen one bleached bone, seen them all and it proved, if proof were needed, that in the end all men come to the skull beneath the skin. There were older graves here, the ones Paternus ran his fingers over now. On one of them, Victor, long dead, lived on in stone, lounging on a couch while a slave filled his goblet with cold, grey wine. How Victor would hate it, that the dust of the slave could now be mingled with his and no man knew who was who. Nearby, Regina of the Catuvellauni to the far south, sat in her basket chair, with a distaff and wool beside her. At her feet was carved her name and tribe in Latin and another line in a language Paternus could not read.

The centurion turned away. It may be, and he thought of this every day, that he had ridden over the grave of his wife that morning or marched past the long-rotted remains of his son. For all his promise to Justinus and his vow to Sol Invictus, these dead ones, these beloved, were at his elbow always and he could never forget them. 'Quin. Quin.'

'Io, Paternus!' He turned at the sound of his name. He had just been thinking of Justinus and here he was, cloak-wrapped against the night, striding over Rutilius' new ditches and piles of timber. 'The General wants a word.'

Those who fought under Maximus in those bitter autumn days reckoned their fortunes by his dog. To the General himself, the dog was a softie, rolling over to have his belly tickled and licking sauce from the great man's fingers. To anybody else, he was Cerberus, the beast that guarded the entrance to hell. On a good day, he would snarl at passers-by. If he snapped, the General was displeased. If he pissed over your boots, you might just as well drive a blade into your bowels and have done.

Paternus did not believe any of this nonsense, but he was not sorry to see that Bruno was curled up and snoring as he entered the general's quarters. All the way from the granaries, Justinus had stayed tight-lipped. Yes, he knew what Maximus wanted. No, he could not say anything. Paternus would have to live with that.

'We've had a message from the south,' Maximus had one leg up on a stool and a goblet in his hand. 'The man came by ship this afternoon. It's from Papa Theodosius. All goes well. He's fortifying Londinium and has seen no sign of Valentinus.' The general threw down the vellum and took a swig from his cup. 'You know, I could get used to this ale stuff. Oh, it's not good Iberian wine, of course ...'

'Will that be all, sir?' Paternus asked.

'Not quite,' Maximus said. 'There's news, too, of your chums of the Wall, your other halves, if you will.'

'Oh?' Paternus was more interested now.

'Theodosius has turned them into pets. They are, apparently, feted wherever they go. Nothing is too much trouble for men who held the Wall.' He paused. 'Just the two of them.' He paused again. 'All seventy three miles of it.'

Paternus stifled a smile. He could not imagine Vitalis going along with any of that nonsense, but it carried all the hallmarks of Leocadius. The man had never met a tale he could not make taller. 'That's good news, sir,' he said.

'Yes, isn't it?' Maximus stood up. 'Well, gentlemen, I mustn't keep you. Tribunes' meeting in half an hour. Something's come up.'

The Wall heroes saluted.

'Paternus, I want you there too,' the general said.

'Sir?' The first centurion was surprised.

'Oh, didn't I tell you?' Maximus smiled. 'Must be this beer. As of now, you're a tribune. Supernumerary, of course. Pay won't come through until hell freezes over.'

'Sir, I ...' Paternus was about to protest and Maximus knew it. He was not sure he liked this man with his strange reclusive habits and his sickening honesty; on the other hand, he could do with more like him when it came to the clash of shields.

'Don't give me all that bollocks about how you don't deserve it.' Maximus wagged a finger at him. 'The sole reason I'm doing this is that the Count has promoted your pals to that glorious elevation – in my opinion, *far* above their ability, but there it is – so it's only right you get the same deal.'

Paternus knew when a deal had been struck and a bargain made and he just saluted and said, 'Thank you, sir.'

Maximus closed to him, all bonhomie gone, the smile a scowl. 'And if you let me down, tribune,' he said, levelly, 'I will break you. Depend on it.' He looked across at Justinus framed in the doorway. 'Still here, tribune?' he snapped.

'I was just wondering, general,' Justinus said. 'The tribunes' meeting – what exactly has come up?'

'"Exactly" would be difficult to quantify, Justinus,' he said, taking the final gulp of his draught. 'All I know is that Valentinus has been spotted north of here. Tomorrow, we cross the Wall.'

As far as anyone in Magnus Maximus' command knew, no Roman soldier had crossed the Wall for over a year. The forts to the west, from Segedunum to Maia, still lay in ruins, their dead unburied, weeds growing from their toppled stones. The engineer Rutilius was itching to get his hands on them and start rebuilding, but Maximus did not have the troops to cover the whole area. He was hurrying slowly, as the old adage had it, because he had no intention of losing a fort again.

There had been rumours before. Valentinus had been seen in Eboracum to the south. He was living in Vindolanda along the Wall. He had stolen Theodosius' transports riding at anchor in the Abus. Magnus Maximus' legions had elected him Caesar and he was on his way to Rome to take up his new position. But *this* was different. Because it came from Dumno.

The little man sat in the centre of a circle of Roman officers that night as the fire crackled. He had a small table in front of him and on it, a platter of bread and cheese into which he tucked heartily.

'Tell these gentlemen,' Maximus said, 'what you told me earlier.'

Dumno stopped chewing and swallowed hard. Of the faces around the room, the only ones he knew were Justinus and Paternus. 'I have heard,' he said, his Latin sounding a little rusty after all these weeks without speaking it, 'that the man you are looking for has crossed into Votadini territory.' He took a swig of Maximus' wine.

'Where from?' the general asked.

'The south. Or west. Maybe the south-west.'

Maximus raised an eyebrow in Justinus' direction. The tribune could not leave it at that. 'Come on, Dumno,' he said. 'You can do better than that.'

'Well, I ...' the arcanus was having trouble with his geography.

'Thirty sesterces,' Maximus said. 'That's my final offer.'

'South-west.' Dumno suddenly saw the light, especially when it flashed from silver coins. 'They say ... but I can't believe this, excellency ...'

'What do they say?' Maximus' patience was wearing thin.

'They say he defeated the Count of the Saxon Shore, wherever that is.'

'Yes, we know that,' Maximus told him. 'Come over here, little man.'

The general had slid back his chair and walked over to a map that his staff had drawn up of the Wall and the lands to the north and south. 'We are here,' Maximus said. 'Arbeia. These,' he pointed north, 'are the Votadini lands. Where do you say Valentinus is?'

'Well, I got it from Raffa. And he heard it from Mog Ruith. But Gwythir thinks ...'

'Yes,' Maximus cut him short, 'I'm so glad you have friends,' although judging by the smell of the man, they could not be very discerning. 'What's your best evidence?'

'Oh, dear,' Dumno frowned at the wall picture. 'I'm not very good at maps. And my written Latin isn't up to much either ... Does this say "Votadini"?'

Maximus nodded.

'And what are these?' The arcanus was pointing to supply depots that the general had set up to the south, complete with ballistae ammunition and spare horses.

'Nothing,' Maximus said, 'that need concern you. Where do your contacts tell you Valentinus is?'

For a long time, Dumno stared at the map, trying to make sense of it all. Then he took a deep breath, screwed up his courage and pointed. 'There,' he said. 'He crossed the river the Votadini call Blyth a week ago. Winter's coming. Can you feel it?' he pulled his hare skin cloak tighter, for all the fire was blazing. 'He'll want somewhere to hole up.' Dumno looked at the officers sitting in their circle. 'Against men like these, I'd be hiding in a hole in the ground,' he said.

'How many men does he have?' Maximus asked.

'Three, four hundred at most,' Dumno said. 'They say – and Mog Ruith was positive about this – his bands have broken up. They won't raid too far from home, you see.'

'And where is home?' Maximus asked. 'Where exactly do these people come from?'

Dumno spread his arms, looking for Justinus and Paternus. 'Ask them,' he said. 'They've seen them.' He looked at the others.

'You've all faced them, haven't you? At the headland of the two bays? Raffa told me you wiped out ten thousand Picts.'

'Oh, we did,' Maximus smiled. 'Before dinner. We got down to the serious business later. All right, arcanus. See my quarter master for the money.'

'Thank you, sir,' Dumno bobbed in front of the general. 'If I can be of further service ...' and he grabbed his last chunk of bread and ducked out into the night.

He had not got far when he felt a hand on his shoulder. The little man stopped in his tracks and spun round to face Justinus. 'Master?' Dumno cringed. He had been beaten by Romans before.

'When I saw you last, arcanus,' he said, 'You were riding south out of Eboracum as I recall.'

'Ha.' Dumno laughed without humour. 'Indeed I was.'

'So what are you doing back here?'

'Have you been to the south?' Dumno's face took on a mask of horror.

'Point taken,' Justinus said.

'Do you know,' Dumno said, a smile playing over his lips, 'On the general's map back there ... I think I read the name "Selgovae". Did I? My homeland?'

The tribune nodded.

'I haven't been back for a while.' Dumno's eyes were suddenly filled with tears. 'Not since my family ...' He cleared his throat and dabbed his eyes with his hare fur. 'Tell me, sir,' he said, 'When you catch this Valentinus, what will you do to him?'

Justinus' smile was dark in the half light of the camp. 'Believe me,' he said. 'You don't want to know.'

They crossed the Wall a little after first light the next day. The Jovii remained behind with orders to hold the camp. Maximus would send a galloper back each day with news and the exact position of his troops. If no rider came, the Jovii were to prepare for a siege. If the siege failed, there would be no falling back to the Abus or Eboracum. Magnus Maximus expected the Jovii to die to the last man.

The savage winds of autumn were biting from the sea, filling cloaks and billowing them outwards, ruffling the scarlet and black plumes of the marching men. The cavalry advanced in open order, using the old army road north, probing the country as they went.

146

The river called the Blyth lay a day's march north but there was no way of knowing which way Valentinus had crossed or whether he was still there.

Maximus had given orders that the marching column must appear bigger than it was. His four thousand soldiers must look like ten thousand and he spaced his units accordingly. On the wings of the column the lines of pedes looked solid, their shields a single line of colour in the morning. In the centre, though, were gaps between the units; and the baggage train, with its ballistae and timbers for the marching camps, was ringed by the largest men.

The general himself rode with his staff and his tribunes at the rear and scouts ahead reported back to him every hour. In the event of an attack, this galloper system would break down, but the general would switch to another plan. And men like Magnus Maximus *always* had another plan.

Surprise was pointless in this gods-forsaken open country. There was no tree to be seen, no thick forest to provide cover for an ambush. So the general ordered his men to sing and the drums to beat. A Roman soldier might march to his death in silence, but on the way there, he would roar his lungs out and the enemy who heard him would fade away ...

Before the sun had set on that first day's march, Maximus halted his column and ordered the camp set up. While the cavalry circled the perimeter and the infantry set to to raise a rampart and double ditch, the general and his staff rode north to where the river wound its way eastward to the sea. Ahead, in the half light, the mountains of Caledonia stood, snow-capped already, a darker purple against the mauve of the sky.

'Justinus,' Maximus turned in his saddle. 'Is this a part of the world you know?'

The tribune shook his head. 'Never this far east,' he said. 'But the Votadini should be friendly.' He smiled at a sudden memory. 'My father always says he dines out on being the last man to cross swords with them. But when he did ... And then he will tell you every bit of nonsense in the soldiers' handbook. They were all twenty feet tall and picked their teeth with fir trees.'

There were chuckles all round.

'Well, then,' said Maximus, 'let's hope your pa is prone to a little exaggeration, shall we?'

Flavius Coelius may have been a *little* prone, but not much. True, the warriors facing Maximus the next day were not twenty feet tall, but too many of them were six feet and they were armed to the teeth. They stood along the far bank of the Blyth, swollen and turbulent with recent rains and looked at the Roman horsemen facing them. They had not moved by the time a galloper had ridden back to Maximus or by the time Maximus had arrived with his numbers.

He ordered the cohorts to fan out in battle array and placed his six onagers between then, rocks piled alongside each, ready to hurl death across the river. Both armies were out of range of arrows and sling shot and they waited until one or the other of them blinked.

'I thought you said they would be friendly,' Maximus grunted to Justinus, sitting his horse alongside him. His dog looked prettier than any of *them*.

'I believe I said "should be", General,' the tribune reminded him.

'All right. Justinus, you and Paternus speak their language, don't you?'

'Sort of,' the tribune said.

'Right. Take a vexillum to let them know who we are and a white flag to let them know our intentions. Do you see a man over there in a silver parade helmet?'

Justinus did not. And he *had* been looking for the past half an hour. That said, Dumno may have been right. Valentinus may not have crossed the Blyth but the Votadini ahead were going to make sure the Romans did not either. He turned his horse's head and walked it over to find Paternus, sitting at the head of his cohort. 'Get yourself a white flag, Pat,' he said. 'We're going to have a nice little chat down by the river.'

As the pair made their way over the grasslands cropped short by Votadini sheep, shouts and insults greeted them. The warriors on the far bank carried huge axes and long, rough spears. Above their heads a boar, bristled and tusked, glowered at them in effigy from the top of a standard and a horned god, carved and painted in gold, watched the invaders come on.

'Think they'll know what a white flag means?' Justinus grunted as they reached the gentle rise which fell away to the river.

'Perhaps they'll think it's target practice,' Paternus said, watching the bowmen carefully. 'There aren't as many of them as I thought at first.'

'True,' Justinus nodded. 'But then, there aren't as many of us, either.' Both men were looking east and west. Fullofaudes had ridden head on against an enemy like this and they had crushed him from both sides and from behind. Perhaps the same had happened to Nectaridus. 'Here we go.'

A knot of horsemen was picking its way along the sheep tracks beyond the river. The ground was steeper over there and the going more difficult. Justinus was relieved to find that one of their number carried a white flag too, a scrap of linen tied to a pole. And just as he carried the vexillum with its woven letters 'Victores', so one of the Votadini held his standard aloft, the horned god Belatucadros, the shining one.

By the time they reached the river, a single rider came forward, mounted on a bay gelding and wearing, unlike most of the others, a mail shirt and iron helmet. Under it, the hair fell in long, dark ringlets.

'This is Gododdyn land,' the rider said, 'that you call Votadini. The shining one lives here. Who are you and what do you want?'

Both men nearly fell off their horses. The rider was a woman, with a melodic voice that sang out over the tumbling, hissing waters of the Blyth. Justinus recovered first. He held up the scarlet flag. 'We are the Victores Legion,' he said, 'General Magnus Maximus commanding.' He passed the pole to Paternus and unbuckled his helmet, looking the woman straight in the eye. 'We mean you no harm. We are looking for the man called Valentinus.'

The woman half turned in her saddle and the horse shifted, tossing its head and snorting. Then she unbuckled her helmet too and let her hair fall free. 'I am Brenna,' she said, haughtily. 'And these are my people.'

'Sol Invictus!' Paternus gasped. He was looking at a ghost.

The spears came down and both armies relaxed. Two miles upstream the river broadened out to shallows, through which the horses could cross. At times like these, Maximus wished he had the Batavi with him, men renowned for water-crossings, but in the event, all was well. There were no buildings on these windswept moors for the leaders to meet in, so Maximus took half his staff and an escort of cavalry across to the north bank and they sat on the ground, facing each other.

The Votadini had milk, bread and cheese which they passed

to the Romans. The Romans in turn gave them creamy almonds and dried apricots, leathery outside but sweet as honey inside. To wash it down, there was wine from the south. When the small talk was over, the general got down to business. 'We have been friends for centuries,' he said, 'the Votadini and Rome.' He was not used to dealing with women on equal terms.

Brenna nodded, sipping the dark red contents of her cup. 'It was always so,' she said, 'since the days of Hadrian. But now ...' her voice trailed away.

'Now?' He looked up. They were speaking through Justinus as interpreter, since Brenna only knew a few words of Latin and the general had no Votadini at all.

'Now the world has turned upside down,' she shrugged. 'Since Valentinus.'

'What do you know of him?' Maximus asked.

'Not much,' the queen admitted. 'Some say he came from the east, from Rome itself. But the people he leads are outlanders, strangers like the Attacotti and northerners like the Picts.'

'You've seen no Saxons?'

Brenna consulted briefly with one of the tall warriors sitting beside her. 'Once, crossing the mountains in the north. They came ashore in great ships, perhaps a thousand warriors.'

'Do you know where Valentinus is now?' Maximus asked her. 'We've heard he is to the north, somewhere near here.' The warriors around Brenna looked alarmed and muttered together.

'We've heard nothing,' she said, resting her hands on her knees as she sat cross-legged. 'Except that you gave the Picts a bloody nose to the south-east.'

'It was our pleasure,' Maximus smiled. 'We know they follow Valentinus, and the Saxons and the Attacotti and the Scotti. Who else?'

Brenna's face darkened. 'Some of the Selgovae from the west,' she said. 'And, I'm ashamed to say, some of my own people.'

'But you have an army here,' Maximus raised his cup to the troops standing in clusters nearby, waiting for Brenna's word of command. She leaned forward, looking the general in the face. The jaw was strong, the cheeks hard and tanned by years of campaign in the sun and the wind. Because she spoke no Latin she could not detect an accent and so had no idea where he came from. But the eyes, the eyes were kindly. There was ambition there, but there was humanity too.

'Can I trust you?' she asked. Justinus duly translated for her.

'As much as I can trust you,' the general said. And they both smiled.

'I have an army, yes,' she agreed, 'but what you see is what you get. There are eight hundred men at my back and that is all I have. From here to our capital, you won't find another fighting man. All the others have gone over to Valentinus. And by the way,' she leaned back, finishing her wine. 'Take a good look at my men. Nearly half of them are grandfathers and children whose voices have yet to break. I'm glad you weren't in a fighting mood today, Roman.' And they laughed.

Paternus was watering his horse on the Votadini bank. On the south side, Maximus had ordered a camp set up and the earth was flying and the hammering of the timbers echoed across the mews. It was dark and the parley had gone on for hours while negotiations continued. All that time, he had rarely taken his eyes off the queen of the Votadini, the way she laughed and smiled, the tilt of her head. Even her eyes, dark and sparkling like the waters of the Blyth, reminded him of ...

'You didn't tell me your name ... last time.' A voice made him turn so sharply that his mare's head came up and the animal skittered. Paternus spoke soothing words to it and stroked its neck. It blew down its nose and shook its head then settled back to its drink. The tribune bowed stiffly. 'It's Paternus,' he said. 'Paternus Priscus. The last time, I didn't know I was talking to a queen.'

'You weren't,' she said, nuzzling the soft cheek of the horse and whispering in its ear. 'My father was still alive then and we were on the run.'

'Your father?'

'Braciaca, lord of the Votadini. I am his only child.'

'And they follow you? Your warriors, I mean?'

Brenna laughed. 'Of course they do,' she said. 'It is our way. Only you Romans refuse to be led by a woman.' She tapped him playfully on the shoulder. 'Don't tell me,' she said. 'A woman's place is down there,' she pointed to the ground, 'with her legs open.'

'No.' Paternus was not smiling. 'No, I didn't mean that.'

'Good,' she said, sensing that she had hit a nerve.

'When I saw you last,' he said, 'There was a boy with you, not much taller than my boot.'

'My son,' she said. 'Named Taran.'

'Where is he?'

'Safe, pray the shining one.'

'And his father?'

Brenna's smile at the remembrance of her boy had gone and she stood at the river's edge, staring into the water. 'He drowned,' she said. 'The will of the shining one.' She looked up at him. 'You have lost someone too,' she said. 'A wife, perhaps?'

'A wife and son,' Paternus told her. 'To Valentinus.'

'Then we both have new lives to find,' Brenna said, looking into the man's eyes.

'We both have lives to avenge,' the tribune answered.

The attack came out of nowhere. A sickle embedded itself into Paternus' ribs and he was sent flying sideways by the impact. The horse whinnied and bolted, splashing back across the river.

'No!' Brenna screamed at the warrior who was standing over Paternus ready for the fatal blow.

'His men killed Segomo,' the warrior growled. 'You were there, lady.'

'His men killed Segomo because Segomo was about to kill him,' she shouted. There was a dagger in her hand and the warrior was not about to cross iron with his queen. 'Put that down,' she was pointing at the sickle, trembling with the shock of the last few seconds. The warrior straightened and let the weapon fall. People were running from both directions, the Votadini grabbing their swords and spears, Romans snatching up shields and javelins.

Paternus saw his men coming, splashing through the shallows in the half light. 'No,' he said, raising himself up as best he could. 'It's nothing. An accident. Everything's all right.' Somehow he managed to stand and held his hand out to the soldiers, already in skirmish order with their javelins raised. 'Go back,' he said. 'You men have a marching camp to finish.' He turned onto his hands and knees, letting his head hang to relieve the pressure on his lungs. After a couple of laboured breaths, he staggered to his feet, stumbling against Brenna, who held him upright. She turned to his attacker.

'You are banished from the lands of the shining one,' she said, levelly. 'You and your kin. And this I swear by Belatucadros, if I see you again, I'll hang you.'

She waited until he had gone, then took the full weight of the wounded tribune on her shoulders. Cold sweat was trickling

152

down his forehead and his skin was clammy and pale. His blood, dark in the half light, was spreading over his mail coat above his belt and staining her armour too.

'I must get back across the river,' he said. 'I must die with my men.'

She held up his drooping head and did her best to keep her voice steady. 'You're not going to die,' she said. 'Do you hear me? You have lives to avenge, remember?'

CHAPTER XII

'Pa, Pa!' Quin's voice sounded in his ear, now soft, now loud.

'What is it, little man?' Paternus asked, rolling over on the bed.

'Pa, get up. Time to play.'

'It's always time to play,' Paternus yawned. 'Go and bother your mother.'

'Come on, Pa,' Quin had been here before. His mother loved him, combed his hair and made him wash. She fed him with her lovely, warm biscuits that smelt of honey and apples, but she did not play. That was what his Pa was for. The boy tried to lift his father's dagger down from the shelf, but it was too heavy and he gave up.

'Uh-huh,' Paternus warned him. 'Too heavy for a little boy. And too sharp. Race you to the stream.' And he dashed up, out of the married quarters he called home in the fort of Camboglanna and down towards the cool, beckoning water. It was hot already, south of the Wall and today was his day off – a semisallis of the VI Victrix did not get many of those. Little Quin tried to get under his feet and the pair of them laughed and tumbled until Paternus picked the lad up and collapsed into the water, flailing around, helpless with laughter, as Quin splashed him all the more.

Suddenly, the boy was gone. He had slipped under the current, his little hands flapping frantically, his terrified face bobbing now above the surface, now below. 'Hang on, Quin,' Paternus found his feet and was striding out into midstream, but he could not reach the boy. Every time their fingers touched, the current swirled and carried him away, inches, feet, then yards and Paternus, swimming with all his strength, could not see him any more. All he could hear was his voice, 'Pa, Pa ...'

'... Paternus, Paternus, wake up. It's all right. It was a dream.'

The Paternus who lay there under a canopy of trees, had been a semisallis attached to the forts of the Wall, a family man, happy and fulfilled, with all his adult life before him. The Paternus sitting up now was a tribune. He had no family. And his life was over.

'You were dreaming.' Warm hands were soothing his forehead and wiping the sweat from his face. He tried to focus, but his eyes were not working. The voice was soft and melodic, not his Flavia's and yet ... His chest was heaving with the exertion of the swim, the dream, the nightmare ... whatever it was. And he sank back to sleep again.

She opened his shirt under the wolfskin covers, seeing the old scar there and turned his body slightly to the left. Carefully, so carefully, she stripped away the bandages and looked at the wound. The sickle had bitten deep but the edges of the cut were clean. There seemed to be no infection now but Paternus' mind was still wandering. He had been like this for two days and all that had passed his lips was some water. True, it was water from the holy well of Verbeia, whose pool they lay beside now, but would that be enough to save him?

Brenna, queen of the Votadini, wrapped mistletoe around the tribune's head and kissed it gently. It was a time of waiting.

While a small escort marched with the queen and the wounded tribune, the rest of the Votadini travelled north-west with Magnus Maximus. Justinus had the job of watching over them because he spoke the language, but in no sense would these tribesmen in their furs and skins ever become a part of the Roman army. They could not march, they rode badly and their idea of a nightly marching camp was to shelter in the lee of some crags or a grove of trees. Too proud to ask for Roman shelter, they gave the earthworks and palisades a wide berth.

It was two days later that Maximus came across the first signs of his quarry. Justinus left the Votadini trudging behind the Victores column, the chill of an on-coming winter turning hands and noses blue. He was riding ahead with the general and a cavalry escort because the scouts reported a village recently burned by a large army moving south.

Justinus estimated they were due north of Brocolitia now, riding on a spur of land that fell away on both sides. He could see for miles, the sweep of the barren landscape under leaden skies. Trees only grew in the hollows where the icy winds of winter did not blast them to twisted, stunted bushes and smoke was rising from one of these hollows and one of those clumps of trees. Justinus was the only man in the general's entourage to know what that burning might be. The Attacotti ate people. And when there was time and wood was plentiful, they cooked them over slow fires, basting and dancing in wild abandon, like insane cooks in the kitchen of some great man's villa.

But this was different. It was black smoke, drifting upwards from a dozen hut-roofs and it had been burning for some time. As the knot of horsemen cantered down the slope, there was a shrill scream from the stand of oaks and a naked woman ran across the open ground, tearing her long hair as she ran, tears streaming down her face.

'Tribune!' Maximus shouted, clawing free his sword and Justinus rammed his heels into his horse's flanks and galloped after her. She twisted this way and that, leaping over tree roots and making for the blackened, smouldering wrecks of what had once been a village. A few geese the raiders had missed squawked and flapped at the thud of the woman's feet and ran ahead of her for a few paces, necks outstretched like a bizarre guard of honour. Turning, she dashed into the darkness of one of the huts.

Justinus swung out of the saddle and let his horse wander. The others were there now, forming a time-honoured circle around the place so the animal was not going to get far. He drew his sword and ducked his head under the half-burned beam. After the brightness of the day he could not see a thing. The smell of burning almost choked him and he felt loom weights and broken pots under his boots. Then there was an ear-piercing scream and the woman he had been chasing was on top of him, beating his shoulders with her fist and trying to wrench off either his helmet or his head. He dropped the sword in surprise and hauled her off, gripping both her flailing arms as she tried to claw his face. She drove first her right foot, then her left into his groin and he doubled up as the sickening pain hit him. She was hurtling out of the door, her hair flying behind her when she came face to face with the flat of a spatha blade and dropped where she stood, out cold.

A rather sorry-looking tribune of the VI Victrix hobbled out of the smoking hut, his eyes brimming with tears, he told himself, from the smoke. Several horsemen sat their animals looking at him. One of them was General Maximus. 'Can't catch a naked woman, laddie?' he shook his head in dismay. 'You've been too long on the Wall.'

Her name, she said, was Fanna, daughter of Cernunnos and Epona. She had never married, although she had been betrothed once to a beautiful man who had horns on his head, like her father. In fact, no man had touched her until *they* came.

'Who are *they*?' Justinus asked. From somewhere, Maximus' horsemen had found a cloak to cover the girl's nakedness and had given her some food. She ate ravenously, eyes constantly on the move, watching them all. Justinus told his soldiers to go away and even Maximus had taken the hint. Now, just the two of them sat in the smoky hut, less choking than it had been, a small, spitting fire between them.

'The painted ones,' she said. 'And the Scotti. They've gone, though, now, haven't they?' She peered over his shoulder, checking in the shadows for lurking monsters. He could see the goose flesh crawl along her arms in a sudden flare as a log fell in the fire.

'Yes,' Justinus said softly. 'They've gone. Did you see which way they went?'

Fanna continued to gnaw on her army hard-tack, sucking through broken teeth and she pointed through the door. The general and his escort stood there, warming their hands around a larger fire. Maximus had sent word back to the cohorts. There would be no marching camp tonight; they were to get here, fast.

'Fanna,' Justinus was careful to make no move towards the girl. 'Did you see a man with a helmet?'

She glanced quickly at the spangenhelm lying next to the tribune. 'No, not like mine. A mask. A mask of silver over the face.'

For a moment she did not move, showed no expression. Her eyes widened. Then her face creased into a smile and she started to laugh. 'He said he liked me,' she trilled. 'Said I was beautiful.' She suddenly stood up and let her cloak fall. Her breasts were bruised and bitten, her thighs and belly covered in scratches. She twirled in the firelight, this way and that. 'He wanted me,' she said, taking up the long fronds of her hair and sweeping them mischievously across her face, 'the one in the silver helmet. Said he had to have me.' She stopped swaying and the smile vanished. 'But I wouldn't let him,' she said. 'He was not of my people, so I wouldn't let him.'

'Didn't you?' Justinus asked. He got up slowly, making sure that his movements didn't bring him closer to her. She was like a strung bow, tensed and ready to fly.

'Well,' she said, coyly. 'Perhaps I did. Just once or twice.' She looked at him through huge, uncomprehending eyes. 'Do *you* want to do it with me?' she asked, hands on hips.

Justinus bent down and picked up the cloak, spreading it over her shoulders and pulling it closed. 'It's late,' he said. 'You should get some sleep. In the morning, we'll see.' And he laid her gently down on the soft earth by the fire.

Outside, Magnus Maximus was still warming his hands. 'Well?' he said. 'Valentinus?'

'Possibly,' Justinus said. 'She's Selgovae by her accent.'

'Did she tell you which way the bastards went?'

'South,' the tribune told him. 'If we can believe her.'

'She's lying?' Maximus asked.

'She's mad,' Justinus stretched out his hands too. 'Whether she was anyway or she's been driven to it by what they did to her, I don't know. Says her father is a horned god and her mother is a horse goddess.'

'She's lucky to be alive,' the general nodded, staring into the flames.

'Lucky?' Justinus looked into the hut and saw by the firelight Fanna of the holy parentage crooning softly to herself and pulling out tufts of her hair. 'Yes, you could say that.'

They took Fanna with them as they marched south and found another village, this time untouched. It took a while to negotiate but in the end, Justinus persuaded the people there to add one more lost soul to their number and they marched on.

There were no roads to the south, just miles of desolate moors, purple with heather that was a hard and springy surface for the marching boots. The cavalry scouts of the Victores had vast experience of trailing armies and this was a large one, perhaps five thousand men. They had carts with them, the wheel-ruts cut into the mud frozen hard now with the coming of winter. And they passed one or two graves, too, fresh dug by the side of the path they travelled. There were wooden carvings there, hideous gods chiselled into oak and ash, no doubt companions who would take the dead to whatever afterlife the barbarians believed in. One thing was certain; if this was Valentinus, he was in no hurry. He had had time to bury his dead and to mark the place. He was probably only a day ahead; less because a raiding party that huge took time to move and the barbarians did not march like the Romans. On a good day the Victores could manage twenty five miles; but who was to say if this was a good day?

Maximus halted his column on the low plain with a thick forest to his right. His scouts had come galloping back with news. They had found a dragon standard.

'Skirmish advance,' the general gave the order and the cavalry fanned out. The first two cohorts slid their shields off their backs and the front ranks hoisted their spears to the upright. The marching column was transformed into a fighting unit in minutes, Maximus and Justinus in the centre, the other tribunes with their cohorts. The wind was whipping through the general's scarlet flag, its gold fringes flying over Maximus' head. But most of the noise came from the solid tramp of the Victores, flattening the heather as they took the gentle rise of a scarp slope.

The cavalry outriders halted, their horses snorting and whinnying with alarm. The ground fell away suddenly, a steep ravine beyond the slope. And the ravine was full of bones, jumbled and picked clean by the crows and the ravens.

'Let me see that again.' Maximus flicked his fingers and his signifer handed him the battered draco. Its bright red paint was peeling badly and the snarling mouth had lost most of its teeth. 'Is this the dragon of the Ala Invicta Brittaniaci?' he asked Justinus.

'It could be,' the tribune said, but he was already looking at the landscape. The dragon standards were carried by so many units and there was rarely any way of telling one from another. But the words of the signifer Metellus were echoing in Justinus' mind. In front of him, the ravine with its bodies. To his left a scarp slope steeper and higher than the one they stood on now; to his right, an oak forest, dark in summer but naked now the leaves had gone. Justinus nodded to himself, then turned to Maximus. 'Welcome, sir,' he said, 'to the mouth of hell.'

They had no time to bury the dead from the ravine. Scattered over the fields ahead, they saw trinkets lying in the grass, the amulets of bone and wood that soldiers carried to keep them safe from harm. Here were the rays of Sol Invictus, like the spokes of a wheel. There the dying bull of Mithras. There was even a Chi-Rho, the looped cross of the Christ. They all knew, the men of the Victores, that what they were looking at was a deadly reminder. They were marching, once again in column, shields on their backs and spears at the slope, over a battlefield. Any more valuable trinkets would have been picked up by the victors of the field. All the weapons and armour would have been taken. So would the horses. This was the way it could go for any of them – bleached bones in a crack in the ground, a ground that had no official name; dead men defending a frontier they could not hold.

Maximus felt it too. Somewhere on this springy turf, the Dux Brittanorum had gone down fighting, a man with a higher rank than him, a man too arrogant, too careless. He turned in the saddle to scan the grim faces of his men, marching over the field of the invisible dead, chasing ghosts that had kept one step ahead of them all the way.

'Close up!' he snarled at them, wheeling his horse round and riding back through the ranks, which parted to let him through. 'Sing, you bastards!' he shouted. 'The Girl from Clusium – let me hear it. And make it loud. I want those poor sods back there in that pit to hear it too.'

A semisallis famous for his golden voice struck up the notes and others joined in. There were sad songs the legions sang, songs of home and the hearth fire. And there was The Girl From Clusium. It was not the sort of song you'd teach your children or even sing in front of your wife and the physical positions in verse four were pretty unlikely, but it always brought a smile to the face of a marching soldier and Maximus knew it. 'Shove, shove, shove, shove!' the refrain thumped out to the thud of the boots.

Maximus swung his horse in alongside Justinus. 'That should keep the buggers happy for a while,' he said. 'Where the hell are we?'

Justinus pointed. 'That should be the Wall,' he said. 'Brocolitia, dead ahead.'

What sun there was lit the Wall just before it died. It glowed fierce and red through bars of purple cloud gilding the stones of the fort of Brocolitia. Maximus' army halted here, their singing stopped, their throats hoarse.

'The bastards have smashed the Mithraeum,' somebody shouted and dozens of men dashed over to look. The roof of the little temple had gone and the top stones toppled into the grass. The bull-pit was full of roof debris and the statues of the torch-bearers, Cautes and Cautopates had had their heads struck off. The three altars at the far end had been daubed in shit, old and caked now by the weather. Of Mithras and the great bull, there was no sign. The Victores muttered darkly, the brighter mood of their singing gone now, in this insult to their god.

'What's this?' Maximus was not with the others, clustered around the desecration to the east of the abandoned fort. He was standing to the west, where the ground was marshy and a stone circle surrounded a pit, dark and deep. Justinus, as the only man there who knew the Wall, took a coin from his purse and threw it into the darkness. 'Listen,' he said.

For two seconds, perhaps three, there was nothing; then an eerie thud, like two wooden plates clashing together. 'That's water down there,' he told the general. 'This is the Well of Coventina. She's a water goddess the Brigantes worship; the Selgovae too as far as I know.'

'Seal it,' Maximus ordered.

'Our men worshipped her too, sir,' Justinus said. 'The garrison here, I mean.'

The general rounded on his tribune. 'Well, shame on them,' he said. 'No man deserves to be butchered, Justinus, but I can't help thinking if you Limitanei had been truer to your vows ...'

He checked himself. He knew he was being unfair and that in these insane days, many a man was losing his religion. 'Seal it,' he said, more softly now. Then he turned to his staff, still sitting their horses some yards away. 'We'll set up camp here, Camp Master. Pickets out. Third and Fourth cohorts to dig.'

They sealed the well of Coventina, goddess of the deep water, with stones from the Mithraeum; and they rebuilt as much of the soldier god's shrine as they could. Usually, Maximus would not have wasted time with this but he knew it did the men good to see their holy place restored and an inconsequential piece of barbarian rubbish destroyed for ever. It helped morale and it kept them busy while the general waited for news.

He had sent his cavalry scouts out at first light and by midday they were back. They brought the news he had expected to hear, but, as was usual with scouts' reports, it could be interpreted a dozen ways. He stood on the ramparts of the Wall that afternoon, his tribunes with him. There had been a time, and that only a year ago, when the guardians of the Wall only looked north because that was where the potential threat came from; not from the Selgovae and the Votadini but from the painted madmen further north. Now, the watchers on the Wall looked in all direction; the south was just as suspect, just as dangerous.

'Valentinus has split his army up,' Maximus told the trib-unes. 'Ten miles to the south. The scouts report at least six different war bands, heading south and west, but none of them north and none of them east. That either means ...' and he was still wrestling with the problem, '... he's going to attack us everywhere, across Brigantia. Or ...' he looked to the north where the sky lay dark and heavy with unshed snow, 'Or he's going into hiding for the winter.' He caught Justinus' eye. 'Yes, I know he attacked out of season last year,' he said, 'but he can't keep an army in the field for ever.' He smiled. 'Only we can do that. Of course, it's possible he's lost con-trol of them. That's the trouble with a conspiracy – there are too many parts that make up the whole. Different tribes, different lead-ers. He's only going to hold them together as long as there's booty and plenty of it. And look at this place.' He waved his hand over the scene, the shattered gate, the smashed walls. 'He didn't do this. At least, not recently. Only the shit on the altars is relatively new. Everything else was done when this fort was hit last year. So he's taking his people over old ground, played out and dead. And the snows are coming. He'll need to find shelter and he has too many men to do that in one place. He's going to find a bolt-hole and so are we.'

Paternus had no memory of being taken north to the holy well. Arbeia, the Wall and all things Roman lay to the south and he had never been this far north before. In the early days, as he lay in Brenna's arms, he had been delirious with fever. His wound had become infected and his mind boiled with demons and things of the night.

Now, all that had changed, and he was himself again. She changed his dressings every day and he sat around the camp fire in the autumn mists, listening to the sad songs of the Votadini. Across the circle, eyes shining in the flames, the queen of the people who called themselves Gododdyn, smiled at him. She was always there, as her little band of people went about their business in the shelter of the holy grove. They rebuilt the huts, piled with stones and the wattle and daub that gave them warmth. While the warriors kept a constant watch from the hills, the women wove their cloth and kneaded their bread.

At first, Paternus was loath to join them. His side was stiff from the rib that had cracked and the wound was still angry and inflamed. He had lost the track of time but the cascading leaves and the chill from the north told him that winter was on the way. He had heard nothing from Justinus, not a word from the army of Maximus. For all he knew they were lying in the heather somewhere, yet more victims of the man in the silver helmet whose very existence had come to blight them all. He wondered, as he wandered the hills above the pool and saw the Votadini patrols letting their horses graze, how it went for Leo and Vit in Londinium. What had Maximus said? They were Theodosius' pets now, feted wherever they went. Leocadius would love that. Vitalis? Well, Paternus was not so sure.

'You're leaving us, aren't you?' A voice made him turn. Brenna stood there, her long cloak around her, the torque around her neck shining in the bright, brittle light that broke the snow clouds.

'Yes,' he said. 'I must. You have saved my life, but I am a tribune of the VI Victrix. I must get back.'

She crossed to him and laid a hand on his shoulder. 'What if there *is* no going back?' she asked.

'What do you mean?' he frowned.

'How long have the Romans been here?' she asked, 'in these islands?'

'In Britannia?' Paternus said. 'I don't know. My father came here from Germania and the Empire was old then. How do we measure this? In years? In men's lives? Who knows? Why do you ask?'

'Perhaps it's meant to be,' she shrugged. 'Perhaps one day the light of Rome will be extinguished for ever.'

Paternus laughed. It was not a sound anyone heard often. 'Perhaps one day, Leocadius Honorius will buy his own drinks.'

'You miss him, don't you?' she laughed as well. She knew all about Leocadius, Vitalis, Justinus, all the heroes of the Wall. The only one she did not know about was Paternus, the silent, the still. Because he never talked about himself.

'A little,' Paternus smiled. 'I miss Vit more. He has a sort of ... I don't know ... vulnerable quality about him. From what little I've heard of Londinium, they'll eat him alive there.'

Brenna closed to him and took his face in both hands, looking steadily into his eyes. 'Don't go, Paternus,' she said. 'We all lose friends, people we love. We've lost already, you and I. Let's not lose anyone again.'

And she kissed him. It may be that she had kissed him before, while his mind had been ranging, in the time of his dreams. But if so, he could not remember it. And this was more than a kiss of friendship, of one comrade to another in this strange war they were both fighting on the frontier. Her tongue entwined with his and they stood, locked together in an embrace, arms wrapped around each other. He breathed in the scent of her hair, her skin and kissed all the harder. His hand slipped under her cloak to feel the swell of her breasts and her eyes closed and she shuddered.

'Rider!' A Votadini voice broke the moment and the pair sprang apart.

'Where?' Brenna was a woman no more. A woman falling in love with a man. She was the warrior queen of the Gododdyn, with the blood of kings coursing through her veins.

'To the south.'

'How many?' Brenna could not see beyond the trees.

The scout who was answering her held up one finger. Obviously the stranger was within earshot now and any more shouts would alert him. Brenna and Paternus scrambled up the bracken-covered slope in front of them and lay at the top, peering through the fronds. The scout was right. All they could see was a solitary horseman, wrapped in a fur cloak against the icy blast of the winter wind. Neither of them was armed, so Brenna signalled to her people to move forward. Four of them urged their horses on, all of them in the shelter of the trees. They halted there, stroking their animals' necks to soothe and keep them quiet. Then they strung their bows and slid the gut into the notch. The rider would have no chance. He was alone and in the open. He would be dead before he hit the ground.

'Io, Justinus!' Paternus shouted and was on his feet, crashing through the bracken now, all stiffness in his side forgotten.

'Belacutadros!' Brenna hissed through her teeth. She was on her feet too, waving to her horsemen to get forward. All four of them rammed their heels against their ponies' flanks and came cantering out of the thicket.

'Pat!' Justinus was laughing, seeing his old friend struggling towards him in a borrowed Votadini cloak. He saw the horsemen seconds later and drew his sword, but Paternus was there first and, not for the first time, stopped the shedding of blood between the Votadini and Rome.

By the firelight that night, the two heroes of the Wall sat nibbling the carcase of a hare. The Votadini had told their tall tales and the old jokes, they had sung and danced, clapping and jumping to the rattles and the drums. Now, as the fire dwindled and everyone had crawled off to bed, warm with the beer inside them all, the Romans were alone.

'How long did you say it's been?' Paternus asked.

'Three months. You missed the Saturnalia last week. I'd have given a year's pay to see Maximus do what he promised and muck out the stables for the slaves.'

'You missed it?' Paternus asked.

'He didn't do it,' Justinus laughed. 'Called away at the last minute. Some urgent business along the Wall.'

Paternus laughed too. 'Yes,' he said. 'There's always some urgent business along the Wall.'

There was a silence and Justinus said, 'You'll miss this place.'

'No,' Paternus shook his head. 'No, I won't.'

'The girl ... er ... sorry, the queen. Brenna. You'll miss her.'

Paternus looked across the deserted camp site, with the huts silent against the dark of the trees and the holy pool darker still in the night. 'No,' he said.

Justinus spat out a bone he had been wrestling with for some minutes. 'You know she loves you, don't you?'

Paternus' head jerked up. 'Since when have you become such an expert?' he asked.

Justinus tapped the side of his nose. 'I've been around,' he said. 'It's not only Leocadius who does the skirt chasing, you know. She loves you. I've seen it all day. The way she looks at you, touches you. She's like a little girl in your presence.'

'No!' Paternus stood up sharply. 'It's not like that. And anyway,' he cleared his throat, 'we have places to be. Tomorrow we'll be off to Arbeia and I'll never see her again.'

CHAPTER XIII

Londinium, Hiems in the year of the Christ 369

Everybody had told Count Theodosius that it never snowed this far south, yet that year it did. His men toiled in the margins of the river mist, their hands freezing to the blocks of stone they lifted. Shovels crunched into mortar that was setting as the engineers looked at it and the great cranes swung against skies heavy with yet more unshed snow.

For three months, young Theodosius had ridden west and north at the head of the Heruli, Stephanus at the young man's back just in case of trouble. The German was too loyal to say so, but he could not warm to the son as he warmed to the father. Where the Count was fair and kind, with a twinkle of humour and the heart of a lion, the boy was mean-spirited and secretive. The face, whether under his elaborate gilded helmet or beaming at some titled tart in the governor's palace, gave little away. Even in his cups, the man remained an enigma, watchful and guarded, as though every word had been measured and weighed, every glance accounted for.

They had met one raiding party shortly before Saturnalia, in what may have been the last of the season before the weather closed in and they had routed them, hacking men down as they fled and hanging two or three, their bodies left to rot in the wind as food for the carrion crows. Most of the booty they carried was returned to grateful villagers and owners of villas, but that took time and Theodosius had people to deal with all that. He himself rode back to the warmth of the palace he had made his own.

At Verulamium, they had never heard of Valentinus. Theodosius and Stephanus rode their horses splashing through the marshes there to find the Londinium gate strong and well-fortified, with ballistae primed and ready. The theatre was doing a thriving business and would the son of the Comes Rei Militaris care to see a play? They were putting Aristophanes *Frogs* on that week – you know, the naughty one? Of course, it would all be done in the best possible taste, in especial honour of the son of the Comes Rei Militaris.

All was quiet, too, at Calleva Atrebatum, its mighty walls intact and patrolled by a vexillation of the II Augusta. There were rumours of raids further west, but these had been small, apparently, and of no consequence. The garrison commander there assured them he was ready for Valentinus, if indeed the man was real. He had started to believe he was just a figment of some mad barbarians' imagination. The local priest here had been about to start divine service and would the great Theodosius care to attend? He would and while Stephanus and *his* barbarians waited outside, the son of the Comes Rei Militaris communed with his god.

Camulodunum, the colony of the deified Claudius, had little to fear from the land and everything from the sea. If the Saxons struck, as rumour had it they were striking along the coast of Gaul, then the town could expect to see some action. And it had seen action before. The old temple of Claudius, now turned into a fortress, had witnessed the slaughter of civilians in the attack on it by Boudicca of the red hair, in the dark early days when the eagle standards were rammed into the granite of Britannia and no one felt safe. Some of the more sensitive souls who strolled the wall-walks at night swore they heard sobbing from the crypt far below them, as if the ghosts of the long-departed still sang to them from the stones.

Leocadius had ridden out with the younger Theodosius twice, trotting on his expensive imported Arab past the trudging, cursing pedes. There was a time when this would have been the height of his ambition – a tribune's rank in the army he had joined as a pedes. Most men spent all their lives as pedes; a few made semisallis; a select minority circitor and, the impossible dream, centurion, primus pilus. *Nobody* rose from the bottom to tribune. The Wall had done that for him, he reflected more than once, as he twisted the black ring on his finger. But somehow, it was not enough. He was bored and restless, tired of supervising building work and the odd ride out into the country, chasing a will o' the wisp. There *had* to be more to life.

She was walking in the palace garden when he saw her and he had not seen her for a while. Snow lay on the ground and the fountains had frozen. Julia's father was not a happy man. Having shown true Roman hospitality to the Theodosii last summer, the arrogant bastards had moved in. They had generously allowed him to stay but the consul's quarters now were just that – a quarter of the palace he had once filled entirely. So he increasingly spent his time in his apartments at the basilica. That was probably just as well; it meant that his appalling wife was not likely to see the procession of girls who trooped in most nights for his delectation and delight.

'Julia,' Leocadius whispered, appearing out of nowhere under an archway. 'How are you?' Before she could stop him, he had taken her hand and kissed it, 'I was hoping to have seen you at the Saturnalia feasts.'

'I wasn't allowed,' she told him, blushing at his touch despite herself. 'Papa is watching.'

Leocadius took her gently by the arm and tucked her away out of the sight of the house's upper window. 'What, now you mean?' He could not see anybody.

'No,' she laughed. 'Not now. He's at the basilica.'

'And your mother?' the tribune wondered. Julia's mother was like a Pictish battleaxe, beautiful enough on the outside but hard as iron and with a tongue as sharp.

'She's here, upstairs,' Julia told him. She folded her arms and gave him a wry smile. 'Why are you asking?' she said.

'Oh, you know,' Leocadius hedged. 'Just wanted to pay my respects.'

'Come on, then,' and she screwed up her courage and took him by the hand.

'Er ... on second thoughts, I have to get back. Duty and all that.'

'When will I see you again?' she asked. Although Leocadius was blissfully unaware of it, Julia Longinus had made it her business over the last few weeks to be anywhere she thought he might be – the barracks, the basilica, the area along the river where they were building the wall. She had not seen him in any of those places.

'Whenever your mama or papa allows it,' he said.

'Don't tease me,' she frowned. The girl was seventeen, but

in many ways was still a child. 'Mama will never allow it unless there are at least thirty people in the room. And Papa won't even concede that. The laws of the deified Constantine ...'

'... have long been ignored,' he smiled. 'Anyway, those laws are about rape.' He looked at her with her suddenly downcast eyes, 'And I don't intend to rape you,' he said. She almost looked disappointed. He half turned, as if to go, then suddenly swung back and kissed her hard on the mouth, pressing himself against her under the trail of ivy from the arch. She struggled at first, beating her little fists on his shoulders and back. Leocadius had been this way before, albeit not with this girl and he knew all the signs. Anyone who wanted to fight him off could do so. They could grab his hair, jab a finger in his eye, knee him in the balls. Julia did none of these things. He felt her lips soften and a little furtive tongue slide around his. When they came up for air she was breathing hard, her heart thumping in her chest.

'Tonight,' he whispered, already hard under his tunic. 'What time does everybody go to bed?'

'That depends,' she breathed, eagerly planning the taking of her virginity. 'Papa and the Count often stay up talking. His stairway leads past my room.'

'Servants?' he checked.

She smiled coyly. 'Deaf, blind and dumb,' she trilled. 'As all good slaves should be.'

He laughed. 'Two by the candle, then,' he said and patted her belly under her cloak. 'Keep warm for me.' And he was gone.

There was a sharp frost again that night, sparkling on the snow that already lay thick on the ridge-tiles of Londinium's houses. The odd dog barked in the distance and along the Walbrook a rowing boat banged against its moorings as the little stream trickled past. The governor's palace stood square against the river, candles still gleaming in its upstairs windows.

Vitalis leaned his back against the building on the street corner. The tabernae were empty now, the cold having driven everybody home. Only the most determined or the most hopeless drunk wandered the night in search of Bacchus, muttering to themselves in their double darkness.

'Hero of the Wall,' a quiet voice said in the shadows. Vitalis stood upright, his dagger at easy reach in the folds of his cloak. 'Are you ready yet to meet the god of the midnight?' Decius Critus opened the fur-edged cloak he was wearing and let Vitalis see his robes underneath. They were strange and eastern, with silk embroidery and gold thread. A bull with huge horns worked in silver stared at the tribune from the man's chest.

'Yes,' Vitalis said. 'I am ready.'

Decius Critus was half a head shorter than Vitalis but he was square and solid and moved silently over the stones. In other times, with other men, Critus would have blindfolded the tribune before leading him through the maze of alleyways. But this man was different; this man he could trust. Vitalis could see the lights of the camp in the far distance, the pin-pricks of fire moving along the ramparts as the guards patrolled, looking out over the sleeping city and the dark forests to the north.

Critus came to a wall at the end of one particularly dark passageway and he tapped on a low door. A grille in the timber slid open with a squeal of iron and a face peered out. 'God of the midnight,' Critus whispered and the door edged open. He went inside, motioning Vitalis to follow him. The tribune had seen a Mithraeum before, but nothing like this one. It was arched over the roof with black stones and columns supported it with vine leaves intermingled with ivy, all carved from granite. 'We saved what we could from the last temple,' Critus told him.

An attendant emerged from the shadows, his shaved head wrapped round with a silk turban and for all it was as cold as the grave in here, wore only a loincloth.

'Prepare him,' Critus said and slipped away through a slit in the wall. The attendant said nothing. That was because he had no tongue and whatever secrets this place held would die with him. He unbuckled Vitalis' cloak and laid it on a bench to one side of the room. Then he unfastened his tunic and pulled it over his head. Finally he knelt to remove his subligaculum, leaving Vitalis naked. The attendant dipped his hand into the pitcher at his side and with practised fingers he ran oil over Vitalis' body, his shoulders and back, his arms and legs until he glistened like a gladiator. As this process had begun he had shivered with the cold, his skin like that of a goose hanging in the marketplace, but now he felt warm and almost glowing from within.

The attendant bowed and held out a hand to indicate the way that Vitalis was to go. He walked into a chamber, as high as a man and half as high again. Pillars like those in the atrium held the curved ceiling and stars sparkled there, lit by candles in a small chamber overhead. There was a wall facing him and he had to turn left. Steps led down into a pit, perhaps ten feet long and three feet wide. Like a coffin for a pair of lovers.

He knew what was expected of him and he lay down. Three figures appeared, one on each side of the pit and the other at the end nearest his feet. This one was Critus, but Critus transformed. The robes were still there, glowing in the sharp candlelight, but on his head was the massive mask of a bull, its eyes like rolling fire, its horns curved and deadly.

'Are you, Vitalis Celatius, ready to embrace the Lord Mithras and receive his kiss?'

'I am,' Vitalis said.

'Cautes, torch bearer of the chamber,' Critus said. The figure on Vitalis' left took one pace forward. He too wore the robes of a priest and the head of a bull, the horns twisted and crooked. He held up a pitcher. 'The first kiss,' he said, his voice booming in the bull mask. He threw the jug's contents over Vitalis and blood sprayed over his head, chest and arms. The blood was warm and smelt of salty death and the initiate fought down the urge to gag.

'Cautopates,' Critus said, 'torch bearer of the chamber.' The third figure stepped forward, this time on Vitalis' right. The same robes, the same mask, the same pitcher. 'The second kiss,' the man thundered, his voice booming off the walls of the eerie chamber. And the blood rained down on Vitalis, trickling off his face around his neck and over his shoulders to drip into the bottom of the pit.

'Come,' Critus said as the torch-bearers turned away. 'Prepare to receive the third kiss.'

Vitalis stood up, the warm blood beading on his oiled skin and running in rivulets down his naked body. He climbed the steps again and followed Critus around the wall into the main chamber. The torch-bearers had taken their places under the stone carvings of the minor gods they represented, Cautes and Cautopates, handsome young men in Phrygian caps and clothes from Pontus Euxinus. Between these statues, a large stone disc was lit from behind by candles that shone through the shafts of the stone to flicker and move on the other walls. In front of the disc, as strangely attired as the torch-bearers, Mithras himself, with smouldering eyes and long, hanging hair was drawing his stone blade across the stone throat of a stone bull.

'Mithras,' Critus intoned, 'God of the morning.'

'God of the morning,' the others echoed, Vitalis too.

'Receive this soul of a soldier,' Critus went on. 'He has carried the sword and the spear. He will bear witness for you. He will withstand the pain.' He nodded, the bull's head lowering towards Vitalis who knelt and bowed his head.

The torch-bearers left their altar places and stood behind Vitalis, one to the left and one to the right. From under their robes, each of them pulled a short whip, of the kind they kept discipline with in the legions, barbed with sharp pieces of bone.

'I will withstand the pain,' Vitalis promised and licked his lips in a vain attempt to get ready. He only tasted blood and would soon taste more. He tensed as he heard Cautes' whip snake through the dense air of the temple, lashing across his left shoulder. His flesh was still quivering from that when Cautopates lashed him with a second, cutting diagonally across the first. Vitalis was still kneeling upright as the third blow hit and the fourth. Each one drove his body further forward until the pain of his knees against the cold, hard stone was almost as bad as the pain in his back. The blood trails of the bull were lost now in the fresh spurts of Vitalis' own and he grunted as he lost count of the blows he received. They had reached an almost hypnotic rhythm, like slow and agonising heart beats, like the fluttering pulse of a dying man.

Throughout it all, Critus was chanting, the low murmurings of the god of the bull, accepting this new sacrifice in the cave of the Mithraeum. Then, as suddenly as it had started, the beating stopped and Vitalis knelt there, trembling with the shock and the pain. He straightened and that move was agony as his shredded flesh shifted position with the flexing muscles beneath. He held out his arms, running with blood and oil and looked up as well as he could at Mithras on his altar. The god and the bull wobbled through his tears.

'I have withstood the pain,' he mumbled and was vaguely aware of Critus standing in front of him. All three of the priests had blood trickling from the necks of their masks, one of those clever little tricks of conjurers, staining their robes as they folded away the whips in their sleeves.

'Welcome,' Critus said. 'Welcome, child of the darkness.'

And Vitalis did not remember any more.

It was rather like that for Leocadius. One minute he was thrusting himself on top of the girl, listening to her feverish gasps turning into grunts and feeling her raking his arms with her long nails. Then he erupted and heard her scream as he slowed down and flopped beside her.

For a moment the chamber was silent, with just slight breathing in the darkness. Then Leocadius let out a sigh that turned into a laugh. 'I thought you said you hadn't done this before,' he said.

'You didn't believe that, surely?' she giggled.

He turned to her. 'No, of course not,' he said. 'It's every man's dream, really, I suppose. To find a virgin who goes like a wild ass.'

'I'll be a virgin for you whenever you like,' she purred, fumbling for his manhood again.

'Yes,' he laughed. 'But I *certainly* won't believe you next time. What *would* your mama say?'

She turned to him and leaned up on one elbow. 'She would say, "Is he up for doing it twice, Honoria? You know how I like these big Roman boys".'

They laughed together. 'And then there's your papa,' he said. 'What would his observations be, I wonder, if he could see us together now?'

'I have no idea who my father was,' she told him, 'which makes me a bit of a bastard. Just like you, Leo. Now, less talk and more action.' And it was her turn to straddle him.

The Paulinus Hupo who visited consul Julius Longinus by day was a general dealer. He never came alone but always with other traders and merchants, usually in some boring enclave with the Ordo. After all, there were regulations. There were weights and measures, cargo manifests, the providing of water, the public baths. It was all up for discussion. And it went on and on.

The Paulinus Hupo who came by night however was a different matter. He came alone or sometimes with a girl for Longinus to look over. Nowadays, he came to the basilica, to the consul's private apartments there because the Theodosii had all but taken over the governor's palace and that meant that Longinus often had to be in the room only two away from his wife.

'I am a *little* concerned, Paulinus,' the consul said, waiting while the slave Albinus, keeper of secrets, poured them both a goblet of wine.

'In what way?' Hupo asked. He had grown his hair back

now, as befitted one of the leading lights of the town but he always kept his dagger to hand, just in case. 'How's that, by the way?'

'Hmm?'

'The wine. I've just acquired a few amphorae of the stuff. From Gallia Lugdunensi. I think it could catch on.'

'It could,' Longinus savoured it. 'It could. No, things generally are getting a little awkward. The Count is breathing down my neck about refortification and that snotty boy of his ...'

'Little Theo?' Hupo sneered. 'What a charmer. Chip off the old block.'

'The hell he is,' Longinus growled. 'He's taking too healthy an interest in accounts. Specifically, *my* accounts.'

'Well,' Hupo yawned. 'Nothing untoward there, surely. You've got more clerks and accountants than I've got fingers in pies.'

'Yes, yes, but this is a cutthroat world, Paulinus. I don't have to tell you that. I just wish the bastards would bugger off and I can have my palace back.'

'Any chance of that?' Hupo asked.

The consul shrugged. 'It all depends on this Valentinus and his bloody conspiracy.'

'Valentinus?' Hupo raised an eyebrow.

Longinus checked the corners of the room to make sure they were alone. 'You know he's sent me what amounts to a threatening letter, don't you?'

'Yes, I heard.'

'Well, there you are. One minute, for us, it's business as usual. The next we're going up in flames like a second Troy.'

'There's no chance of that,' Hupo said.

'What do you mean?' Longinus asked.

'I mean,' the general dealer quaffed his wine and stood up, 'that I must be going. Oh, by the way, it *is* the Ides of Februarius ...'

'Yes, yes,' Longinus waved him aside. 'Albinus will leave the money in the usual place. What about that girl you mentioned? The one from Cyrenaica?'

'Oh, yes,' Hupo smiled. 'The athletic one.' Then he frowned. 'Are you sure you're up to it, Julius? I mean, a man of your years?'

'My years are fine, thank you,' he said, affronted.

Hupo laughed. 'Just say the word, then. I'm keeping her warm for you.'

'Consider the word said,' the consul smiled.

Albinus, the keeper of secrets, left the money in the usual place and one of Hupo's people, who could keep secrets too, collected it. Then Hupo threw a banquet, a modest one, it was true; in fact it was more of an intimate supper and there was only one guest. It was the tribune, Leocadius Honorius.

'How's the wine, Leo?' Hupo asked. 'An amusing little palate-tickler from Gaul.'

'It's good,' Leocadius said. From somewhere a lyre was playing a gentle love song and scantily clad girls brought in the various courses. The food was magnificent; Leocadius' palate was honed on fine foods now and he savoured every mouthful. The fish sauce alone was to die for.

''Have you given any thought to my offer?' Hupo asked.

'Would that would be the one you made me when I was chained to your floor?'

'Yes, I'm sorry about that,' Hupo frowned, as if he meant it. 'But these are dangerous times, tribune. I can't be too careful. Let me show you something.'

He clapped his hands and two slaves emerged from behind a curtain carrying a large chest between them. It was bound with iron bands and padlocked. Hupo opened it with a curiously shaped key and hauled open the lid. Inside was more money than Leocadius had seen in his life. It could have built five forts along the Wall and kept a Wall soldier in clover for ever.

'That's quite a fortune,' he managed after nearly a minute in silence with his mouth open.

'And that's only part of it,' Hupo said. 'Unlike these barbarians who I understand bury their loot in one place, mine is sensibly scattered.'

'Where does it come from?' Leocadius asked.

Hupo laughed. The lad was more naive than he thought. 'Hush money, protection money, a few dues creamed off here and there. You might say I'm a farmer. I farm taxes.'

'I'm a soldier,' Leocadius shrugged. 'I don't see how I would fit into all this.'

'Exactly,' Hupo smiled. 'You're a soldier.'

Without warning, the general dealer was on his feet, a knife in his hand, thrusting at Leocadius through the air. One of the girls screamed. The tribune dodged sideways, rolling off the couch and caught Hupo's wrist. He banged it hard on a marble stand and the dagger clattered to the floor. Now it was Leocadius' turn. His knife was glittering at Hupo's throat and the man fell backwards until there was nothing but wall behind him. The slaves hurtled through their curtain but Hupo flicked his fingers and they stood still. His eyes were wide because Leocadius' blade tip was still pricking the skin of his neck.

'What's going on?' Leocadius asked, wondering how he could take on all three of these men.

'Call it a little test,' Hupo's voice was rather strangulated. 'You passed with flying colours.'

'Good for me,' Leocadius said. 'What's your point?'

'You're a soldier,' Hupo said, easing the blade-tip aside. 'You kill people for a living. And you're pretty good at it too. I sensed that when you gave my man Gillo a bloody arm. But you were pissed that night. I wanted to see what you can do when you're sober.'

'So,' Leocadius lowered the dagger. 'You've seen. Now what?'

Hupo ordered the slaves away and slammed the chest shut. He would pick up his dagger later when Leocadius would not be there to misconstrue the move and when the swelling in his arm had gone down. He sat back on the couch and waited as a girl mopped the floor and refilled their cups. 'My people,' he said, clearing his throat, 'call themselves the Black Knives. Oh, I know, it's deliciously melodramatic, isn't it? But that side of my business needs work – the protection side. I've got enough men but up against a wharf rat sometimes, it doesn't go so well. Can you give them a few tips? For serious money, of course.'

'What, you mean, train them, like an army?'

'In a manner of speaking, yes.'

Leocadius laughed. 'You want Flavius Coelius for that,' he said.

'Who?'

'Never mind.' Leocadius' smiled faded. 'Just someone I used to know along the Wall.'

'All that's behind you, Leo,' Hupo said. 'All that Wall non-sense. This is Londinium, by Bacchus. It's a city that's going places, believe me. One day it'll rival Rome itself.'

Leocadius laughed but he saw that Hupo was not joining him.

'You can be part of it,' Hupo went on. 'It won't interfere with your duties overmuch. There's a handsome salary. As much wine and as many girls as you can handle.'

'Sounds like a soldier's dream,' Leocadius said.

'So you accept?' Hupo asked.

It was the end of Martius when Decius Critus sent for Vitalis. He sent for others, too, many more children of the darkness, but they did not meet in the secret temple by the Walbrook. Bishop Dalmatius was on the warpath again, he whose cult demanded that men love each other and turn the other cheek. So Critus hired a room over one of the tabernae to the east of the city where each day Theodosius' troops were climbing ladders with stones and bricks, fortifying sections of the wall and building towers, the bastions of which jutted out into the river mud.

One by one the adherents of Mithras made the sign of the bull's horns with their fingers and ducked under the low portico. There was a table in the centre and on it an ewer chased in silver. Beside it stood a goblet, carved in ivory and brought all the way from Egypt and the edge of the world to the south. Critus sat at one end of the table, the torch-bearers to his left and right. They were the priests of Mithras and only they were allowed to speak.

'The time is now,' Critus said. 'Dalmatius and his Christians have pushed us too far. They destroyed our old shrine and now we are told they are looking for the new one. Well, no more. We will strike first. Your job, all of you, whatever your walk of life, is to seek these Christians out. Discover their plans if you can. Above all, find out their festivals.'

'We know,' 'Cautes' said, 'that they have stolen the Saturnalia and pretend that that was the time of their Galilean's birth.'

'But there is another festival coming,' 'Cautoprates' said, 'when the Romans of Judea put him to death. On the third day, they believe, he rose from the dead ...'

There were guffaws and there was table-thumping.

'That is when we will strike,' Critus silenced it. 'But we need exact times.' He looked along the table. 'Vitalis,' he said. 'You are the newest of our band. That will be your job.'

Vitalis wanted to speak, to protest, but he knew the rules of the order and he could not.

'Cautes' poured the wine into the goblet and passed it to Critus who drank from it.

'Behold,' he said, 'the blood of the bull that died for us.'

'Behold,' the torch-bearers intoned, 'the blood of the bull.' And the goblet passed from both of them along the table, man to man. When it reached Vitalis, he put the cup to his lips, but he did not drink. Had he embraced one god, just to kill another?

CHAPTER XIV

Londinium, Ver

'But why didn't you come?' Julia whispered, 'like you said you would?'

Leocadius spread his arms wide. 'Duty, my lady,' he lied. 'A tribune has many duties. But,' he glanced around the corner, 'I'm here now. Tell me, are your slaves still blind, deaf and dumb?'

'Oh, yes,' she giggled. The cold of the winter had given way to a warm spring but it was nearly two by the candle and a chill breeze was blowing off the river. Julia's apartment lay to the north-east, furthest from the appalling smell of the Walbrook and armed guards from the garrison patrolled the forecourt, with its twinkling fountains and its sentinel lions of stone. A tribune of the VI attached to the staff of Count Theodosius could simply walk past these men and they would jump to attention and salute, but that was not how Leocadius wanted to play it. Rolling in the bed of Honoria or any other lady of the Londinium night was one thing, but Julia came of a titled family, the daughter of the Consul, no less and he had to be careful. Besides, it all added to the adventure of the thing.

It had been some weeks since he had promised to come to her and if she had, indeed, been keeping herself warm for him as he had asked, she must be at boiling point by now. She took his hand and led him through the garden, along paths edged with clipped hawthorn, the slight fragrance from the few open blossoms promising that spring was really here at last. Damn Luna – her moon was huge tonight, making the grounds of the governor's palace as bright as day. They tiptoed up the steps to the side door – at least it was dark in the shadows here and he listened to the crunch of the guards' boots as she fumbled noiselessly with the latch. Inside it was cool and dark and this was not a part of the palace Leocadius had been to before. Still holding his hand, she led him along a landing open at one side where the trees of the atrium stood. She held her finger to her lips as both of them heard talking. They flattened themselves against the plaster of a wall along which naked nymphs and cherubs cavorted, dancing with Bacchus in a frieze that stretched out of sight. Leocadius peered over the rail. The Count was saying goodnight to the consul, each man in his cups, clapping the other on the back and ambling towards the front door which slaves swung open for them and they disappeared outside.

'He'll be back in a minute,' she hissed. 'This way. Quick.' She let go of his hand so that she could lift her dress and ran, sandal-footed across the landing, the tribune running behind. He was not wearing his regulation boots tonight or the whole escapade might have come to an end then and there. As it was, Julius Longinus, returning across the atrium, caught sight of a fleeting shadow; but he put that down to too much wine and went to bed.

In the doorway, Julia pointed along the corridor,' Mama's room,' she mouthed, almost silently. Leocadius nodded. She was the last person in the entire palace he wanted to wake up. He pressed against the girl in the doorway and it opened gently. With a practised hand, he closed it behind him and locked it, all the time kissing the girl's cheeks and neck. When both his hands were free, he held her face in his and kissed her full on the lips. They were parted for him already and before she knew it, he was untying the thongs of her dress and letting it slip to the ground. Naked in the moonlight, she shuddered for him and he ran his tongue over her bare shoulders and down to her breasts. Her breathing was ragged now, but he would take his time, teasing her, making her wait.

Julia had never been this way before but it was a road the tribune knew well. He lifted her off the ground in his powerful arms and carried her over to the bed. While he fondled her and she opened her legs for him, she kept her eyes wide open the whole time, willing him to be gentle, trusting herself to him. She was trembling all over, breathing heavily as he took her, increasing the tempo imperceptibly until she wrapped her legs around his body and he stifled her screams with the deepest of kisses.

Stephanus was out early with his Heruli cavalry the next day. They were travelling north-west, in the direction of the forests, following the Roman road that led to Verulamium. There was a village off to the left, perhaps ten huts, with lazy smoke climbing to the blue of the spring sky. All was calm, as it should be and Stephanus had passed this way a dozen times before. The sun was in the sign of Aries and Venus, the goddess of love herself, presided over the time.

Little children were playing at the edge of the village as their mothers milked the goats and fed the geese. They seemed to be squabbling, as children will, over something being passed from hand to hand.

'It's my turn!' one of them shrilled.

'No, it's not. You've already had it once!'

'I want it!'

Stephanus had been in Britannia long enough to be able to pick up the gist of this conversation and he was about to ride on, with his patrol smiling indulgently at his back when he hauled hard on the rein and sat still. His black mare shook her head and champed the bit at this sudden command from the man on her back.

As he looked, one of the children picked up something from the grass and put it on his head. It was much too big for him and it was a cavalry parade helmet, the dull, flat visor carved into a blank face of solid silver, except for the eyes and mouth. The little boy wearing it laughed and ran about, chased by the others shouting 'Me! Me!' until he fell over, unable to see where he was going and dizzy at the same time.

But it was not a playfellow who pulled him upright; it was a huge man in a coat of mail with long blond hair and a vast moustache. The boy screamed, the sound eerie in the echo of the helmet. The women came running, one or two with knives and pots in their hands. Stephanus ripped off the helmet. 'Where did you get this?' he asked, his Latin strange and guttural.

'Tell the nice gentleman,' his mother said, holding out her hand. The boy ran to her and buried his face in the folds of her rags.

'Sextus found it,' the lad whispered.

'Sextus?' another woman said. A taller boy walked reluctantly across to her. 'Did you find that helmet?' She shook him until he felt his teeth rattle.

'Yes,' he admitted, tears bubbling in his eyes.

'Where?' Stephanus wanted to know.

The boy pointed.

'Show me,' the German said and, springing into his saddle, bent down and scooped the boy up, pushing him over the pommel, his body held in place by Stephanus' arms. He looked down at the woman. 'If I like his answer, I'll bring him back,' he said. 'If not, I'll eat him.'

The men of the patrol chuckled grimly and wheeled away, riding behind their leader at the boy's direction. About half a mile away the ground fell away to the side of the road to form a cleft in the hillside. Stone had been quarried here at some time in the past, but the place was disused now and a tangle of brambles covered the weathered blocks and crevices.

'Down there,' the boy pointed. Leaving the lad on the horse, Stephanus dismounted and scrambled down the crumbling rocks. At first he saw nothing, hacking through the brambles with his sword. Then he gave a shout and two of the riders swung out of their saddles and joined him. Half way into the undergrowth lay the body of a man. Most of the flesh had gone from his bones and the tendons of the jaw had gone so it looked for all the world as if the corpse was laughing at some long forgotten, obscene joke. The sword had gone but the belt was still there, studded with brass and turquoise. So was most of the armour – a coat of overlapping scales each one forged from beaten brass; a coat like that would pay the Heruli for six months.

'Was it on his head?' Stephanus asked the boy, secretly impressed if young Sextus had had the nerve to remove it.

'Nearby,' the lad said. 'Over there.'

All that lay there now was moss clinging to the dead trunk of a fallen oak. Whatever trail there may have been had gone cold. Stephanus climbed out of the quarry with the others. He pointed his sword briefly at Sextus, then laughed and slammed it into his scabbard. 'All right,' he said in his clipped Latin. 'Let's get you home. I'm not very hungry today, anyway.'

That day of the Sun, Vitalis went to Bishop Dalmatius' church that had once been a temple. The sun was streaming in through the high windows where the statues of Jupiter Highest and Best had once stood and the light flashed on the plain brass cross on the altar.

One by one the celebrants trooped up to the rail, kneeling before the bishop in his tall mitre and snow-white stole, the cope beneath it worked in gold and silver thread. He passed each man, woman and child a goblet etched with the Chi-Rho of the risen Christ and said, in ringing Latin, 'O Lamb of God, that takes away the sins of the world.' The congregation mumbled their responses, in Latin more garbled than his and a priest held up a banner with the Agnus Dei, woven in gold. 'This is the blood of Christ,' Dalmatius boomed. 'Drink this in remembrance of me.'

When everyone who had gone to the high altar had drunk and taken the bread which was the body of Christ and returned to their places, Dalmatius mounted a pulpit set to one side and scanned the upturned faces. Children were told to be quiet and to stand still by parents anxious not to offend either their God or his bishop.

'This,' said Dalmatius, 'is the day of Saint Georgius, who died in the service of the Lord.'

'Praise the Lord!' the congregation boomed. All of them, that is, except Vitalis, who stood at the back, watching the throng of Christians before him.

'He was a soldier,' Dalmatius said, 'whose father was a soldier before him. And he rose to the rank of tribune in the days of Diocletian.' His eyes fell on Vitalis, the same Vitalis who was a child of darkness and whose back still carried the marks of the Mithras whips. 'We have a tribune with us today,' the bishop said, 'in these days of Valentinian.'

All eyes turned to follow the bishop's gaze and Vitalis wanted the ground to swallow him up.

'When Diocletian ordered that all Christians worship pagan idols, Georgius refused. He gave his fortune to the poor and suffered as our Lord suffered, not on the cross of martyrdom but by the pincers and the red-hot iron. He cried to God in his agony to bring down fire and destroy the pagan temple that Diocletian had set up. Just as we destroyed the temple of Mithras that the Evil One allowed to exist in our midst.'

His voice was raising in a relentless crescendo. 'They cut off the head of the tribune Georgius,' he screamed, 'as we cut off the head of their bull. So the enemies of Christ shall be scattered and He will triumph.' He waited until his fiery words had sunk into the brain of everyone there, then, with calm restored, he raised his hand and blessed the congregation. 'Go in peace,' he said, 'with the kiss.'

And each man, woman and child turned to the one next to him and kissed him.

Next to Vitalis stood a young man about his own age. He leaned across and kissed the tribune on the cheek. He whispered in his ear, 'It's about now,' he said, 'that the candles go out and we all fall on each other, in an abomination of incest. Isn't that what you pagans believe?'

'Us pagans?' Vitalis frowned as the congregation filed out, careful to leave their donations in the cup of the attendant by the door.

The young man smiled. 'My name is Pelagius,' he said. 'Have you got a minute?'

Stephanus threw the silvered helmet down on Count Thoedosius' desk. It rolled so that it seemed the face was looking up at him, chilling and deadly.

'A child found it,' the cavalryman said, easing off his boots after the long ride. 'Near a dead body.'

The Theodosii, father and son, looked at each other. 'This body,' the younger man said. 'Could it be our friend?'

'Valentinus?' Stephanus grunted, squeezing his toes. 'It's possible.'

'No, no, wait a minute,' the Count was thinking this through. 'Theo, have you come across a war band, any that he might have ridden with?'

'Where was this, Stephanus?' Theodosius asked.

'On the road to Verulamium,' the German crossed to the Count's wall map, the one superimposed on a pastoral scene that was once Julius Longinus' pride and joy. 'About ...' he found the approximate spot and fixed it with a finger, 'here.'

'No,' Theodosius shook his head. 'I came across a little trouble further south than that, along the Thamesis. Stephanus, you were with me.'

The cavalryman nodded. 'They were locals,' he said, 'cashing in on the situation.'

'We hanged them, anyway,' Theodosius remembered.

'And the last serious clash I had,' the Count said, 'was shortly after the Ides of Ianurarius, due north in Trinovantes territory. I certainly didn't see this,' he picked up the helmet, as though somehow by looking at it and handling it, he could see the face of Valentinus peering out of the eyeholes at him. 'It's like a play, isn't it?' he said, half to himself. 'A tragedy by Pacuvius perhaps. The man's an actor and a bloody good one, always hiding behind his mask. What does he want us to think now; that he's dead and we can all go home?'

'It's a ruse,' Theodosius said. 'It's got to be.'

'What if it's not?' Stephanus asked. He crossed back to his masters and sat forward in his chair. 'What if he's finished, not actually dead, but beaten? We've all faced barbarians before. We know they can't hold a field for ever. Over winter his men will have had a chance to think; to wonder. There's no more booty, no more loot. The villas have been plundered and the towns are too strong. What about the wife? What about the children? They'll leave, desert him in numbers.'

There was a silence. 'I hope to whatever gods the three of us believe in that you're right, Stephanus,' the Count said. 'And time will tell. If we hear of no more attacks in the coming weeks, with spring upon us, we can assume that the owner of *that*,' he pointed to the helmet, 'has indeed given up the ghost. In the meantime, Theo, get a rider off to Maximus. Tell him what we've found. See if he can shed any light.'

'How did you know I was a pagan?' Vitalis asked again. He was walking through the market place with the strange young man who had given him the kiss of Christ in the church. The stalls were doing a roaring trade for all it was the Christian Sabbath; lambs bleating in their pens, ducks quacking and hens fluttering. There were skins for sale, tooled leather, aprons, pots and pans. Samian ware from Gaul and German trinkets carved in dark wood. The city that would one day rival Rome was on its way.

'The responses,' Pelagius told him. 'You didn't join in. So, unless you're deaf, you're an unbeliever.'

Vitalis caught the man's sleeve. 'Where are you from?' he asked. 'I can't place the accent.'

'Hibernia,' Pelagius said. 'To the west at the edge of the world.'

'Attacotti,' Vitalis said, stone-faced.

Pelagius frowned. 'Those godless bastards? No, I've nothing to do with them. Why were you at our church, tribune?'

'Let's just say I was intrigued,' Vitalis murmured.

Pelagius looked hard into the man's eyes. The tribune had a strong face, but there was pain there; and loss and bewilderment. 'If you took off your tunic,' he said, 'would I find whip scars on your back?'

Vitalis blinked. Pelagius smiled.

'You are a child of the darkness,' the Hibernian said. 'I am a child of the light.' And he walked on.

Vitalis caught up with him, half stumbling over a stand of pots in front of a stall. 'You're very sure of yourself,' he said.

'Of course I am,' Pelagius smiled. 'All you can see is me. But I know the Lord Jesus is walking with us.' He looked around at the screaming, cackling market and the flash of coins changing hands. 'And that's a comfort, believe me.'

'You go along with all that rubbish of the Bishop?' Vitalis asked.

Pelagius stopped by the conduit that brought drinking water from the river and took a swig from a gourd hanging there. 'No,' he said, wiping his mouth on his sleeve. 'Not all of it. Dalmatius would have us believe that we are all sinners – it has been that way since the Fall.'

'The Fall?' Vitalis was confused.

'Drink, tribune?' he offered him the gourd. Vitalis shook his head and the Christian poured the water away. 'There,' he said. 'That's where the Bishop and I disagree.'

'I don't understand,' the tribune frowned.

'You chose not to drink, yes? That was your free will?'

Vitalis still looked doubtful. 'Yes.'

'Dalmatius won't have that. Since the serpent tempted Eve, and she in turn tempted Adam, we are all born sinners. Only the Lord can save us, at the end of time.'

'And you don't believe that?'

'That the Lord can save us, yes, but not the rest. We all have choices to make; places where the road diverges and we must choose one path. I chose the way to my God; you chose the army and, I am guessing, Mithras. Look there,' Pelagius pointed to a baby suckling his mother's breast alongside a market stall. 'There is one of Dalmatius' sinners.' The man winked and nudged Vitalis. 'You can tell he's evil incarnate, can't you?'

'That's rubbish,' Vitalis said.

'Exactly,' Pelagius walked on.

'It's all rubbish.'

'Ah.' Pelagius stopped. 'Not all, Vitalis. Some of it is quite profound. Some of it is the truth.'

Vitalis stood and watched the man go. He had a strange sense of calm about him, almost of peace. And the tribune had never seen that in a man before. At the corner of the market square, just where dark alleyways led to the sunlight, Pelagius turned. 'Will we see you in our church again?' he asked.

'No,' Vitalis said quickly. 'No, you won't.'

North of the river, beyond the city's eastern wall where Theodosius' new towers were all but complete, the forest was thick and dark. For all it was Iunius by now, the sun only dappled through the green canopy of the oak and the ash here and there, creating little circles of light in the gloom.

Over the past few weeks this had become the haunt of the Black Knives. They preyed on travellers from Caesaromagnus and Camulodunum further north, the merchants passing through the territory of the still-peaceful Trinovantes to the hub of the universe that was Londinium. Leocadius visited when he could because they had set up a permanent camp, a cluster of thatched huts past which a stream ran. They fished in the Thamesis but those men were not hunters. They had all been born in the city and their fathers before them and they found the country strange and wild. The alleyways were their hunting ground, the quiet courts after dark and the rat-infested wharves. They took turns to camp out here in the wilderness, never more than six of them and they brought their women and children with them.

This morning, Paulinus Hupo had turned up to watch his tame tribune put the Knives through their paces. He stayed back in the trees for a while, leaning on the neck of his horse and watching the display.

'Right, Lucius,' Leocadius said. 'One more time, then. I am a citizen ... er ... a dealer in wines, say. I'm carrying a purseful of silver because I've just done a deal at the quayside. What do you do?'

'I stop you.' Lucius was not the sharpest of the Black Knives, but he showed some promise.

'Where will you do this?'

'Er ... somewhere dark.'

'Good, good,' Leocadius was watching the others to make sure they were watching him. 'Right. Here I am. I have unwisely left the Via Principalis and I'm plodding on, minding my own business.'

'Whoa!' Lucius slammed the flat of his hand into the tribune's chest.

'No, no, not yet,' Leocadius said. 'What do we always do first?'

'Um ... oh, check the road.'

'Do it, then.'

Lucius looked backwards and forwards along the dark alleyway of his imagination. 'All clear,' he said cheerfully.

'Right.'

'Whoa!' he slapped his hand against Leocadius' chest again, but this time, the tribune grabbed his wrist, wrenched it hard behind the man's back and kicked his legs away from under him.

'And if you do that,' Leocadius said, 'three things will happen. One, you will have got nothing from your unwary traveller. Two, he may have broken your arm. And three, he might well decide to cut your throat as you're lying there, just for annoying him.' He hauled the man upright. 'Now, we'll do it again. And this time don't touch me.'

Lucius pulled his tunic into place and cleared his throat. 'Whoa!' he said, keeping well out of the tribune's reach.

'Yes?' Leocadius put on a silly, middle-aged merchant sort of voice which had the others sniggering.

'I want your purse,' Lucius said.

'You can't have it,' Leocadius was staying in character.

'Then I'll have to take it,' the lout said and made a grab for it. The tribune whirled away like a dancer in the arena and Lucius missed. He straightened and tried again and again Leocadius darted to one side.

'Let me try,' a voice grunted from the trees. It was Gillo, the man whose arm Leocadius had ripped the first time he was introduced to Paulinus Hupo. He had not attended these sessions before but he had heard all about them from the others and he was not sure he approved. From his hiding place in the trees, Hupo sat upright. He was about to ride forward, put a stop to this nonsense, when something made him hang back.

Lucius got out of the way, vowing to work on his technique and Gillo stood in front of Leocadius. He was half a head taller, with massive shoulders and brawny arms. And he was swaying from side to side, ready to pounce whichever way Leocadius ran.

'I'll take the purse, tribune,' he growled, 'but first I'll take the dagger.'

Leocadius' left hand flashed under the mock sagum he was wearing in his role as the merchant and his knife hissed through the air. The blade thudded into Gillo's right shoulder and he staggered back two or three paces, clutching at the air with his good hand as blood spurted down his sleeve.

'You bastard!' he hissed, more in disbelief than pain. Leocadius had crossed the space between them in two strides and gripped the knife hilt. 'Now,' he said, looking Gillo in the face, 'Either I take this out or I push it in further. Either way it's going to hurt like hell and you may never use that arm again. Of course, if I push it in, you'll probably bleed to death anyway. Oh, and by the way, you haven't got my purse yet.'

'All right!' a voice bellowed from the trees. 'That's enough.'

Paulinus Hupo walked his horse into the clearing and swung out of the saddle. He pushed past Leocadius and wrenched the knife out of Gillo's shoulder. The man winced and grunted and had to be steadied by the others. 'Get that cleaned up,' he barked, 'and get him back to the city. It'll need stitches.'

He looked at Leocadius. Then he swung an arm around the man's shoulder and handed him his dagger, pommel first. 'Let's have a chat, Leo,' and he took him off into the forest.

Here, out of sight and earshot of the others, Hupo hauled a wineskin off his shoulder and took a swig before passing it to Leocadius. He smiled. 'I knew I'd made the right decision,' he said.

'About what?' the tribune asked.

'About you,' Hupo sat down on a treestump. 'You actually *like* hurting people, don't you?'

Leocadius shrugged. 'It goes with the territory,' he said.

'Perhaps. Perhaps not,' Hupo said. 'I know tribunes who have never drawn a sword in anger.'

'Ah, yes,' Leocadius smiled, taking another swig, 'But they weren't heroes of the Wall, were they?'

Hupo's laugh was bitter. 'You know he let you all live, don't you?' he said, the smile fading.

'Who?' Leocadius asked.

'The man with the silver helmet.'

'Valentinus?' the tribune frowned. 'What do you know of him?'

'Only what I hear on the streets,' Hupo shrugged. 'I'm just a

191

general dealer, remember.'

'General dealer, my arse!' Leocadius growled. He took a step towards Hupo. 'If you know something ...'

The leader of the Black Knives held up his hand. 'You're not going to throw your dagger at me, are you, Leo?' he chuckled. 'That would be very unwise.'

'What do you know of Valentinus?' Leocadius asked again, his eyes flashing fire.

Hupo saw that look and read it well. 'You really want him, don't you?' he said. 'Old scores, eh?'

'You could say that,' the tribune said. A wind suddenly blew through Leocadius' soul. For a moment he was back again on the windswept, barren moors with the rooks and the ravens for company and corpses burning on the Wall.

'I may be able to help,' Hupo said.

'How?'

The general dealer shrugged. 'A lot of tittle-tattle comes my way, Leo, from travellers in the tabernae, sailors on ships. Oh, most of it is inconsequential rubbish, but just occasionally, there are nuggets of pure gold. Your man could be dead.'

'Valentinus? Dead?'

'You know about that helmet they found?' Hupo checked.

'Yes,' Leocadius nodded. 'I've even seen it. They keep the bloody thing at the governor's palace like some damned Celtic talisman.'

'So do you think he's dead?'

Leocadius thought for a moment. 'I'd want to see his corpse myself,' he said. 'A big man, on a black horse, they say.'

Hupo snorted. 'They also say my city was founded by Aeneas, the hero of Troy. Pure bollocks.'

'So how do you know about Valentinus?' Leocadius persisted.

'I don't,' Hupo shrugged. 'At least, not yet. But I know people who know people. I'll get back to you, I promise.'

'Marvellous!' Leocadius took another swig of wine.

'In the meantime, did I tell you that, I have even bigger plans – Aedile for life.'

'Aedile?' Leocadius frowned.

'Yes,' Hupo smiled. 'I run the Games. The arena. The place where they kill people. Interested?'

CHAPTER XV

Valentia, Ver, in the Year of the Christ 370

Justinus knew he should not have ridden out onto the moors alone but he also knew he had no choice. A slow spring was coming to the north, the streams running free of ice and snow and babbling a welcome of sorts as his horse padded over the heather.

The Jovii and the Victores, under the watchful eye of the engineer Rutilius, had rebuilt the Wall from Arbeia to Camboglanna, deepening ditches, piling stones, lashing palisades to a double thickness. Where there had been one platform for a wild ass, there were now two and every fort had its ballistae, every milecastle its beacon. Lovingly, the legions had restored the graveyards to the south and where they found bones, they gave them a decent burial. And they rebuilt the shrines as they found them – the temples of Oceanus and Neptune at Pons Aelius; Atrenocitus at Condercum; the Mithraeum at Brocolitia; and the grave of the greatest hero of them all, the centurion Lucius Castus of the VIth Victrix, who had lived and died defending Vindovala.

Milestones were hauled upright and resunk into the clay. The building of the towns and villas to the south would take longer, although the townsfolk themselves were already at work on them, putting up new roofs, re-glazing windows, hacking down trees for the framework of buildings. The north was Roman again. And of Valentinus there was no sign.

Justinus reined in his horse north of Camboglanna. There the Jovii had established themselves, but the little town that led to the river had no families yet. This legion was a field army. It was up to General Maximus if they left or if they stayed. Their wives and children were far away in all the wide reaches of the Empire.

Justinus was back where all this had started, as it seemed to him, so long ago, looking at the overgrown ruins of Banna. The outlying forts to the north, in the Selgovae country that had once been Valentia, had not been rebuilt yet. Justinus was the last Roman to leave this place alive and now he was the first one to return. He half expected to see the grisly corpse of Ulpius Piso, the first centurion, spread-eagled above the tower wall. All he saw now was grass and weeds sprouting in every corner. And he heard the wind, that damned wind that moaned and sang along the Wall.

He dismounted and looped the reins to a milestone, half sunk in the grass. He wandered into the courtyard with its crumbling, shattered stones and remembered the dead who had lain there; Clitus the Hand player, Drusus with his easy laugh, Lucullus the eagle-eyed. He saw their faces, a deathly white with eyeless sockets that stared at him and gaping mouths that seemed to say 'Where have you been? What kept you so long?'

He shook himself free of it and climbed to the top of the tower. The land stretched into the distance with the pale purple mountains of Caledonia fading into cloud as far as his eyes could see. Some movement caught his eye. Far below him, a stag and his does were moving over the heather, silent and free. There were no hunters here; no ravens wheeling in the sky.

Justinus clattered down the steps and reached into his saddle-bag. He pulled out the phalera, the Medusa's head he had once taken from the breastplate of Ulpius Piso and he buried it in the good earth, murmuring the old words, 'Mithras, also a soldier, teach me to die aright.' Almost without conscious thought, he pulled the black ring from his finger and dropped it into the hole with the Medusa. It lay there, a black hole into his past, pulling the brightness of the silver into its heart. He crumbled some earth over it, and the image faded. Then he realised the past could not be buried so easily. And scarcely looking at the ring, he snatched it up and replaced it on his finger.. He brushed the soil over the head until it was covered, patted the surface flat and strode to his horse. He did not look back.

'You sent for me, sir,' Justinus saluted in the general's tent on the slope before Camboglanna. The fort was finished but there were far too many men to be accommodated within the stone and earth perimeter so the leather tents stretched over to the river bank.

Maximus' dog looked up from his morning nap and sniffed the air. He knew the smell of this one and went back to sleep with an approving whiffle.

'A message from Theodosius,' Maximus sat in front of his campaign table, the heavy one it took four slaves to carry. He was waving a piece of parchment, 'We're going to set up Valentia again.'

'Valentia?' Justinus smiled. 'That would be good. Just like old times.'

'Only more so,' Maximus got up and stood at the tent entrance looking up to Rutilius' new tower. 'It'll be a client kingdom again. The Votadini, the Selgovae. We'll draw up a new treaty with them. In the meantime, you're in command along the Wall.'

'Sir?' Justinus was astonished. Two summers ago he had been a circitor, with twenty men under him; now he led two legions.

Maximus read the man's face. 'Oh, I know you don't have seniority,' he said, turning back to face the tribune, 'and there are many good men I could give the job to. But you know the Wall, Justinus. You speak native and you have a feel for the country. You'll have Paternus with you.' He closed to the man until their noses almost touched, 'And this time, hero of the Wall, you'll hold it.'

Justinus said nothing. Ever since the stupid bragging of Leocadius, all four of them had been haunted by this. It was something the tribune would have to live with. 'Where will you be?' he asked.

'This will only work if the VIth can man the Wall again,' the general told him. 'My legions won't be here forever. I'm going to Eboracum to see the Praeses. If that man is looking for an early retirement, he can forget it.'

While the tribune Justinus doubled the night guard at every fort and milecastle and kept four cohorts with him at Camboglanna, Magnus Maximus took a turmae of cavalry and rode south, the mastiff plodding along at his horse's side, sniffing the ground and cocking his leg all over the territory of the Brigantes. It was four days' ride to Eboracum and Maximus did it in three, his lathered horses wheezing their way towards the north wall of the city and the camp of the VI Victrix.

The Praeses Decius Ammianus was glad to see the general, for all he was not overfond, and shook the man's hand heartily. Maximus had kept him informed of progress along the Wall but even so, Ammianus had not relaxed or lowered his guard. There were patrols night and day, riding out in the noonday sun and every phase of the moon, quartering from east to west, south to north, keeping the Praeses informed. And still no strangers were allowed into the camp, the canabae or the colonia. Eboracum was still a military base under siege.

After the officers had held their discussions and pored over their maps, a clerk inking in the re-occupied forts as they spoke, it was time for a bath and a change for dinner. Timing meant they had missed the late afternoon cena, so it was supper instead. Augusta Ammianus purred over the handsome general, who seemed to be even more rugged after his campaign in the north. But one who was not purring was Lavinia, the Praeses' daughter. She entered the room on the arm of a civilian, and she wore the robes of a matron.

'Allow me to introduce,' Ammianus beamed, 'my son-in-law, Marcellus Musa – General Magnus Maximus.' The men shook hands, but it was Lavinia who Maximus was looking at as he went on looking at her throughout the meal. There was small talk and there were speeches and then the party broke up. Not however before Maximus managed to catch Lavinia alone. The girl, it was true, was two years older than when they had last met and the silly little girl with the fluttering heart had become a woman, cold and aloof.

'Not a soldier, then, your husband?' he murmured as they found themselves together in the atrium of Ammianus' private quarters.

'No,' she said, not looking him in the face. 'He owns half the colonia and his money comes from wool. Not, sir, that it is any business of yours.'

Maximus smiled. And he thought of what might have been. And what was. Lavinia was not the first girl to wave a teary goodbye to him on his way to the war. She would not be the last. He reached inside his tunic and pulled out a crumpled love-knot, made from the reeds of the Ussos. One end of it was brown with somebody else's blood and he took her hand and pressed it into her palm. 'It kept me safe,' he said. 'Thank you.'

She turned and swept away. And he did not see her tears

start to flow.

'A marriage?' Paternus frowned. He was standing in the barrack block at Aesica, duties over for the day and he was unbuckling his armour.

'Best way, Maximus says, to cement an alliance,' Justinus explained.

'Why me?' Paternus asked. 'Doesn't he know about my family?'

'He knows,' Justinus told him. 'But he's looking at the bigger picture.'

'Bollocks to the bigger picture.'

Justinus took his old friend firmly by the shoulders, the Wall ring glinting in the candlelight. 'Pat, I saw the way she looked at you,' he said. 'The woman loves you.'

Paternus said nothing, then, 'I *am* grateful to her; she saved my life.'

'This isn't about feelings,' Justinus said. 'It's about politics. It happens every day, all over the Empire. Money marries money. Senators get their ends away with other senators' daughters. It's the way of the world. You don't have to love her. You don't even have to stay under the same roof if you don't want to. Maximus says ...'

'Well, you can tell General Maximus he can go to hell!' Paternus yelled.

'Why don't you tell him yourself?' Magnus Maximus strolled into the room and the candles guttered in the wind. There was an awkward silence. The general looked at Justinus. 'I gather that didn't go too well.'

Justinus shrugged.

'All right,' Maximus said. 'Justinus, give us a moment, will you?' When the tribune had gone, the general turned to Paternus. 'I asked him to talk to you first,' he said, his face hard, his eyes cold, 'because he is a friend and I know what you Wall men mean to each other. But if you're not amenable to suggestions, Paternus, then it's simply a matter of obeying orders.'

'There's nothing in the Emperor's Regulations ...' the tribune began.

'Don't talk to me about Regulations,' Maximus snapped. 'I wrote the bloody things! There *are* no regulations about what's happening now, what we're doing here. These are uncharted waters, Paternus, believe me. A year ago we had no forts on the Wall still standing. The Empire was crumbling like old rocks pounded by the sea. There may still be a bastard out there we can't catch and we can't second guess. My job is to rebuild the Wall and hold it, and by Jupiter Highest and Best, that is exactly what I'll do. And if I have to lie, cheat, steal and kill to do it, then so be it. And that includes telling you to marry a queen of the Votadini.'

There was a silence. 'I asked Justinus,' Paternus said, 'and now I'm asking you – why me?'

'You know the woman. I understand she has feelings for you.' Paternus turned away, but Maximus spun him back to face him. 'Do you think you're the only one who's lost a family? The men who died on the Wall, at the mouth of hell, everywhere we've fought Valentinus, they had families too. And what about the villas and the villages these bastards have ransacked?' Maximus let stillness fill the room, then he clapped a hand on Paternus' shoulder. 'Nothing,' he said softly, 'can ever replace your loved ones. And I'm not suggesting that you try. But it's time for healing, Pat. There's been too much blood on the Wall, for too long. You can help put that right. Bury the past as you were never able to bury your family.'

Paternus looked into the general's eyes. Could he read compassion there, after all? Was Sol Invictus smiling down on the two of them as they stood there in the glow of the candles?

They came in all their splendour that Junius, as the Romans further south mowed their hay with their long, sweeping scythes and made sacrifices to Hercules and Fors Fortuna. Their drums announced their coming, marching for the Wall at Aesica. They were the Votadini and the Selgovae, the client tribes of Rome who had come to make their peace with Rome again.

Maximus had no way of knowing how many of these people had remained loyal to Rome or how many of them had fallen to Valentinus' sword or gone over to his promise of silver. But this was a fresh start, a new Wall and a new beginning. The Empire had stood for four hundred years; today was the time to drink to the next four hundred.

The client kings and their huge entourages camped in the open facing the Wall, the sun above the clouds sending huge shadows moving slowly and silently over the tents and horse-lines. Women had built fires and children brought water. The smell of cooking wafted over the Wall and it was not long before the camps merged and Votadini drank with Selgovae and the legions joined in. Little boys ran about with Roman helmets on their heads and tried to lift Roman shields. Market traders set up on the camp's perimeter, rivalling Londinium for the few days they were there, selling skins and piglets in exchange for grain and wine and the ever-welcome hard currency of the Jovii and the Victores.

Lenumio of the Selgovae was in a particularly jovial mood when Magnus Maximus came to see him. He was an old man now, too fond of his wine and too fond of his fish sauce to be much of a general. But in his day, as he kept telling Maximus through the interpreter Justinus, he could have had him and the Count for breakfast. And talking of breakfast, was there any fish sauce in Aesica?

'Paternus.' Brenna, queen of the Votadini, had come with her people too and they had camped alongside the Selgovae and their women nattered like neighbours over a wall and their children kicked around a ball of rags, laughing and hooting with delight.

'Paternus,' she said again. He turned away from watching the children at play and looked at her. The warrior queen he had last seen at the holy pool was gone. Brenna's hair trailed to her waist and her eyes were shining. 'How are you?'

He cleared his throat. 'Well, lady,' he said. 'Thanks to you.'

She smiled and pushed a little boy forward who was trying to hide in her skirt. 'Paternus, this is Taran, my son.'

'Taran?' Paternus had heard that name before.

'Taranis,' she explained. 'Our god of the wheel.'

'Our Jupiter,' he said. 'The sky god.'

'His is a different sky,' she said. 'But it doesn't have to be. Taran, this is Paternus.'

The little boy was perhaps six. He had seen the tribune before, outside a smoky hut near a grove of hanged men but he had no clear memory of it. Helmets frightened him. And snorting horses. And fire. But here was a tall man without armour and he had a kind face. Taran squared his shoulders and walked right up to him, extending his right hand. 'Pleased to meet you, sir,' he said.

Paternus blinked. If Quin were alive, he would be about this boy's age now, practising with a little wooden spatha and learning to throw the legionary's darts. He wanted to kneel down, sweep him up into his arms and bury his face into the boy's neck. But that was not to be. He was not his Quin but a stranger's child. He took the little fingers in his own right hand, careful not to squeeze too hard. 'And you,' he said.

Taran decided he had been brave enough for one day and he dashed off, brushing past his mother to play with the others.

'He'll make a fine king one day,' Paternus said.

'If Rome will let him,' Brenna watched him go.

'Why shouldn't she?' Paternus asked, pouring them both a cup of wine.

A cold smile swept over Brenna's face. 'Oh, Paternus, are any of us free to do what we want? Not so long ago, I had a kingdom, whole and entire. Now my people are frightened. They say Valentinus is dead, yet everyone jumps at the sound of a closing door or the crowing of a cock. She looked at him and moved closer. 'You had a wife and a son ...'

He turned away.

'And now,' she said, taking a deep breath, 'Rome is back and the Wall is manned again ... until the next time.'

He turned back to her. 'Will there be a next time?' he asked her.

'Taranis himself could answer that, but we can't. Not even your General Maximus. Isn't that what this wedding is all about?'

At last she had raised the subject. One of them had to and over the last few days, when they had avoided each other and in the last few moments while they made small talk, it had stood like a ghost between them.

'Brenna ...' he tried to say something.

She closed to him and pressed her fingers to his lips. 'I don't ask you to love me,' she said. 'Not as I love you.'

Paternus looked into those sad, dark eyes. So Justinus had been right and Maximus had been right. He wanted to tell her that it was hopeless, that he would never love another woman, that the spirit of his Flavia would always be there between them. He could not tell her that. He could not tell her anything. In the end, he pulled her to him and held her tight, looking out over the sunlit field where the Votadini and the Selgovae children played; and she buried her face into his chest and cried softly to herself.

'Brings tears to your eyes, doesn't it?' the scruffy little man said, wiping his face with his hare-skin cuffs.

'Dumno!' Justinus turned to see who was talking to him. 'You little shit, I thought you were dead.'

'Me, tribune? Never. My, but they make a handsome couple, don't they?'

Justinus had to agree they did. The wedding of Brenna, queen of the Gododdyn called the Votadini, to Paternus, tribune of the VI Victrix, was happening under a smiling sky, the clouds gone and the crickets, assuming they could be heard under the thud of drums and tabors and crackle of the shell rattles of the children, sang their approval too. The only nod in the direction of Rome was the scarlet awning under which the couples stood. And the wall of shields of the Victores to the west and the Jovii to the east.

The ceremony was taking place on the vallum below the Wall at Aesica, on the lands of the Votadini that were, once again, from today, Valentia, the land of the Emperor Valentinian, all power to him. Brenna wore a long dress of green and gold, the snow white of virginity long behind her. Her veil, of translucent cloth, covered her face and her train was held by a little boy, determined not to stumble or drop the precious load his mother wore. Paternus wore the parade armour of a tribune, the bronze breastplate curved and oiled like muscles and with a scarlet cloak that swept the ground.

Brenna's women, dressed in a simpler version of her robes, formed a circle around the pair and, singing one of their strange songs, of the stream and the heather, they wove white ropes of soft cloth around them both. When they had finished, the music of the harps stopped and Paternus held out his right hand. In a clear voice, he said, 'Hand on my hand in the morning,' and Brenna clasped her fingers to his. 'Hand on my hand in the night' she said.

'Touch to my touch in the dawning,' he chanted.

'Walk with me to the light,' they both intoned, their voices together in the new beginning that was Valentia.

There was an audible 'Aah,' from the crowd, even Dumno and he nudged Justinus again. Then the drums struck up and the ropes were unwound and the time was right for music and dancing and, Lenumio hoped fervently, serious drinking into the night.

'Well, well,' Dumno said, striding alongside Justinus. 'I never thought I'd see the day.'

'It's been a long time coming,' the tribune said. 'What news from you, arcanus?' Justinus picked up a goblet and nodded to Dumno to help himself.

'Well,' the man gulped the wine gratefully. 'It hasn't been easy, I can tell you. I've been in the west for a while.'

'The west?'

'The islands. I thought it would be safer there.'

'Any news of Valentinus?'

'Ah,' Dumno took another quick swig and checked before and behind to make sure the coast was clear. 'Somebody told me he was dead.'

'Really?'

'But then somebody told me he was in Gaul, causing havoc over there.'

'I just wish he was in hell,' Justinus sipped his wine. 'Then he could cause as much havoc as his liked. Excuse me, I must go and congratulate the happy couple.'

But the tribune never reached Brenna and Paternus under their different skies. He was crossing the vallum, weaving in and out of the dancers and the children and the drunks when he stopped dead in his tracks. A tall, dark man was looking at him, blinking in the sunlight. He had a sword at his hip and a goblet in his hand. Justinus was unarmed, but this was no time to let that bother him. He threw his own cup to the ground and made for him, but the man had vanished. A dancer caught him, her hair flying, her breasts bare and she swung him round. No sooner had he extricated himself from her but another one grabbed his hand and rubbed herself sensuously against his groin. He pushed her aside and tried to find his quarry again, only to be offered a goat-skin of wine by a drunk Selgovae. By the time Justinus had shaken him off the tall dark man was no longer at the feast.

The tribune ran up the slope towards the Wall's ramparts. From here he could see the whole field, the rigid lines of the legions broken up now as girls flirted among them and the wine began to flow. Paternus and Brenna sat in the centre under their awning, receiving gifts and donations and fawning speeches from Celt and Roman alike. From this distance, they looked like any other happy couple, married for love.

'Talassio!' Justinus heard the old Roman wedding greeting he had not heard for years as one of the older officers scattered petals over the newly weds.

The fires were still bright over Aesica that night and lovers lay entwined under the stars. The distant guard calls of the Wall watch echoed across Valentia. The muttered curses of the watchers themselves, those who had missed out on the festivities, carried no further than the nearest semisallis, who immediately told the grumblers their fortunes. Horses whinnied and stamped at their tethering ropes and the music had dwindled to a single, lonely harp and the irregular tap of a drunken drum. Away on the edge of the camp, a single voice, plaintive on the evening air, sang a love song which everyone understood, whatever their native tongue. It wove into the brain and told of loss and longing. The lonely felt even lonelier, the loved held their beloved tighter as the song wound to a minor chord and stopped.

Paternus and Brenna lay in their huge tent, her hair still studded with petals. For a while they both lay there, on their backs, staring at the roof-joists overhead. Then she turned to him and ran her fingers over his naked chest. He could feel her breasts pressed against him and her thigh sliding over his.

'I know you cannot love me,' she said, her voice a honeyed whisper in the darkness.

He looked down at her upturned face, earnest, pleading. Then he turned away. It had been a long time since he had lain with a woman and he had never lain with a queen. He was expected to do his duty, not just as a husband but as the living link between Valentia and Rome. He lifted her chin and kissed her full on the lips. She ran her fingers through his hair and he returned her caresses. The ghosts that lay between them never said a word.

'This had better be important, tribune,' Magnus Maximus hauled on his shirt and turned to talk to someone in the inner tent. 'Don't go away. I won't be long.'

Justinus had been on his feet now for hours. Ever since he had seen the man at the wedding, he had been scouring the ground, looking for him. He had seen no one ride away to the north of the Wall and the guard had orders to let no one pass to the south. He had peered into every tent, looked under every market-stall awning and had found nothing.

Maximus splashed his face with cold water and helped himself to a jug of Votadini ale. He did not offer one to Justinus. 'Well?' he snapped. 'I've got a hot woman waiting for me in there. What do you want?'

'Do you believe in ghosts?' Justinus asked him.

Maximus blinked, looking at the beer in case that was responsible. 'Goodnight, Justinus,' and he turned to go.

'No, sir,' the tribune held his sleeve. 'I'm serious.'

The general frowned. 'All right,' he said. 'No, I don't. Now, what is all this nonsense about?'

Justinus paced backwards and forwards in the entranceway. For some time he had been worrying this, wondering how he could put it so that it made any sense at all. 'Earlier,' he said, 'Soon after Paternus made his vows, I saw someone.'

'Anyone in particular?' Maximus asked.

'Artabanus, the arcanus.'

The general blinked. 'No,' he said. 'Meaningless.'

'Artabanus,' Justinus repeated. 'Do you remember the tale Metellus told?'

'Er ... the signifer of the Ala Invicti Britanniciaci? I heard about it, yes.'

'Artabanus was the arcanus, the scout, that rode out with Fullofaudes.'

Maximus shrugged. 'So?'

'So,' Justinus was making his point. 'No one survived. Except Metellus. That was the whole point. Valentinus let him live to carry his tale back to us. *No one else survived.* Yet, earlier today, I saw Artabanus, as clearly as I'm seeing you now.'

'The signifer got it wrong,' Maximus explained it away. ' I heard he went to pieces afterwards.'

'No, sir,' the tribune stood his ground. 'He didn't get it wrong. Do you remember, when we found the mouth of hell?'

'I do,' Maximus nodded.

'A good choice of field, was it, for us, I mean?'

'Decidedly not,' the general said, taking up his ale again. 'The worst possible.'

'What did you put that down to?' Justinus asked.

'Bad luck,' Maximus murmured. 'Or bad generalship. I'd never heard much good of Fullofaudes.'

'What if it was neither?' Justinus said. 'What if Fullofaudes was taken straight there, to the mouth of hell by someone working for Valentinus? Artabanus didn't go down under the dragon standard, he helped to cut it down.'

'I see.' Maximus paused in mid-swig. 'So ...'

'So what if Artabanus has been here all along? Count Theodosius believed there was a spy in Eboracum, didn't he?'

'It seems likely,' Maximus said.

'What if that was Artabanus, sneaking into the colonia, sniffing us out and stirring things up?'

'Do we need these arcani?' the general asked.

'They have their uses,' Justinus had to admit.

'I'm not sure they do. If there are any more of the bastards lying pissed out there by morning, round them up. We'll ask a few questions and tell them their services are no longer required.'

'Magnus ...' a sweet voice wheedled from the inner tent.

'Yes, yes,' the general yawned and drained his cup. 'But before you round up the arcani, Justinus, find yourself a woman, will you? This bloody Wall has taken over your life.'

LIBER III
CHAPTER XVI

Autumnus, in the Year of the Christ 370

The room was silent save for the faint hiss of needles busily employed mending linen and the room was soft with sunlight. The women sat around a low table, with a bowl of olives, slick with oil, some bread and a salty cheese set out for the midday meal. A slave added a plate of smoked fish and a pitcher of wine. The consul's wife set aside her sewing and, leaning forward, began to pile her plate with food. She had been a beautiful and lascivious girl when she had met Julius Longinus, back in the day when he was a thrusting young merchant but now she was fat and lazy with more than a suggestion of a moustache across her lip. She looked up at her daughter, who was still sewing.

'Julia,' she said, in a harsh voice which set the consul's teeth on edge whenever he heard it and made him long for one of Hupo's compliant girls, 'eat.' She filled her mouth with soft cheese and bread as she spoke, reaching out with her free hand as she did so.

Julia put her sewing aside but didn't reach for a plate. She sat back instead and smiled a small smile at her mother. 'I'm not really very hungry, Mama, thank you,' she said. 'I'll have a piece of bread, just to keep you company.'

Her mother looked at her, almost uncomprehending. Matidia Longinus had always had a good appetite. Once it had been for lying with her husband but that had not lasted, to their mutual satisfaction. On the occasions that she felt the need, there was always a slave handy but those times were few and far between. Now, her appetite was for food and that her daughter didn't share her enthusiasm was beyond her. She took another bite.

Julia took a small piece of bread, dipped it in some oil and put it on her plate, untasted. 'I don't feel very hungry most of the time, Mama, if I told you the truth.'

Through a mouthful of bread, Matidia snapped at her child. 'I hope you always tell the truth, Julia. I have brought you up to be honest, at least. Yes.' She nodded complacently to herself, her chins compacting with each move of her head.

Julia took a deep breath. 'I don't want to disappoint you, Mama. I am as truthful as I can be.'

Matidia's little eyes were suddenly piercing. 'Do you have something to tell me, Julia? Nothing to upset me, I hope. You know my health is not good.' She put a greasy hand to her bosom but she was not built to look frail.

Julia dropped her head and muttered something her mother did not catch.

'What?' the woman grated. 'What was that?'

'I have been ... I have been seeing a man. In my room. At night.'

Matidia had a sudden flash of memory, of her legs squeezed tightly around the young Julius Longinus, of her stifled screams that her mother must not hear. She shook her head and stood up, plates and bread and fish going everywhere. 'You slut!' she screamed. 'If it's that slave ...'

'No, Mama. It is the tribune, Leocadius Honorius.'

Matidia had heard stories about the tribune that did not redound to his credit, but this was not the time. It seemed her daughter may have caught herself a man who was on the rise, just as she had years ago and by a similar method.

'He loves you?'

Julia was startled. It had never been something that she had considered. 'I ... don't know,' she said, finally.

Her mother sat back, legs apart, a meaty hand on each knee. 'You don't know?' she echoed. 'What do you talk about, then, in your room at night?'

'We ...' Julia's voice sank to a whisper. 'We don't seem to

talk much ...'

Her mother leaned forward, her own appetite gone. 'Then ... you are making sure you don't bring disgrace on us, I hope.' Matidia was proud of herself for not grabbing the slut's hair and banging her head on the table. She was behaving as a loving mother should. The screaming could come later.

'I don't know what that means,' Julia said, a tear rolling down her cheek. 'I ... I just let him take me.'

'You didn't sneeze? Use rue? Nothing?' Matidia's voice was rising to a crescendo and outside the door a small gaggle of sniggering slaves was beginning to gather.

'I didn't know any of those things,' Julia was on her feet now, her hands protectively across her belly. 'I am with child. Leocadius' child and I don't know what to do!' She collapsed back on to her couch, curled up and sobbing.

Matidia sighed and helped herself to another piece of cheese. It wasn't how she would have chosen to get a tribune as a son-in-law, but now it was here, it was as good a way as any.

Honoria knocked on the door of her mother's apartment and receiving no reply, opened it and peeped round into the room. It was dark, despite the sun outside, the small, high window being draped with gauze. As her eyes adjusted, she saw that the bed was occupied and withdrew her head. Before she had quite closed it, she heard her mother call.

'Honoria? Is that you?'

'Yes, Mama.' She waited with her ear to the gap.

'Wait a moment, darling. I won't be long.' Her mother's voice was always full of laughter and this was no exception. She heard her say, in honeyed tones, 'You won't be long, will you?' Her question was answered by a grunt. Then another and another. Her mother spoke again, a congratulatory note in her voice this time. 'Well done, Plautius. I knew we'd get there in the end. Just leave the money on the dish by the door as usual and tell my daughter to come in as you leave.'

The door swung open and a merchant Honoria knew well as a customer of Hupo's slunk out, holding the brim of his straw hat well down over his face. Honoria called a greeting, but just got yet another grunt in reply. She pushed open the door and went over to the window to pull aside the gauze. Her mother sat up in the bed and patted the edge of it for her to sit.

'I need to talk to you, Mama,' Honoria said.

'Will it take long?' her mother said.

'Do you have another caller expected?' Honoria asked, looking round at the door.

The woman smiled. She looked scarcely old enough to be out by herself, let alone be Honoria's mother. Partly this was because she was adept with makeup, partly it was because she was beautiful to start with and partly because she had had Honoria when she was only fourteen. 'No, darling,' she said, patting her daughter's knee. 'When old Plautius is my customer, I always give him the whole day. He sometimes takes a while.'

The women laughed. Honoria had not had the pleasure herself, if that was the word, but Plautius did not have a high reputation amongst Hupo's girls.

'No, I just need to ... well, I don't need to tell you, dear. Wash. You don't want a little brother or sister, now, do you?'

Honoria looked at her mother. 'No,' she said. 'How do you feel about a little granddaughter or grandson?'

Her mother leaned back on the pillows and looked long and hard at her daughter. This had been a good while coming. The girl had been in Hupo's household these five years now and she knew she had been giving herself for free for years before that. She smiled and held the girl's hand.

'I hope the little bastard has got a rich papa,' she said. 'Anyone I know?'

'I haven't decided yet,' Honoria said, with a smile.

'If it's the tribune, take care,' her mother said. 'If it's Hupo ... well, you could do worse. He has no other bastards that I know of.'

'I'll see,' Honoria said.

Her mother swung her legs out of bed and walked away from her daughter, reaching for her sponge. 'Off you go, darling,' she said, rolling up her gown. 'Mama is busy.'

She didn't turn as her daughter softly closed the door. Both women would have been surprised to see the tears on the other's cheek.

Decius Critus sat in the darkness of the Mithraeum that night. The prayers had been said and the blood had been spilled. 'We haven't seen you, Vitalis,' he said to the man sitting next to him, watching the candlelight flicker between the horns of the great bull.

'No,' said the tribune. 'Affairs of state.'

'The Christian calendar,' Critus said. 'Their ceremony to mark the resurrection of their Christ ...'

'We missed it,' Vitalis said. 'I sent you word.'

'Yes,' Critus nodded, his eyes closed. 'We got your message. But it changes nothing. That church is an abomination. We can burn it down any time; we don't need to wait for one of their ceremonies.'

'But that's when you'll find most people there.'

'Exactly,' the priest smiled. 'There's not much point in making a protest if there's no one there to see it. If I wanted Dalmatius dead, any one of my people could knife him in some back alley. No, this has to be a celebration of Mithras, a triumph of our god over theirs.' He looked at Vitalis. 'We are in no hurry,' he said. 'The time will come. And I can count on you, Vitalis, can't I? As a true child of the darkness?'

'You can count on me,' Vitalis said.

On the windswept moors north of Aesica, a huddle of peasants stood looking at the line of shields ahead of them and the grim-faced soldiers who held them. General Magnus Maximus was walking his horse to and fro, waiting until the little group was assembled. Then he reined in and spoke loud and clear, Justinus translating his words on the wind.

'You arcani,' he said. 'You secret people; Rome thanks you for your hard work in the past. You have supported us. You have fed us precious pieces of information. You have befriended us against the barbarians.' He watched their faces as Justinus' dialect sank in. The Votadini understood him and the Selgovae. It was the end of an era. 'Now, we have, as you see, a new Wall. And we have a new Rome. There will be peace.' He did not believe it himself, but it sounded impressive there, with the dragon standard snaking in the wind and the Wall high and solid. 'There is silver for each of you. May your gods go with you.'

He wheeled his horse away and the cohorts stood firm until the arcani had broken up and had crossed to the tables where clerks were handing over coins and keeping careful accounts in their ledgers.

Dumno went over to the tribune. 'Io, Justinus,' he said, half-smiling. 'The end of the road, eh?'

Justinus had dismounted and walked along the little track

with the arcanus. The little man looked up at the Wall ramparts. 'I'm going to miss all this, you know,' he sighed.

The tribune laughed. 'You're going to miss our silver, Dumno,' he said. 'Anything else, I'm not so sure.' He stopped and his smile vanished. 'Have you seen Artabanus?' he asked. 'I don't see him here this morning.'

'Artabanus?' Dumno frowned. 'Have you forgotten, sir – he died at the mouth of hell.'

'Did he, Dumno?' Justinus said. 'Did he really?'

And the little man collected his silver and rode away.

Count Theodosius had set up a new camp to the west of the city. He was within half an hour's ride to the west wall, an hour for the marching men. If truth were told, he was tired of Londinium and found himself dreaming more and more of the warm lands of his birth where the orange groves bloomed and the sky was an eternal blue. Here the summer was fading already and he sat on the ramparts as the light dimmed, watching the harvesters carting in their corn, the barley a dull russet where, at home, it would be sparkling gold.

Vitalis found him up here, watching the fishing boats sail upriver to their little jetties beyond the Thamesis' bend. He was wearing his parade armour, the plumed helmet tucked into the crook of his arm and he stood to attention. Theodosius reached across to help himself to more wine. 'Tribune,' he nodded.

'I want to offer my resignation, sir,' Vitalis said.

The Count raised an eyebrow. 'Well,' he sighed. 'No sense in beating about the bush. Thank you for coming to the point. Now ...' he poured another cup for Vitalis and handed it to him. 'Why don't you tell me what all this is about?'

'I ... don't believe I am needed here, sir,' the tribune said. 'We've heard nothing of Valentinus now for months and all seems quiet.'

'It does,' Theodosius had to agree. 'Anxious to get back to the Wall?'

'No,' Vitalis said coldly. 'No, I shall never go back there.'

The Count chuckled. 'I don't think I can promote you any higher, tribune,' he said, 'Wall hero or not.'

'I don't want promotion, Count,' Vitalis said. 'I have other callings now.'

'Indeed?' Theodosius was on his feet, looking into the boy's face, trying to read his mind. Then he sniffed, took a swig of wine and said curtly, 'Well, technically, you're on my son's staff. Have it out with him.'

'Resign?' the younger Theodosius slapped the backside of the slave girl who was lolling on his lap and sent her packing. 'What in God's name for?'

Vitalis had become quite used to visiting the governor's palace. It was always full of officers and merchants and the army of quill pushers who always surrounded a Roman general these days. Occasionally, he saw a harassed-looking consul hurrying towards his litter. The man would nod to him and disappear into the bowels of the city he was trying to run.

'I have my reasons, sir,' the tribune said.

'What are they?'

For a while, Vitalis said nothing. He had rehearsed this moment over and over again in his head and nothing sounded right. 'I am thinking of becoming a Christian,' he said.

Theodosius got to his feet and put down the wine goblet he had been sipping from. His eyes narrowed as he closed to Vitalis. 'I frequent Bishop Dalmatius' church,' he said. 'I've never seen you there.'

'Not that kind of Christianity,' Vitalis said.

'What other kind is there?' Theodosius asked.

'The world is wide,' Vitalis hedged. He had no intention of mentioning the name of Pelagius, the strange young man he had met and could not now forget. 'Didn't Christ tell us to turn the other cheek?' he asked. 'To love our neighbours as ourselves?'

'Your point?' Theodosius arched an eyebrow. A thinking tribune? What was the army coming to?

'I am at present a soldier, sir,' Vitalis said. 'Rome pays me to kill. That cannot be right.'

Theodosius looked at the man, then burst out laughing. 'I am a soldier too, tribune. And I would think no more about killing an enemy than I would swatting a fly.' He was suddenly serious. 'The enemies you kill are the enemies of Christ. Those barbarians are only our neighbours in the sense that we let them live. You have misread the Scriptures.'

'I have never read any Scriptures,' Vitalis admitted.

'Then keep your mouth shut until you have!' Theodosius screamed. He grabbed Vitalis' hand and held up the ring. 'As long as you wear this,' he said, 'you are useful to me and useful to Rome. Will you take it off, throw it to the garbage that infests our market place and watch them kill each other to obtain it?'

Vitalis looked at the ring. He hated it. He hated the lies it stood for. But four other men still wore theirs and he could not break that bond. 'No,' he answered.

Theodosius stepped back, feeling himself vindicated. 'Then your resignation request is denied, tribune,' he said. 'See yourself out.'

If the Wall had been cold once the autumn came, the winds that moaned over Din Paladyr were far worse. The sea here churned grey and misty, spray flying over rocks that desperately tried to hold it back and the roar of the surge echoed far inland.

In the weeks that followed their wedding, Paternus and Brenna had gone north with her people to this ancient hill fort, the largest in the whole of Valentia. Paternus had been made Praefectus Gentium by Maximus, ruling with the queen as Praeses of the area. Most days he kept asking himself how it was that a semisallis of the VIth should have risen so far so quickly. And every day the answer lay on his finger – the Wall ring with its four helmets carved in jet. And most days, too, he would look out from the wind-blown ramparts of the fort to the grim, grey estuary of the [Forth] with the wind chiselling the ridges of the water. To the west Brenna had told him lay the ghosts of the Roman camps that had once been the Antonine Wall, a wall that not even Theodosius and Magnus Maximus could restore, where the spirits of the Wall guardians roamed the heather, seeking peace. The Votadini stayed away from these places and the palisades had long rotted and deer and hares cropped the grass.

To the north lay Caledonia with its terrible, beautiful mountains, a deep purple in summer and lost in the mist by the time Septembris came. There, in the hidden glens and secret valleys, an army may still be hiding and a man called Valentinus, with or without his silver helmet, might yet be biding his time.

Every day he rode out across the heather, half a turmae of cavalry at his back. He was teaching them, slowly, to abandon their hell-for-leather charges and to ride or march in hand, ready for any eventuality. But the Votadini were a wounded people, scarred by their losses to the barbarians and even more by the desertions of men who they believed were family and friends. Learning would take time.

Little Taran rode out with him, a special saddle made to keep the boy safe. His feet did not reach the belly of his pony and the pony only came up to Paternus' chest. While Brenna carried out her duties as queen, dispensing justice and offering prayers to Taranis and Teutates, to the horse goddess Epona and the spirits of the sky, Paternus did his best to train an army.

That evening, as the sun sank low over the stunted oaks and the taller firs moaned in the wind, Paternus wrapped Brenna's boy in his furs and stroked his face. The lad had been gabbling about this and that because it had been an exciting day. He had shot his first grouse with a legionary's dart and he had tussled with the dog to bring it triumphantly back to camp. Then, quite suddenly, he had fallen asleep, just as he had when he was a baby. Paternus looked at him, the shadow of Quin still hovering on the goose-feather pillow.

He felt a hand on his shoulder and Brenna stood there, smiling at them both. 'Pat,' she said. 'There's something I have to tell you. I am with child.'

'You've been avoiding us, tribune,' Pelagius said, smiling at Vitalis over the steam of the Baths. 'I'm crushed.'

There was a time when Vitalis would only use the baths to the north, the one designated for the garrison. Increasingly now he was using the public Baths, where civilians like Pelagius were welcome. Even so, he had not seen Pelagius here before.

'I thought it was time I saw how the other half lived,' he said, soaking in the hot water and watching the steam swirl into patterns in the half light.

'You don't approve?' Vitalis asked.

'What's not to like?' Pelagius chuckled. 'Although I can't see this idea catching on in Hibernia. Tell me, are you still with Mithras?'

Vitalis looked around him. Half the men there were soldiers. Half of those worshipped the dying bull. The other half were probably Christian; it was hard to tell. 'I have not left the Temple,' he said, 'if that is what you mean.'

'I haven't seen you in Dalmatius' church,' Pelagius said.

'I told you I wouldn't be back,' the tribune reminded him.

'Yes, you did,' Pelagius laughed. 'And I didn't believe you.'

'I'm surprised you're still there,' Vitalis said.

'You are? Why?'

The tribune shrugged, sending little ripples of water eddying into the candlelight. 'With your different views on what the Christ intended. You're a damned heretic, Pelagius.'

'I may be,' he said, leaning forward to Vitalis. He suddenly grabbed his hand and pulled it out of the water, looking at the black ring. 'But I, at least, have free will.'

'With child?' Julius Longinus was aghast. He got up and crossed the room in what seemed like a single stride, slapping his daughter across the face so that she staggered backwards and collapsed sobbing on the couch.

'Oh, Julius,' his wife scolded. 'There's no need for that.'

'No need for that?' He looked at Matidia in disbelief. 'No need for that? What are you thinking about? I'm ruined.'

'Ruined?' she repeated, throwing a cloth to her weeping daughter but not taking her eyes off her husband. 'What on earth are *you* thinking about?'

'May I remind you,' Longinus stood upright, 'both of you, that I am Consul here in Londinium? The Count, no less, is my guest ... albeit perhaps a rather long-staying guest. People come to me with their problems. I dispense the law, I arbitrate, I run the Ordo, I ...'

'Yes, yes,' Matidia was almost yawning. 'We know what you do for a living.' Then she flashed a scowl at him. 'And what you do in your spare time.'

He ignored her. 'That a daughter of mine ... I shudder to think what Dalmatius will say about this.'

'Dalmatius?' his wife frowned. 'What has that pederast got to do with it?'

'Pederast?' Longinus repeated. 'No, no. The Bishop is simply celibate. He is married to his church. There's nothing odd about Dalmatius, I assure you. Anyway, you're changing the subject.'

'No, I'm not,' she insisted. 'You brought the degenerate into it.'

'Merely because as a Christian he does not approve of bedroom hanky-panky before marriage.'

'Or after it, it would seem.'

The two had worn themselves out following their usual argument as soon as Dalmatius' name came into it and the only sound in the consul's quarters was the steady sob from their daughter.

'Shut up, Julia!' they chorused, briefly united.

'Well?' Longinus turned on the girl. 'Who is it? Lentulus Marcellus? Proclivius Parbo?'

'For Jupiter's sake, Julius,' Matidia shrieked. 'They're *your* cronies. No girl who wasn't getting paid would be seen dead with them. Tell him, child.'

Julia sat up, sniffing, her eyes red and puffy, her cheek still stinging from her father's slap. 'Leocadius Honorius,' she almost whispered.

'The tribune?' Longinus' eyebrows almost disappeared under his hair. 'Are you mad?'

'Oh, come now, Julius,' his wife stepped in again. 'He *is* rather good looking, in a plebeian sort of way. *And* he's ambitious. *And* he's a hero of the Wall.' She ran through in her mind all the old reprobates who were her husband's friends and counted her daughter lucky.

Longinus dithered, glaring at the two women who were clearly bent on making his life hell. Then he pulled himself up to his full consularly stature and said to the girl, 'Well, you'll have to marry him, Julia. But you'll do it without my blessing and you can't live here. Neither will I have you living in his quarters, like some bloody camp follower. I expect I can find you a small villa on the edge of town somewhere.'

'Oh, papa!' Julia's face broke into a smile.

'Three slaves and that's it. Matidia – you'll have to make all the arrangements, with Honorius, I mean.'

'Don't be ridiculous, Julius,' she snorted. 'Since when was a Roman woman allowed to conduct marriage contracts? Get a message to the man. Tell him you want to see him face to face. It wouldn't hurt to put the fear of the gods into him.'

Count Theodosius sent a message by fast ship to the north. He himself had received an urgent summons from the Emperor. There was trouble in Gaul and now that all seemed quiet in Britannia, could the Theodosii come east? Legions were available; there was no need to abandon the western islands. Why not put Maximus in charge? He was a good man and loyal to his Emperor.

'So Papa Theo's going home. I'm going to miss the old boy,' Maximus was reading the Count's letter and fondling the battered ear of his dog. 'We won't miss the younger one, will we, Bruno, eh?'

He sighed and looked out of the Principia to the deserted parade ground of the VI. 'Dux Britannorum, eh? Well, well, well ...'

Somewhere in the cold of northern Iberia, a white-haired old lady would be very proud of her boy.

'Will you go south, sir?' Justinus asked. 'To Londinium?'

'No, not yet. The forts are all but finished up here, it's true, but the Count seems to have had little trouble in the south. I'd just like to stay up here a while longer. Then we'll see.'

There had never been a farewell like it. The Heruli and the Batavi marched out of the gates of Londinium, over the bridge they had kept so well and made their way east. The cornicines blasted, the drums thundered and the cohorts let rip with the old songs again, songs that died away with their marching boots.

There had been speeches and banquets and the crowds had lined the streets, throwing flowers and trinkets, girls running alongside the soldiers and kissing them for all the world as if they would never see them again. In fact, they were marching to Rutupiae and all of them, except a handful to provide an escort for the Theodosii, were coming back again.

The night before, the Count had said his farewells to Julius Longinus and his perfectly ghastly wife and that sweet daughter of theirs who seemed to have put on some weight. The consul was a happy man once again; happy that is for one who was about to have Leocadius Honorius for a son-in-law. He was about to get his palace back, all of it, and he could stretch and preen and fart to his heart's content. That German fellow ... what was his name? Stephanus? He was in charge of the legions until General Maximus came south. And Stephanus was such a boring bloody soldier, he would stay in the camp to the west. From what Longinus knew of him, the idea of fountains and feather beds and hot and cold running slaves in every room filled him with dread. Longinus had shaken his head. If he wasn't mixing his races too much, these Germanii were so bloody Spartan!

Leocadius unbuckled his helmet once the ceremonies were over. From the Count's new towers, he watched the man's entourage shrink into the distance, until only the scarlet vexillum was visible as a tiny dot of red, like a ladybird in a cornfield.

He wrapped his arm around Honoria, the woman who was carrying his child and kissed her on the forehead.

'Paulinus will be a happy man today,' she said.

'Oh?' Leocadius asked. 'Why?'

'Well, with the Theodosii gone, he can hold those bloody Games he keeps going on about. Hasn't he mentioned them to you?'

'Yes,' Leocadius said. 'Once or twice.'

'Leo,' she looked up at him, her eyes serious for a moment. 'Don't get involved with any of that, will you?'

'The Games?' he laughed. 'What, because they're illegal?'

'No.' She wasn't laughing. 'Because the Games are all about death. And death is Paulinus' stock in trade.'

He fondled her breasts briefly before the patrolling guard swung back towards them. 'See you tonight,' he whispered, 'usual place.'

'Right, Gillo,' Paulinus Hupo sprawled in the atrium of his town house, the one north of the river. 'Take this note to the consul, will you? Tell him it's time we talked Games. Tell him there's a fat little backhander in it for him once he has officially appointed me Aedile. And Gillo,' the man paused in the doorway. 'Dress up, there's a good lad. And be polite. The Longini are quality, after all.'

He downed his wine and straightened his robes. It was time he found Honoria, the woman who was carrying his child.

CHAPTER XVII

Now that the Arcani had gone, melted into the snows of Valentia which lay thick on the land, Magnus Maximus had had to increase his patrols north of the Wall. Rutilius' engineers had worked miracles to rebuild the forts, but the outlying fortlets like Banna would have to wait for another spring.

Justinus' patrol that day was routine like any other. He rode at the head of two turmae, wearing their fur caps now that the Pax Romana had been restored. Their helmets they carried strapped to their saddlebows and their shields hung there too. Flurries of snow were powdering their cloaks and the breath of men and horses snaked out on the frozen air. He had no signifer with him because this was simply a reconnoitring expedition. The last thing Justinus Coelius expected was trouble. Yet there it was, at the river in front of him. Cavalry.

He halted the column and the men huddled closer for warmth. The river itself was still free of ice but everyone knew how cold that water would be. Just wading through it up to the horses' knees could take its toll. Justinus checked the horizon. Nothing. No sign of other units. No one lurking in the forests ready to spring an ambush. Just a handful of cavalrymen letting their horses drink.

He called his decurion to him. 'What do you make of them, Labienus?'

'They're ours, sir,' the young man said after a few minutes squinting against the glare of the snow.

'That's what I thought,' Justinus nodded. 'But what the hell are they doing there?'

'Shall I find out, sir?' the keen young man asked. Justinus

looked at him. He was not that much younger than the tribune but he had come with the Jovii from Gaul and had never seen the Wall until a few weeks ago. And the Wall was covered in the blood of men like Labianus.

'No,' Justinus said. 'We all will. Skirmish order.' The command was not shouted and the trumpeter kept his cornicen strapped across his body. The Ala Jovii drew their swords as one, but slowly, as though they were advancing on a doe by a water hole and were anxious not to surprise her.

It took a few moments, but the disoriented riders at the water's edge seemed to panic when the lines of the Jovii trotted forward out of the mist. Their hooves padded softly on the snow and it was only the whinny and snort that gave the advance away.

'Io, circitor!' Justinus shouted to the shaven-headed man trying to calm his bay. The man snapped something to the men nearest to him and they all came to attention. Those who had already mounted, sprang down again from the saddle and stood to their horses.

'Who are you?' Justinus asked as his horse's hooves splashed through the shallows on his side of the river.

'Second Augusta, sir,' the circitor said, smiling. 'We're a bit lost, I'm afraid.'

'Second Augusta?' the tribune replied. 'Lost indeed. I thought your men were based in the south west - Isca Dumnoniorum?'

'That's right, sir,' the circitor called back. 'We got cut off with Count Nectaridus. Butchered, he was, with most of his command.'

'Where was this?'

The circitor turned to the man next to him. 'Oh, now you've asked me, sir,' he grinned. 'I don't rightly know.'

Justinus looked harder at the man in front of him. All vestige of uniform had gone from this unit now and they were wrapped in hare and squirrel fur. Here and there a Pictish axe gleamed at a saddlebow.

'Trophies of war?' Justinus asked.

The circitor followed the tribune's gaze. 'Oh, them. Well, you know how it is, sir. You pick up what you can.'

'Indeed you do,' Justinus' smile was as icy as the ground. 'Especially when you're four hundred and fifty miles from home, give or take a yard and you can't remember where the Count of the

Saxon Shore was butchered, when you were, I presume, standing alongside him.'

'I ...' the circitor was fast running out of ideas.

'Especially when some of the things you picked up are the horses of the VI Victrix from Vinovia. I'd know that brand anywhere.'

The circitor squinted at the tribune's face under his fur cap. 'Justinus Coelius? Is that you?'

'It is, Malo. And don't feel badly about it. I didn't recognize you, either.'

Malo licked his lips, cracked and salty in the cold. 'I heard you'd been promoted,' he said. 'You're a tribune now, eh?'

Justinus nodded coldly. 'And you're a damned deserter,' he growled.

All hell broke loose. A dart hissed from behind a shield to thud into the prong of Justinus' saddle and his horse shied to the right, caracoling back from the water's edge.

'Horse archers!' he heard the decurion yell on the slope behind him and the shafts hissed over his head to thump into the milling mass of men and horses on the far bank.

Justinus knew he had to hurry. He had caught the deserters unprepared, in open country, but once they were mounted, it might take him all day to hunt them down and night was never far away at this time of the year. 'Turmae,' he bellowed. 'Charge!'

There was no time for the parade ground niceties, the formal walk, march, trot of General Maximus' handbooks. Justinus whipped free his sword and steadied his nervy animal until the front rank were crashing at the gallop through the shallows. Then he rammed his heels home and charged with them. Helmets still dangled uselessly from harness, shields stayed where they were. The cavalry were just swordsmen now, hacking and scything at the men trying to mount. The horse archers could not fire for fear of hitting their own men.

It was all over in minutes, the deserters showing their colours again and throwing their weapons away. If Justinus had had the VIth with him, he knew that that would be their last action, but the Jovii had lost no-one on the Wall and Mars Ultor did not ride with them that day. One horseman, however, had mounted and was making a break to the north-east, his body low over his horse's back to make himself less of a target.

Justinus had reined his own mount in and he yelled up the

slope, 'Semisallis Porsena?'

'Sir?' the horse archer urged his horse forward.

'See that rider galloping to your right?'

'Yes, sir.'

'See if you can hit a horse's arse at sixty paces.'

It *was* a long shot; there was no doubt of that, but if any man in the turmae could do it, it was Octavius Porsena. He gripped his animal's barrel with his thighs and drew the bowstring back to his lips, kissing it briefly before the shaft sang on the air. There was a whinny of agony as the galloping horse staggered a few paces, then went down, screaming and kicking as the arrow point inflamed every nerve in its body.

Justinus was impressed, but he would never let Porsena know that. He kicked his horse forward, out of the river, icy water pouring down from his boots and the sodden fringes of his cloak. The deserter had fought his way from under the wriggling, shrieking animal and was dashing across the snow, but the drifts were too deep and he stumbled. Justinus wheeled his horse in front of him, then swung the animal round as the deserter tried to double back. Whichever way he floundered, he was facing a tribune of the VI. He was facing a hero of the Wall.

At last, exhausted and his lungs in agony, he stood still, his sword still in his right hand, his left clutching his side in pain. Then he straightened. Whatever fight the others had shown initially had left them and they were being rounded up and herded up the hillside, dragging their stolen horses with them. A body, weeping blood in the weeds, floated downstream. The deserter threw his sword into the snow where it all but disappeared.

'Go on, Artabanus,' Justinus said, grim-faced, 'Pick the sword up again. Give me a reason to kill you.' Two of the Jovii had reached the fugitive arcanus and dragged him away. Justinus swung out of the saddle and picked up the sword. It was a Saxon weapon, heavy but sharp along one side. Civilized men did not fight with anything like that. But as he looked at it, reflecting the glow of the snow in the metal, he wondered how many Romans had gone down before it and whether it had flicked out the eyes of Fullofaudes as a choice morsel for the Attacotti.

'None of those bastards rides!' Justinus shouted. 'Tie them to your horses' tails. We'll make them eat snow all the way back to Aesica. Decurion?'

'Sir?'

'You will have the pleasure of returning these horses to Vinovia. Take five men. I expect them there by tomorrow night.'

'Very good, sir.' He was even beginning to sound like Magnus Maximus.

The garden of the consul's palace had never looked so beautiful, smelled so aromatically of the afternoon's burning leaves, been so loud with the song of autumn's last nightingale. Julius Longinus leaned back against the wall in his favourite quiet corner and breathed in, knowing that the air he breathed was his again, now that the Theodosii had really gone. If it hadn't been for this other business, he could be quite happy, he thought. His wife all a-twitter at the impending grandchild, a nice warm woman waiting for him in his chamber in the basilica, a goblet of wine by her side.

'Papa?' His daughter's voice broke into his thought. 'He's here somewhere,' he heard her say.

He pushed on his knees and stood up, emerging from his hiding place. 'Is it time?'

'The priest is here, Papa,' she said.

Ah, yes, the priest. But which one? Matidia had insisted on a sacerdos of Minerva as well as Dalmatius' church. She had taken to paying great attention to signs and portents as Julia's belly grew and she was making sure she offended no one, god or man.

He extended his arm and Julia nestled beneath it, just as she had when she was a little girl. He kissed the top of her head. Suddenly, foreboding swept through him like a wave of ice. 'Julia,' he said, quietly, 'are you sure ...?'

'Papa,' she said, turning her head. 'Leocadius is a tribune. He is an important man. A hero of the Wall.' It took a *very* important man to impress the consul.

'Does he love you? Do you love him?'

For reply, she swept her hand over her swollen belly, smoothing the gown around it. It was a little late for love, now. The priests were here, the Christian and the pagan, eyeing each other suspiciously. The few guests gathered closely, trying to make light of an awkward situation. It was time to step up and marry this man she hardly knew, the profile against the dim window in the dark of her room, the urgent hands pressing her against the bed. She shivered and stepped forward.

Leocadius stood back in the doorway to the garden, looking at the little group assembled under the lanterns under the trees. He had always known this day would come, that he would marry, but he had always thought it would be another day. A far future day. And, though no romantic, he had assumed he would love his wife. He wondered as he stood there whether he even liked this girl. He turned to Vitalis, standing at his shoulder and tried a smile.

'Well, Vit,' he said, his voice coming out more huskily than he intended. 'Let's do this thing, eh? We are heroes of the Wall. Surely I can get married without my knees knocking.'

Vitalis didn't smile back. He too had always known that Leo would be caught one day although he had always expected that it would be by the knife point of an angry husband. Marriage to the consul's daughter seemed to be too good for him, in his opinion. The priest from Dalmatius' church was looking over the bride's head into the darkness and catching the gleam of Leocadius' lorica gestured impatiently and the two men walked forward to join the others.

Matidia, baulked of the full wedding ceremony by Longinus' political necessity of placating the Christians, had nevertheless made sure that Julia wore the flame coloured veil, the very one she herself had worn at her wedding to Julius and which she had kept in her cedar chest ever since, waiting for this day. She stood on the edge of the little group and cried with regret for all the preparations she had made so many times in her head and which would now never be real. The gown, specially woven, the girdle, the knotted cords, all the days spent with Julia planning her special day. And what had it come to, in the end? This hole in corner ceremony with a Christian priest mumbling his rites, annoyed because he was not in a proper church; the priest of Minerva in his bronze crown consigned to a corner, taking no part. She cried for the loss of her special day and for the loss of her daughter, but mostly, she cried for herself.

The Christian priest felt no more comfortable about this ceremony than did Matidia. He knew these people were not Christians, they just wanted to do what was expedient. This woman was clearly with child, the man was clearly impatient to be elsewhere and the soldier standing at the groom's shoulder looked as though he were carved from stone. He gabbled through the vows, scarcely giving them time to repeat them, clasped their hands, proclaimed them man and wife and stepped gratefully aside. He knew what to expect later – a sermon from Dalmatius on why *he* had not been called on to officiate. Pausing only to grab his fee from Julius, he was gone.

Vitalis looked at Leocadius, standing there, still holding Julia's hand. He hadn't kissed her, had hardly looked at her. Vitalis' heart turned over in his chest with sorrow for them, two people bound together for life for what? A few nights of grunting and rolling on a bed. He agreed with Pelagius about original sin, but there were lots of sins a man could do later and Leocadius had a list as long as his arm. He couldn't wish him well, the words would stick in his throat, so he melted away into the shadows and was on the heels of the priest as they hurried through the palace to the world outside.

Matidia wiped her eyes on the corner of her gown and stepped forward. Julius was standing there like an idiot, seemingly lost for words. Although there would be no maidenhead taken tonight, there were things which must be done and so she nudged the two women she had coerced into attending and, with a reasonable facsimile of merriment and rejoicing, they took Leo and Julia by the arms and led them through the palace to the bridal chamber. Matidia had spent a great deal of Julius' money on the room and it did look quite incredible, hung with fragrant boughs and with an enormous, silk-swathed bed in the centre, pulled out from the wall to be the centrepiece of the room.

Leocadius tried to step through the door, but was prevented by the women, who led Julia in and closed the door in his face. 'Stay there,' Matidia snarled to him, opening the door a crack. 'We must prepare your bride.'

Inside the room, the women removed Julia's jewellery and clothes and wiped her body with sweet oils. They tactfully avoided looking at her belly, tight and round in the candlelight. They put her in the bed and plumped the pillows behind her. Then, Matidia blew out all the candles but one and tiptoed from the room. Julia lay there like a sacrifice. She felt more nervous about this night than the one when she had given her virginity to Leocadius. She stifled a sob, tweaked the covers across her breasts and waited.

Outside the door, Matidia leaned up so her face was as close to Leocadius' as she could make it. 'Your bride is waiting for you,' she hissed. 'Your consummation is at hand.' Leocadius' eyes widened. This woman was really taking this too far. He opened his mouth to speak but she clamped her hand over it. 'You will go in there and take my daughter, do you understand me?' she said. 'In case you don't know what to do, I have arranged for a musician to sing dirty songs outside your door all night. Because I know it can be hard for a man when he has to persuade a virgin to give herself to him.' She leaned in further and he caught a gust of wine on her breath. 'Do you understand me, Leocadius?' She reached down and caught hold of his balls and gave them a squeeze. 'Do you?'

He nodded.

'Good. Here comes the musician. I'll see you both in the morning. And my daughter had better be smiling.' She let go of his face and turned away down the corridor. She passed a lute player coming the other way. He gave Leocadius an embarrassed grin and struck a chord.

Leocadius opened the door of the bedroom and looked in. He closed the door softly behind him and walked up to the bed. Julia lay there silently, following him with eyes grown big in the shadows of the flickering candle. He reached out with one hand and drew the covers back from her breasts, tracing down and circling one nipple, grown dark as the child grew inside her. He traced further, pushing the covers ever lower and she tensed, clenching her fists by her side and arching her back to meet his questing touch. He brushed his palm down over her tight skin and cupped it between her legs. She gave a groan and closed her eyes. The pressure of the hand left her and she waited, waited for the weight of him to press her into the mattress, as he had not done for so many weeks. But she waited in vain. With a swish of his scarlet cloak and the soft thud of a closing door, Leocadius was gone.

The torches on the walls threw weird reflections at Aesica that night. Artabanus stood shivering in the gatehouse, listening to the calls from the watch outside. From where he stood, wrists still bound from being dragged behind a horse, he could see flurries of snow whirling down through the night. He had lost all feeling in his fingers and toes and his legs felt like lead.

'Tribune!' a guard shouted and everyone except the arcanus clicked to attention. Justinus marched in, still in his mail from the day's raid, but bareheaded now. He sat down on the campaign chair and waited while an orderly filled his cup with wine. He took a sip, then got up and offered it to Artabanus. At first, the man did not move, except to turn his head. Then he thought better of it and gulped the wine greedily. It was the first liquid to pass his lips all day.

Justinus jerked the cup away from him and sat down again.

'How long had you been in Eboracum, sending your messages out of the city?'

Artabanus looked blank, 'I have never been to Eboracum in my life,' he said.

'Very well,' Justinus changed tack. 'Tell me,' he said, 'about the mouth of hell.'

'What's to tell?' Artabanus shrugged.

Justinus was across the room in one bound and slapped the man across the face, the Wall ring drawing blood from his lip. 'The truth, you bastard!' he growled.

Artabanus' head was ringing and he knew that, in terms of pain, this was just the start of it. His shoulders hunched and all he wanted to do now was to get this over with.

'I had my instructions,' he said. 'I was to take Fullofaudes to the mouth of hell because it was a perfect place for an ambush. He had no idea. He thought he could beat us with a handful of cavalry. I was too far away to see the look on his face when he realised exactly what he was up against.'

'What was he up against?'

'Picts. Attacotti, Saxons, Scots. We were all there. In our hundred then.' He lifted his head defiantly. 'In our thousands now.'

Justinus rested his elbows on the carved arms of the chair. 'Tell me about Valentinus,' he said.

Artabanus hesitated. 'He's going to kill you all,' he said.

'Is he?' Justinus asked. 'When and how is he going to do that, precisely?'

Artabanus' throat was still choked from his hours being dragged across the frozen moorland and his laugh was a hoarse cackle. 'You'll know it when it happens,' he said. 'Just like Fullofaudes did.'

'They say Valentinus is ten feet tall,' the tribune said. 'Rides a black horse from hell and wears this terrible helmet.'

Artabanus chuckled again. 'He has many horses,' he said, 'and helmets too. As for his height ...'

Justinus smiled and shook his head. 'Come on, Artabanus, time to stop this charade now. We both know he's dead, don't we? That's why you're with that pack of renegades outside. You've lost. You're broken up into little war bands and I'm going to swat you like flies.'

Artabanus was not smiling. 'He's not dead, tribune,' he said. 'He's biding his time. You'll see. Come the spring.'

Justinus was on his feet again, crossing to the bound man. 'What will I see, arcanus?' he asked.

'He will come out of Valentia like the end of the world,' he said, his eyes bright with the thought of it. 'And death shall follow him.'

'Yes,' Justinus said solemnly. 'It will.' His left hand came up hard and fast, driving his dagger into Artabanus' stomach. The man gasped and doubled up, his bound hands twitching as he tried to remove the blade. Justinus did that for him, twisting it and pulling it free. As Artabanus' head slumped onto his shoulder, he whispered in his ear, 'Your big mistake,' he said, 'was going to a wedding.'

He stepped back and let the man fall, his blood oozing onto the gatehouse floor. 'Circitor,' he said. 'Get rid of that. And tomorrow I want the others hanged.'

'All of them, sir?' the circitor frowned.

'All of them.'

The sweat stood out on Brenna's brow and a rivulet ran down the side of her face, trickling coldly into her hair. Nevertheless, she pushed away the well-meaning hand that went to mop her cheek.

'Will you stop fretting?' she said, through clenched teeth. 'It's sweat, that's all. I don't need you to mop my sweat, you're here to get this baby born. Why won't the baby be *born*?' The last word was a howl that echoed through the open door and into the night. Paternus and Taran, sitting on the far side of the flickering fire, looked at each other and as quickly looked away. They both had things to think about. The last time Paternus had caused a woman to scream like that, his Flavia had presented him with Quin. Taran, as the last person to make his mother scream like that, had more complicated thoughts and they weren't for sharing with Paternus. Nevertheless, in the dancing shadows of the fire, the boy's hand sought the man's and both felt comforted.

The knee-women who were there to help the queen give birth to the Roman's son looked at each other across her head. She had spurned many of the birthing rituals of her people, in deference to the baby's father, but they had insisted on the undoing of knots in her clothes, on the open door which was a mercy anyway in the heat of summer. She had been like this now since midday and there was not even a full moon to help the baby out. They had tried her sitting, lying, walking around. Rituals or no rituals, the elder of the two had hidden a stone axe under the queen's bed. It had been good enough for her and for her mother, it was good enough for any queen alive.

Brenna screamed again, throwing her head back so that the sinews stood out on her neck. She had her hands on her knees and she pushed down, the muscles on her arms bunching with the effort, her fingers claws digging into her own flesh.

Paternus took Taran by the elbow and raised him to his feet. 'Let's go for a walk, boy,' he said. 'This is women's work.'

Taran nodded silently and the two walked out of the compound towards the high ground, so they could fill their ears with the scream of gulls and the wind off the distant sea.

'Is my husband outside?' Brenna panted.

One of the women leaned across so she could see out of the door.

'No, lady. He and your son have gone.'

'Good,' Brenna choked out a laugh. 'If they have gone, I can scream.' She looked from one stricken face to another and gave another hoarse chuckle. 'Oh, yes,' she said. 'I can scream louder than that.' And she bent forward, one of the midwives at each shoulder and she pressed down on the ground on either side of her hips. The scream this time could tear skin and as it receded, leaving the women with ringing ears, she took a deep breath and with it, her son slid into the world, in a rush of water and blood.

'There,' she said, falling back on the bed. 'A boy. We will call him Edern.'

One of the women scooped up the child and was about to give him a quickening slap when he opened his mouth and yelled. The other picked up twine and a knife and with deft hands tied and cut the cord. Brenna held out her arms and another prince of the Votadini was put to her breast.

CHAPTER XVIII

Aestivus

Magnus Maximus went south that summer, leaving his northern command to his one remaining hero of the Wall. The winds were with him in the German sea and his little flotilla saw no Saxon sails at all, just the odd fishing coracle off the coast and one or two swan-necked merchant ships making for their havens along the mouth of the Witham.

He had sent messengers ahead to Stephanus the German to meet him at the broad estuary of the Thamesis where the marshes stretched forever before the forests began. The general travelled light, with a single cohort of troops, his staff and his dog. For months now he had received regular messages from Londinium; all of Maxima Caesariensis seemed to be quiet and travellers coming into the city spoke of no trouble on the roads. But Magnus Maximus did not know this part of Britannia and he needed to see it for himself.

It was a stifling night it the city, the shutters of the day having made no difference in the narrow streets. Most of the tabernae had closed now and the alleyways that never slept became broad thoroughfares for the rats. In the governor's palace, Matidia slept the sleep of the dead, snoring gently through the night. But in his quarters in the basilica, her husband was still awake, the candle burning soft and slow beside him as he peered to read the small print of the parchments before him. God and Jupiter highest and best, who would be a consul?

233

He had heard earlier in the day that General Magnus Maximus was on his way to the city. More clash and carry. More military mouths to feed. What would this one do? Put up another bloody wall? There was no hope of paying for the last one. And then, there was his beloved palace. He had heard that this Maximus was an oaf, with the eating habits of a pig. At least the Theodosii were gentlemen and had left Longinus' statuary alone. He shuddered to think what this one might do.

The candle fluttered and a breeze lifted one of the pieces of parchment on his table. 'I said "no disturbances", Albinus,' the consul said, without looking up.

'If you'd rather I went away,' a soft, melodic voice wafted from the shadows behind the curtain.

Longinus put down the quill. 'Who is it?' he asked in his official consular voice. 'Who's there?'

She undulated into the light, her golden hair tumbling over her cloak. 'Honoria,' she said, smiling. 'You can call me Honoria.'

Longinus' smile turned into a chuckle. 'My dear,' he said, getting to his feet. 'I shall be delighted to call you anything you like.'

He looked her up and down. Lovely. Half a grain sack lighter than his wife, but curving in all the right places, not like the last one Hupo had sent him. The girl had gone like a wild ass, but had the statistics of a hop-pole. He took her hand and led her to the couch at the far side of the room, lovingly unbuckling her gold brooch and removing her cloak. 'Sit here,' he said, 'beside me.'

'I am disturbing your work,' she looked at the clutter of papers on the table.

'Oh, that ...' Longinus poured them both a goblet of wine. It was only his second-best stuff but this girl, for all her fine cheekbones and expensive jewellery, was not likely to notice. 'Affairs of the day,' he said with a sigh. 'I much prefer affairs of the night.'

'You naughty man!' she tapped his shoulder with her dangling sleeve.

'Did Hupo send you?' he asked.

'In a manner of speaking,' she said.

'Er ... a bite to eat, perhaps?' he said, remembering his manners. No need to rush things; he was going to savour this one. 'Where's that slave?' He was on his feet, but Honoria held his arm.

'We don't need him,' she said. 'And anyway, I'm not hungry. Not for food, anyway ...'

She let him take her hand and he kissed it. Then he placed a finger in his mouth and sucked it, keeping his eyes on her all the time. Her other had roved down to his lap and his hardness reared up. 'Oh,' she purred. 'So it's true.'

'What is, my dear?' He was now sniffing and licking her neck under the glorious cascade of her hair.

'What they whisper about you in my part of the city.'

'Do they?' Longinus was gratified. 'What part of the city is that?'

'Any part where you are, Julius .. I may call you Julius?'

'My dear,' he said, sliding his hand inside her robe to fondle her breasts. 'I wouldn't have it any other way. Shall we?' He used his free hand to indicate a curtain across an archway behind him and he helped her up. He couldn't help noticing his shadow on the wall, erection and all and felt a surge of pride. So, they were talking about this in the city, eh? Well, it was hardly surprising.

He led her into a bedroom which was in total darkness.

'I'll get a candle,' he said.

'No, no,' she stopped him. 'I like it in the dark.'

'Do you?' he murmured. She was already pulling his pallium over his head. She threw it to one side and stroked her long nails down his chest. Then she reached up and kissed him.

'Naked, though, surely?' he said.

'Is there any other way?' She undid the ties of her robe and let it fall. He could see almost nothing in the darkness but he felt the weight of her breasts and fondled her nipples before sliding his hand down over the curve of her hips. She pushed him gently backwards so that his legs hit the bed and he fell back. Then she felt for his manhood and rubbed it gently, getting faster and faster until the consul was squirming on the bed.

'Straddle me,' he gasped. 'I'm nearly there.'

She lowered her head to his and murmured, 'So am I.'

The next thing Longinus felt was an excruciating pain in his chest. A thud. Followed by a second. What sort of love-making was this? Hupo had sent him some very imaginative girls over the years, but none who ... He could still see nothing, but he felt something warm and wet trickling over his chest and down both sides onto the sheets. He heard a sucking sound and felt the pain again. He could not breathe. There was the most terrible agony in his lungs and he could not feel his fingers. He tried to move but he could not. He tried to speak but could make no sound. He was vaguely aware of the girl moving away from him, standing up; he heard the rustle of clothes as she was dressing again.

Then, Julius Longinus did what every consul must do one day. He died.

Honoria swept up the curtain and wiped the broad blade of her dagger on it. She finished her wine on the way out and made for the stairs. The slave Albinus met her halfway up. She looked at him and slid the dagger away into its hiding place. Then she pressed a small heavy bag into his hand. 'As agreed,' she said. 'Our bargain.'

'Our bargain,' Albinus bowed and went on up the stairs. He took the candle and pulled aside the curtain. Justinus Longinus lay on his back, stark naked. There was blood all over his chest, oozing from three wounds. His eyes and mouth were open as if something had surprised him. Albinus slapped the still-warm corpse across the face. 'You've had this coming for years,' he whispered, 'you hypocritical old bastard.'

'Dead?' Paulinus Hupo could not believe his ears. 'Gillo, are you sure about this?'

The man shrugged. 'It's the talk of the forum,' he said.

'What was it?' Hupo asked. 'Apoplexy?'

'Knife.'

'Really?' Hupo was intrigued. He quickly ran through in his head the names and faces of men who would have wished the consul dead. The problem was that it was rather a long list and his own name was at the head of it. 'Well, well,' he was pacing his chamber, vaguely aware of the lute playing in the corner. 'This *is* good news.' A sudden thought struck him. 'He was always going to be a stumbling block to the Games. But with him already halfway across the Styx ... Gillo, get a message to the barracks. I've got a strange feeling that our friend Leocadius knows all about the sad demise of his father-in-law ... he's probably still cleaning his dagger. Tell him the Games are on.'

'Dead?' Leocadius blinked. 'Jupiter Highest and Best.' He quickly wrapped the sobbing Julia to him at their villa beyond the east wall and kissed the little one on the head. Try as he might – and it had to be said the tribune did not try very hard – he could not warm to the little, wriggling thing. She had her father's eyes, except they were blue and what might develop into her father's nose. That said, she had her mother's demanding whine, and that far outweighed the rest.

He left his young family weeping with the three slaves Longinus had allowed him, as well as four of his own and rode west, the guards at the gate hauling the timbers open for him. He clattered into the courtyard of the basilica and dashed up the consul's back stairs.

'Albinus,' he met the slave on the landing. 'What price this? What do you know about it?'

'Nothing, sir,' the slave assured him. 'It was my night off.'

Leocadius barged past him and into the room where the ex-consul of Maxima Caesariensis lay half in his winding sheet, his wounds dressed and stitched, the blood washed away. The tribune took one look at the punctured chest and murmured, 'Hupo.'

It was three days later that Magnus Maximus reached Londinium. Unlike the Theodosii, he approached from north of the Thamesis and he brought no army with him other than his single cohort and the escort provided by Stephanus the German.

'This place is like a morgue,' he said to the two heroes of the Wall who stood before him. 'I didn't expect a triumph but a few smiles wouldn't have come amiss.'

'It's the consul, sir,' Leocadius told him, standing to attention with his plumed helmet in the crook of his arm. 'Julius Longinus; he's dead.'

'Murdered,' Vitalis added. He had had no love for the consul but the man's murder was something else. In this city on the edge of pandemonium, every faction would be bound to blame every other. There would be blood.

Maximus looked at his tribunes. Rumours had already reached him long before he left the north. Leocadius had married the consul's daughter and was rising in the world. On the other hand, he was rarely at his post and found the office of tribune a little arduous these days. And Vitalis ... well, Vitalis was lost. He had tried to resign. And, to Maximus, a man who resigned from the army might as well resign from life.

'Who's running the place in the meantime?' the general asked.

'Er ... the Ordo, sir,' Leocadius told him.

'The Ordo!' Maximus slammed down his goblet. 'You can't run a city by committee,' he thundered. 'Shuffling old bastards lining their own purses and bickering over the cost of a whore. Leocadius. You're it.'

'Sir?'

'The new consul of Maxima Caesariensis. It's you.'

For a moment, Leocadius stood rooted to the spot. 'Sir, I know nothing about politics.'

'And you knew nothing about the army until you joined. Trust me, lad, it's like falling off a log. You'll have a garrison to back you and me and my legions for as long as we're here. And don't worry about me getting under your feet. I shall be Stephanus' guest at the camp outside the walls. You'll have the governor's palace to yourself.'

'Well,' Vitalis murmured under his breath, 'You and the mother-in-law.'

Leocadius shook his head.

'Is there a problem?' Maximus asked him.

'Sir,' the tribune had been storing this up for some time and now it all came tumbling out. 'May I speak freely?'

The general spread his arms.

'I'm a pedes,' Leocadius said. 'A stupid child who was tired of foot-slogging with the army. I wanted to leave, drop my shield and get the hell out. Then ...'

'Then the Wall,' Maximus said.

'We didn't fight anybody,' Leocadius shouted and the silence that followed stunned everybody. The man was calmer now. The little devils that had haunted his nights for all these months had at last fallen silent and he felt a huge weight lifted from him. 'We ran,' he said quietly. 'Vitalis was there. He'll tell you.'

Maximus looked at the man.

'It's true,' Vitalis nodded. 'All we found at Banna and Camboglanna were corpses. We ran south to Eboracum dodging barbarian patrols.'

'So the whole thing is a lie!' Leocadius shouted. 'Heroes of the bloody Wall!' He tore off the black ring chiselled with its four helmets and ripped his knuckle before throwing it across the room. He looked at Vitalis. 'For the last four years we have been living a lie.'

Maximus turned and crossed the room. He picked up the ring where it had bounced off the wall and looked at it. The light caught its facets and the gold that gripped them. He reached out and took Leocadius' hand and slipped the ring back on the bleeding finger. 'I know,' he said softly.

The tribunes looked at each other. 'You know?' It was Vitalis who found his voice first.

'Of course I know,' the general said, turning away to pour more wine. 'Just as the Count knew and praeses Decius Ammianus before him.'

The silence was palpable.

'You arrogant bastards,' Maximus grated. 'This isn't about you, either of you. And it's not about Justinus or Paternus either. Haven't you got it yet? It's about Rome and what is best for her. It will always be about Rome. And whether you're a foot-slogging pedes, or a consul of a province ...' he smiled to himself, 'or the Dux Britannorum, we just do our duty by her. And that's all.'

For a moment, no one moved. No one spoke.

'You, Vitalis ...' Maximus broke the moment first.

'Sir?'

'You want to leave the army, I hear.'

'Yes, sir, I ...'

'Request denied.'

'You, Leocadius ...'

The man stood to attention.

'Do not wish to be consul. Request denied.'

He slammed the goblet down.

'Whatever happens,' the general said, 'You two will always be on the Wall. So will Justinus. So will Paternus. There is nothing else.'

Just as Julia's wedding was held behind closed doors and no one shouted 'Talassio' or strewed her with flowers, so the funeral of her father was a quick and quiet business. In the old days, the death of a great man was followed by the munera, an orgy of death in which gladiators faced each other over the purpling corpse and human sacrifices followed the man to his grave. Matidia did not have the strength left in her to fight for the man now that he was gone and she abandoned centuries of tradition and let Bishop Dalmatius have his way. The Christians laid Julius Longinus in a lead box inside a stone sarcophagus, his fast-decaying body packed with chalk. But there were no grave goods with him. His rings passed to his widow and his staff of office to his successor, Leocadius Honorius. When they laid Longinus in the ground, his head faced to the west, to wait for the Second Coming of a god he had never really believed in.

As the summer unfolded and the sun grew hotter, general Maximus rode out with Stephanus most days and Vitalis was often with them. The harvest was rich in the golden fields and the vines and hops ripened under a cloudless blue. Of barbarians and conspiracies and Valentinus there was no sign. Leocadius did indeed enjoy the sweep of the governor's palace, with or without his mother-in-law. He sold the little villa on the edge of the city and now he had more slaves than he knew what to do with. He largely let the Ordo do the routine work, the day to day, because he knew nothing about sewerage systems and cared even less.

Paulinus Hupo was a frequent visitor in those first weeks and various members of the Black Knives came and went under cover of darkness. It was Hupo who called the west wing the House of the Women because two of them lived there. One was an increasingly sullen Roman matron, beginning each day to look more like her mother and when she was not doting on the sickly, mewling girl she had given birth to and named Aelia, of the sun, she was snapping at Leocadius. She was intrigued by the new compound her husband had had built beyond the orchard, but the walls were high and she could not see in. Neither was she allowed through the gate where garrison soldiers stood guard.

It was here that Honoria spent most of her time. She had never had servants before and found her new life strange and unsettling. Her boy was getting stronger every day and was even beginning to show signs of wanting to stand. He ate everything that was in reach and his nursemaid was kept busy making sure that everything he ate was food. She had breastfed the boy herself, despite the expensive nutrix bought for her by Hupo. Her mother, who knew all there was to know about preventing children although little about children themselves, had recommended it as a sovereign remedy against more appearing like peas in a pod and Honoria had embraced the idea, enjoying both the closeness with her son and also the freedom it gave her in bed with Leocadius and, when it was politic, Hupo.

She knew about Julia; Julia did not know about her. But the old consul's daughter was not a stupid woman and she knew that when the new consul was away at night, he could be anywhere, carousing with the low-life beyond the Walbrook, rolling in the sheets with someone else. Yet despite this, she could not rouse herself to seduce him back into her bed. Her daughter had become her world and, when she looked back on it, sharing her bed with Leo-cadius had not been so very wonderful even at the first. He visited her occasionally and made desultory love to her, which she received politely. Other than that, they barely spoke. Her mother looked at the girl with pity in her eyes; it was like looking into a mirror, one that reflected, in the distorted brass, all the years of pain.

Dalmatius' church that had been the temple of Jupiter was crowd-ed that Die Solis as the summer was dying and the last rays of the sun glanced off the coloured windows, dappling the standing con-gregation with reds and blues and golds.

'Let us pray,' the bishop intoned and there was a shuffling and murmuring as everyone stretched themselves on the cold stone of the floor, face down. Even the old were helped into that position of the Christ, with arms outstretched so that the fingertips of the faithful touched, creating a web of prayerfulness across the whole church floor.

But one man was not lying down. He was not even kneeling. He was standing like an ox in the furrow looking at Dalmatius.

'Pelagius,' the bishop said. 'Time to pray, my son.'

There was muttering from the floor and the craning of necks as people tried to see what was happening. Pelagius did not move. 'You are wrong, bishop,' he said. There was an audible gasp and Dalmatius' attendants were on their feet, scowling at this outrage and waiting for the word from their lord and master.

'Wrong?' Dalmatius' voice rang around the stone.

'There is no such thing as original sin.'

For a moment, nothing moved. It was as if the dust motes, twirling in the air, had stopped and hung suspended.

'You would deny your Lord, blasphemer?' Dalmatius roared.

'No, bishop.' Pelagius' voice was clear and sharp. 'I would deny you.'

'I speak for the church of Rome,' Dalmatius said. His voice held the note of one who knows that he has ultimate right on his side. He allowed himself a smug nod to his henchmen, who flexed and shifted, awaiting that the moment to strike the heretic down, if God did not do it first.

'Then the Church of Rome is wrong,' Pelagius answered.

Another gasp and this time people were on their feet, all

eyes turned to the heretic in their midst.

'Stone him!' Dalmatius thundered. It was a dramatic order, but ammunition in that church was hard to come by. Pelagius held up his hand and parried the first blow with his arm. The second caught him on the forehead and he staggered backwards. Hands were clawing at him, fists and feet lashing out, people screaming and spitting. He felt himself being forced backwards out of the door and knew he had to keep his footing no matter what. Once he went down under this mob, there would be no getting up.

'Forgive them,' he muttered, 'for they know not what they do.'

He slipped as he reached the courtyard and rolled in the dust, his face a mask of blood. Still they were coming for him, snarling faces and snapping curses. Then they stopped and fell silent. Pelagius twisted round to a half-kneeling position to see a tribune of the VI Victrix, his mail glinting in the sun, his sword drawn. The mob had not been stopped by one man alone. It had been stopped by the power they knew he had at his back. Few in that crowd of Christians had seen a legion take a city, but they knew it was possible. And to take a church was the work of moments. One by one they fell back and the bishop's assistants, the deacons in their Chi-Rho robes, ushered them all back inside.

'Vitalis,' Pelagius gasped, spitting the dust from his mouth. 'I think I owe you my life.'

The tribune helped him up. 'Been upsetting people again?' he asked.

'I thought it was time,' Pelagius said, 'for a little truth.'

'That's why I'm here,' Vitalis sheathed his sword and led the man away. The square was surprisingly deserted at this hour of the morning and the chanting of the Christians was dying away. 'You probably don't want to hear this now, or then again, perhaps you do.'

'I'm not sure I'm up to riddles at the moment.'

'There is to be an attack on Dalmatius' church. By the children of darkness.'

Pelagius stood still, looking into the tribune's face. 'How do you know?' he asked. 'Are you still part of it?'

'From what I've just seen,' Vitalis said, 'if that's an example of your Christ, I'll stay with Mithras any day.'

'No,' Pelagius said sadly. 'That's not an example of my Christ; it's an example of Dalmatius. That's very different, believe me.'

'So you wouldn't mind if they burned his church down, then?'

'Of course I would,' Pelagius told him. 'There are innocent women and children in there.'

'Not according to Dalmatius, there aren't,' Vitalis reminded him.

'When will this happen?' Pelagius asked, 'the attack?'

'I don't know exactly. I've done my best to deter them already. It's only a matter of time.'

'I'll see consul Leocadius,' Vitalis said. 'And if that doesn't work, General Maximus. One of them will have an answer.'

'What the hell has it got to do with me?' Leocadius asked. He was lounging on a couch that night, sampling some excellent oysters. Honoria lay on the couch next to him, the mistress and the love of the consul of Maxima Caesarensis.

'I thought you had some sort of role in this city,' Vitalis snapped. 'Over and above whoremaster, that is.'

Leocadius was on his feet in a second and Honoria sat upright. Not that it was needed, but her dagger was never *very* far away. The consul's jaw twitched as he faced the man. Then he took a deep and relaxed, 'I'm going to forget you said that, Vitalis,' he murmured, 'because it's you.' He turned away and poured himself more wine. He stood staring at the wall for a moment, ignoring the others. Then he turned back.

'I can issue warnings,' he said, 'in my official capacity. Slapping Dalmatius and Critus into gaol isn't going to achieve much.'

'Why not?'

'Because behind them both there are other religious maniacs hell-bent on destroying each other.' He looked at Vitalis, wondering what had happened to the carefree young lad he had known on the Wall before each of them wore these rings. On the other hand, he was not so surprised; Vitalis had always had a moral streak a mile wide. He was too good for this wicked world, really.

'I'll see what I can do, Vit,' he promised. 'But if I were you, I'd have a word with Maximus.'

'What's it got to do with me?' the general asked. He was sitting in the principia of his camp to the west that night, drinking with Stephanus and feeding his dog strips of venison.

'You *are* Dux Britannorum, sir,' Vitalis was standing to attention, dressed in parade armour, hoping for the impossible.

Stephanus sucked his teeth and shook his head. He had got to know Magnus Maximus fairly well over the last months, better than he knew Vitalis. But he did recognize a man with a death wish when he saw one. In the event, the general was quite restrained. He toyed with unleashing the mastiff on the man, slicing through his breastbone with the spatha lying in the corner. In fact, he did neither. 'Thank you, tribune,' he said, 'for reminding me. I'm sure you can find your own way out.'

Stephanus breathed again.

The sun was still bright on the hills above Din Paladyr and a couple of men were wrestling on the grass kept short by the wind and the sheep. It was rather a one-sided contest. One of them was a warrior, tall and powerful, a tribune of the VI Victrix and Praefectus Gentium of Valentia. The other was a seven year old, wiry, tough, laughing and tumbling as the man broke all the rules by tickling him. And yet the boy won every bout.

She watched them on the hillside, holding her other boy to her. It would not be *that* long before little Edern took to the rough and tumble with Taran and the man they both looked on as their father. There was still something between them that she could not remove, like a river in full spate or a mountain ice-clad in winter. When they were alone, just the two of them, by the fire's glow, when they made love, he was never *quite* with her, not completely. It was just something she would have to live with. And it would be well.

Paternus saw him first. With all his years on the Wall, his old instincts had never left him. He rolled upright, holding the struggling Taran under one arm. It was a rider, on one of the short-legged shaggy ponies of the north, galloping up from the ravines that scoured the land, calling out to the queen of the Votadini. Brenna stood up, resting the baby on her hip and waited. The horseman reined in, the animal's flanks flecked with white.

'An army, my lady,' the rider gasped, chest heaving.

'Where?' Paternus asked. 'And how many?'

'More than the eye can see,' the rider told him. 'Led by a man in a silver helmet. They're making for the Wall.'

CHAPTER XIX

Paulinus Hupo had been to the eternal city once, when he was a boy. He had been to the Coliseum, that huge arena where men died for the pleasure of the mob. He had been one of the mob that day and it was an experience he would never forget. Clowns had come on first, wearing grotesque masks, dancing and cavorting, hitting each other with pigs' bladders. Then, as the sun rose and the seats emptied, the Noxii were brought on, haggard criminals roped together and unarmed. There were no Christians among them – all that had gone with the deified Constantine who had embraced the peculiar Galilean cult on his deathbed. But the Noxii died anyway as the gladiators whirled around them, practising their deadly art, pirouetting and posturing, going through their paces as they did in their training schools, but with living human beings as their targets. The crowd shouted hysterically as the sharp blades bit home and the tridents slid through skin and flesh to rip limbs entangled and already captured in the nets.

For years he had pestered Julius Longinus with the idea. All the man had to do was make him Aedile, official Games organizer and he, Hupo, would do the rest. Nothing too ambitious; no lions or bears; just man against man. It happened all the time in the real world. It was the way of that world. Only the toughest survive; the weak and the puny go to the wall; or at least, they are dragged out of the arena through the gate of death. For years, Longinus had had his answer ready – he could not offend Dalmatius nor the Christian church generally; the city's amphitheatre had fallen into rack and ruin – it was full of undesirables sleeping rough and a

245

whole army of feral cats.

Now, things were different. Leocadius Honorius was consul of Maxima Caesarenius; good old Leo. Hupo had the bent bastard in the palm of his hand anyway. It was going to be a picnic.

'No,' Leocadius said flatly, looking at the man. Hupo had come to him in the night-time, as was his custom when there were dark doings to be discussed. 'Out of the question.' Leocadius knew that Hupo had murdered his father-in-law although he also knew he would never be able to prove it. And the more he had to work with this degenerate, the less he liked it. Increasingly these days, there was a little voice inside his head, the voice of his conscience. And it sounded exactly like the voice of Vitalis.

'What's your objection?' Hupo asked him. He knew that Leocadius had butchered his predecessor to get his job and that could be useful in the blackmail stakes if the consul persisted. What was the matter with the man? He had gone along with everything so far, taking Hupo's backhanders without demur. He had continued to pay the going rate for the protection of the Black Knives and knew his accountants were able to make it all right in his annual report to the Emperor. 'You could be the star, you know.'

'What?'

'Of the arena. The Emperor Commodus, they say, killed one hundred and thirty seven men in the Coliseum.'

'Yes, I'd heard that,' Leocadius smiled, 'but weren't their swords made of lead?'

'We can arrange that,' Hupo said.

'The hell we can,' Leocadius laughed. 'If I'm going into the arena, it'll be a fair fight.'

'To the death?' Hupo asked.

'To the death!' the consul answered.

Hupo smiled. What a vain bastard this man was. One minute he was refusing, the next he could not wait to die in the sand.

'There's one proviso,' Leocadius said. 'We'll have to hold the event at night. And outside the city. I don't know how Maximus will stand on any of this and the last thing either of us wants is to have the army stepping in.'

'Agreed,' said Hupo, 'and I know just the place.'

The torches threw flickering reflections into the boughs of the oaks as the trickle grew to a flood. Half of Londinium was on its way east, beyond Theodosius' towers manned by the Batavi that night.

They gabbled happily under the fitful moon, peeping out from the clouds now and then, as eager to watch the spectacle as the people on the ground. Men carried pitchers of ale and wine; women nattered about whatever it is women natter about; children ran and played and frightened each other jumping out from behind the dark trees.

Tonight the camp of the Black Knives was transformed. Deep in one of those forests that Stephanus the German so hated, a circle had been marked out with timbers and makeshift seating set up on raked angles so that the crowd would miss none of the entertainment. The acoustics would have to take care of themselves, but the ever-obliging Hupo had set up a special stand for the ladies so that they could best hear the screams and groans of the wounded.

Hupo's people were everywhere, selling wine, olives and oysters from their brightly painted stalls. Little clay effigies of gladiators were available, hoplomachi and retiarii, the barley-men of the sword and net; myrmillons with their fish-crested helmets and secutors with their huge oblong shields. Children buzzed around them, pestering their parents to let them collect the set. There was the crash of drums and the clash of tambourines and Hupo himself welcomed the great and good of Londinium to the best seats. It had been years since the Games were held in this city and old men were boring everyone to death with their reminiscences and grumbling because the Aedile had got this wrong; and that was not right either.

Hupo himself could not have cared less. Whatever he had spent on tonight's entertainment, he was recouping handsomely on the gate money and that was before the betting started. He was suitably dressed for the occasion, wearing all the splendour of a bygone age. Nobody wore a toga anymore, but Paulinus Hupo was draped in one tonight, trying not to fall over the damned thing with its heavy purple fringe. His face was painted white with large red circles on his cheeks like a clown and on his head he wore a wig of crimson, coiling like the snakes of Medusa. He satisfied himself that all was well in the filling auditorium and slipped beyond the bushes to where his gladiators waited.

In the ancient days these men would have stood in the animal pens below the arena, listening to the roars of the crowd as they bayed for blood. The oak forest was the best that Hupo could do, but it was cold out of the circle of the torches and away from the throng and several of the fighters were shivering with the tension of the moment. They were slaves, bound by every custom of Rome, to do their master's bidding. And tonight, that master was Paulinus Hupo. He had bought them and it was their duty, if the crowd wished it, to die.

It was that that brought the city in their thousands, both sexes, all ages, all classes; the rumour, carefully spread by the Aedile, that there would be at least one fight to the death. Hupo checked the weapons, feeling the cutting edge of the Thracians' sicas, the deadly curved swords with the wooden hilts. He weighted the nets of the retiarii, the trident men and checked the padding on arms and legs. He would have dearly loved to have had a matched pair of female fighters but the time had been too short and Honoria had positively refused. She did not object to mixing it with another girl; she had been doing that in the stews of Londinium for most of her life. What she objected to were the terrible hairstyles and all that sweating and grunting in public. She kept that sort of thing for the bedroom. At the mention of bedroom and at the sight of her lowered lashes, Hupo had capitulated, albeit unwillingly.

Honoria was sitting in a place of honour that night, her rich cloak hung with gold clasps, watching the musicians and the acrobats in the arena, twirling with their flaming brands and somersaulting over the bark-sprinkled ground. Her mother, refusing to be upstaged, sat beside her. Julia and Matidia had not replied to their invitations, so Leocadius would be going alone.

There was more than a smattering of soldiery there, as the Heruli, the Batavi and several of the city garrison, had left off their armour and jostled for good positions on the stands. If general Maximus did not approve of this reversion to the barbarism of old, he had not let the consul know that; but neither was he there in person. Hupo scanned the crowd as he returned to the arena. There was no Stephanus either, no Vitalis. He knew there would be no churchmen there; that was a given. But he smiled to himself as he caught sight of old Proclivius Parbo, the ex-consul's old friend. The man was a thorough-going Christian, having booked his west-facing place in Dalmatius' own personal graveyard beyond the Bishop's Gate. Yet here he was, pissed as a fart, with a girl on each arm and a wreath of Bacchus' ivy leaves lop-sidedly around his head.

'We know,' Dalmatius was holding the attention of his flock, rather smaller than he would have hoped that night, in his church to the west of the city, 'what abomination goes on in the woods to the east. We know it, Lord, and we are here to beg you to put a stop to it, to end this sacrilege of slaughter once and for all. The deified Constantine himself spoke out against it. You shall not kill, you have told us, again and again. And yet, the wicked will not listen, because they have black evil in their hearts.'

'Tonight,' Decius Critus spoke in the cave of Mithras, the candles flickering behind his head, looking for all the world as if the fires of hell shone from his ears, 'we will strike such a blow that Dalmatius and his Christians will never forget.'

The men in darkness with him murmured. Half of them, soldiers and ex-soldiers, would have loved to have been in the forest to the east where iron rang on iron and men died. But this was their greater calling. There would be other Games. Now that Paulinus Hupo was Aedile and Leocadius Honorius consul, they could count on it. Tonight, they would ring iron of their own. And Londinium would remember. At a word from Critus, they filed out into the night.

Consul Leocadius made his grand entrance at last, an army of scribblers and denarius-counters fluttering behind him. The tubas sounded his arrival with a fanfare and the crowd roared their delight. The acrobats stood still in the arena and, at a signal from Hupo, extinguished their brands in the bark. The Aedile made his way up the temporary staircase below Leocadius' dais with its scarlet awning and its guttering torches and made a handsome speech of welcome. The consul replied in equally fulsome tones, neither man meaning a word of it and the Games could commence.

Leocadius took the white linen from a flunkey and raised it high. In front of him, a sea of expectant faces looked at him, eyes and teeth shining in the light of so many fires. He gave a half smile, enjoying the silence; enjoying the moment of absolute power. For those few seconds, Londinium and nearly everyone in it, belonged entirely to him. Then he let the cloth fall and the roar from the crowd was deafening. Hupo announced the first pairing, although nobody heard what he said and the betting started in earnest.

The pair circled each other, the Hoplomachus in his huge iron helmet with the black feathered crest. His right arm was bound in white fabric from shoulder to wrist, as was his left leg. Over this was strapped a greave of bronze. The torches shone on the silver studs that held his subligaculum at his waist. The short straight sword of his opponent, the Provocator, banged on the man's round shield and they broke apart. The faces of both men were hidden completely behind the iron grilles and under the rims of their helmets. They grunted and wheezed as they traded blows, iron ringing into the night and dust and bark flying as their sandals slipped. The crowd roared delightedly as first one man, then the other, drew blood. The Provocator's sword licked over his opponent's shield to slice his forearm and as the wounded man stumbled he jabbed his spear into the Hoplomachus' thigh, making him drop to one knee with the sudden pain and shock. The crowd were on their feet, screaming hysterically, their hands in the air, drawing their thumbs across their throats. But Hupo shook his head and laughed. As Aedile, he would say who lived or died tonight and this was not billed as a fight to the death. Besides, no man had given up yet as the Hoplomachus was on his feet again. The crowd groaned, disappointed that the wounds were only slight.

Again they swung to the attack, but this one was short-lived. The Provocator banged hard on his opponent's helmet, twisting the iron so that his skull hit the side. Padded or not, the man fell, his senses gone, his brain damaged for all time. Again the crowd were on their feet and again the thumbs slashed horizontally. *Now* they begged the Aedile, *now* was the time for the coup de grace. Hupo raised the hand of the tired Provocator and the medici scurried over to carry the unconscious man away.

The children of darkness had left their lair by the Walbrook and were making their way silently through the streets. They were dressed in dark clothing so that they would not easily be seen and they covered their faces so they would not easily be recognized. They travelled in threes and fours, the brands that would light their way and burn Dalmatius' church still mere sticks in their hands. Critus alone wore the robes of his calling, the bull flashing silver on his chest and his long, tasselled sleeves trailing the ground.

The few drunks still rolling along the alleyways saw them and scurried away. Men in shadows was bad news in a city like Londinium; it usually meant death.

Paulinus Hupo's timing was immaculate. He knew what pleased a crowd. Make them laugh. Make them cry. Make them wait. The wine and beer were flowing fast and the trinket sellers moved among the crowd, anxious to milk the moment for all it was worth. There was a roar as the Aedile announced the second pairing and two huge men strode into the arena – the Thracian against the Myrmillo. Money flew thick and fast and the stakes were high. Hupo was delighted; above the appreciative roar of the crowd, he could hear the sound of serious money.

The Myrmillo's helmet was sculpted into myriad facets, so that it glittered like fish scales and a huge white plume stood tall like a fountain above it. His shield was large and rectangular, of the type the army used to carry long ago and it curved around his body. Diana the huntress was carved on the greave buckled to his left leg and his sword was short, straight and double-edged. The Thracian's curved weapon clanged against it, the blades flashing sparks in the torch light. Their shields locked for a moment, then they pulled apart, hacking and parrying to the delight of the crowd. The Thracian lunged and lost his balance and the Myrmillon was on him, swinging his sword down so that it hit the neck defence of the man's helmet and he sank to his knees.

Hupo dashed into the arena. The crowd would have *his* blood if the bout ended so quickly, so he barked at the Myrmillon to wait until the Thracian had recovered. For a moment, the man sat in the scattered bark, his sword and shield still in his hands, waiting for his vision to clear. All around him the mob were hissing and booing, throwing anything at him that came to hand. 'Get up, you bloody coward!' 'What are we paying good money for?' 'Call yourself a Thracian?'

Then he staggered upright and the fight went on.

They reached the square of the old temple of Jupiter, Highest and Best. Lights were twinkling in the small high windows and those nearest could hear the chanting of the faithful inside Dalmatius' church. Critus lit his torch and passed the flame to the next man, who passed it to another. Suddenly, in the eerie semi-silence the alleyways that led to the square burst into light.

Critus raised his flaming brand. 'Mithras, god of the midnight!' he yelled and the cry was taken up by the others, hundreds of determined men rushing across the square with hatred in their hearts.

In front of the main doors two men stepped forward out of the shadows. One was a tribune of the VI Victrix, although tonight he wore no armour and carried no weapon except his sword. The other was Pelagius and he carried no weapons at all.

It was time for the final bout of the evening. To nobody's surprise the concussed Thracian had gone down to the Myrmillon and there were shouts of 'Fix!' and 'Resign!' – both of these delivered to the Aedile. Being Master of the Games was a two-edged sword but Hupo knew that the best was yet to be. He walked into the centre of the arena and stood there in his ceremonial robes until the clamour had died down.

'Tonight,' he said, 'we have a special contest.' He clapped his hands. 'I give you, Hermes Psychopompus.' There was an ecstatic shout as two of the long-suffering slaves who had been hauling seating and scenery all day appeared at the Aedile's elbow wearing masks and carrying red hot irons, glowing in their hands. The tension in the auditorium was electric. These were the guides who would take the dead to the underworld. The irons would be used on any gladiator whose nerve left him and he refused to fight.

Again, Hupo the consummate showman waited for quiet. He raised his hand high and boomed out, 'Behold, the Ferryman.' This time the roar turned to a boo, not against Hupo but against the black-cloaked figure with the hook-nosed mask of the death demon, Charon. In his hand, he carried a two-handed stone-headed hammer, ready to shatter the skull of the gladiator who lost.

'This,' yelled Hupo, although he had absolutely no need to tell the crowd, 'will be a fight to the death.'

The roar in that strangely haunted forest was deafening and everybody was on their feet, shaking their fists in the air, turning to each other, gabbling excitedly and slapping each other on the back. A tall man with blond curls sauntered casually into the arena, waving and smiling at the crowd, loving the moment. He wore a scarlet sublicagulum, fringed with gold and a chequered band around his head which was otherwise bare. His legs below the knee were padded with white fabric, bound and strapped and he had a bronze plate strapped to his left shoulder. In one hand he trailed a nine foot square net hung with little lead weights to ensnare his opponent and in his other a trident, five feet long and ending in three murderous iron prongs. His body gleamed with oil in the torchlight and there were adoring 'oohs' and 'aahs' from the ladies and, furtively, a few of the men.

'This is Danaos,' Hupo shouted once the noise had dropped a little. 'He has forty nine kills to his name. Who will make it fifty?'

'That's far enough, Critus!' Vitalis shouted. The chants and curses of the children of darkness died down and the only sound then was the hiss of iron as the tribune drew his sword and held the blade naked in the torchlight. 'There is no place here for you.'

'Nor for you, traitor,' the Mithras priest growled. 'I should have known. When you did not come to the Mithraeum, I should have known. Are you a damned Christian now?'

'I may or may not be a Christian,' Vitalis said, 'but I am probably damned.'

Pelagius murmured out of the corner of his mouth, 'You don't have to do this, Vitalis. Get out of here while you can. You owe nothing to those people in the church.'

'No,' Vitalis said, 'I owe it to myself.'

The doors of the church crashed back and Bishop Dalmatius stood there, wearing his robes just as Critus was wearing his. He stepped forward into the light of the torches, facing the children of darkness with a growing army of muscular Christians fanning out from the building and facing the square. The lines of battle were drawn.

'I accept the challenge!' a voice shouted in the darkness of the gate of death. Charon raised his hideous masked head and cradled the hammer in his arms. The crowd fell hushed as Leocadius Honorius, the consul of Maxima Caesariensis, walked into the centre of the arena. He was wearing the armour of a Thracian, a broad silver belt holding the green sublicagulum and oil gleamed across his shoulders, back and chest. Bronze greaves glowed in the torchlight on both legs and his right arm was encased in articulated iron, overlapping plates as oiled as he was.

No one, other than those sitting nearest him, had noticed the man slip away earlier, during the last bout. He carried a small shield in his left hand and a large, griffin crested helmet in his right, the high horsehair crest trailing the ground now as he walked. The crowd would have roared anyway, but when they saw who it was, they roared even louder. No one, in that insane cockpit of butchery, was asking themselves the question – why? What had possessed the new consul that he should lay his life on the line for a wager? What would make a man like him risk all for the roar of the mob?

Only one woman was asking herself all this and more as she looked down at him. Honoria was on her feet, not screaming delight with all the others, but covering her mouth in horror, her eyes wide. Hupo caught the moment, saw the girl who was the mother of his child, shouting animatedly at her own mother sitting beside her, pulling the girl's cloak, trying to calm her down. Hupo caught the moment and remembered it.

He turned to face the fighters, who stood before him, bare-headed and with legs apart. They gave the Aedile the ritual greeting, chanting together, 'We who are about to die, salute you.' Then, Leocadius buckled on his helmet, clashed his curved sword blade on the prongs of the retiarius' trident and stepped back. Many in the auditorium that night had never seen a fight to the death. This in itself was worth the entry fee and Hupo found himself smiling while Honoria sat high on her stand, frozen with the horror of it all. The man she loved was facing a professional killer and she knew he stood no chance at all.

'You will not violate this sacred ground!' Dalmatius' voice carried across the square.

'What sacred ground?' Critus bellowed back. 'Look around you, you blinkered buffoon. You are worshipping in the Temple of Jupiter. Your Galilean carpenter has no more place there than he has in my Mithraeum.'

'You're wrong, Critus,' Pelagius said. 'The Lord Jesus has a place everywhere. In the Temple of Jupiter. In the Mithraeum. In my heart and in yours.'

The first torch sailed into the air high over Pelagius' head to bounce off the plaster wall and do no damage. The second hit the thatch of the barn next door and the third landed in the centre of the Christian mob, one of the deacon's robes exploding in a roar of flame. Both sides closed together, punching, gouging, kicking and somewhere in the middle of it all, Vitalis and Pelagius were trying to stay alive.

Leocadius was trying to stay alive too. The sword in his hand was not the weight he was used to. It was shorter, lighter and curved. The shield was too small, although what use it was against that bloody net, he had no idea. His bigger problem was the helmet. The thing was heavy and the retiarius bobbed in his vision through the eye-holes of the grille. He could hear his own breathing in that bronze bucket, echoing and re-echoing like the rattle of chains in hell. The noise of the crowd, at least, was muffled and he was grateful for that. He did not have time to watch them, to pick out faces. He was too intent on the net and the trident in front of him.

It was no consolation at all to remember that the net man had done this at least forty nine times before and this was Leocadius' first fight. Twice the net slapped over his head, the lead weights pinging off his helmet and peppering the skin of his back. He drove the taller man back with his shield and hacked with the sword. The trident whirled across and caught the blade on its hooks and he twisted sideways, throwing Leocadius off balance. He dropped heavily to one knee, then thrust upwards, grazing the retiarius' thigh as he did so. The man fell back, cursing under his breath as the blood began to trickle from the open cut.

The crowd were screaming, 'Kill! Kill!' as though they could literally smell the blood. The pair circled each other, Leocadius finding breathing ever more difficult in the suffocating helmet. He saw the trident coming for his face and parried desperately with the sword. Then the net hooked around his ankles and he went down, the fall knocking the wind out of him. The blond killer stepped onto his sword arm and the fight looked to be all over. Leocadius saw the trident raised and turned his head. Charon in his blackness stared back at him and he knew, although he could not see them, that the crowd had their thumbs at their rthroats while the Aedile made his lightning count.

Hupo smiled. It was gratifying to know that most of them wanted Honoria's darling dead. And the best news of all was that Hupo himself would have no responsibility for his death. It was the will of the people of Londinium; what consul could wish it any other way? He raised the white cloth in his hand, the one he would soon dabble in Leocadius' blood once Charon had demolished his skull. But first the honour of actually killing the man would go to the retiarius. Hupo dropped the cloth and the trident came up, held by the gladiator in both hands, ready for the final, downward thrust.

'The city!' someone yelled. 'The city's on fire!'

'Fire!' that was Magnus Maximus' voice yelling on one side of the square.

'Fire!' that was Stephanus the German's on the other side. With roofs blazing at their backs, solid lines of Heruli and Batavi archers were emptying their quivers into the crowd. Longbows hissed, crossbows thudded. Christian and Mithraean went down to the deadly shafts and the tide of battle drew back.

There were bodies everywhere, men with broken arms and legs, pressed to death in the crush. Once-flaming brands lay burned out on top of corpses and the fight in a Londinium square was over.

The only sound now, apart from the groaning and whimpering of the wounded, was the crackle of the flames. 'Put that out!' Maximus yelled and half a cohort jumped to it, grabbing buckets, ewers, pitchers, anything they could and forming a human chain to the Walbrook.

The general walked into the heart of the battle. 'If any of you people want to continue this,' he said, 'now would be the time. I've got two legions primed and ready and they don't care who they kill. The Christ or Mithras – it's all one to them.'

Nobody moved. Then Vitalis stuck his head up from under a pile of the injured and the dead. 'Nice to see you proving useful,' Maximus grunted to him. He grabbed Bishop Dalmatus by the cope, dark blood staining the gold cloth. 'You're lucky you're alive, Christian,' he said, although he didn't care for the pallor of the man's skin. 'You,' the general dragged another man to him. 'You're the priest of Mithras, yes?'

Critus mumbled something, which was the best he could do with a broken jaw. He had hold of both of them by the scruffs of their necks and he banged their heads together. 'If you two can't behave,' he said, like a dominus telling off his pupils, 'I shall have to take further steps. You, Mithras man, will have your throat cut. You, Christian, will be crucified. Right here. Right now. Do we understand each other?'

Both men, numbed and in pain, nodded.

Vitalis had found his sword under the debris of the fight. He walked over to Maximus, raised the weapon and broke it over his knee, before letting the pieces clatter to the ground.

Pelagius, bruised and bloody, waited for the man to come back. 'Was that wise?' he said, 'to make an enemy of him?'

'It's finished,' Vitalis said. 'Before, I asked if I could leave his bloody army. Now I have.'

Maximus turned to the soldiers still lining the square as the water was thrown over the thatch with a hiss like a thousand snakes. 'Has anybody seen the consul?'

The consul dragged himself upright. Only three men still stood in the arena and the crowd had gone. Most of the torches had been abandoned as everybody had rushed away to save their homes. Fire in the city was the one dread they all shared. It caused panic like nothing else.

'Here's to the next time, Consul,' the retiarius shook Leocadius' hand, 'and I should work on that wrist action if I were you.'

'To the next time,' Leocadius hauled off the helmet. Then he turned to the Aedile. 'You still here, Hupo? Haven't you got the odd silver-chest to save?'

The Aedile scowled at him, threw off his red wig and strode to the west.

On the platform high above the arena, old Proclinus Parbo woke up. His ivy wreath had fallen off and the girls had gone. He looked down at the solitary figure in gladiator's armour in the centre of the ring.

'Did I miss anything?' he called.

CHAPTER XX

The message from Paternus arrived in the middle of the night and the circitor of the watch knew it was too important to wait for morning. The Votadini scout was exhausted and a horse had died under him as he thrashed the animal, galloping south. An army was coming out of Caledonia, an army perhaps ten thousand strong. It was the army of Valentinus.

Justinus had yelled at his scribes to get up and in the flickering candlelight, ink flew and quills scratched. In the canabae below Aesica, riders from the Ala Victores were saddling their horses, fitting bits and tightening girths. They were to ride along the Wall in both directions, as far as their animals would take them. When the dumb beasts could go no further, they were to find new mounts and ride on. From Arbeia to Maia, every fort must be told because no one knew where Valentinus would strike.

As the gallopers mounted, a day's food and water in their saddlebags, Justinus ordered the beacons to be lit. He paced the wall-walk as the first light of dawn broke, and he watched the mountains to the north. The flames burst into light in the brazier overhead, the signal that would spread from milecastle to milecastle that there was trouble in the wind. The scouts could confirm what that trouble was but the flames themselves would give the warning.

And Justinus sent gallopers north too, to the outlying forts of Blatobulgium and Banna. Their tiny garrisons were to pull back to the shelter of the Wall; now. There would be no surprise attacks this time, not if Justinus could help it. Valentinus was welcome to the stones of those forts, but he would not have its people; not this time. The tribune sent riders south that same morning. They were to ride to the Abus and take the fastest bireme south to Londinium. The Dux Britannorum was there and the Wall needed Magnus Maximus and his legions. The Ala Jovii were sent north, scattered into small patrols, watching every road and every area of open ground. They had orders not to engage the enemy but to watch which way they went and report back.

Justinus stood on the ramparts of Aesica once all this flurry of activity was over. He could do no more for the moment. Now it was all about waiting.

Paternus held his little son in his arms, kissing his soft forehead and stroking his cheek. He had little curls that tangled at his neck and a little bubble burst on his lips. He never thought he could love another as he had loved his Quin, yet here he was and he had never been apart from the boy for the whole of his young life.

Brenna hugged them both and Paternus turned to her. Her eyes were soft in the morning but she would not cry. For most of the night she had argued with him that she should ride out with him. She was queen of the Gododdyn, for Belatucadros' sake. *She* should be leading her people. Paternus had been as stubborn as he had been right. She was a mother. Mother of the kings of the Votadini. If she was not there any more, what would happen to them?

He kissed her deeply as he passed the baby back. The Votadini army, the men he had trained, sat their horses or stood silently in the ranks, the pale autumn sun gleaming on their armour and spear-points. He looked across to where Taran held his helmet and beckoned the boy over. He knelt down so that he was on the lad's level. 'Look after them for me,' he said, as a tear rolled down the lad's cheek. 'And don't take any lip from that little one. You're the man now.'

Taran flung his arms around Paternus, sobbing helplessly as he hugged his neck. Paternus squeezed him back, so hard he thought he might break. Then he snatched the helmet, touched Brenna's cheek once and swung into the saddle. The Votadini marched south.

As the last of the little column became blurs on the horizon, Brenna passed Edern to her woman. Taran had run away, unable to watch any more. He too had argued, in his childish way. Why could he not go with Paternus? He could ride with the best of them, could shoot a dart and a bow. A sword was still quite hard for him, but with two hands ... But it had not worked and Paternus had said no. The queen of the Votadini walked into her private quarters and opened an elm chest that stood in a corner. She lifted out a leather bag and carried it out beyond the ditches of the camp that Paternus had had dug for their protection. She dug into the soft earth with the broad blade of her dagger and dropped the bag into the hole, covering it over and replacing the turf. Through her tears she walked back. Paternus, the man she loved, had, over the last months, lost some of his demons of the night. Had his new family at last replaced the old? Could she hope for that? She had just buried one of those demons on the lonely hillside; that part of Paternus, at least, was behind him. It was the shrivelled head of the Pict, Talorc.

The whole nightmare was starting again, as it must have started those long months ago when the barbarians had first banded to-gether and Valentinus had come from the north, the general with no real name, the warrior without a face. Paternus watched the smoke drifting, casting shadows over the sunlit moors. He was half a day, he estimated, behind the barbarians. They had bypassed Trimontium, the old fort abandoned since Agricola's time but were in no hurry to reach the Wall. A chill wind was blowing across the moors heralding the winter that was to come, but Valentinus was no respecter of seasons and that meant nothing to him.

As they trailed his army, Paternus wondered whether the man knew the Wall had been rebuilt, that a welcome awaited him along that bloody ridge, a welcome made of Rutilius' earth and stone and Justinus' wild asses, archers and slingers. He had taken the Wall before because no one had been ready; no one could be-lieve the sheer scale of the attack. This time it would be different. When Valentinus camped, Paternus camped. If he burnt a village, they let him. There would be no heroics in this war. But when it came to it, it would be a fight to the death.

Order had been restored to Londinium. It was one of those things, people said. In a city as great and restless as that, things like that happened. All right, so a few Christians were knocked about – they used to be thrown to the lions. Some of the Mithras people had headaches – long overdue. Whatever happened, Londinium would go about its business, the usual dog-eat-dog business that made it the capital of Maxima Caesariensis and indeed, the whole of Britannia.

Paulinus Hupo should have been a happy man. He was richer than any god in the pantheon now and people would talk of the Games for years to come. It was a shame there were no actual deaths in the arena, but you couldn't have everything. Next time would be better. But Paulinus Hupo was not a happy man. That was because he was looking at his baby in a new light. Honoria was crooning to it, swaying around the atrium with the boy in her arms. He was heavy but she did not mind that. She looked at the drooping eyelids that were closing over eyes that had darkened from the bright blue of birth, to midnight and now to the moleskin depth of his father's. She kissed the little ringlet curling over the ears, ringlets that looked so like the much longer ones of Leocadius. Hupo watched them in silence and they did not know he was there. He had seen, at the arena, how she had reacted when the consul was in the ring, when his life was on the line. He did not mind that; Honoria could give her heart to anyone she chose. But the boy. That was different. He vanished into the shadows.

'The bastard's yours, isn't he?' the Aedile-for-life yelled across the landing of the basilica.

Leocadius looked furious and swept up the curtain to his private apartments. Albinus and the other slaves were suddenly nowhere in sight. 'Do you mind keeping your voice down?' Leocadius hissed.

Hupo looked at him and burst out laughing. 'Listen to you,' he said. 'You even *sound* like Julius Longinus. I thought with you in the corridor of power I might at least get some honest dishonesty.'

Leocadius looked at the man with a new loathing. 'Yes,' he said, with a certain smugness. 'Honoria's boy is mine. Can that matter so much to you?'

Hupo closed to him. 'From now on,' he said, 'You'd better watch your back, consul. You won't always have Magnus Maximus to wipe your arse for you.'

'Consul! Consul!' It was something Albinus had been shouting now for years. The slave had suddenly materialised from nowhere and was on the steps that led to the courtyard. 'General Maximus is at the gate, sir. There's news from the north.'

Decius Ammianus, praeses of the VI Victrix, had been closeted away all morning with his tribunes and his staff. He had, it was true, been counting down the days to his retirement and dreaming of those vine-clad slopes below Vesuvius where the mountains ran down to a sun-kissed sea. And now, this. But Decius Ammianus knew the score; into every life a little rain must fall. And once again, it was pouring cats and dogs.

On the way out, as he was on his way to join Augusta for their prandium, a grizzled out warrior of the VI stopped him.

'Any news, sir?' he asked, 'of my boy Justinus?'

'None of him specifically, Coelius,' the praeses said, 'but don't you worry. He can handle himself.'

'Oh, I know he can, sir,' Flavius said. 'I taught him. I just thought ...'

The praeses looked up at the man. 'Well, out with it. What's on your mind?'

The weapons master drew himself up to his full height. 'I'd like to volunteer, sir,' he said. 'Go north to the Wall ... you know, help out a little.'

Ammianus smiled. 'Come here,' he said, and doubled back into the principia to his wall map. 'Valentinus' army was sighted by the Votadini here. He's marching south and if it was a Roman army it would take him four days. But it's not a Roman army; those barbarian bastards will loot and pillage and sacrifice to whatever gods they have to their hearts' content. Justinus will be ready for them.'

The weapons master did not seem convinced. 'Flavius,' the praeses said, clapping his arm around the man's shoulder. 'We're too old for all this, you and I. Better let the lads handle it, eh? Besides, I have it on good authority that General Maximus is on his way north. All Justinus has to do is to hold until then.'

'Maximus?' Flavius smiled. 'Why didn't you say so?' He flicked a coin out of his purse and it glinted in the light from the window. 'I once bet the man that one of our contubernae would make fifteen circuits of the parade ground in full pack.' He winked at his commanding officer. 'Like taking honeycomb from a baby.'

Vitalis took some finding. Leocadius had sent his people out to all quarters of the city. Critus, the priest of Mithras, would have spat at the mention of his name, except that his jaw was not working well enough. Bishop Dalmatius was not receiving visitors at all but he had called upon his God to send his thunderbolts against the man. In the city's barracks and Maximus' camp to the west, it was the same story and an adjutant had pointed to the tribune's name on the army roster; it had been struck off.

When Leocadius finally found his man he was sitting in the forum, of all places, a spear's throw from the consul's offices in the basilica. Pelagius was with him.

'Could you leave us, Christian?' the consul asked.

Pelagius got up, bowed slightly and left. Leocadius did not sit down because he had not been invited to sit. 'I hear you've left the army,' he said.

'You hear right,' Vitalis told him.

'Why?'

Vitalis looked up at him. To be honest, he did not know where to start. 'Do you know, Leo,' he said, 'in the time I've served the eagles, I've never actually killed anybody.'

'So?' the consul shrugged.

'So, I've found myself, Leo,' Vitalis said. 'Ever since the Wall, I've been ... lost, looking for ... and I didn't even know what. Now, I do. I've found the Christ. And that means no killing. Young Theodosius does not have an issue with that, but I do. The way he looks at it, a Christian soldier is killing the enemies of Christ. I can't believe that.'

'That's a pity,' Leocadius said.

Vitalis shrugged. 'I'm sorry,' he said. 'That's just the way it is.'

The consul sat down. There were no flunkies with him now, no purple-shirts concerned with protocol and politics. It was just Leo and Vit, the lads from Banna with all their lives before them. 'No, I mean it's a pity because Valentinus is back; that mad bastard who murdered Paternus' family and the gods know how many more north of the Wall and south of it. He's back and Maximus is marching to meet him. And I'm going with him.'

'You are?' Vitalis frowned. 'But I thought ...'

'What, this?' Leocadius flicked the gold fringes of his pallium, waved his arm over *his* forum, *his* basilica. 'This is nothing, Vit. Nothing. Your God is nothing, too.' He grabbed his friend's arm and forced his hand into a fist, clunking their Wall rings together. '*That's* what matters,' he said. 'Before everything else and after it, we're heroes of the Wall. And we've got some unfinished business.'

Magnus Maximus did not have enough transports to ship his legions north, so he stripped the camp completely, leaving Londinium to its garrison. He marched by road, the columns of Heruli and Batavi singing as they marched and the less-than-delicate refrains of the *Girl from Clusium* echoed in the valleys of the Catuvellauni as they trekked north. Eight thousand men, six hundred horses, three dozen ballistae and wild asses, two silver eagles and a mastiff, all on the road to the Wall.

Bremenium had been abandoned long before anyone had heard of Valentinus. It lay forty miles northwest of Arbeia and the thistles grew in the crevices and the rooks wheeled overhead. They were watching two armies far below them through the broken cloud. One was huge and loud, with laughing, tumbling horsemen and foot-soldiers, some painted like the sky, some carrying the hacked-off heads of their enemies at their belts and from their saddlebows. The other was far smaller and silent, trailing the others with a sparse handful of miles between them.

Paternus could move faster than Valentinus with his wild, unruly mob but the tribune had over-reached himself that day and had got too close. The Wall was still a day and a half's march to the south and if the Votadini got too close, they would get a bloody nose for their pains.

It was late afternoon when the solitary horseman trotted over the rise. Paternus halted the column and gave the old command, 'Skirmish order!' He had trained his men well and they broke into groups of five, each band with an archer and crouched in the heather. Beyond them lines of archers stood three deep, ready to fire in volley and the horsemen had cantered to the flanks. The solitary rider coming towards them was one of Paternus' own scouts. He was not returning with a message, at least not one he could deliver himself, because he had no head. He had been propped into the saddle with a broken spear strapped to his shoulders and his coat of scales was dark brown with his blood.

There was no sound on that hillside below the old fort, just the wind singing in the stones and the steady hoof-falls of the horse. One of the Votadini ran forward to catch the animal's reins and bring it to a halt. Paternus was not looking at the headless scout; he was looking at his men. Their eyes were wide in horror and the cavalry on the wings were calming their skittish horses. The tribune barked an order. 'Get that out of sight,' he said. 'The rest of you; fall back. On the fort.'

While the Votadini formations broke up and made for the higher ground, Paternus kept his place, watching the horizon ahead. He felt his throat tighten as he saw, coming over the ridge, a silver helmet on the head of a man on a black horse. At first, he was alone, as though he was offering a challenge to the tribune, man to man between their two armies.

'Are you the one they call Valentinus?' Paternus called. He had never seen the man in the flesh before and his skin prickled. Now he knew what Fullofaudes had seen; and Ulpius Piso and Nectaridus; every man who had faced this faceless demon. Even he had begun to wonder whether the man was real; and yet here he was. He was not as tall as he had expected and there were no thunderbolts flashing from his eyes.

'I am Valentinus,' the horseman shouted back, his voice echoing and distorted through the helmet. 'And are you Paternus?'

The tribune's horse bucked and pranced to the left, annoyed by the last droning flies of summer. 'You know me?' he frowned.

'Of course I do,' Valentinus said. 'We all do.' And the horizon was suddenly thick with a forest of spears, solid phalanxes of horsemen sitting their horses silently and fanning out on both sides of the man in the silver helmet.

'You are everybody's lapdog,' he went on, 'licking the arse of Rome and that whore of the Votadini. What do you want of me, tribune?'

Paternus could not believe this. The man seemed to know more about him than Paternus knew about himself. But he refused to be shaken. He glanced behind him. His men had taken post in the still-standing tower and behind the crumbling ramparts of the fort. That did not fill him with confidence because he remembered how the Picts had hacked their way into a new fort not so long ago, a fort manned by Romans. But none of these misgivings were apparent as he shouted to Valentinus, 'I want your head, you renegade bastard,' he said, 'on a pole briefly before I shove it up your own arse.'

There was a cackle of laughter from Valentinus' men and when it had died down, he said, 'Go home, Paternus. Go back to the Votadini hovel you came from. You've lost one family; you don't want to lose two.'

Paternus muttered under his breath every curse he could lay tongue to. He wheeled the horse away and galloped for the fort. Now it would be a waiting game. Valentinus had clearly lost patience with the army trailing him like a flea he could not scratch and now he was doing something about it. The tribune dismounted and slapped his horse's flank so that it trotted a few yards away and waited, snickering nervously. Bremenium had been well chosen in the days of Agricola. There were no forests on the northern slopes to provide cover for the barbarians. On the other hand, the fort was a ruin, protection in name only and Valentinus' troops outnumbered Paternus' at least five to one. He buckled on his helmet and summoned a lad of the Votadini to him.

'Can you ride, boy?' he asked.

'Yes, lord.' The boy could not have been more than fourteen, his voice still squeaking as he adjusted to manhood.

'Take my horse and get back to Din Paladyr. Tell the queen ... Tell her what happened here.'

The boy looked into Paternus' face, calm and steady. For the past year he had run behind the man, hunted with him, learned the passage of arms the Roman way. Then he looked beyond, to the huge silent column of barbarians moving down the slope into the valley, the dying sun flashing on their spearheads and axeheads. And he understood. No power on earth could stop that. He turned in search of the horse.

Paternus had taken up a position in what was left of the central tower where the men of the II Augusta who had built the place once stood, standing guard at the edge of the world as Paternus was standing now. Valentinus' column was a sight to see, as drilled and Roman a formation as anything that Paternus knew, narrowing at the foot and widening at the back into the swine's head array that the Romans had inherited from the Greeks. There was a single shout from those ranks, deep and guttural as the spearheads came down and the march forward increased to a jog and then to a run.

Valentinus had not moved from his ridge. He and a knot of horsemen were watching the outcome of the battle from a safe distance and Paternus knew he had to get through a human wall before he could reach him. He raised his hand. The swine's head was crossing the flat ground now, making short work of the little stream that meandered through the valley and making its way up the hill. The single grunt was growing in the throats of the barbarians, rising and echoing off their shields as they took the slope. This was the barritus, the war cry the Romans had stolen from the barbarians who had stolen it back again. Paternus had not taught this to his men, but the Votadini had been fighting battles long before the murderous bastard of the silver helmet was in his cradle and they had battle cries of their own. The roar began along their battle lines too, spears thrusting to the sky. The tribune looked at their faces, at men downtrodden for too long, kicked by Roman and barbarian alike. They had been waiting for this moment for months, perhaps years, perhaps centuries.

'I'll kill the first man who leaves the Wall,' he yelled at them. 'Stay where you are. They'll break on the stones.' Apart from numbers, the Votadini had all the advantages. They had *some* protection, at least, from the walls. They had the rise of the ground in their favour and the sun was dazzling low in the barbarians' eyes. Paternus could see them now; the painted people with their blue swirls; the Saxons with their one-edged swords; the Scotti in their dark plaid trousers. The Attacotti were probably down there too, jogging up the slope, but there was no way of knowing an Attacotti until he was flicking out your eyes with his skinning knife.

'Loose!' Paternus roared and there was the deep throated thud as the arrows left the bows, the whine and hiss as they tore the air and the thump as they hit the lime-wood shields. Screams and yells punctuated the barritus as men in the front line and the second went down, the third line stumbling over bodies and leaping clear, running at full pelt now for the wall. Paternus knew he did not have to give further orders as long as his archers had arrows left. Wave after wave sailed over the ground, crumpling the first ranks of the swine array and slowing it down. Individual men who had dashed forward out of formation were brought down with arrow shafts slicing through their throats, thudding into their heads. A carynx on the far hill with Valentinus brayed its orders, the ghastly scream like all the furies of hell and the swine array changed formation, swinging to its left to hit Paternus' men in the flank.

'Archers! Right!' Paternus screamed, seeing the danger. The Votadini obeyed, sending their arrows hurtling into the barbarians who had nearly reached the wall. Soon there would be no time for the bowmen to reload before the enemy were on them. The Picts were in the front line, swinging huge axes in both hands as they reached the stones, only waist high at that part of the wall.

'Now!' Paternus yelled to the cavalry he had hidden behind the slope and the horsemen rammed home their heels, driving the tough little ponies forward, spearing the Picts as they tried to get a foot-hold on the stones. Spears slammed into teeth, their crimson points jutting out through skulls and helmets. Swords swung in the afternoon, lopping off arms and splitting heads. Blood was spraying in the early autumn air and the barbarian attack had come to a standstill.

Again, the carynx on the hill spoke and the swine array split, one half of it breaking the engagement on Paternus' right and going for the left. The tribune, in the centre, saw at once the problem. In the end, it had simply come down to numbers. He did not have enough men and the archers of the swine array had time to find their own marks now. Out of nowhere, a shaft bit deep into Paternus' shoulder and the impact threw him backwards so that he bounced off the tower wall behind him and swayed for a moment as he regained his footing. The attack was coming from two sides simultaneously now and Valentinus had enough men to encircle the old fort completely.

The Votadini cavalry lurched forward on their left to try to stop the latest attack but it was useless. The spears came up from the ground, skewering the horsemen as they tried to negotiate the wall. Men were hauled from their saddles and their skulls were smashed by a dozen trampling boots. There was no quarter anywhere along the wall and Paternus' centre was collapsing as men ran to support the floundering wings.

There was no hope of stopping this now. The Votadini were going down in their tens and their scores, dying as the men of the VI must have died along the Wall not far to the south almost exactly four years before. Command was gone and Paternus knew he could not make himself heard above the screams and terrible din of battle. He drew his sword for the first time and, forcing his numbing arm to work, swung into the enemy, scything first one down, then another. His iron slashed the throat of a Pict and lopped off the ear of a Scotti. He lunged for a third man, but the press of battle carried him back from the wall and he found himself floating on struggling bodies, his sword gone and his helmet dented. His men were floundering all around him and the barbarians were still coming on, over the wall and through the gate, battering the Votadini aside.

He felt a sudden pain in his chest but did not hear the thud as a Pictish axe head bit through mail and tunic and flesh to crack a rib. He lost his balance and rolled under marching feet, covering his head and waiting for the end.

Paternus had not heard the blast of the cornicines, nor the Roman shouts of command. Horsemen were galloping in formation across the high ground behind the fort and the barbarians were falling back. He did not see them scatter, leaping back over the bloody wall with the exhausted, shattered Votadini half-heartedly chasing them. And he certainly did not see the bastard on the black horse lift his silver helmet to the sky at the approach of the Roman reinforcements. He knew those shields. They were the Jovii. And this was no scouting patrol. It was not even a vexillation. Valentinus knew it was a whole bloody army.

The sun was dying as the dead were dragged away and the weapons picked up in the heather. Paternus was sitting on the blood-slick ground, his back against a half-buried milestone. The sounds around him were strange, muffled, far away. So were the faces, even though they were close to him.

'You couldn't have waited, I suppose?' he heard a familiar voice say.

'Justinus?' Paternus' own voice was as distant as any of the others. 'Is that you?' The man was a dark shape against the gold of the sky.

'Yes, Pat,' the tribune said. 'It's me.'

'I'm glad it's you,' the man said. 'Because I was afraid I wouldn't have a chance to thank you.'

'Thank me?' Justinus knelt beside his friend, looking grimly at the man's wounds. 'What for?'

'Brenna,' he said. 'And Taran. And little Edern. Thanks to you, I've got a family again. Tell them I love them, won't you?'

'You can tell them yourself, Pat. We just need to get you back up there to Din Paladyr. Brenna's herbs will do the trick.' Justinus held his friend's hand lightly. It was sticky with drying blood.

Paternus leaned his head back against the milestone, and opened his eyes a little wider. He frowned, looking beyond Justinus and he smiled, a sweet smile that Justinus had never seen on his face before. His pressure on the tribune's hand grew stronger and he tried to pull himself more upright. Justinus put his arm behind him and took his weight and Paternus leaned his head against his supporting shoulder. His whisper was faint, but Paternus could just hear it, above the noise of the wounded.

'Justinus, look,' the Praefectus Gentium of the Votadini murmured, trying to raise his ruined arm to point. 'It's Quin. I

knew he would come for me. He's been waiting all this time, waiting ...'

Justinus knew from the weight of his friend's head that he
had gone. He fought back tears and gently disengaged his arm. He
looked down at the bloody face and closed Paternus' eyes. 'Mithras,
also a soldier,' he murmured, 'Teach me to die aright.' He looked
up to the sky. 'Ave, Sol Invictus,' he said, although he knew that
Paternus was saying that for himself by now, hand in hand with
Quin and Flavia. Then he stood up, looking at the four battle vet-
erans of the Votadini who stood there.

'Take him back to Din Paladyr,' he said, 'the body of your
lord. All solemnity, now. All the songs of glory. Tell your queen ...
well, tell her it was her name on his lips at the end. Tell her that.'

CHAPTER XXI

Justinus pulled his army back the next day. The Votadini told him that Valentinus had attacked them with four thousand men. That meant that the bulk of his army were elsewhere; east, west, north? Who knew? They themselves went home, to lick their wounds and fight another day. Paternus was dead; they would bury him as Justinus had asked, on the windswept headland of Din Paladyr. And if they had to die too, it was there they would do it, in their own heartlands, not on Selgovae territory.

Justinus did not know exactly what had made him come north from the Wall when he did. He left the Victores at Aesica with vexillations out to the west. The milecastles were held by the VI again, as they had been for years, but no one believed that everything was back to normal. Perhaps it would never be. *Something* had told him to move out the Jovii in full marching strength and *something* had made him ride in the direction he had, to the sound of battle.

The five rings of the Wall were five no longer. Theodosius wore one but the Count had long ago left Britannia's shores and was fighting somewhere in Gaul. The last Justinus had heard was that the man had won a great victory and the Emperor had made him Magister Militum, commander of the army. The next step from there was at Jupiter's right hand above the clouds. Paternus' ring would not lie in the grave with him, along with the wine and the salt and the weapons he would need in the Gododdyn afterlife, back with his old family until the new one should join him, unknown years from now. It would gleam on on Brenna's finger, and then her son's. One ring glinted on Justinus' finger as he led the legion back to Aesica, a strong cavalry rearguard halting every mile to reconnoitre. And the other two? They shone on the fingers of two tribunes who were no longer tribunes. One was a politician these days, lining his purse and making speeches. The other had gone mad. And both these men, back in armour though without a specific rank, were riding north with the army of Magnus Maximus.

For ten days, all was quiet on the Wall. There were no more wild rumours about Valentinus. In fact, there was no information at all. Justinus was beginning to wonder whether Maximus had been right to give the arcani their marching orders; little Dumno was like a good deed in a naughty world. Yes, he would eat any garrison out of house and home, and his eyes lit up at the sight of Roman silver, but he brought useful news. And news of any kind was better than nothing.

On the eleventh day the cornicines of Magnus Maximus woke the morning and Justinus gave his thanks to Mithras. He would make his sacrifice later, when he had time. There were formal greetings and informal ones, much back-slapping and hugging as old comrades met for the first time in months. There was no room for them all at Aesica, so the leather tents went up and new earthworks were dug to the south to accommodate the newcomers.

The general sat with his commander of the Wall and all his tribunes the next day, tablets and scrolls of parchment in front of him on his table. Justinus had told him of the attack at Bremenium and that Valentinus himself had been there. Earlier he had told Leocadius and Vitalis about the death of Paternus and a sadness descended on them all.

'We're none of us the same,' Vitalis said. 'Not since Theodosius gave us these.' He held up his hand with the ring still there. 'I've thrown this away once, but it just came back.'

'So did I,' Justinus admitted. 'I was going to bury it at Banna, put it under the earth with good men. Something made me pick it up again.'

Leocadius nodded. 'I wore mine in the arena,' he said. 'It kept me alive. Or something did. But Vit's right. We're none of us the same.'

Now all three of them sat in front of the general, stony-faced and he told them all their future. They would find this man, the elusive ghost of the silver helmet. And they would kill him. 'Tomorrow, gentlemen,' Maximus said, the mastiff rolling at his feet, 'We are going to collect a debt.'

Maximus led his men out in a two-pronged attack, one to the north west, the other to the north east. They were five miles apart and riders from the Ala Heruli, the general's best cavalry, rode between them under the command of Stephanus the German. Maximus led one army, his legions from Londinium, tired though they were from the long march north; and Justinus led the other, his fresher troops from the Wall.

No one sang that morning and everyone was fully armed. The onagers groaned against their timbers and the ballistari walked alongside them, putting their shoulders to the wheels over rough ground and keeping the torsion ropes greased and ready. Behind them, mules dragged the heavy carts of shot, the round stones which the ballistari had been painting all night. 'This one's for you, Valentinus,' some said; others said, 'Kiss my arse.' General Maximus' favourite read 'This is what eagle shit feels like'; always a lover of nature was Magnus Maximus.

There was plenty of water on the moors of Selgovae country and hunters went out daily with their snares and darts. Hare and venison went into the huge stew pots every night. For three days, Maximus' column on the left followed the retreating tracks of Valentinus. He was moving slowly north west, beyond Banna that Justinus' men had been ordered to abandon, into the open country beyond.

Stephanus' advance cavalry sighted them first and they came galloping back to tell him. He in turn sent half a turmae west to find Justinus and took the others east to the general. The German reined in his black and saluted, thumping his chest and extending his arm. 'They're in a forest, Maximus,' he said. 'They're in a bloody forest.'

'Are they?' the General threw a sliver of venison to his mastiff, padding along beside him. 'Well, we'll just have to smoke them out.'

He swung down from his saddle and touched the grass. Tinder dry. It had not rained north of the Wall for three weeks and that made conditions perfect. The ground was iron hard for his cavalry and tough going for the pedes, but for lighting fires it was heaven sent. Maximus rode forward with Stephanus and his staff and looked at the ground ahead.

Valentinus had chosen well. The thick woods , of mountain fir, dark against the morning sky, stood on a ridge. That meant that Maximus' foot sloggers would have to march uphill into the teeth of whatever missiles the barbarians could throw at them. On the other hand, no reports had reached the general of any siege equipment with Valentinus' army. It would be the old way, spear to spear and sword to sword. Maximus could not see a single warrior in the trees but he knew instinctively they were there.

'Take post, gentlemen,' he said to his tribunes and they galloped to their units to open the day's dance.

Five miles to the east, one of Stephanus' riders had reached Justinus. He rode with Leocadius and Vitalis on his staff but, to be honest, he could no more rely on them now than he could four years ago when their lives had been turned upside down at Banna. Leocadius seemed his old self, laughing, cracking jokes, giving everybody the benefit of his company. But none of these things made him a good soldier. As for Vitalis, the man seemed ill at ease. He wore his mail coat as if it hurt him and refused to wear the scarf of a tribune because he was not part of this world anymore.

The death of Paternus had hit them all very hard. And it was only that that kept Vitalis in the field at all. He had come north, arse and thighs aching, through the woods and valleys of the south, because Leocadius had shamed him into it. But he would not fight and the scabbard hung empty at his side.

'The general's orders, sir,' Stephanus' rider wheezed, looking as blown as his horse. 'Valentinus is in a wood five miles to the west of here. The general's compliments and could you join him?'

'I would be delighted,' the tribune said and gave orders for his column to wheel left to follow the Heruli horseman. 'This is it, lads,' he murmured to Leocadius and Vitalis. 'We've got our hooks into the bastard at last.'

Julius Amiterra was the general's commander of artillery. His men said he had the guts of a two-wheeled carroballista and his balls were made of stone. Neither of these things was said within his earshot. He had drawn up his onagers, on Maximus' instructions, at the base of the hill. Shooting upwards was always a bit of a bastard for the artillery, but the ground, at least, was hard and the machines would not sink into a morass of mud and become immovable. Amiterra's men had clothed half their stones with pitch-soaked straw, wrapped with sacking and tied with twine over the carefully-painted words of love they were about to unleash on the enemy.

Behind them, Maximus' legions were drawn up in battle order, the Batavi at the front and the Heruli in reserve. He sat his horse and looked along the lines – grim-faced men standing in the total silence he expected, watching the dark trees of the forest on the ridge.

'No talking!' he heard the bark of a centurion somewhere in the tight formation and heard the thud of the man's cane as it hit somebody's back. What he could not hear were the whispered words that followed it. 'I'll have you, Orno, you snivelling little soldier. And fasten that strap, man. Where *do* you think you are?'

Talking in the ranks at moments like these would not do. It was never about the weather. It was always about the enemy – his numbers, his strength, what so-and-so said what's-his-face had told him about what they did to prisoners. Best keep silent.

Maximus looked at the sky. There was a sun up there, he knew, above the grey northern clouds, but he could not see it. It must be mid-morning. Along the Thamesis about now he would be inspecting the perimeters with Stephanus or entertaining some of the dignitaries from the city, putting his cohorts through their paces as titled ladies tittered and whispered together about the men's taut bodies. He shuddered. Give him a killing ground any day.

'Io, Valentinus!' He cupped his mouth to make sure his voice carried to the trees. 'Come out, come out, wherever you are.' He allowed the ripple of laughter from the ranks nearest to him.

For a moment, perhaps two, there was silence. Then, 'Good morning, Maximus,' echoed from the tall firs. A solitary figure rode forward out of the deep shadows, a man on a black horse. A man wearing a silver helmet. The front ranks craned their necks to see him, this monster they had heard such things about. He looked surprisingly small at this distance, but that was probably a trick of the light. The general's mastiff growled and whiffled as though he tasted the man's bones already. 'How nice of you to come so far to pay your respects.' His Latin was perfect.

'Respect is something you have to earn, bastard,' Maximus shouted. 'Oh, I know you're good at knocking over milecastles and murdering children. Let's see what you can do against a legion or two, eh?'

'Pretty shields,' Valentinus shouted back. He was still the

only enemy in sight, as his horse shifted and snorted, scenting battle. 'The Batavi and the Heruli. I don't see the others with you – the Jovii, the Victores. Where are you hiding them, eh? Up your arse?'

Maximus exchanged smiles with his staff. 'Cocksure bastard, isn't he?' he said. Then his smile vanished. 'And a bit too well-informed for my liking.'

'How is it in the sunny south?' Valentinus was making small talk and Maximus did not yet know why. 'And how's my old friend Paulinus Hupo?'

Maximus' horse skittered to one side. Had the general heard right? He did not know Hupo personally, but he knew *of* him; the sort of gutter-life that every city throws up now and again. Was *that* why Valentinus had not attacked Londinium as he had threatened? Did he *know* that Theodosius' walls and Theodosius' artillery were too strong for him?

This prattle had gone on for long enough. 'Talking of old friends,' he called, 'Have you met *my* old friend, Vulcan?' He brought his raised arm down. 'Now, Amiterra!' he roared. 'Now's your time!'

Along the artillery line, the pitch burst into flame and the ballistae crashed into action. The wild asses kicked and bucked, the ropes flying free as the burning rocks were hurled into the air. They sailed high up the hill to smash into the tree tops, ripping boughs and splintering timber. The sap-rich fronds went up like tinder and the flame shot along branches and down trunks.

'Reload!' Amiterra bellowed with lungs long used to yelling over ballistae-fire. The second wave of missiles fell shorter, hitting the trees half way up the trunks and sending showers of burning foliage crashing to the forest floor.

Valentinus had long gone, vanished behind the black smoke and Maximus called a ceasefire. The troops, jabbering away excitedly at the roar and scream of the bombardment, fell silent again. The general cursed. The wind was changing, blowing the choking smoke back into his own lines as the fire took hold and the whole thick stand of trees began to burn. Where the hell were they? Maximus had expected to smoke the barbarians out, to watch a terrified rabble with their bodies writhing in flame, come tumbling down the hillside where his legions would destroy them. But there was nothing.

'Reload, sir?' Julius Amiterra had hurried across to the general's position.

'No, stand your men down.' Maximus wheeled his horse and cantered along the line, shouting to the tribunes. 'He's pulled his people back. East, west, I don't know. Be ready to move on my command.'

The shields came up from the ground, forearms bunched and sinewed in the arm-straps. The spears were erect, probing the sky. Maximus reached the cavalry wing extending to the east. 'Stephanus. Take yourself on a run. Ride east and find that slippery bastard. And get a message to the left wing to do the same. He's moving somewhere beyond that hill and I've just given him a smoke-screen to hide behind.'

The German chuckled. 'Ah, where's Papa Theo when you need him, eh?'

Maximus growled, 'Get on with it, you insubordinate shit!' but he could not help smiling as he said it.

'Battle order!' Justinus yelled. Ahead of him he saw black smoke billowing across his front from a large stand of trees on the high ground. He could not make it out clearly, but it looked like Maximus' two legions drawn up at the bottom of the slope. They were not moving, as if Valentinus had fixed them with his Medusa's stare and turned them all to stone.

What concerned him more was what lay directly in his path. If the barbarians had been hiding in that wood, they were hiding no longer. A solid mass of them stood on the reverse slopes below the flaming trees where the timbers cracked and fell. Justinus could see the blue bodies of the painted ones and knew the standards of the Scotti – the boar and the stag and the bear. He also knew he was outnumbered and the bastards were massing to attack.

'Archers!' he yelled and the bowmen of the Jovii dashed to the front while the foot-sloggers hurried into their cohort attack formations, ready for the swine array. Justinus looked at the army that lay before him. There was infantry in the centre and cavalry on the wings, just like a Roman formation.

'Jupiter Highest and Best,' Leocadius murmured at Justinus' elbow and pointed straight ahead. A solitary horseman was walking his animal forward, a sudden flash of pale sun striking the silver of his helmet.

'Well, well,' the voice rang in the metal cask, distorted and strange. 'Is that Leocadius I see with you, Justinus? And young Vitalis? How nice. All the heroes of the Wall. Oh, except Paternus. Shame about him, wasn't it?'

Leocadius clawed free his sword and raised his reins to force his horse forward. But Justinus held him back. 'Don't be a bloody fool, Leo,' he growled. 'That's exactly what the bastard wants. How far do you think you'd get?'

The consul frowned. His blood was up and this bastard had lived too long. But he knew that Justinus was right.

'You didn't think just rebuilding the Wall would stop me, did you?' A sinister laugh echoed across the field. 'Let's face it, you're still a circitor. And those over-promoted shits with you are still pedes. You're out of your depth, circitor. Go home.'

Justinus looked at the lads with him. Their faces were calm and grim now, ready for the inevitable, ready to avenge everything. Because everything that had happened to them since Banna, since they had run with their tails between their legs, had been because of Valentinus. This, as Maximus had said, was the time to collect the debt. And to offer a quick prayer to Mars Ultor, the avenger. The commander of the Wall buckled on his helmet and yelled to Valentinus, 'I am home!'

His hand came down and the bows sang out, the hiss of arrows hurtling across the valley, the iron tips thudding into cheek bones and eye-sockets, the rest bouncing off shields. The barbarian archers loosed their arrows back and Justinus' men fell back to the protection of the Jovii shields. Iron smashed into them and the front line recoiled a little with the impact. First blood to nobody and the day had only just begun.

Stephanus sent his galloper back, his horse's hooves thudding across the heather. He had ripped off his helmet and was waving to Maximus, sitting under his scarlet banner, waiting for word.

'Enemy to the east, sir,' the man gasped. 'They're engaging the other legions.'

At last. 'Cornicen,' Maximus shouted to the man standing behind him. 'The Batavi will wheel right, Heruli in support. Double time.' And the whole line swung and wheeled, boots thudding as one as though on a parade ground and the whole unit jogged forward.

Now, Valentinus was on the march. His swine array was moving forward, the carynxes at their head blasting out their terrifying noise. This was the moment that every Roman had dreaded since they had first crossed the Tiber to spread the eagle's wings far and wide. All of hell was coming up out of the ground against Justinus and his men knew it. It was more than sinew and iron and the guts of individual men. It was a monster, the darkest demon of the night, thousands moving as one, terrifying, unstoppable.

And Valentinus' words hammered in Justinus' head. He was a circitor. What the hell was he doing here in command of two legions, in command of the Wall? Around him, any one of his staff had more experience than he did. Anyone except Leocadius and Vitalis and he could not read their faces now. Leocadius had clapped his tribune's helmet on, with its fancy scrollwork and only his eyes flashed in the reflection of the distant fires. Vitalis showed no emotion at all, the wail of those terrible horns echoing through his head.

'Ballistae!' Justinus roared and the wild asses kicked. Rocks hurtled through the air as the frames bucked and shuddered, sending their messages straight into the heart of the swine array. A barbarian's head was ripped off his shoulders and the carynx scream became a series of disjointed wails as the hornmen went down, trampled by the chanting warriors behind. Shields buckled and split, heaps of men collapsed in the path of the attack, but they kept coming anyway.

'Shields!' Justinus bellowed and the front rank of the Jovii knelt, locking their shields and pointing their spears upwards. The second tilted their bodies so that the shields overlapped and the spears were held level, ready to smash into eyes and teeth. The ranks behind still had their shields slung across their backs and they were ready to hurl their spears into the sky. A more experienced commander might have met the enemy running, with a crash that would reach the heavens, but the moment had gone and there was no time to move forward.

'Spears!' Justinus thundered and the javelins hissed through the air, sailing over the heads of the kneeling and standing Jovii and thudding into the swine array. Men went down under this deadly rain, skewered by iron that pelted them from above. There was no need for Justinus to roar the next command. It was instinctive. The shields came up to the horizontal, to lock above the heads of the Jovii. This was the testudo, the turtle and everybody braced themselves as the barbarian spears clattered off the shield bosses and fell harmlessly to one side. A few found their mark, iron slicing through shoulders and necks; and screams and groans filled the air.

Still the Jovii stood fast. And still the swine array came on.

Stephanus the German reined in his black on the eastern slopes of the hill. The trees were still burning but very few of them were still standing now. The smoke had darkened the sky completely and he could not even see the sun, but he reckoned it was midday. Ahead, he could see the running line of the barbarians glittering in their armour. No one had beaten these bastards yet and they knew it. He shook his head. Justinus was a man of whom the general had spoken highly and over the last few days Stephanus had got to know and like him. But the man was standing still to receive the shock of the attack and he might not stand at all. The cavalryman read the signs, scouring Justinus' back line to watch for stragglers. He knew the men at the front could not run because they had nowhere to go. All retreats began at the back. No one was breaking yet and he could see the centurions at the rear, their sticks in their hands, watching for just such a break.

Stephanus would have liked to have waited for Maximus' infantry to catch up, but he did not have the time for that. He swore in the guttural language of his homeland and drew his sword. 'First turmae,' he bellowed at his horsemen. 'Direct. Second and third, I want you up our arses.' He slashed the air with his blade and the cavalry moved forward, at a walk at first, the dragon standard fluttering just behind Stephanus. Each man rode knee to ham with his comrade. Keeping the horses in check until the right moment. A cavalry charge was all well and good and the thunder of the hooves shook the ground, but it was best delivered against a weakened enemy, men already cracking and exhausted. Against a legion in defence, it was suicide. And against other cavalry? Well, that was the question, wasn't it?

The Ala Heruli rose to the trot, spears erect still, jabbing the air while the turmae behind carried their spatha blades at the slope on their shoulders. The cornicen with Stephanus judged the moment and blasted out the canter. The spear points came down and the sword blades shot upright to the vertical. Valentinus' horsemen were racing in a wide circle, trying to prevent Stephanus from reaching the swine array, but they were not in position as the German struck.

'Sound the charge!' Stephanus roared, ramming his heels home as the black broke into a gallop. His men were shouting their battle cries of the Rhenus and the Ister, their horses champing their iron bits and breathing hard.

The shock on the Jovii front line was like nothing most of them had felt before. Huge Picts were hurling themselves onto spear-points, impaled bodies with blood bubbling from their mouths. The front line jarred and held for a moment, then it broke and the second stepped forward on Justinus' command, their spears level. Swords hacked against shields and bounced off helmets, teeth and blood flying over the swine array. The barbarians had lost all formation, but their sheer weight of numbers carried them forward. Justinus' front line had all but gone, his kneeling men hacked down and the spears of the second line, where they had not found their mark through gristle and bone, were being batted aside like toothpicks.

Now it was shield to shield and the heaving began. In the centre, and only yards from Justinus' scarlet flag, men were locked in the grim dance of death that all battles come down to. Where iron failed and men lost their weapons in the press, both sides spat at each other, kicking, gouging and tearing with their bare hands. Leocadius saw it first – a vexillum of the VI with its gilt letters, the one hacked from the arm of the signifer from Camboglanna. The consul had had enough. For nearly two hours now he had sat his horse and waited. But he would follow Justinus no more. He was not part of this army any more, with its rules and its traditions and he broke every one of them now.

Leocadius slammed his heels into his horse and forced the animal forward. Around him the centurions were smashing their sticks onto the shoulders of the wavering back line, snarling at them to hold their places and pushing them forward. He saw, in his mind's eye, the butchered, headless Ulpius Piso, looking out with eyes he no longer had, over the ground he had failed to hold. His sword rang on the shield of a Pict, battle-mad and foaming at the mouth. He parried the man's attack and slashed him from shoulder to groin, watching him roll to the ground. A spear thudded into his horse's chest and the animal whinnied and stumbled, throwing Leocadius out of the saddle. For brief seconds, he was stunned by the fall, unable to catch his breath, rolling among the milling feet of the Jovii, Roman boots he knew so well, sliding and scraping in the dust. Then he was on his feet, checking his grip on his sword and whirling back to the attack in search of the captured vexillum.

Stephanus ducked the slash of the Pictish sword and rammed home his own, driving the point of the blade through the man's ribs and out through his back. He wrenched it free and hacked off the hand of another who was riding at him. The Ala Heruli were everywhere that day, driving the barbarian cavalry back, breaking their formation, scattering every attempt to stand against them. The German cursed under his breath, his spangelhelm sprayed with barbarian blood. He knew he could not reach the Jovii and Maximus was still a mile away, running forward with all speed, urging on his men and hitting them with his whip. As for Justinus, he was on his own.

The tribune had lost sight of Leocadius but that was the least of his worries. He signalled to the Victores and the legion moved forward. He could hear, even above the cacophony of slaughter, the screams of the centurions. 'Close up! Close up!' The Jovii were crumbling. All four lines were engaged now, pushing and grunting with the exertion. Boots had churned the ground to a mass of slippery grass, mud and blood; and dead men were held up by the living, their limbs cooling, their eyes sightless.

Valentinus was not sitting at the edge of the field now, watching like a spectator at the Games. He had brought his horsemen along the flank of the swine array and was hacking about him left and right, his murderous spatha drawing blood wherever it flashed.

Justinus had no reserves left. His cavalry were committed to right and left although he could not see them. Behind the rear rank of the Victores, he had nothing else to stand between him and the Wall. The press had reached him now and the cornicen beside him went down, an arrow through his throat. The scarlet flag wavered as the signifer fell, blood spraying over his wolf's skin headgear. An axe bounced off Justinus' helmet and he parried for his life, dazed by the blow.

All day, Vitalis had sat his horse in the middle of this mayhem. Now something shook him and he seemed to spring to life. He took the flat of a sword on his arm and lashed out with his right boot, knocking the attacker off balance. Then the press carried him away and Justinus could not see him any more. The commander of the Wall caught a sword blade on his own and scythed horizontally, slashing a scarlet line across the blue-painted chest ahead of him.

Then, something happened. And it was difficult to see what

it was. There was activity away to the west and the press was breaking. The swine array was falling back, the carynxes silent, the battle cries and the roars dying away. The only sound now was the barritus, deep from the bowels of hell, the death knell of many a barbarian from the Ister to the Wall. It came from the throats of the Batavi and the Heruli. General Maximus had arrived.

Iron still rang around the field and battle-mad men who had not heard it, had no idea that the tide had turned. Vitalis was on his knees, an ugly gash across his forehead and the blood was dripping into his eyes. His lungs felt like broken bellows, wheezing and grinding, as he tried to make sense of what was happening. Then, suddenly, there he was, the rider still mounted on the black horse and yelling frantic commands in the eerie echo of the silver helmet. And in that moment, Vitalis knew what he had to do. The Christian who had sworn to kill no more, the soldier who had never killed, the child of the darkness, grabbed a broken sword lying beside him. He snatched the reins of the black horse, the animal whinnying and shying in panic in the middle of the chaos and he tugged hard. Valentinus lost his balance and pitched forward, the sword gone from his grasp. Vitalis stood over the man for a second, then lunged downwards. The broken blade sliced through the throat below that ghastly, immobile face. There was a gurgling sound and a bubbling of blood through the mouth of the mask. Valentinus' limbs shook uncontrollably and he died.

Vitalis dropped the sword. Axes and spears were clashing all around him but he knew peace in that moment, a peace he had not known in four years. He knelt beside the dead barbarian general and reached forward. He unhooked the little latch at the top of the mask and wrenched it open, staring at the dead face inside that stared back at him.

Dumno.

CHAPTER XXII

The battle was over. The barbarian dead lay in heaps strewn across the valley floor, the Roman dead on the higher ground where Justinus' line had held. For years, wherever soldiers met, in contuberniae or tabernae they would talk of this day and argue who had won. Was it the Batavi or the Heruli, running to the rescue? Or was it the Jovii and the Victores who had fought them to a standstill?

They collected the weapons and the armour that could be re-used and Stephanus' exhausted cavalry spent two days rounding up the scattered horses. For two days and two nights the fires threw sparks into the sky, darkening the blue by day and lighting the darkness by night. The man called Valentinus was stripped of his armour and his little dumpy, naked body was rolled onto a common funeral pyre with his warriors. There would be no grave marker for him.

'Dumno, eh?' Leocadius was shaking his head as that first darkness descended. He had won back the vexillum from Camboglanna and vowed to return it to the fort on his way south. 'Who would have thought it?'

'We all should have,' Maximus said. 'He was just too ordinary to be true, wasn't he? Turning up at Eboracum, bringing sad news for Paternus. When he started asking about my supply depots, I should have realised.'

'What I can't get my head round,' Leocadius said, 'is that he was working with Paulinus Hupo as well, *that* far south. Are you sure that was the name he gave, general?'

Maximus nodded. He stared out of the tent to where the

dead were burning, their souls rising to the heavens or fragmenting as ash to the earth, depending on where a man's gods lived.

'I'm sending them home tomorrow,' Maximus said, 'the prisoners. He turned to the surprised faces. 'Papa Theo's way,' he said, smiling. 'Oh, we'll escort them as far as Caledonia. And they'll be unarmed. And on foot. But I don't think there'll be any more trouble.'

'Who was it who said Valentinus was ten feet tall?' Justinus asked.

Maximus turned to him with a strange look on his face. 'We all did, Justinus,' he said. 'That was what he relied on. In fact, he was just a man, like the rest of us.'

Justinus walked out in the Selgovae night to where Vitalis stood alone, watching the flames. The gash across his forehead was bruised and both his eyes were swollen and dark. 'Are you all right, Vit?' the commander of the Wall asked.

'No.' Vitalis said after a while. 'But I will be.'

That had to be enough.

In the days that followed, Leocadius Honorius went south with an escort of the Ala Heruli and laid the vexillum of the VI Victrix in its niche at Camboglanna. He stood with bowed head while the garrison officially welcomed it home and then he rode south. He had pressing business along the Thamesis that could not wait. It involved Paulinus Hupo, already a dead man.

Justinus remained commander of the Wall, riding the cold ridges where the rooks and ravens wheeled. In the winter he went south to Eboracum and chopped wood with old Flavius Coelius, who clipped his son around the head when he called him old.

Stephanus the German asked permission from the Dux Britannorum to leave the Britannia command and go east to Papa Theo. If truth be told, the country had become a little tame now that Valentinus was dead and a man like Stephanus longed for the sound of battle in his ears and the rush of blood through his veins.

The winter became the summer and there was peace in Britannia. Far to the north, a woman and her two boys put flowers on a grave on the windswept heights of Din Paladyr. And the boys grew and the seasons turned. And all was well ...

The galloper thundered out of the east as dawn broke over Londinium. He clattered over the bridge, wreathed in river mist where the ships rode at anchor and the sails were lifting with the new day. The guard stood aside for him, recognizing the insignia of the younger Theodosius on his sleeve.

Justinus had come south for the first time in his life. He had been born at Verulamium but had no memory of the place. Londinium however was new to him. He was not that sure he cared for it and after a week or so was missing the cold and the winds of the Wall. Leocadius was the perfect host and Justinus had the run of the governor's palace, except that newer bit, the area behind the wall. The gate to it was locked and Justinus heard laughter and merriment behind it occasionally, but it was none of his business and he left it alone. He never saw Honoria with her little dark-haired boy; Leocadius wanted it that way. Justinus was dutiful to the frigid Julia, the consul's wife, making small talk with her while dutifully dandled her little golden-haired girl on his knee from time to time.

As for Leocadius, Justinus saw little of him. The man had many duties that kept him in various parts of the city at all hours of the day and night. What about Paulinus Hupo, Justinus had asked, the man who had played the spy for Valentinus? Dead, Leocadius had told him. Knife, apparently. This was Londinium, one of the most dangerous cities in the Empire. What can you do?

The messenger was told to ride west. He would find General Maximus in the camp beyond the western wall. The man lashed his lathered horse and clattered through the narrow streets, street-sellers scattering as he rode.

'Dead?' Magnus Maximus looked hard at the messenger. Sometimes, men died for news like this and the messenger knew it.

'I don't have details, sir.' The man was still on one knee, head bowed.

Maximus looked at Justinus. 'Do you believe it?' he said.

'Sir,' the messenger held something in his hand, outstretched to the general. 'I was asked to give you this.'

Maximus took it. It was a black ring, chased with gold and carved with four helmets. It was the ring of the late Count Theodosius, who had been executed at Carthago three weeks ago. With him had died a faithful warrior, Stephanus, but the messenger knew nothing of the whereabouts of Theodosius' son.

'Papa Theo,' Maximus said grimly, squeezing the ring in his

hand. He looked at Justinus. 'This is the Emperor's doing,' he snapped. 'The man never could abide successful generals. Well ...' he crossed to the window where a cohort of the Batavi were going through their paces, their boots crunching on the parade ground, their shields locking in the morning. 'Well, he wasn't the only successful general around.' Maximus dismissed the messenger, who was only too glad that he still had his head and he slipped the Wall ring on his finger.

'Call the tribunes for me, Justinus,' he said. 'All of them. I want the legions here, all four of them. As well as any of the limitanei you can spare.'

'Why, sir?' Justinus was afraid to hear the answer.

'Because I want them to elect me as Emperor,' he said. 'It's been done before. And here in Britannia. Here,' he hauled off the eagle insignia he wore around his neck, 'In my absence you will be Dux Britannorum.'

'Me?' Justinus could not take this in.

Maximus clapped a hand on the man's shoulder. 'Some have greatness thrust upon them,' he said. 'To be honest, I'd like you with me in whatever adventures might befall me across the German Sea, but I need a man here I can trust.'

'Sir, shouldn't you consider ...?' But Justinus was not given the chance to finish the sentence.

'Count Theodosius is dead, Justinus,' Maximus said, 'and it's my guess, on the Emperor's orders. Well, as of now, there is another Emperor in the West. And I need you here to hold the fort. Will you do that for me?'

'I hear the legions have elected Maximus Emperor.' Pelagius was weaving a basket in the dying light of the evening.

'They have,' Vitalis nodded, standing for a moment before hoisting the heavy kit-bag onto his shoulder.

'Quo vadis, Vitale?' Pelagius asked him. 'Where are you going?'

'I don't know,' Vitalis said. 'But I can't stay here.'

'Valentinus?' Pelagius asked. 'He's still with you, isn't he? His ghost?'

Vitalis nodded. 'That will always be,' he said, 'wherever I go.'

'You could come with me,' Pelagius said.

'With you?' Vitalis frowned. 'Where are *you* going?'

'Across the sea with Maximus. Not as part of his army, of course. He is looking for the man who killed his old friend, with murder in his heart. Mars Ultor sails with him.'

'And Jesus sails with you,' Vitalis smiled.

'Always,' said Pelagius.

Justinus rode north that autumn, back to where it had all begun. It was cold on the heather ridges and the distant mountains stood like grey ghosts in the early morning. The only sound was the guttural scream of the rooks wheeling on the air currents. Their bright eyes saw everything; the hares darting in the tangled purple; the water, bright and babbling over the stones

MAP

GLOSSARY OF PLACE-NAMES

Abona: Bristol
Aegyptus: Egypt
Aesica: Great Chesters, Northumberland
Anderitum: Pevensey Castle, East Sussex
Aquae Sulis: Bath, Gloucestershire
Aquileia: Italian city near Venice
Arbeia: Fort in South Shields, Tyne and Wear
Augusta Treverorum: Trier, Germany
Belgica: Tribal region that roughly covers modern Belgium
Boderia: Firth of Forth, Scotland
Bononia: Bologna, Italy
Branodunum: Saxon Shore Fort, Norfolk
Britannia Prima: One of five provinces of Britannia, covering Wales and south-west England
Britannia Secunda: One of five provinces of Britannia, covering north England
Caeseraugusta: Zaragoza, Spin
Carthago: Carthage, Tunisia
Cataractonium: Catterick
Clausentum: Bitterne, Hampshire
Clota: River Clyde
Constantinople: Istanbul, Turkey

Dal Riata: Irish Kingdom which ruled lands in Ireland and Scotland
Deva: Chester
Din Eidyn: Edinburgh
Din Paladyr: Traprain Law, Scotland
Dubris: Dover
Durnovaria: Dorchester
Eboracum: York
Flavia Caesariensis: One of five provinces of Britannia, covering central England
Gallia: Part of the Roman Empire that roughly covers modern France, Luxembourg and Belgium
German Sea: North Sea
Hadrianopolis: Edirne, Turkey
Hasta: Asti, Italy
Hebros: River Maritsa, Turkey
Hibernia: Ireland
Hibernian Sea: Irish Sea
Hierosolyma: Jerusalem
Icena: River Itchen
Isca Augusta: Caerleon
Isca Dumnoniorum: Exeter
Lindum: Lincoln
Llyn Tegid: Bala Lake, Wales
Maxima Caesariensis: One of five provinces of Britannia, covering south-east England
Mediolanum: Milan, Italy
Mona: Anglesey
Narbonensis: Province in Gaul
Natiso: River Natisone, Italy
Oceanus: Atlantic Ocean
Onnum: Halton Chesters, Northumberland
Pinnata Castra: Inchtuthil Fort, Perth and Kinross
Pollentia: Pollenso, Italy
Portus Adurni: Portchester Castle, Hampshire
Portus Leminis: Lympne Fort, Kent
Regulbium: Saxon Shore Fort, Kent
Rutupiae: Richborough Castle, Kent
Saxon Shore: Coastal defences from Norfolk to Hampshire
Sorviodunum: Old Sarum, Wiltshire

Tarraconesis: Roman province of Spain
Thamesis: River Thames
Tynus: River Tyne
Valentia: Short-lived fifth province of Britannia, perhaps north of Hadrian's Wall
Vectis: Isle of Wight
Venta: River Wensum
Verulamium: St Albans
Vienna: Vienne, France
Viroconium: Wroxeter
Vindolanda: Bardon Mill, Northumberland
Vindovala: Rudchester

GLOSSARY OF TERMS

Ala(e): Cavalry regiment(s)
Alans: Nomadic tribe
Alemanni: Germanic tribe
Aquilifer: Roman military eagle-standard bearer
Baestasians: Germanic tribe
Belatucadros: Celtic god of war
Cena: Mid-afternoon / evening meal
Circitor: Rank above semisallis in Roman army
Chi-Rho: Christian symbol and monogram
Comes Litoris Saxonici: Count of the Saxon Shore
Contubernium: Roman squad of eight (or ten) soldiers
Contus: Cavalry lance
Cornicen: Roman military horn player
Danaan: Faery race of Irish folklore
Deceangli: Celtic tribe of North Wales
Decurion: Member of the nobility
Donativum: Special payment to soldiers on the accession of a new emperor
Draconarius: Roman military dragon-standard bearer
Dux Britannorum (Britanniarum): Military general in Britain
Farum: Lighthouse
Flagrum: Cat-o'-nine-tails
Fustuarium: Cudgelling

Germani: Collective term to describe the various peoples beyond the river Rhine

Gododdin: Celtic tribe north of Hadrian's Wall

Goth: Germanic tribe

Gustatio: First course of a meal

Heruli: Germanic people serving in the Roman army

Hiberni: Roman term for the Irish

Imbolc: Celtic festival

Isis: Egyptian goddess

Jentaculum: Breakfast

Juti: Germanic tribe from Denmark

Lancea: Spear

Limitanei: Border soldiers

Lorica: Armour

Magister Militum: Commander of the Roman Army

Mansio: Official inn for travellers

Medicus / Medici: Doctor(s)

Necropolis: 'City of the dead', cemetery

Nemesis: Roman goddess of revenge

Optio: Rank below centurion in the Roman army

Ordo (curia): Council / court

Pedes / Pedites: Foot soldier(s)

Praeco(nes): Town crier(s)

Primus Pilus: 'First Spear', senior centurion of a legion

Sacristan: Role within the Roman Church

Scotti: Roman term for the Irish

Schola Palatina(e): Emperor's Bodyguard(s)

Semisallis: Rank above pedes in the Roman army

Signifer: Roman military standard bearer

Solidus: High-value Roman coin

Spangenhelm: Military helmet

Spatha: Sword carried by Roman army

Spiculum: Javelin

Subligaculum: Undergarment

Suebi: Germanic tribe

Tartarus: Roman underworld

Turma: Cavalry squadron

Valetudinarium: Hospital

Vallum: Defensive earthworks

Vandals: Germanic tribe

Vexillation: Detachment of soldiers

Vexillum: A military standard
Vicarius: Governor of a diocese
Votadini: Roman name for the Gododdin
Vulcan: Roman god of fire

BLKDOG

www.blkdogpublishing.com

Made in the USA
Monee, IL
30 December 2022

23944497R00184